Praise for
New York Times bestseller
PATRICK ROBINSON
and **HUNTER KILLER**

"Robinson is one of the crown princes
of the beach-read thriller."
Stephen Coonts

"Talk about 'ripped from the headlines':
bestseller Robinson's latest international political
thriller reads like the evening news on speed . . .
The main characters come off as real people
caught up in a frightening scenario."
Publishers Weekly

"A master craftsman of the techno-thriller . . .
No one does it better."
Carlo D'Este, author of *Decision in Normandy*

"If you like your techno-thriller in ripping yarn
form, you'll love this . . . It's all stirring stuff, with
lots of sabotage and hunter-killer submarines,
frogmen and mercenaries—lots of things that
fans of Clancy, Higgins, Forsyth and the like
will just love."
San Jose Mercury News

"[Rashood] is one of Robinson's most inspired
creations."
Guardian (London)

"Patrick Robinson has tapped into our fear."
Herald Express

Books by Patrick Robinson

GHOST FORCE
HUNTER KILLER
SCIMITAR SL-2
BARRACUDA 945
SLIDER
THE SHARK MUTINY
U.S.S. SEAWOLF
H.M.S. UNSEEN
KILO CLASS
NIMITZ CLASS
TRUE BLUE
ONE HUNDRED DAYS
(with Admiral Sir John "Sandy" Woodward)

PATRICK ROBINSON

HUNTER KILLER

AVON BOOKS

An Imprint of HarperCollinsPublishers

AVON BOOKS
An Imprint of HarperCollins*Publishers*
10 East 53rd Street
New York, New York 10022-5299

First Avon Books paperback printing: May 2006
First HarperCollins hardcover printing: May 2005

Avon Trademark Reg. U.S. Pat. Off. and in Other Countries, Marca Registrada, Hecho en U.S.A.

Printed in the U.S.A.

10 9 8 7 6 5 4 3 2 1

Author's Note

Because my principal publishers are in New York and London, I have chosen to work, essentially, in miles, yards, and feet. In terms of weight I have stuck with pounds and tons, except where military and naval protocol requires something different in the area of missile warheads.

However, in instances where serving French Naval officers and Special Forces are quoted directly, I use the correct metric measurements of their native language, the actual words they would have spoken.

Anyone mildly confused by all of this needs only to know that a meter is roughly a yard—the Olympic metric mile, 1,500 meters, is about 130 yards short of a proper mile. And a kilometer is roughly two-thirds of a mile.

I would also like to point out I have no wish to portray the French nation as cunning and unscrupulous. I am merely selecting one single nation to suit the purposes of this fictional work, in the year 2010, five years into the future from the date of publication.

I could have chosen Great Britain, but they are too close and loyal to the United States. I suppose I could have chosen Germany or Spain, or even Ireland. But none of them has quite the naval muscle and know-how of France.

Hopefully I have treated the French fairly and reasonably, despite casting them sometimes as heroes and sometimes as villains. It's one of the hazards of writing "techno-thrillers"—the villains are all fictional, but I write on a pretty broad canvas, and occasionally entire nations are scorched by the white-hot lance of my keyboard! No hard feelings (I hope).

PATRICK ROBINSON
October 2004

Cast of Principal Characters

United States Senior Command

Paul Bedford (President of the United States)
Adm. Arnold Morgan (Supreme Commander, Operation Tanker)
Gen. Tim Scannell (Chairman of the Joint Chiefs)
Adm. Alan Dickson (Chief of Naval Operations)
Adm. Frank Doran (C-in-C, Atlantic Fleet)
Adm. George Morris (Director, National Security Agency)
Lt. Cdr. Jimmy Ramshawe (Personal Assistant, Director NSA)
Adm. John Bergstrom (SPECWARCOM)

United States Foreign Services

Charlie Brooks (Envoy US Embassy, Riyadh)
Agent Tom Kelly (CIA Field Officer, Marseille)
Agent Ray Sharpe (CIA Brazzaville, Congo)
Agent Andy Campese (CIA Chief, Toulouse)
Agent Guy Roland (CIA, Toulouse)
Agent Jack Mitchell (CIA Field Officer, North Africa, Rabat, Morocco)

United States Navy

Capt. Bat Stimpson (Submarine Commanding Officer, *USS North Carolina*)

Capt. David Schnider (Submarine Commanding
    Officer, *USS Hawaii*)
Capt. Tony Pickard (Commanding Officer, *USS Shiloh*)
Lt. Billy Fallon (Helicopter aircrew, *USS Shiloh*)
Lt. Cdr. Brad Taylor (SEAL Team Leader)

French Senior Command

President of France
Pierre St. Martin (Foreign Minister)
Gaston Savary (Head of the Secret Service, DGSE)
Gen. Michel Jobert (C-in-C, Special Operations)

French Navy

Adm. Georges Pires (Commandant Fusiliers Marine
    Commandos, COMFUSCO)
Adm. Marc Romanet (Flag Officer, Submarines)
Capt. Alain Roudy (Commanding Officer, hunter-killer
    submarine *Perle*)
Cdr. Louis Dreyfus (Commanding Officer, hunter-killer
    submarine *Améthyste*)
Lt. Garth Dupont (Commander Frogmen, *Améthyste*)
Cdr. Jules Ventura (Commander, Special Forces in Gulf,
    Perle)
Lt. Reme Doumen (Leader, Assault Team Two,
    Saudi Loading Docks)
Seaman Vincent Lefevre (assistant to Commander
    Ventura)

French Special Forces Commanders, Saudi Arabia

Maj. Etienne Marot (2/IC Team Three, Khamis
    Mushayt)
Maj. Paul Spanier (Commanding Officer Team One,
    Air Base Assault)
Maj. Henri Gilbert (Team Two, Air Base Assault)

French-appointed Military Commanders, Saudi Arabia

Col. Jacques Gamoudi (ex–Foreign Legion, C-in-C Saudi Revolutionary Army, Riyadh, aka Hooks)
General Ravi Rashood, C-in-C Hamas, C-in-C Southern Assault Force, Saudi Arabia (aka Maj. Ray Kerman)

French Foreign Services

Agent Yves Zilber (DGSE, Toulouse)
Michel Phillipes (DGSE Field Chief, Riyadh)
Maj. Raul Foy (DGSE, Riyadh)
Envoy Claude Chopin (French Embassy, Brazzaville, Congo)

Members of the Kingdom's Royal Family

Prince Khalid bin Mohammed al-Saud (playboy)
King of Saudi Arabia
Prince Nasir Ibn Mohammed al-Saud (Crown Prince)

Saudi Military Personnel

Col. Sa'ad Kabeer (Commander, Eighth Armored Brigade, Diversionary Assault Air Base)
Capt. Faisal Rahman (al Queda battalion, Riyadh)
Maj. Abdul Majeed (Tank Commander, Airport Assault)
Colonel Bandar (Tank Commander, Revolutionary Army, Riyadh)

Israeli Connection

Ambassador David Gavron (Washington)
Agent David Schwab (Mossad, Marseille)
Agent Robert Jazy (Mossad, Marseille)
Daniel Mostel (*Sayanim*, Air Traffic Control, Damascus)

Key International Personnel

Cpl. Shane Collins (British Army electronics intercept operator, JSSU, Cyprus)

Sir David Norris (Chairman, International Petroleum Exchange, London)

Abdul Gamoudi (father of Col. Jacques Gamoudi)

Wives

Kathy Morgan

Shakira Rashood

Giselle Hooks, aka Giselle Gamoudi

European "Royalty"

Princess Adele (South London)

HUNTER KILLER

Prologue

PRINCE KHALID BIN Mohammed al-Saud, aged twenty-six, was enduring a night of fluctuating fortunes. On the credit side, he had just befriended a spectacular-looking Gucci-clad blonde named Adele, who said she was a European princess and was currently clinging to his left arm. On the debit side he had just dropped $247,000 playing blackjack in one of the private gaming rooms.

The casino in Monte Carlo was costing Khalid's great-great-uncle, the King, around the same amount per month as the first-line combat air strength of the Royal Saudi Air Force. There were almost thirty-five thousand Saudi royal princes bestowing a brand-new dimension upon the word *hedonism*. Like young Prince Khalid, many of them loved Monte Carlo, especially the casino. And blackjack. And baccarat. And craps. And roulette. And expensive women. And champagne. And caviar. And high-speed motor yachts. Oh boy, did those princes ever love motor yachts.

Prince Khalid pushed another $10,000 worth of chips to his new princess and contemplated the sexual pleasures that most certainly stood before him. Plus the fact that she was royal, like him. The King would approve of that. Khalid was so inflamed by her beauty he never even considered the fact that European royalty did not usually speak with a south London accent.

Adele played on, with gushing laughter, fueled by vintage Krug champagne. She played blackjack as thoughtfully as a fire hydrant and as subtly as a train crash. It took her nine minutes and forty-three seconds precisely to lose the $10,000. When this happened, even Prince Khalid, a young man with no financial brakes whatsoever, somehow groped for the anchors as well as Adele's superbly turned backside.

"I think we shall seek further pleasures elsewhere." He smiled, beckoning a champagne waitress with a nod of his head and requesting a floor manager to settle his evening's account.

Adele's laughter carried across the room. But no one turned a head as the young Saudi prince blithely signed a gambling chit for something in excess of $260,000.

It was a bill he would never see. It would be added to his losses of other evenings that month, totaling more than a million dollars. And it would be forwarded directly to the King of Saudi Arabia, who would send a check, sooner or later. These days, later rather than sooner.

Prince Khalid was a direct descendant of the mighty Bedouin warrior Abdul Aziz, "Ibn Saud," founder of modern Saudi Arabia and progenitor of more than forty sons and God knows how many daughters before his death in 1953. The young Prince Khalid was of the ruling line of the House of Saud. But there were literally thousands of cousins, uncles, brothers, and close relatives. And the King treated them all with unquestioning generosity.

So much generosity that the great oil kingdom of the Arabian Peninsula now stood teetering on a financial precipice, because millions and millions of barrels of oil needed to be pumped out of the desert every day purely to feed the colossal financial requirements of young princes like Khalid bin Mohammed al-Saud.

He was one of literally dozens who owned huge motor yachts in the harbors along the French Riviera. His boat, *Shades of Arabia*, was a growling 107-foot-long, sleek white Godzilla of a powerboat that could not make up its mind whether to remain on the sea or become a guided missile. Built in Florida by the renowned West Bay Son Ship corporation, it boasted five staterooms and was just about the last word in luxury yachts. At least for its size it was.

The Captain of *Shades of Arabia*, Hank Reynolds, out of

Seattle, Washington, nearly had a heart attack every time Prince Khalid insisted on taking the helm. And this was a reaction that did not abate even on a calm, open sea. Prince Khalid had two speeds. Flat out or stopped. He had five times been arrested for speeding in various French harbors along the Riviera. Each time he was fined heavily, twice he ended up in jail for a few hours, and each time the King's lawyers bailed him out, on the last occasion paying a fine of $100,000. Prince Khalid was an expensive luxury for any family, by any standards, but he could not have cared less. And, anyway, he was certainly no different from all the other young scions of the House of Saud.

Slipping his hand deftly around the waist of Adele, he nodded to the other ten people in his entourage, who were gathered around the roulette wheel, playing for rather smaller stakes. They included his two "minders," Rashid and Ahmed, both Saudis, three friends from Riyadh, and five young women, two of them Arabian from Dubai and wearing Western dress, three of them of European royal lineage similar to that of Adele.

Outside the imposing white portals of the casino, three automobiles—two Rolls-Royces and one Bentley—slid immediately to the forecourt, attended by a uniformed doorman from the world's most venerable gaming house. Prince Khalid handed him a hundred-dollar bill—the equivalent of more than two barrels of oil on the world market—and slipped into the backseat of the lead car with Adele. Rashid and Ahmed, each of them highly paid servants of the King himself, also boarded the gleaming, dark blue *Silver Cloud,* both of them in the wide front seat.

The other eight distributed themselves evenly among the other two cars, and Prince Khalid instructed his driver. "Sultan, we will not be returning to the Hermitage for a while. Please take us down to the boat."

"Of course, Your Highness," replied Sultan, and moved off toward the harbor, followed, line astern, by the other two cars.

Three minutes later they pulled up alongside *Shades of Arabia,* which rode gently on her lines in a flat, calm harbor.

"Good evening, Your Highness," called the watchman, switching on the gangway light. "Will we be sailing tonight?"

"Just a short trip, two or three miles offshore to see the lights of Monaco, then back in by one A.M.," replied the Prince.

"Very good, sir," said the watchman, a young Saudi naval officer who had navigated one of the King's Corvettes in the Gulf Fleet headquarters in Al Jubayl. His name was Bandar and he had been specifically selected by the C-in-C to serve as First Officer on *Shades of Arabia,* with special responsibilities for the well-being of Prince Khalid.

Capt. Hank Reynolds liked Bandar, and they worked well together, which was just as well for Reynolds, because one word of criticism about him from young Bandar would have ended his career. The Saudis paid exorbitantly for top personnel from the West, but tolerated no insubordination directed at the royal presence.

Gathered in the magnificently presented stateroom, which contained a bar and a dining area for at least twelve, Prince Khalid's party was served vintage Krug champagne from dewy magnums that cost around $250 each. On the dining room table there were two large crystal bowls, one containing prime Beluga caviar from Iran, about three pounds of it, never mind $100 an ounce. The other contained white powder in a similar quantity, and was placed next to a polished teak stand upon which were set a dozen small, hand-blown crystal tubes, each one four and a half inches long and as exquisitely turned as Adele's rear end. The contents of the second bowl were approximately twice as expensive as the Beluga. It was also in equal demand among the party.

Including the cost of the two stewards in attendance, the refreshments in that particular stateroom represented the sale of around six hundred barrels of Saudi crude on the International Petroleum Exchange in London. That was 6,600 gallons. Prince Khalid's lifestyle swallowed up gas faster than a Concorde.

Right now he was blasting the white powder up his nostrils with his regular abandon. He really liked cocaine. It made him feel that he was the right-hand man of the King of Saudi Arabia, the only country in all the world that bore the name of the family that ruled it. His name.

Prince Khalid tried never to face the undeniable fact that he was close to useless. His bachelor of arts degree from a truly expensive California university was, so far, his only true achievement. But his father had to persuade the King to build a vast new library for the school, *and* furnish it with thousands of books, in order for that degree to be awarded.

These days the Prince wandered the glorious seaports of the Mediterranean all summer, reclining in the opulence of *Shades of Arabia*. It was only when he took his nightly burst of cocaine that he felt he could face the world on equal terms. Indeed, on the right evening, with the precise correct combination of Krug and coke, Prince Khalid felt he could do anything. Tonight was one of those evenings.

The moment his head cleared from the initial rush, he ordered Bandar to the bridge to tell Captain Reynolds that he, Khalid, would be taking the helm as soon as the great motor yacht had cast her lines and was facing more or less in the right direction. "Have the Captain call me as soon as we're ready," he added, making absolutely certain that Adele could hear his stern words of command.

Ten minutes later he took Adele up to the enclosed bridge area with its panoramic views of the harbor, and assumed command of the yacht. Captain Reynolds, a great burly northwesterner who had spent most of his life on freighters on Puget Sound, moved over to the raised chair of First Officer Bandar, who stood directly behind him. Adele slipped into the navigator's spot, next to Prince Khalid.

"She's ready, sir," said Reynolds, a worried frown already on his face. "Steer zero-eight-five, straight past the harbor wall up ahead, then come right to one-three-five for the run offshore . . . and watch your speed, *please*, Your Highness . . . that's a harbor master's patrol boat right off your starboard bow . . ."

"No problem, Hank," replied the Prince. "I feel good tonight. We'll have a nice run."

And with that he rammed open both throttles, driving the twin 1,800-horsepower DDC-MTU 16V2000s to maximum revs, and literally thundered off the start-blocks. Princess Adele, whose only previous experience with water transport had been an economy day trip on the ferry from Gravesend to Tilbury in southeast London, squealed with delight. Hank Reynolds, as usual, nearly went into cardiac arrest.

Shades of Arabia, now with a great white bow wave nearly five feet above the calm surface, charged through Monte Carlo harbor at a speed building to twenty-five knots. Her wake shot both crystal bowls clean off the dining room table, and the white dust from the billowing cloud of cocaine caused even the ship's purebred Persian cat to believe that it could probably achieve anything. Its purring could be heard in the galley, fifty feet away, like a third diesel engine.

Meanwhile, ships and yachts moored in the harbor rocked violently as the massive wake from *Shades of Arabia* rolled into them, causing glasses and crockery to crash to the floor and even people to lose their footing and slam into walls. In that briefest of scenarios anyone could understand the reason for the draconian French laws about speeding that were enforced in every Riviera harbor.

Prince Khalid never gave them a thought. He hurtled past the harbor walls, missing the flashing light on the wall to his portside by about ten feet, and roared out into the open sea. With all care cast aside by the Krug–coke combo, he hammered those big diesels straight toward the deep water, less than a mile offshore.

And out there, with over sixty fathoms beneath his keel, the Prince began a long, swerving course through the light swell, which delighted his guests, who were all by now on the top deck aft viewing area, marveling at the speed and smoothness of this fabulous seagoing craft.

No one took the slightest notice of the big searchlight a mile astern, which belonged to the coast guard patrol launch, summoned by the harbor master and now in hot pursuit, making almost forty knots through the water.

The night was warm, but there were heavy rain clouds overhead, and it was extremely dark. Too dark to see the massive, dark shape of the ocean liner that rode her gigantic anchor one mile up ahead. In fact there was a light sea mist, not quite fog, lying in waxen banks over the surface of the sea.

One way or another the 150,000-ton Cunarder, the *Queen Mary 2,* was extremely difficult to see that night, even with all her night lights burning. Any approaching vessel might not have locked on to her, even five hundred yards out, unless the afterguard were watching the radar sweeps very carefully, which Prince Khalid was most certainly not doing. Captain Reynolds was so busy staring at the blackness ahead that he, too, was negligent of the screen. But at least he had an excuse—mainly that he was frozen in fear for his life.

At length he snapped to the Prince, "Steady, sir. Come off fifteen knots. We just can't see well enough out here . . . this is too fast . . ."

"Don't worry, Hank," replied Prince Khalid. "I'm feeling very good. This is fun . . . just for a few minutes I can cast aside the cares of my country and my responsibilities."

Captain Reynolds's eyes rolled heavenward as his boss tried to coax every last ounce of speed out of the yacht, despite the fact they were in another fog bank and visibility at sea level was very poor.

The watchmen on the largest, longest, tallest, and widest passenger ship ever built did however spot the fast-approaching *Shades of Arabia,* from a height close to that of a twenty-one-story building. They sounded a deafening blast on the horn, which could be heard for ten miles, and at the last minute ordered a starboard-side reverse thrust in order to swing around and present their narrower bow to the oncoming motor yacht rather than their 1,132-foot hull. But it was too late. Way too late.

Shades of Arabia came knifing through the mist, throttles wide open, everyone laughing and drinking up on the aft deck, Prince Khalid tenderly kissing Adele, one hand on the controls, one on her backside. Hank Reynolds, who had heard the *Queen Mary*'s horn echo across the water, yelled at the last moment, "JESUS CHRIST!" He dived for the throttles, but not in time.

The 107-foot motor yacht smashed into the great ocean liner's port bow. The pointed bow of *Shades of Arabia* buried itself twenty feet into the *Queen Mary*'s steel plating. The colossal impact caused a huge explosion in the engine room of the Prince's pride and joy, and the entire yacht burst into flames. No one got out, save for bodyguard Rashid, who had seen the oncoming steel cliff and hurled himself off the top deck twenty feet into the water. Like Ishmael, he alone lived to tell the tale.

Two days later, in a palatial private residence in the northern suburbs of the city of Riyadh, Prince Nasir Ibn Mohammed al-Saud, a fifty-six-year-old devout Sunni Muslim and the heir apparent to the King, was sipping dark Turkish coffee and staring with horror at the front page of the *London Daily Telegraph*.

Beneath a six-column-wide photo of the badly listing *Queen Mary 2*, was the headline: DRUNKEN SAUDI PRINCE ALMOST SINKS WORLD'S LARGEST OCEAN LINER; *High-speed motor yacht rams QM2, causing mass evacuation in 100 fathoms off Monaco.*

The photo showed the remains of the *Shades of Arabia* jutting out from the bow of the ship, the heavy list to port on the forward half of the mighty ship, and worst of all the French coast guard helicopters swarming above the stricken liner, evacuating some of her 2,620 passengers and 1,250 crew.

The lifeboats were also being lowered, even though there was no immediate danger of the great ship's sinking. But she could not propel herself, and would have to be towed into port to be pumped out and temporarily repaired, in preparation for the two-thousand-mile journey to the mouth of the Loire River, to the shipyards of Alstom-Chantiers de l'Atlantique, in Saint-Nazaire, where she'd been built.

Prince Nasir was appalled. An inset picture of young Prince Khalid was captioned: HE DIED IN A FIREBALL PRECISELY AS HE LIVED—RECKLESS TO THE END. The story named the dead companions, chronicled the champagne in the casino. It referred to Prince Khalid's losses at the tables, his womanizing, his love of cocaine, his incredible wealth. It quoted Lloyds insurance brokers' ranting and raving about their losses, bracing themselves for a huge payout to the Cunard shipping line for collision damage to the $800 million ship, loss of income, lawsuits from passengers, and compensation to the French government for the costs of the evacuation.

Prince Nasir knew perfectly well this was the biggest story in the world, one that would sweep the television and radio stations of the United States and Europe, as well as every newspaper in the world. And it would go on doing so for several days yet.

The Prince loathed everything about it. He hated the humiliation it brought upon his country. He detested the plain and obvious defiance of the Koran. And he hated the sheer self-indulgence of Prince Khalid and the terrible harm to Saudi Arabia's image caused by this lunatic spending of petro-dollars by young men in their twenties.

Prince Nasir would one day be king. And the only obstruction that stood between him and the throne of Saudi Arabia was his well-publicized and vehement disapproval of the lifestyles of the royal family. For the moment, however, he was the nominated Crown Prince, a wise and pious Islamic fundamentalist who had made it quite clear that when he ascended the throne the shame was all going to end.

Nasir was the outstanding political and business mind in the kingdom, at home in the corridors of power in London, Paris, Brussels, and the Middle East. The King valued his counsel in a wary and cautious way, but of course Prince Nasir had countless enemies: sons, brothers, and grandsons of the King.

There had been three attempts to assassinate him. But the Saudi populace loved him, for he alone stood up for them, gave interviews revealing the real reason for the drop in their state incomes from $28,000 to $7,000 over fifteen years—the astronomical cost of the royal family.

He was a tall, bearded man, descended like most of the royal family from the great Ibn Saud. The call of the desert for him was never far away. Most evenings, he would be driven out to the hot, lonely sands north of the city, where he would rendezvous with friends. His servants would cast upon the desert floor a vast, near-priceless rug from Iran. A three-sided tent would be erected. And there they would dine, talking of the great revolution to come, a revolution that would surely one day topple the ruling branch of the House of Saud.

Today the Prince rose to his feet muttering, as he had done many times before, "This country is like France before the Revolution. One family bleeding the state to death. In eighteenth-century Paris, it was the Bourbon kings. In twenty-first-century Riyadh, it's the al-Saud family."

And then, louder now, as he hurled the newspaper aside, *"THIS HAS TO STOP!"*

Tuesday, May 5, 2009
King Khalid International Airport
Saudi Arabia

THE BLACK CADILLAC stretch limousine moved swiftly around the public drop-off point to a wide double gate, already opened by the two armed guards. On each wing of the big American automobile fluttered two pennants, the green-and-blue ensigns of the Royal Saudi Naval Forces. Both guards saluted as the instantly recognizable limo swept past and out toward the wide runway of terminal three, the exclusive enclave of Saudia, the national airline.

Inside the limousine was one solitary passenger, Crown Prince Nasir Ibn Mohammed, deputy minister of the armed forces to his very senior cousin Prince Abdul Rahman, son of the late King Faisal. Both sentries saluted as Prince Nasir went by, heading straight for the take-off area where one of the King's newest Boeing 747s was awaiting him, engines idling in preparation for takeoff. Every other flight was on hold until the meticulously punctual Prince Nasir was in the air.

Wearing Arab dress, he was escorted to the outside stairway by both the chief steward and a senior naval officer. Prince Nasir's own son, the twenty-six-year-old Commodore Fahad Ibn Nasir, served on a Red Sea frigate, so his father was always treated like an Admiral wherever he traveled in the kingdom.

The moment he was seated in the upstairs first-class section, the door was tightly secured and the pilot opened the throttles. The royal passenger jet, reveling in its light load, roared off down the runway and screamed into the clear blue skies, directly into the hot south wind off the desert, before banking left, toward the Gulf, and then northwest across Iraq, to Syria.

He was the only passenger onboard. It was almost unheard of for a senior member of the royal family to travel alone, without even a bodyguard. But this was different. The 747 was not going even halfway to Prince Nasir's final destination. He used it only to get out of Saudi Arabia, to another Arab country. His real destination was entirely another matter.

A suitcase at the rear of the upstairs area contained his Western clothes. As soon as the flight was airborne, Prince Nasir changed into a dark gray suit, blue shirt, and a maroon print silk tie from Hermès, complete with a solid-gold clip in the shape of a desert scimitar. He wore plain black loafers, handmade in London, with dark gray socks.

The suitcase also held a briefcase containing several documents, which the Prince removed. He then packed away his white Arabian *thobe*, red-and-white *ghutra* headdress with its double cord, the *aghal*. He had left King Khalid Airport, named for his late great-uncle, as an Arab. He would arrive in Damascus every inch the international businessman.

When the plane touched down, two hours later, a limousine from the Saudi embassy met him and drove him directly to the regular midday Air France flight to Paris. The aircraft already contained its full complement of passengers, and although none of them knew it, they were sitting comfortably, seat belts fastened, awaiting the arrival of the Arabian prince.

The aircraft had pulled back from the Jetway, and a special flight of stairs had been placed against the forward entrance. Prince Nasir's car halted precisely at those stairs, where an Air France official waited to escort him to his seat. Four rows and eight seats, that is, had been booked in the name of the Saudi embassy, on Al-Jala'a Avenue. Prince

Nasir sat alone in 1A. The rest of the seats would remain empty all the way to Roissy–Charles de Gaulle Airport, nineteen miles north of Paris.

They served a special luncheon, prepared by the cooks at the embassy, of curried chicken with rice cooked in the Indian manner, followed by fruit juice and sweet pastries. Prince Nasir, the most devout of Muslims, had never touched alcohol in his life and disapproved fiercely of any of his countrymen who did. The late Prince Khalid of Monte Carlo was not among his absolute favorites. The great man knew, beyond any doubt, of the antics of that particular deceased member of his family.

They flew on across Turkey and the Balkan states, finally crossing the Alps and dropping down above the lush French farmland that lies south of the forest of Ardenne, over the River Seine, and into northwest Paris.

Again, Prince Nasir endured no formalities nor checks. He disembarked before anyone else, down a private flight of stairs, where a jet-black, unmarked French government car waited to drive him directly to the heavily guarded Elysée Palace, on Rue St. Honoré, the official residence of the Presidents of France since 1873.

It was a little after 4 P.M. in Paris, the flight from Damascus having taken five hours, with a two-hour time gain. Two officials were waiting at the President's private entrance, and Prince Nasir was escorted immediately to the President's private apartment on the first floor overlooking Rue de l'Elysée.

The President was awaiting him in a large modern drawing room, which was decorated with a selection of six breathtaking Impressionist paintings, two by Renoir, two by Monet, and one each by Degas and Van Gogh. One hundred million dollars would not have bought them.

The President greeted Prince Nasir in impeccable English, the language agreed upon for the forthcoming conversation. By previous arrangement, no one would listen in. No ministers. No private secretaries. No interpreters. The following two hours before dinner would bring a meaning to the word *privacy* that was rarely, if ever, attained in international politics.

"Good afternoon, Your Highness," began the President. "I trust my country's travel arrangements have been satisfactory?"

"Quite perfect," replied the Prince, smiling. "No one could have required more." The two men knew each other vaguely, but were hardly even friends, let alone blood brothers. Yet.

The door to the drawing room was closed, and two uniformed military guards, summoned from the exterior security force, stood sentry in the outside corridor. The President of France himself poured coffee for his guest from a silver service laid out on a magnificent Napoleonic sideboard.

Prince Nasir complimented the President on the beauty of the piece and was amused when the President replied, "It probably belonged to Bonaparte himself—the Palais de l'Elysée was occupied by Napoleon's sister Caroline for much of the nineteenth century."

The highly educated Arabian Prince loved the traditions of France. He not only had a bachelor of arts degree in English literature from Harvard, but also a *maîtrise* (master's degree) in European history from the University of Paris. The knowledge that Bonaparte himself may have been served from this very sideboard somehow made the coffee taste all the richer.

"Well, Your Highness," said the President. "You must tell me your story, and why you wished to have a talk with me in this most private manner, at such very short notice." He was of course keenly aware of the traditions of highborn Arabs: talk about almost anything else for a half hour before tackling the main subject.

Prince Nasir knew that time was precious at this level. The balding, burly politician who stood before him had, after all, an entire country to run. The Prince decided to speak carefully, but with heavyweight intonations.

"Sir," he said, "my country is in terminal decline. In the past twenty years the ruling family—my own—has managed to spend over a hundred billion dollars of our cash reserves. We are probably down to our last fifteen billion. And soon that will be ten billion and then five billion. Twenty years ago my people received a generous share of the oil wealth that Allah has bestowed upon us. Around thirty thousand dollars per capita. Today that figure is close to six thousand. Because we can afford no more."

"But, of course," replied the President of France, "you do own twenty-five percent of all the world's oil . . ."

Prince Nasir smiled. "Our problem, sir, is not the creation of wealth," he said. "I suppose we could close down modern Saudi Arabia and all go back to the desert and sit there allowing our vast oil revenues to accrue, and make us once more one of the richest nations on earth. However, that would plainly be impracticable.

"Our problem is the reckless spending of money by a ruling family that is now corrupt beyond redemption. And a huge percentage of that expenditure goes on the family itself. Thousands and thousands of royal princes are being kept in a style probably not seen on this planet since . . . well, the Bourbon royal family's domination of your own country. I have stated it often enough. Saudi Arabia is like France before the Revolution. *Monsieur le Président,* I intend to emulate your brave class of warriors of the late eighteenth century. In my own country, I intend to re-enact that renunciation of the rights of the nobility."

The President's early left-wing leanings were well known. Indeed he had risen to power from a base as the communist mayor of a small town in Brittany. In a previous incarnation, this particular French President would have stormed the gates of Paris in the vanguard of the Revolution. Prince Nasir realized the word *Bourbon* would elicit instant sympathy.

The President shrugged, a deeply Gallic gesture. And he held out both hands, palms upward. "I knew of course some of the difficulties in Saudi Arabia . . . but I put it down mostly to your closeness to the Americans."

"That, too, is a grave problem, sir," replied Prince Nasir. "My people long for freedom from the Great Satan. But this King is a vigorous globally ambitious man, aged only forty-eight, and under him it would be impossible. We are bound up with the infidels so tightly . . . even though the majority

of Saudis wish devoutly they could be once more a God-
fearing nation of pure Muslims. Not terrorists, just a religious people in tune with the words of the Prophet, rather
than the grasping material creeds of the United States.

"I tell you this, sir. If Osama bin Laden suddenly materialized in Riyadh and ran for President, or even King, he
would win in a landslide."

The President of France chuckled. "I imagine there are
many Saudi Princes who would not agree *exactement* with
your views," he said. "I don't imagine that young man who
almost sank the *Queen Mary* last week would have been . . .
er . . . too *sympathique*."

"He most certainly would not," said Prince Nasir, frown-
ing. "He is a prime example of the endless corruption in my
country. There are now thirty-five thousand members of the
Saudi royal family, all of them drawing up to one million
dollars a month, and spending it on private jets, ocean-
going yachts, gambling, alcohol, and expensive women.
And if it goes on, we are in danger of becoming a godless
Third-World country. To stand in one of our royal palaces is
to watch something close to the fall of the Roman Empire!"

"Or the British," countered the Frenchman, again chuckling. "More coffee from Napoleon's sideboard?"

Prince Nasir had always liked the French President, and
he was extremely glad to know him better.

"Thank you," he said. The two men walked across the
room toward the silver coffeepot. They were already in step.

"Well, Your Highness, you are outlining to me a very sad
state of affairs. And I agree, if I were the Crown Prince of
such a nation I, too, would be extremely exercised by the
situation. But to the outside world, Saudi Arabia looks very
much like the one constant in a turbulent Middle East."

"That may have been so twenty years ago, but it is most
certainly not so today. It is my belief that this corrupt ruling
family must be overthrown, and its excesses removed, the
lifestyles of the Princes terminated. And the colossal spending on military hardware from the United States ceased
forthwith. Everything has to change if we are to survive as
the prosperous nation we once were."

The Prince rose to his feet and paced across the room and back. "Remember, sir, as a nation we are not yet eighty years old. The active members of this family are just a generation, maybe two, from men who grew up in goat-hair tents and followed the rhythms of the great desert, from oasis to oasis, eating mainly dates and drinking camel's milk . . ."

"You are surely not advocating a return to those days?" asked the President, smiling.

"No, sir, I am not. But I know we must return part of the way to our Bedouin roots in the desert, to the written creeds of the Prophet Mohammed. I do not wish to see our sons spending millions of dollars on Western luxuries. *"Wallahi!"* he exclaimed. *By God!* "What could that boy Khalid possibly have been doing with those cheap women on a yacht fit for a President, under the influence of drugs and alcohol, having just lost more than a quarter of a million dollars in the casino at Monte Carlo? I ask you that. What could he possibly have been doing with such a lifestyle?"

"Very probably having the most wonderful time." The French President smiled. "But I do of course understand. It plainly is not right that there should be thousands of these young men ransacking the Saudi Treasury every month, at the expense of the people. I think you are very probably correct. Something will soon need to be done. Otherwise the people will rise up against the King, and you might be looking at a bloodbath . . . as we had in Paris in the eighteenth century. And by the sound of it, equally justified."

Prince Nasir sipped his coffee. "The problem is," he said, "our King is quite extraordinarily powerful. Not only does he pay all of the family's bills—none of the young Princes ever sees a bill, for anything. Every charge they incur goes directly to the King, from all over the world. "But he also controls the Army, the Air Force, and the Navy, plus all of the security forces. Only he can pay them. And they are loyal to him alone."

"How large is the Saudi Army these days?"

"Almost ninety thousand—nine brigades, three armored, five mechanized, and one airborne. They're supported by five artillery battalions, and a separate Royal Guard regiment of three light infantry battalions. The armored brigades have almost three hundred highly advanced tanks, the MIA2 Abrams from the United States. Of course, one of our armored brigades is entirely French equipped."

The President nodded sagely, though well out of his depth. "And the Navy?"

"It's the smallest of our services. Just a few Corvettes in the Red Sea, and a few guided-missile frigates, purchased, you will know, from France. But the Navy is not our greatest strength."

"And the Air Force?"

"This is our best force. We have more than two hundred combat aircraft in the Royal Saudi Air Force, with eighteen thousand personnel. They are deployed at four key airfields. And their mission is very simply to keep the kingdom safe, in particular to keep our oil installations safe."

"Well, Your Highness. I would assess that is a *magnifique* amount of firepower to put down a revolution. If our Bourbon Kings and Princes had possessed half of that, they'd still be here, raping and pillaging the land."

Prince Nasir laughed despite himself. He took another sip of coffee and then said, "Sir, the Achilles' heel of the Saudi King is not the ability of the military to fight. It's his ability to pay them."

"But he has all the money in the world, flowing in every month to achieve that," replied the President.

"But what if he didn't?" said Prince Nasir Ibn Mohammed. "What if he didn't?"

"You mean someone takes all the oil away from him?" said the President. "That sounds most unlikely given all those armored brigades and fighter jets."

"No, sir. What if the oil was taken out of the equation? What if it simply no longer flowed, and the King had no income to pay the armed services? What then?"

"You mean, supposing someone destroyed the Saudi oil industry?"

"Only for a little while," replied the Prince.

Wednesday, May 6, 2009, 5:00 A.M.
Foreign Office
Quai d'Orsay, Paris

Pierre St. Martin, the Foreign Minister of France and a hopeful future President, stood beside a large portrait of Napoleon placed on an easel on the left-hand side of his lavish office. Before him stood Monsieur Gaston Savary, the tall saturnine head of the French Secret Service—the Direction Générale de la Sécurité Extérieure (DGSE), successor to the former internationally feared SDECE, the counterespionage service.

The two men had never met before, and the elegant Monsieur St. Martin, was, quite frankly, amazed that he had been ordered to his office at this ungodly hour in the morning, apparently to converse with this . . . this spy from La Piscine—the kind of man patrician politicians in London refer to as Johnny Raincoat.

La Piscine was the government nickname for the DGSE, derived from the proximity of the bleak ten-story Secret Service building to a municipal swimming pool in the Caserne des Tourelles. Savary operated out of 128 Boulevard Mortier, over in the twentieth arrondissement; that was about as far west as you could possibly go and still be in the City of Lights. It is not the kind of neighborhood in which you'd expect to locate an urbane Foreign Minister. The suave and expensively tailored St. Martin had never been to La Piscine.

Nonetheless, they had both been ordered to the sumptuous offices on the Quai d'Orsay by the President of France himself. And the current resident of the Elysée Palace was due there in the next few minutes.

St. Martin, who had spent the night at the apartment of one of the most beautiful actresses in France, was a great deal more irritated by the intrusion into his life than Savary.

Both men were around the same age, fiftyish, but the Secret Service chief was a lifelong career officer in undercover operations. For him the call in the middle of the night was routine. No matter the time, he was instantly operational, and he had been for ten years responsible for the planning of black operations conducted on behalf of the government of France, using both military forces and civilian agents.

A lithe, fit, and slightly morose man, Savary had even taken part personally in various French adventures. He would, as ever, admit nothing, but he was reputed to have been operational in the attack and subsequent sinking of the Greenpeace freighter in Auckland Harbor, New Zealand, in July 1985. Interference with the Pacific nuclear tests conducted by France?

NON! JAMAIS! was Savary's view of that.

"Would you like to remove your raincoat?" asked the Foreign Minister. "Since we are shortly to be in the presence of our President."

Savary, without a word, took the coat off and slung it over the back of a near-priceless Louis Quinze chair, owned originally by the Duchess of Bourbon, the King's sister, for whom the massive next-door Palais Bourbon had been built. Stormed and captured by the mob during the Revolution, today the former private residence served as the French Parliament, but retained its original name, Bourbon. It was a reminder of the blistering pace in opulence that those old French aristos had set for the Saudi royal family to emulate.

St. Martin stared at the spy's raincoat over the back of the late King's chair, and . . . well, winced.

He pressed a small bell for the butler to bring them some coffee, but his prime purpose was to get rid of the garment owned by *Jean-Claude Raincoat or whatever his damned name was*. St. Martin had always harbored a sneaking regard for the Bourbons and their excellent taste.

"I don't suppose you have the slightest idea what this is all about?" he said.

"Absolutely none," replied the intelligence chief. "I just received a phone call from the Palais Elysée and was told that the President wished to see me in your office at five-fifteen A.M. Here I am, *n'est-ce pas?*"

"My summons was exactly the same. My mobile phone rang at one-thirty A.M. God knows what this is all about."

"Maybe *le Président* is about to declare war?"

"Not, I hope, on the United States."

Savary smiled for the first time. But just then their coffee arrived, for three, as requested. St. Martin had the butler pour just two cups and asked him to hang Savary's raincoat in the hall closet.

Almost immediately a phone rang on his enormous desk and a voice announced that the presidential car had arrived at the portals of the Foreign Office. Pierre St. Martin poured the third cup of coffee himself.

Three minutes later he was most surprised to see that the President was entirely alone: no secretary, no aides, no officials. He closed the door himself and said quietly, "Pierre, Gaston, thank you for coming so early. Would you please ensure that our discussion is conducted entirely in secret. Perhaps a guard outside the door."

St. Martin made a short phone call, handed the President a cup of coffee, and motioned for everyone to be seated, the President on a fine drawing room upright chair, the Secret Service chief on the Louis Quinze number lately occupied by his raincoat, while the Foreign Minister himself retreated behind his desk.

"Gentlemen," said the President, "approximately two hours ago, one of the most important Princes in the Saudi Arabian royal family left my residence to fly home in a French Air Force jet to Damascus, and then in his own aircraft to Riyadh. His visit with me was so private, so confidential, not even the most senior staff at the Saudi embassy here in Paris were aware of his presence in the city.

"He came not just to inform me that the financial excesses of the Saudi Arabian ruling family would shortly bankrupt his country, but to propose a way out of the problem—to the very great advantage of himself, and indeed of France."

St. Martin swiftly interjected, "Doubtless inspired by that young Saudi Prince who nearly sank the *Queen Mary* last week?"

"I think partly," replied the President. "But the problem of thirty-five thousand princes, all members of the family, spending up to a million dollars a month on fast living has been vexing the reformist element in the Saudi government for several years. According to my visitor, the time has come for that to cease."

Savary spoke for the first time. "I imagine he mentioned that the Saudi King is heavily protected by a fiercely loyal Army, Air Force, and Navy. So an overthrow of that part of the family is more or less out of the question."

"Indeed he did, Gaston. He mentioned it in great detail. And he pointed out that the only person in the entire kingdom who could pay the armed services is the King, who receives all the oil revenues of the country and pays all the bills for his family."

"So the armed services would be most unlikely to turn against him," said Savary.

"Most unlikely," agreed the President. "Unless for some reason the vast revenues from the oil fields ceased to exist."

"And the King could no longer pay them, correct?" said Savary.

"Precisely," replied the President.

"Sir, I have no doubt you are as aware as I am that those Saudi oil fields are guarded by a steel ring of personnel and armaments," said Savary. "They're just about impregnable—understandably, since the whole country is one hundred percent dependent upon them, from the richest to the poorest."

"Well, we have not reached that point in the conversation yet, Gaston. But I would like to inform you, in the broadest possible terms, what the Prince was proposing."

"I, for one, am paying keen attention," said Pierre St. Martin.

"Excellent," replied the President. "Because the information I am about to impart might be of critical importance to our nation. His Highness, Prince Nasir—you need know nothing more of him—proposes the following. Someone hits the oil fields and knocks out the main pumping station and the three or four biggest loading terminals on both the Red Sea and the Persian Gulf.

"Two days later, with Saudi Arabia's economy effectively laid to waste, a small, highly trained fighting force attacks the Saudi military city in the southwest of the country near the Yemen border. And while the military is in disarray, another highly specialized force goes in and takes Riyadh, the capital city.

"They knock out a couple of palaces, gun down the royal family, take the television station and the radio station, and sweep the Crown Prince to power. He then appears on nationwide television and announces that he has taken control, and the corrupt regime of the present King has been summarily swept away."

"And you are proposing we somehow take part in all this?" asked St. Martin incredulously.

"Certainly not. I am suggesting we examine the feasibility of doing so."

"And if the military coup were carried out, with our assistance, and the Prince took over Saudi Arabia, what could be in it for us?" asked Gaston Savary.

"Well, as his best friends and closest allies, and a sworn opponent to the ambitions of the United States, we would be awarded every single contract to rebuild the oil installations, and we would become the sole marketing agents for all Saudi Arabian oil for the next hundred years. Anyone wishes to buy, they buy it from us. Which means we effectively control world oil prices."

"And how long would it take us to rebuild the oil installations?"

"Maybe two years. Maybe less."

"And what about that big Saudi Army and Air Force?"

The President shrugged. "What about them? They would have no alternative but to switch their allegiance to serve the new King. After all, they cannot serve a dead one, *n'est-ce pas*? And no one else could possibly pay them, save for the new ruler. And even then things would be rather tight for a few months, until some oil began to flow, probably in the Gulf terminals."

"You really think this could be achieved, sir?" said Savary. "Militarily, I mean?"

"I have no idea. But Prince Nasir does. And he says that if it is not achieved, Saudi Arabia is doomed."

"What kind of a premise will he campaign on?" asked St. Martin.

"Well, he won't really need to campaign, will he? Not if he simply seizes power. But he will immediately assure the populace that the massive financial stipends for the princes will end forthwith. Which will save his treasury maybe two hundred fifty billion a year.

"He will also advocate an immediate return to pure Muslim worship of the Wahhabi persuasion. You understand— strict rules of prayer, no alcohol, the strict word of the Koran, and the teachings of the Prophet. There will be no more cozying up to American politicians, and the country will return to its basic Bedouin roots, to the old ways of life. They will heed the call of the desert, and bring up their children according to the old traditions, as indeed Prince Nasir has brought up his own. And there will certainly be no more financing of terrorism. And no further need to pay vast sums of protection money to groups who might otherwise attack Saudi Arabia. I speak of course of hundreds of millions of dollars directed to al-Qaeda.

"Once Prince Nasir has severed his ties with the United States, there will be no further danger from the fundamentalist groups. And of course we may also expect a far greater Saudi support for the Palestinians."

"But surely this will cause chaos on the world oil markets?" said St. Martin. "Absolute chaos."

"I have no doubt it will. But this won't affect us, because we will rid ourselves of our Saudi contracts long before anything happens. We will sign new two-year agreements with other Middle Eastern countries for all of our oil and gas requirements."

"But what about the world oil shortages? This would just about bankrupt Japan and cripple even the mighty economy of the United States. Our European partners would also be hurt. Gasoline could go to a hundred fifty dollars a barrel." St. Martin was just beginning to look particularly distraught.

"I agree," said the President. "But if Prince Nasir is correct, all this will happen anyway, if the Saudi population takes to the streets in protest against the royal family. As for the oil prices going through the roof—well, can you imagine anything more appealing to the country that effectively controls world sales of Saudi oil?"

"But, sir," said St. Martin. "The Saudi fields are the only stabilizer in all of the world's markets. Remember how they saved everyone by producing millions of extra barrels in 1991, and then again after 9/11 when they pumped almost five million extra barrels to save the market? Petrol prices hardly went up by a single franc.

"Saudi Arabia *is* the world market. The savior of the world's economy in times of crisis. It's the only nation that can produce extra oil. What are its reserves—two to three million barrels a day, if necessary, at any one time? Can you imagine the reaction of the United States if anyone ever found out we were in any way implicated?"

"What if no one ever found out we were implicated?" replied the President. "What if no one ever knew? What if it all appeared to be just an Arab matter—a military coup by the people against their corrupt rulers; a kind of insurrection that spread, most unfortunately, to the oil wells?"

"Sir, do you think it possible such a momentous action by France could ever be kept secret?"

"Again," said the President, "I have no idea. But the reason we are in this room, at this unearthly hour of the morning, is that we have been asked for help by a senior representative of one of our major trading partners . . . a partner that would feel obliged, in future, to purchase all of their military hardware from France—warships, fighter aircraft, and weaponry worth billions. Thus, gentlemen, please find out what we could do, how quietly we could do it, and whether we could stay sufficiently remote never to be proven guilty of anything. Meanwhile I shall behave as if this conversation had never taken place. You are the only two people in France who know anything of the prince's visit, and of the proposals he made. Perhaps you would be good enough to contact me when you have formulated your thoughts."

And with that, the most powerful man in the European Union stood up, replaced his coffee cup on the tray, and walked to the door.

Neither Pierre St. Martin nor Gaston Savary could recover swiftly enough even to open it for him. Both the French Foreign Minister and the head of France's Secret Service were in shock. And they just stood there, gawping, at the departing President, momentarily stunned by the enormity of the task he had set for them.

"*Sacré merde!*" muttered Pierre St. Martin.

Friday morning, May 8
Paris

Gaston Savary was alone, driving his black Citroën staff car through heavy commuter traffic into the remotest outpost of the northwest suburbs of the city. He was going against the incoming traffic, but it was still outlandishly busy, with queues of buses, vans, and trucks all the way, as always, in both directions. Over three and a half million people fight their way into, and out of, Paris every working day.

He reached the outer suburb of Taverny and drove up to the guardhouse at the entrance to one of the most secretive compounds in Europe—the headquarters of France's Commandement des Operations Speciales (COS), the joint service establishment that controls the worldwide special ops activities of all three French armed forces.

As head of the largely civilian French Secret Service, Savary was a regular visitor, and both duty guards wished him "*Bonjour*" before waving him through to a waiting escort who slipped into the front seat of the Citroën.

They drove toward the offices of the First Marine Parachute Infantry Regiment, the prime special ops unit in France, the direct equivalent of Britain's SAS, and the U.S.A.'s Navy SEALs and Rangers. This is a formidable black ops outfit, which clandestinely provides special training and even assistance to foreign countries; plus offensive action if necessary. It also conducts its own military intelli-

gence gathering and in recent years has been at the sharp
end of most French counterterrorist operations. Two heavily armed helicopter squadrons are under its command.

Gaston Savary instructed his escort, a young Army Lieutenant, to park the car. He let himself out at the main entrance, where another young officer wished him *"Bonjour"*
and took him immediately to the special ops C-in-C, General Michel Jobert.

The two men were old acquaintances, but nonetheless
Savary handed over a letter, certified by the office of the
Foreign Minister of France, instructing the General to work
carefully and in the strictest confidence with the bearer, ex-
amining the project scrupulously, before arriving at one of
two conclusions: possible or impossible.

And in the most clandestine manner, the two most senior
undercover warriors in France began their feasibility test on
behalf of their government and, in a sense, on behalf of
Prince Nasir Ibn Mohammed of Saudi Arabia.

In the next fifteen minutes General Jobert's dark, bushy
eyebrows rarely descended to their normal position on the
lower part of his forehead. He was truly astounded at the
scale of the proposition. Gaston Savary reckoned Jobert
softly exclaimed, *Mon Dieu!* about twelve times.

But the proposition was real enough. The President of
France wanted a professional opinion; whether the Saudi
oil industry could be brought to its knees by military attack
for a period of around two years, and whether, in the ensuing days, with the Saudi economy in ruins, it would be possible to subdue the Saudi armed forces and then take the
capital city of Riyadh. All with France, to all appearances,
having not the slightest involvement.

The first three items—the oil, the surrender of the army,
and the capture of Riyadh—were probably possible. In the
opinion of General Jobert the collapse of the economy
would leave an army somewhat disinclined to fight anyone.
The problem was the fourth item: could France somehow
make it all possible, with a substantial military involvement, and yet remain anonymous?

General Jobert, on reflection, thought absolutely not. So

did Gaston Savary. Which essentially meant that the President would have to decline the offer of the Saudi Prince to make France his sole supplier of future military hardware, and the sole world agent for all Saudi oil products. And that particular *non* would ultimately represent the rejection of an opportunity for the hard-pressed French Republic to earn several hundred billion dollars.

And that was a scenario both General Jobert and Gaston Savary suspected might not sit too well with a President whose country had been known, traditionally, to operate almost exclusively from a sense of unfettered self-interest.

The General, who had not received the slightest indication as to why he was meeting with Savary, read again the second page of the letter from Pierre St. Martin. It contained the briefest outline of the requirements that Prince Nasir considered would cripple the Saudi oil industry.

Priority number one was the destruction of the world's largest processing complex, at Abqaiq, which was situated twenty-five miles inland from the Gulf of Bahrain. Abqaiq was the destination of all crude oil from the Saudi south, particularly from Ghawar, the most productive oil field on earth. Beneath the shifting desert sands, right there, sixty miles southwest of Dhahran, lay 70 billion barrels.

Close to Abqaiq, Pump Station Number One sent some 900,000 barrels of light crude per day, seven hundred miles, up and over the Aramah Mountains, to the Red Sea oil port of Yanbu al Bahr.

If Pump Station Number One went down, the massive loading terminals of both Yanbu and, ninety miles to the south, Rabigh would be finished. So would the huge refineries in the area, including the enormous complexes at Rabigh, Medina, and Jiddah.

Nonetheless, Prince Nasir believed the Red Sea terminals should be hit and destroyed. On the Gulf coast, the largest offshore oil field in the world, at Safaniya, 160 miles north of Dhahran, was another of the Prince's prime targets. The reserves out there, below the warm, sandy Gulf seabed, numbered 30 billion barrels—around 500,000 barrels a day for about 164 years.

The biggest terminal on the Gulf was Ras Tannurah, which had capacity for 4.3 million barrels of oil a day out at the end of a narrow, ten-mile-long sandy peninsula. The colossal loading dock was offshore, at the Sea Island complex, where Platform Number Four pumped more than two million barrels a day into the world's waiting tankers. In Prince Nasir's opinion, a direct hit at that platform would virtually wrap it right up for Ras Tannurah. Especially if someone banged out the pipeline from Abqaiq, which the Prince had thoughtfully mapped out for the President of France.

In Nasir's opinion, the final, critical hit should be slightly north, on the 4.2-million-barrel-a-day complex at Ju'aymah, principal loading bay for liquid petroleum—propane, that is, the prime source of all Japanese cooking. If Prince Nasir's plan ever came off, the Japanese would find themselves eating a whole lot of sushi, accompanied by stone-cold sake.

The terminals of Ras Tannurah and Ju'aymah, plus the Red Sea ports, loaded Saudi Arabian oil products into a staggering 4,000 massive tankers a year. Unsurprisingly, Aramco (Arabian American Oil Company), 100 percent owned by the Saudi government since 1976, was the largest oil company on earth. Its headquarters were in the Eastern Province city of Dhahran and its capability was approximately 10 million barrels a day, though in the twenty-first century it had pumped considerably less.

Twenty-six percent of all the oil on the planet lay beneath the Saudi desert—that's around 262 billion barrels, which, at 5.5 million a day, ought to last around 130 years. The Saudi royal family were the sole proprietors of Aramco, which owned every last half-pint.

"You want me to hit that lot?" asked General Jobert incredulously. "That's probably ten different targets. Three would be difficult. I suppose we could get three hit squads in there. But they'd need backup, and the explosive would weigh God knows how much. We'd need forty men in each team. But ten targets? *Mon Dieu!* I'd say that would be impossible. We'd have a better chance bombing it."

"That, of course, is out of the question," said Gaston Savary. "Remember, the President's prime requirement is secrecy. If we sent in a squadron of fighter bombers, they'd know the nationality of the attackers in about ten minutes. The Saudis have a lot of very sophisticated U.S. surveillance kits."

Both men ruminated over the apparent hopelessness of step one, and a mood of tacit acceptance prevailed. The critical path of the operation required a succession of ten swift, devastating hits on the greatest oil-producing network in the Middle East. And so far as General Jobert could see, it was militarily impossible, either by land or by air—at least, without getting caught it was.

General Jobert paced the room. He was an impressive man—not tall, but built like a middleweight fighter, with thick, black, curly hair and a swarthy complexion, very French, with the merest suggestion that somewhere in the family tree there may have lurked a North African ancestor.

He was a man in stark contrast to the lean, pale-skinned, six-foot-two-inch Gaston Savary, whose mournful expression concealed a cool sense of irony and a somewhat sarcastic turn of humor. However, on this morning they were thinking as one, both of them aware that an outright rejection of the President's request was not a great idea—for either of them.

The General mused. Land attack? *C'est impossible.* Air attack? *Non, absolument non.* Then he brightened somewhat. "How about by sea?"

Gaston Savary looked up sharply. "You mean frogmen, brought in by submarine, swimmers who could fix sticky bombs on the offshore rigs?"

"Exactement!"

"Have you checked the depth of the water lately? I mean around Abqaiq, which is not only in the middle of the desert but is also the key to the entire operation?" Savary loved the rhetorical question.

But the General smiled. His smile was that of a man one move from checkmate. "As a civilian, you of course do not understand everything about the military mind," he said. "However, I expect you have heard of cruise missiles, and these days there are some very effective ones, that fly out of nowhere."

"In these days of intense surveillance, nothing comes out of nowhere," replied the Secret Service Chief. "There's always someone watching."

"True," replied the General. "But the chances of detecting a missile fired from a submerged submarine are very low. I'm talking about a missile programmed to fly over the ocean and then over the middle of the desert. I assure you no one will pick that up. The element of surprise is too great."

Savary knew when an important sentence had been uttered. He paused for a moment, nodding his head slightly. And then he asked, "Do you really think we could put a submarine in the Gulf without anyone knowing? And then have it unleash a barrage of cruise missiles at the shores of Saudi Arabia without anyone finding out?"

"They'd find out when the oil terminals, pumping stations, and refineries went up in smoke. But they'd never guess, in their wildest dreams, who the culprits were or, above all, how they did it."

"And what about the other coast?" asked Gaston Savary. "The Red Sea? You can't even get in there without traveling on the surface."

General Jobert shrugged. "A submarine would be logged through Suez. But so would many, many other ships. But it would not be logged through the southern end. The Red Sea can be transited underwater, and it is not unusual for a French submarine to make that journey. Also, that sea is extremely deep in places."

"And we also have the element of motive in our favor," said Savary. "We are great friends with Saudi Arabia. And why would anyone, in their right mind, want to blow up the oil system that keeps not only us but most of the civilized world in business? No one would suspect us. No one."

"I have no doubt the President of France considered that most carefully before he asked us to conduct this feasibility test."

"Do you think the whole operation could be carried out using cruise missiles alone?"

The General frowned. "I cannot say, but my instinct is no. We certainly could hit the refineries and the pumping stations, because pinpoint accuracy is not a requirement. But the loading platforms and offshore rigs would require real accuracy, and I don't think we could count on a cruise to hit such a small target in exactly the right place. And anyway, someone working on the rig might see a wayward cruise come in. They're supposed to be accurate to ten meters. But that's too big a margin if you're trying to hit the upper deck of a drilling rig. Better to attack from below the surface."

Gaston Savary could see why Michel Jobert had been made a general, and he could most certainly see how he came to spearhead the French Army's Special Forces.

"Well, General," he said. "I think we must agree it is the most interesting plan. Because if it succeeds, the new King of Saudi Arabia will owe us *everything*. Certainly we will have enormous power over him, because he could *never* admit he was the mastermind behind the destruction of his own country's oil industry."

"Well, no, he could not," replied Michel Jobert. "And that would mean French companies would undertake the entire rebuilding program. There would be huge contracts awarded to us, just as the Americans claimed almost all the rebuilding contracts for Iraq."

"And there'd be a lot of very grateful French industries," said Savary. "And the riches for the oil industry would be incalculable. Imagine owning the sole marketing agency for all Saudi Arabian oil. *Mon Dieu!* That would be something, eh?"

"And I would not be surprised if that led to a long and comfortable retirement for both of us," said the General. "But for now, let's not get too excited. I would like to call Admiral Pires over for a half hour."

"I don't believe I know him."

"He's COMFUSCO."

"Who the hell's COMFUSCO?"

"Commandement des Fusiliers Marines Commandos. It's the French Navy's special ops outfit. Admiral Pires is the head of it. But he's an ex-submariner. And right now he is in overall command of all naval assault commandos, plus the Commando Hubert divers unit and the Close Quarters Combat Group—that's naval counterterrorist—both assigned to COS."

"That's every kind of assault from the sea, correct?"

"*Absolument*. That's beach reconnaissance, assaults on ships, intelligence gathering, amphibious landings, small boat operations, raids, rescue ops, and of course combat search and rescue—CSAR."

"Of course," said Savary, who was always amazed by the military's detailed, meticulous operational structures.

General Jobert ordered coffee for three, and a young Army Lieutenant pushed open the door to announce that the Admiral would be there in ten minutes.

Gaston Savary privately thought the entire scheme was a boundless exercise in naked ambition that would probably end up being abandoned. As a kind of super-policeman, he was used to bureaucrats conducting relentless searches, desperately trying to find reasons not to do things. And if ever there was an opportunity to say no, this was surely it. Offhand he could think of about ten reasons himself.

But, like many of his fellow spies and spy masters, Savary was an adventurer at heart. And he knew how to work the system. No one had asked him to blow up the oil fields. He had merely been requested to find out if it was possible to do so without getting caught. And he was most certainly doing that.

Admiral Pires arrived on time, with the flourish of a man who had better things to do than talk to Secret Service agents. Six minutes later, having received a sharply worded briefing from General Jobert, he was reduced to utter silence.

"*Mon Dieu!*" he said. "That is the most dangerous plan I have ever heard."

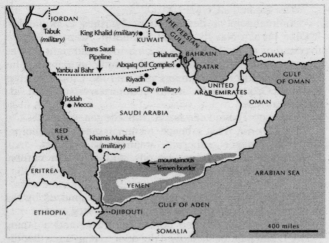

THE ARABIAN PENINSULA, WITH THE FOUR SAUDI MILITARY CITIES MARKED

Savary gave him the benefit of his own wisdom. "Admiral," he said, "we are not being asked to blow up half of Saudi Arabia. We are merely being asked to decide whether it can be done, in secret . . . to the inestimable advantage of France."

"Well, technically we could put one of our new SSNs into the Gulf, making an underwater entry through the Strait of Hormuz. It's deep enough, and it's been done before."

"Is that one of the old Rubis-class boats?" asked Savary.

"No. No. This is one of the new Project Barracuda boats we have been building in Cherbourg for several years. You may have read about them. We have just two that will become operational this year. They're bigger than the old Rubis, around 4,000 tons, nuclear hunter-killers with torpedo and cruise missile capabilities. They actually carry ten MBDA SCALP naval missiles. That's a derivative of the old Storm/Shadows. They're good, quiet ships with very good missiles. We're conducting sea trials right now, off the Brest navy yards."

"What would you consider the likelihood of getting in and out of the Gulf undetected?" asked the General.

"Oh, very good. And the missiles are all pre-programmed. Yes. I suppose we could launch them at a given target along the Saudi coast."

"Would anyone see them in flight?"

"Most unlikely. The Saudis are quite sophisticated. But I'd be very surprised if they picked up low-flying missiles like these on radar. They would not be expecting such an attack."

"Certainly not from their next king," said Savary, helpfully. "Any thoughts on operations on the other coast?"

"The Red Sea?" said the Admiral. "Well, that is more difficult, because you'd come through the Suez Canal on the surface. But I don't think that would attract undue attention. And you might manage to exit the southern end, off Djibouti, at periscope depth; assuming you wanted to stay out of sight. That's the Bab el Mandeb, the narrow straits that lead out into the Gulf of Aden—shallow, sometimes under 100 meters deep.

"Anyway, a half-submerged submarine might look a bit suspicious to the American radar, *if* they picked us up—especially with oil fields ablaze four hundred miles astern of the ship. It would probably be better just to go straight through, on the surface, in the normal way, the very picture of innocence."

Gaston Savary really liked this suave and knowledgeable Admiral, who looked extremely young to hold such a high office and rank. But he was not young in thought, and he had grasped the significance of the problem very swiftly, as indeed had General Jobert.

"I should of course like to speak to Admiral Romanet first," said Georges Pires, looking at Savary. "He's our Flag Officer Submarines in Brest. And I don't want to second-guess him. But I would say we could hit our missile targets on both coasts from submerged SSNs. And, certainly, in my own area of operations, we could send in teams of commandos to take out the loading platforms and offshore rigs . . . the Saudi Navy has never been up to much. They'd be no trouble whatsoever."

The Admiral paused, looked thoughtful. Then he said, "Those platforms are big constructions though. We'd probably need a mix of RDX (research-developed explosive), TNT, and aluminum. And the frogmen would have to swim in with twenty-five-kilogram watertight satchels. And we'd use timers, so the swimmers and perhaps an SDV and the submarine, could get clear before the blast. But we could do it. Most certainly we could do it."

Admiral Pires again paused. And then he added, "But the Navy's role is only the beginning, correct? And so I will leave you, while I confer with Admiral Romanet."

"I'd prefer you bring him here," said General Jobert. "I think at this early stage, while we are just appreciating the situation, all discussions should remain under this roof."

"Aha," said Admiral Pires. "Already we are slipping into the black ops mode, already it is occurring to you that we may be ordered actually to carry out this assault on our robed brothers in the desert. Or, at the least, on their oil wells."

"That's the trouble with you guys. You always say yes," said Gaston Savary.

"That's because we are loyal servants of the republic," replied the General. "We are here to do the bidding of the politicians. And we try, if asked, to achieve the impossible."

"But a half hour ago, you thought this would be impossible, without getting caught."

"I do not think that now," replied the senior commander of COS. "I believe we could smash the Saudi oil industry with missiles and frogmen from those two SSNs. And never be detected." Gaston Savary stood up. "Gentlemen," he said, "I have been entrusted to conduct this study on behalf of the Foreign Minister and the President himself. I would be grateful, Admiral, if you would stay for the second part of our discussions. I have enjoyed listening to your views and I think you may have more ideas to give us."

Savary was not the first high-ranking French official to single out the forty-six-year-old Georges Pires as a top-flight military intellect, a career officer who may yet find himself in the Palais Bourbon as a member of the French Parliament.

"Honored sir, I assure you," replied the beefy Commando Chief, whose splendid family summer home, for three generations, was situated on the waterfront of St. Malo, less than 100 miles from the great French naval base at Brest. The Navy had always been his life, although he had found time to be married twice and divorced twice before his fortieth birthday. There was a slightly roguish look to Georges Pires, but his rise to high office in the principal assault section of the French Navy had been exceptionally swift.

Savary continued. "Well, General Jobert, perhaps you could outline for us anything you may know about the Saudi military defenses—on land, I mean."

"Yes, of course," Jobert said. "Let me switch on this big-screen computer, and I will tell you what I know, which is fairly standard but will show you the size of the task." General Jobert stood back and used an officer's shiny wooden baton to point to the map of Saudi Arabia. "They have an overall strength of around a hundred twenty-six thousand," he began. "That's the four elements, Army, Navy, Air Force, and the Royal Saudi Air Defense Force. They don't have regular garrisons. The army is widely dispersed, but its strength is concentrated at four large military cities, built at huge expense in the 1970s and '80s with the assistance of the United States Army Corps of Engineers. The first one to note is right here . . . Khamis Mushayt, in the mountains of the southwest, about 100 kilometers from the Yemeni border.

"The second is up here at Tabuk, which protects the northwest of the country—in particular these routes that lead in from Jordan, Israel, and Syria. A third site, Assad Military City, is at Al-Kharj, 100 kilometers southeast of Riyadh, right in the middle of the desert. That's where the Saudis' national armaments industry is located.

"But the really big one is right here, facing the border area toward Kuwait and Iraq, right outside this city marked here—Hafa al-Batin. This is the King Khalid Military City.

You can see it's sited, deliberately, near the Trans-Arabian Pipeline (TAPLINE), which connects the big southern oil center of Ad Damman with Jordan.

"King Khalid is huge. It houses something like sixty-five thousand people, military and civilians. It's got everything—cinemas, shopping arcades, power plants, mosques, schools, the lot. It's built in the shape of a massive concrete octagon, with several smaller octagons inside it. Right outside the main complex they have a hospital, a racecourse, maintenance and supply areas, underground command bunkers, and the anti-aircraft missile sites. Gentlemen, you will not be attacking the King Khalid military base."

"What's the surrounding country like?" asked Admiral Pires.

"Absolutely wide open desert, swept by radar, no cover. We'd be facing the Saudi missiles and artillery."

"Can they shoot straight?"

"Definitely."

"Are they all like that?" asked Gaston Savary.

"Not quite so bad. But none of them is likely to be easy. Not for a small group of Special Forces. To tell the truth, Gaston, I can see no way for any small group to take, and force the surrender of, these strongholds. The Saudis have excellent communications and air cover. In the end, we would not have a chance.

"And in addition they have a well-armed National Guard, which is specifically tasked with defending the oil installations. The Saudis are not stupid. They know those huge complexes represent their lifeblood, and they've protected them very thoroughly."

"What's their Air Force like?" Admiral Pires asked.

"Very modern," said Jobert. "Well-equipped. U.S. and British fighter bombers. F-15s, Tornadoes. Strong offensive capability. They also have airborne surveillance and tactical airlift capability. In brief, the Royal Saudi Air Force can move people around at will, they can see from the sky, and they have a serious strike force."

"My notes from Prince Nasir say the Air Force bases may be vulnerable," said Savary.

"Well, maybe. But they have two substantial air wings—that's the F-15s and the Tornadoes. And they are divided into strike force air bases at each of the four military cities. It's a bit confusing, but they call the base at Khamis Mushayt the King Khalid Air Base. Same name as the place in the north. See? Down here by the Yemeni border."

"That King Khalid must have been some kind of a leader," said Savary. "Half the country's named after him. But this is the air base Prince Nasir mentions. He plainly thinks it's vulnerable."

"We need to have a very careful look," said General Jobert. "Very careful indeed. Because it must be obvious to each of us that the consequences of any French soldier being caught, captured, or even killed would be absolutely calamitous for France. The Americans would immediately surmise we had blown the oil fields, and there'd be all hell to pay."

"It sounds to me as if the destruction of the oil fields is several times more important than everything else put together," said Admiral Pires. "Just imagine. The lifeblood of the people suddenly gone. An entire nation, the majority of whom can never even remember poverty, suddenly facing the fact they could all be back on camels. No oil, no wealth, no more prosperity. I think the nation would go into shock."

"That's Prince Nasir's view entirely," said Savary. "He thinks the armed forces will have no will to fight. Who for? A penniless king no longer able to pay them?"

"More like a dead, penniless king," said Admiral Pires. "Because if this goes ahead, the Saudis will plainly rally to the cause of the Crown Prince. Especially if he promises to end the patronage of the royal princes and to put the country back together. Let's face it, he's the military's only hope."

"That is all true," said Jobert. "The collapse of the Saudi economy would be an earth-shaking experience. But there still has to be an armed attack to subdue the Army and the Air Force, then to capture the main palaces in Riyadh and take out the King and his principal ministers. In the end, you always have to win it on the ground."

"According to Prince Nasir," said Savary, "the feeling against the King is so strong, the people are so angry, they would rally to the cause of *anyone* who could lead them to victory over the royal family. And Crown Prince Nasir is extremely popular."

"Which leaves us with two tasks," said Admiral Pires. "Number one, to get into the King Khalid Air Base and either take or destroy it. Then, almost simultaneously, to capture Riyadh and remove the King of Saudi Arabia from office."

General Jobert smiled. "One thing, Admiral. Taking the air base needs to be so decisive it will cause the entire military city at Khamis Mushayt to cave in, and then cause the other three military cities to decide there is nothing left to fight for."

"With Prince Nasir on the television appealing for calm, assuring everyone he has everything under control, it just might work," said Admiral Pires. "Just so long as the collapse of the oil industry has the shattering effect we think it will."

"The thing is," suggested Savary, "this whole operation has to look like a totally Arab matter. It will simply appear that the Crown Prince has pulled off a palace coup d'état. For the good of the people. And that may be an end to it. It just so happens that Prince Nasir chose France to help his country get back on its feet. America does not enjoy sole rights to everything it wants, you know."

"So long as no one gets caught, eh?" muttered the General.

"Precisely that," responded the Admiral. "So long as no Frenchman is ever discovered anywhere near the action."

"And who, precisely, does the President have in mind for an operation like this?" asked the General.

"Oh, he's never even thought about that," said Savary. "He just wants to know if we think it is possible. At this stage no more."

"Do you have the feeling that if we say yes he will start thinking about it very, very quickly?"

"I do," replied Savary. "And we may as well have a few

answers. So let me ask a question: King Khalid Air Base—
who goes in, us or an Arab force?"

"Oh, that would have to be a French assault force," said
the General. "I doubt anyone except us, the Brits, the Americans, or the Israelis could possibly pull that off . . . but it
seems so incongruous to have a French force, out there on
its own, attacking that Saudi air base."

"There would have to be some Arab involvement," offered Admiral Pires. "Maybe a 2/IC, or a couple of locals,
men who understand command and may know the terrain,
and speak Arabic."

"I see that," said Savary. "I see it very clearly. We could
provide the force, if we approve the plan. But Prince Nasir
will have to provide some leadership or, at worse, some
high-level advice."

"I don't know that any Arab army has the kind of man we
are looking for," said the Admiral. "We need a skilled Special Forces operator with a sound knowledge of high explosives, close combat fighting, and making detailed plans."

"I don't think they have anyone to fill that bill," said the
General. "And anyway, how the hell do we get in there? We
can't suddenly drop sixty parachutists into Saudi Arabia.
Too high a risk."

"Then they'd have to come in by sea," said Admiral
Pires. "But it would be difficult by submarine. The SDV
holds only a half-dozen. A ferry service like that would take
hours and hours. And they couldn't swim in. Too far. Too
dangerous."

"That's the kind of problem that gets solved by an Arab
who knows the territory," said Admiral Pires. "And understands what's required. The kind of Arab who probably
doesn't exist."

"I know of one," said Savary.

"Oh? Who?" asked General Jobert.

"He's the Commander in Chief of Hamas. Name of Gen.
Ravi Rashood. From what I hear, he's ex–British SAS. He
could do it. The Americans think he's pulled off some terrible stuff these last few years. He could take the air base."

"But would he?" wondered the General. "Why would he?"

"Because he's a fanatical Muslim fundamentalist," replied Savary. "And he hates the Americans, and he wants them out of the Middle East forever. And he knows that without Saudi support and Saudi oil they would have to go. I think you'd find General Rashood more than willing to talk, but I think you'd have to pay him, and Hamas, for the privilege of his involvement."

"Hmm," said the General. "Interesting."

"And now," continued Savary, "for the biggest question of all . . . who commands the Saudi mob in Riyadh? Who recruits, organizes, arms, and rallies thousands of citizens who hate the King, but have no idea what to do?"

"I know one thing," said Admiral Pires. "You need a top-class soldier for that. And top-class soldiers become well known to many people. In all of France, it might be impossible to find such a man, who had the right qualifications and a properly low profile. Those kinds of leaders become public figures. And one sight of this man, leading an attack on the Saudi royal family, would end all of our chances of anonymity."

"You speak wisely, Admiral," said Savary. "But there must be someone. A trained fighter somewhere who has been in combat yet has not reached the highest rank. Someone who has perhaps retired in recent years. Someone who would perhaps consider undertaking such an operation for, say, ten million U.S. dollars. Enough to allow him to live his life free of all financial worries."

All three men grew silent. Savary seemed to be at a loss, but the two military men pondered the problem, each of them running their minds back over a working lifetime in the armed services.

Eventually, surprisingly, it was Savary who spoke up. "There was such a man, you know, who worked for my organization, Secret Service, the DGSE. I never met him, because he was mostly based in Africa, rose to be deputy regional director of a large area—northern, sub-Saharan, and western Africa. He operated out of Dakar."

"Did he have combat experience?" asked the General.

"And how," replied Savary. "I believe he started off in the Foreign Legion. And I think he distinguished himself in Chad, that battle against the rebels at Oum Chalouba, 1986. He was decorated as quite a young officer for conspicuous bravery. I'm not sure what he did after that, but he definitely joined the Special Forces."

"Do you remember his name?" asked Michel Jobert.

"Yes. He was Moroccan by birth. Gamoudi. Jacques Gamoudi. Had some kind of a nickname, which for the moment escapes me."

General Jobert ruminated. "Yes, Gamoudi. I think I've heard that name. He was involved with COS, after his service in the Legion. But I can't remember precisely what he did."

Jobert walked over to a computer desk at the far end of his office and keyed in the information he had. "This ought to come up with something," he said. "It's an amazing piece of software, gives detailed biographies of all French serving officers of the past twenty-five years."

They waited while the computer buzzed and whined. Then the screen brightened. "Here he is," said the General quietly. "Jacques Gamoudi, born 1964 in the village of Asni, in the High Atlas Mountains. Son of a goatherd who doubled as a mountain guide."

"Hell, that's a big step. Moroccan farm boy to a commission in the Foreign Legion before he was twenty-two." Admiral Pires was baffled. "Those guys can't usually speak French."

"Looks like he had some kind of sponsor. Man called Laforge, former Major in the French Parachute Regiment. He was wounded in Algeria, 1961, medically discharged. Then he and his wife bought some kind of hotel in the village, and young Gamoudi worked there. Looks like Laforge helped him join the Legion.

"Jesus. There's a copy of his original application form, Bureau de Recrutement de la Légion Etrangère, Quartier Vienot, 13400 Aubagne. That's fifteen miles from Marseille. He went down there a few weeks later, in 1981, passed his physical tests, and signed on for five years."

"You're right," said the Admiral. "That's a hell of a piece of software."

"Any sign of his nickname?" asked Savary. "I'd know it if I'd heard it."

"Can't see it," said Michel Jobert, scrolling down the computer pages. "Hey, wait a minute, this could be it. Does Le Chasseur sound familiar? There's a bunch of mercenaries he led in some very fierce fighting in North Africa. According to this, they always called him Le Chasseur."

"That's him," said Savary, thoughtfully. "Jacques Gamoudi, Le Chasseur." He flattened his right hand, and drew it across his throat. Which was a fair indication of the reputation of Colonel Gamoudi—Le Chasseur, the Hunter.

One Month Later, Early June 2009

THE TROUBLE WITH Le Chasseur was he had essentially
vanished into the crisp, thin air around the high peaks of the
Pyrenees, somewhere up near the little town of Cauterets,
which sat in the mountains 3,000 feet above sea level,
hemmed in by 8,000-foot summits. Snowy Cauterets was
normally the first French Pyrenean ski station to open and
the last to close.

It was common knowledge that Col. Jacques Gamoudi
had taken early retirement from the Army and headed with
his family to the Pyrenees, where he hoped to set himself
up as a mountain guide and expedition leader, as his father
had done before him, in faraway Morocco.

Indeed an inspired piece of guesswork by Gaston Savary
had brought him, in company with Michel Jobert, to the
town of Castelnaudaray, thirty-five miles southeast of
Toulouse, where Le Chasseur's military career had begun.
Quartier Lapasset, home of the Foreign Legion's training
regiment, was in Castelnaudaray, and the young Gamoudi
had spent four months there as a recruit.

Savary and the Colonel had made extensive inquiries,
and not without some success. But there were no details,
only that Jacques Gamoudi, with his wife, Giselle, and two
sons, now aged around eleven and thirteen, had headed east
into the mountains, maybe four years previously, and had
not been seen since—though a veteran Legionnaire Colonel

thought he had heard that the family had settled near Cauterets.

And now their staff car was winding its way through the spectacular range of mountains that divided France from Spain. They took no driver: Savary himself was at the wheel.

Things had moved forward in the month since first they discussed the operation in Saudi Arabia. But now the pressure was on, directly from the President of France. Their mission was simple: find Col. Jacques Gamoudi. Savary was beginning to wish he had never suggested the man's name in the first place. Not only were they lost, but it was growing dark, they had no hotel reservation, and, generally speaking, they had no idea where they were going.

Cauterets had seemed a reasonable plan. They had run southwest from Toulouse for more than 100 miles into ever higher ground. Now they were driving through steep passes south of Soulom, climbing all the while, up past rugged, treeless peaks.

"This road ends at Cauterets," said the General helpfully.

"So does the world, I shouldn't be surprised," replied Savary, faintly irritably, as he stared ahead at the darkening mountains. "God knows how we'll ever find this character."

"Oh, let's not be negative," said the General. "I doubt there are that many mountain guides in the area. And they'll all know one another."

"You'd need to be a mountain guide to live up here," said Savary, who was a Parisian to the tips of his well-polished loafers. "Shouldn't be surprised if the whole population were mountain guides."

General Jobert chuckled. Twenty minutes later, now in the pitch dark, they ran past a sign that said, at last, CAUTERETS. And there before them was the brightly lit resort town with its cheerful hotels, bars, and restaurants.

They drove on down Route 920 and swung into the Place Marechal Foch. Right ahead of them were the lights of the Hotel-Restaurant Cesar. Simultaneously, both men exclaimed, more or less word-perfect, "This'll do for us."

Anxious to disembark after the long journey, they heaved

their bags out of the car and found their way to reception, where they booked a couple of rooms and a table for two in the hotel's surprisingly crowded dining room.

Twenty minutes later, a few minutes before ten o'clock, they were dining in the best restaurant in Cauterets, with crisp white tablecloths and napkins and an excellent selection of regional wines.

Savary chose a Chateau de Rousse from the historic Jurançon district, southwest of the town of Pau, which was located about thirty-five miles to the north of Cauterets. The General looked at the label, which mentioned Pau, and he wondered if that might be their next stop—since Jacques Gamoudi had completed his specialist parachute training for the Foreign Legion right there in Pau before embarking for peacekeeping duties in Beirut. *Let's face it,* he thought, *we have precious little to go on.*

Between courses, Savary tried an elementary check of the phone book, but there was no Jacques Gamoudi. There was no Gamoudi whatsoever. If Le Chasseur was living up there in the mountains, he was probably using another name.

"You know, I've never asked you, Michel, but what was Colonel Gamoudi actually doing for the Special Forces after he left the Foreign Legion?"

"Well, he had a glowing service report," said the General. "And he quickly made the First Marine Parachute Regiment. He was recommended for a commission, which is a considerably more difficult task than a similar rank in the Foreign Legion. So he went to the French Military Academy at St. Cyr.

"From there he went to the Central African Republic, and made Major at an incredibly young age. He commanded his squadron in a highly dangerous long-term reconnaissance operation. That led to the successful evacuation of 3,000 French civilians and a crushing defeat of that particularly vicious rebel movement, the FACA.

"They decorated him again, and then he was invited to join the Secret Service, which he did. In June 1999 he masterminded the rescue of the U.S. Ambassador from the

Congo. The French Special Ops team went with the diplomat to the Gabon, but Colonel Gamoudi stayed behind and directed the remaining French troops, the ones who had done the fighting.

"He earned his nickname in the murky world of North African politics, where regional conflict was rife and rebellions frequent. He was always in the thick of it, frequently commanding ex–French and Legionnaire officers who were fighting as mercenaries, and protecting French oil interests, and private French companies with involvement in the diamond industry. They say he was even involved in a truly daring plot to assassinate the President of Côte d'Ivoire five years ago." The General hesitated briefly, before adding, "Jacques Gamoudi always seemed particularly at home in a Muslim environment. And I'm telling you, one way and another, he was one hell of a soldier."

"I imagine it can take its toll, a life like that," said Savary. "In that god-awful climate. Always watching your back, always concerned for those who rely on you . . ."

"No doubt," said the General. "I understand many people were most surprised when he turned his back on the army. But he was, apparently, disenchanted. And wanted nothing more to do with it."

"It's often that way with very brave men," mused Savary, sipping his Château de Rousse. "They seem to wake up one morning and wonder why they are doing so much more than everyone else, for the same basic salary. He might be a hard man to turn around. Unless we have a lot of money."

"We do have a lot of money. And I assure you, the President and his royal cohort from the Saudi desert will not hesitate to spend it, if we believe this is the right man to take Riyadh." The General put three photographs on the table. "Take another good look at these, Gaston, because I think he might even deny who he is when we find him."

"*If* we find him," said the Secret Service Chief. "If we find him."

By now it was a little after 11 P.M. And as they left the dining room, the General asked the headwaiter if he had heard of a man named Jacques Gamoudi. Col. Jacques Gamoudi. He was greeted with the blankest of Gallic looks. So the General showed him the photographs, but the response was the same. It was a pattern that would be repeated with the concierge, the receptionist, and indeed the hotel's owner. No one had ever met Le Chasseur.

The following morning was bright and warm. Under cloudless skies they made their way up to the cable cars that linked Cauterets to the Cirque du Lys, a skier's paradise with its twenty-three runs covering twenty-five miles of fast downhill slopes. Not in June of course. But the cable car loading station was a regular starting point for mountain guides, and a gathering place for walkers and climbers from all over Europe.

For two hours, Savary and the General stood beneath the great peaks, mingling with the guides, asking the question, showing the photographs, watching for the slightest sign of deceit or secrecy. But there was none. Le Chasseur had surely vanished, if indeed the Legionnaire in Castelnau-daray had been correct. By lunchtime the two searchers were pretty certain the Legionnaire had been mistaken.

There were just a few hikers gathering now, and they appeared not to have a guide who would walk with them. At least not an adult one. There was a boy, of about fourteen, showing them a map, but that was all.

It was virtually a last-ditch effort, but as the hikers moved off, Savary walked over to the boy who was still folding up his map. His ten-euro tip was still in his hand.

Savary wished him *"Bonjour"* and showed him the photographs. Without hesitation the boy exclaimed, "Hey, that's a good picture of Monsieur Hooks."

"Monsieur who?" said Savary.

"Hooks. He's a mountain guide, lives over in a tiny little place called Heas, right up in the mountains, far above Gedre. That's him. Definitely. The man in your picture."

"Do you know his first name?"

"No, no. He's Monsieur Hooks. No one calls him by his first name."

"Has he lived there a long time?"

"Not too long. But I remember when he came. I was ten, and I was in Monsieur Lamont's class. I used to live over at Gedre, and my school went on a few expeditions to the mountains around the Cirque de Troumouse. Monsieur Hooks was always our guide. He takes all the school parties up there."

"Where exactly did you say he lives?"

"Heas, it's called. But it just a few houses with a shop and a church. You go south from Gedre. It's on the map, on the way to the highest mountains around here. But you could go right past without noticing the village."

Savary thanked the boy and gave him another ten-euro note. Two hours later he and General Jobert were driving along a slow, winding mountain road approaching the small town of Gedre along the tumbling Gavarnie River.

There was only one road out of the town, heading south toward the Spanish border, back into the highest peaks. Savary gassed up the car and noted the signpost, which said: Cirque de Troumouse. Underneath it was written, Heas 6km.

This was another mountain road even more twisting than the last. All around were great craggy escarpments, hardly any trees. It was grandeur rather than beauty. And this little road would eventually become almost a spiral as it headed up into the astonishing ten-kilometer wall of mountains that formed the Cirque de Troumouse.

Heas was the last stop before the big climb. The traffic to see the views was such that the French had shrewdly made the last part a toll road up to the edge of the Cirque, in the time-honored Gallic tradition of always making a buck when the chance was there.

Gaston Savary and General Jobert pulled into the village a little before three o'clock in the afternoon. They inquired at a shop about Monsieur Hooks and were told, politely, that he had gone into the mountains that morning with a coach load of schoolchildren and their teachers. He usually returned to Heas at around 4 P.M. Meanwhile they could certainly talk to Madame Hooks, who had just gone to meet the school bus from Gedre, and would certainly be home in a few minutes . . . four houses up the street, on the left. Number eight.

Savary thanked the shopkeeper and bought a couple of bottles of orange juice. He and Jobert sat on a wall outside in the sunlight and drank them, waiting for a lady with two children to come up the hill toward them.

They did not have to wait long. A slender, pretty woman, late thirties, appeared almost immediately, laughing with two young boys. General Jobert stepped forward with a cheerful smile. "Madame Hooks?" he asked.

"Yes," she said carefully. "I am Madame Hooks."

"Well, I am very sorry to startle you. But my colleague, Monsieur Savary, and I have come a very long way to see your husband on a most urgent matter."

"What about?" she said. "You are looking for a guide through these mountains?"

"Not exactly," said the General. "But we have something to tell him that he will most certainly find interesting."

Madame Hooks appraised the two men, noting their excellent manners, their well-cut clothes and polished shoes, and indeed the big Citroën government car parked outside the shop. Every sense told her that these were men from the military, but she chose not to betray her thoughts. However, she knew better than to antagonize such people, so she said quickly, "Please come up to the house, and we will have some coffee . . . this is our son Jean-Pierre and this is Andre."

The General held out his hand in greeting. "And this," he said, "is a very important man from Paris: Monsieur Gaston Savary."

They walked up yet another hill, about fifty yards, and entered through a gate into a small walled garden, which surrounded a white stone house with a red-tiled roof, a classic French Pyrenean building.

The living room was also classic French country style, large with a heavy wooden dining table at one end and a sitting area around an enormous brick fireplace at the other.

The kitchen was separate, through a beamed archway, and all the furniture was of a high quality. There were some very beautiful rugs, possibly North African in origin, spread over the oak floorboards. A large framed photograph of Monsieur Hooks and his new bride, taken in 1993, was hanging on the wall beside the kitchen. General Jobert noted instantly that Monsieur Hooks had been married in the dress uniform of the First Marine Parachute Infantry Regiment.

Madame Hooks took the boys into the kitchen. When she emerged, she was carrying a tray of four mugs, three of them full, plus a coffeepot. She asked the two men to call her Giselle. "Jacques will not be long," she said. "That school bus he's on is supposed to be back in Gedre by four o'clock."

She was correct in that. Four minutes later, the door opened and Monsieur Jacques Hooks, a medium-size, bearded man, not one ounce overweight, walked inside. He was wearing leather work boots, suede shorts, and a T-shirt, with a green rucksack over his shoulder. Jammed into his wide studded belt was a large sheathed knife.

Monsieur Hooks was surprised, but mannered. "Oh," he said. "I was not expecting visitors. *Bonjour,* I'm Jacques Hooks."

General Jobert was the first to his feet. "*Bonjour,*" he said, "I'm Michel Jobert, and this is my colleague Gaston Savary. We have come a very long way to see you."

Monsieur Hooks seemed to freeze. His face was expressionless. "I don't suppose there would be much point in hiding my true identity from you," he said. "I'm assuming you are both from some branch of the military, but I should warn you right away, I am retired. I have a wife and family, as you already know. And I have no intention of leaving my little mountain paradise."

Gaston Savary held out his hand. "Colonel Gamoudi, I'm honored to meet you," he said. "For what it's worth, I'm head of the French Secret Service. And General Jobert here is Commander in Chief of the First Marine Parachute Infantry . . . your old regiment."

"I'm afraid I knew precisely who General Jobert was the

moment I walked in," said Jacques Gamoudi. "I do stay in touch with a few old friends. And I most certainly would recognize my commanding officer." He smiled gently, poured himself some coffee, and shook his head. "It's been a while now," he said. "But we're very happy here in the mountains. It's a good place to bring up a family. Clean, lovely, no crime, friendly people."

"How about that very large dagger you carry with you?" said Savary, chuckling. "You expecting trouble?"

Gamoudi laughed. "No, but I work in some pretty desolate places with some pretty helpless people. These mountains are just about the last refuge of the Pyrenean brown bear. And he's big and dangerous. This hunting knife is my last line of defense."

"I'm not sure even a knife that size would fend off a Pyrenean bear," said Savary.

"That depends on how well you know how to use it," replied Gamoudi. "Most of God's creatures lose heart for a fight with a knife this big rammed into their left eye."

Savary thus ascertained that the Colonel was right handed. He stared at the heavy forearms, the bull neck, and the wide, swarthy face. He noted the jagged scar below Gamoudi's right ear, the tight military-cut hair, the straight back of his natural stance, the hard brown eyes. Ex–Foreign Legion, ex–Special Forces, ex-mercenary in North Africa. Parachutist. Combat fighter. *What the hell did I expect him to look like? Yves St. Laurent?*

"Before we start to talk," Gamoudi said, "I should perhaps explain that I am not hiding in any way. But in my line of business one is apt to make a few enemies, and so I changed my name. I thought it wiser not to return to Morocco, since I was in North Africa on behalf of the French Republic for so long. But I always wanted to live in France, and the mountains suit me well. I can make a good living up here, so I changed our name, and we just vanished into the mists. Giselle's parents live in Pau."

"Did you meet her during parachute training with the Legion?" asked the General.

"Very perceptive, sir. Matter of fact, yes, I did. I was

twenty years old. She was only fifteen. I had to wait for her to grow up."

"She waited for you," said the General. "Nine years, according to that photograph."

"You don't miss much, sir, I'll say that."

"In our business, Jacques, we can't afford to, eh?"

"You have that right, General."

Both men smiled, almost shyly, that most fleeting sign of camaraderie among combat soldiers.

"Now perhaps you should explain to me why you have traced me to my mountain lair."

"I will let Gaston outline for you the background to our visit. It involves a foreign country, and indeed the President of France . . ."

And for the next ten minutes the Secret Service Chief outlined the interior problems of Saudi Arabia, the prolific spending of the royal family, the monumental cost of that family, the deep unrest within the kingdom, the savage cuts in every family's income from the oil, the offensive ties to the United States of America, the loss of the true Islamic religion in favor of the ideals of a different, godless world to the West.

Jacques Gamoudi nodded. One of four million Muslims resident in France, he still tried to obey the laws of the Koran, although it was difficult to attend a mosque up there in the mountains. But his parents had been devout in the teachings of the Prophet, and there was no question in the mind of Colonel Gamoudi: *There is only one God. Allah is great.*

On their twice-yearly trips to Paris—one at Christmas with the boys—Jacques always took Giselle to the great Moorish-style Paris Mosque, with its towering minaret, almost one hundred feet high, located directly opposite the Natural History Museum in the *Jardin des Plantes*. This was the home of the Grand Imam, and it was extremely important to Jacques that he attend the mosque whenever he reasonably could.

Years of military service in North Africa had kept his religious upbringing alive, and he understood implicitly what so many millions of Saudi Arabians felt about their ruling family. He could not imagine life without the Koran and its teachings, but he could imagine the desolation any Muslim might feel watching the systematic erosion of religion in the day-to-day life of a country like Saudi Arabia.

"There are many great problems in Saudi Arabia," he said. "But I am at a loss to understand why they should concern me, and why you have journeyed here to see me."

"Well, Jacques," said Savary. "One month ago, the President of France had a private visit from one of the most senior princes of the Saudi royal family. And he has asked us for our help in overthrowing the present regime and returning the Saudis to their pure Bedouin roots. And now General Jobert will explain to you what has happened, and what we intend to do to help them."

The following ten minutes were, possibly, the most astounding in Colonel Gamoudi's not uneventful life. He listened wide-eyed to the plan for the Navy to knock out the entire Saudi oil industry, bringing that vast and fabulously wealthy country financially to its knees.

He nodded in general understanding of the plan to hit the air base at King Khalid when the Saudi armed forces' morale was at its lowest possible ebb. And he indicated his general acceptance of the need to take Riyadh, and for the people to rise up and perhaps storm the palace. All in the moments before the Crown Prince appeared on television to announce he had taken command of the country and that the old King, one of his one hundred-odd uncles, was dead.

He also understood that these two men were here in his home seeking his advice.

But when General Jobert coolly told him that he, Col. Jacques Gamoudi, was the man chosen by the French Army to command the operation in Riyadh, he almost shot hot, scalding coffee straight up his nose.

"ME!" he shouted. *"YOU WANT ME TO CAPTURE THE CITY OF RIYADH?* You have to be dreaming!"

To tell the truth, stated like that, Gaston Savary thought they might all be dreaming. But General Jobert was dead serious. "You have all of the required qualifications, Jacques. And we believe you will be leading a revolution against which there will be no opposition. We expect the Army will have given up by then . . . you just need to take the palace."

"But what about the guards? What about the King's bodyguards? What about the protectors in the palace?"

"I don't recall such trifling matters ever having discouraged you before," said Michel Jobert drolly.

"TRIFLING!" snapped Gamoudi. "About a hundred armed men with AK-47s firing one thousand rounds a minute at you?"

"I was rather thinking we might hire one of those Muslim suicide bombers," said the General. "Have him flatten the main royal palace without much fuss—same as all those Saudi terrorists on 9/11. No one was firing AK-47s that day."

"General, am I supposed to be taking this seriously? I mean, who's going to arm this throng? Who's going to train them? Get them to move forward as a fighting force? What about supplies? Hardware? Ordnance?"

"I assure you, Jacques, there will be endless supplies, every last request granted. For this operation there will be no expense spared."

"Well, General, when I read about it in the *Le Figaro*, at least I'll know what's happening. But I could not possibly partake, not in any way whatsoever. I'm retired now. I don't have the stomach for it anymore."

"But you are still a young man, Jacques. What are you, forty-five years old? And by the look of you, very, very fit. Climbing mountains all day, you should be."

"General, I want to make myself very clear: I cannot, will not, be involved. I have my wife and family to consider. General, I would not undertake this for a million dollars."

Michel Jobert smiled. But he did not answer for a few moments. Then he did. "How about ten?" he said.

On a day of truly outlandish suggestions, this one beat them all.

"HOW MUCH?" exclaimed Gamoudi.

"I think you heard me," said General Jobert. "How about

ten million dollars, with a further five million bonus when Prince Nasir assumes the throne of Saudi Arabia?"

Jacques Gamoudi was absolutely stunned. He rose to his feet and walked from one end of the room to the other. He walked back, shaking his head, reflecting on the outrageous proposition. It was outrageous in its assumptions, outrageous in its arrogance, outrageous in its rewards.

The Moroccan-born Colonel had been around in his time. But never had he heard anything to match this. He spoke slowly. "You want me, General, somehow to smuggle myself into Saudi Arabia, then into Riyadh, then find myself a headquarters, and start recruiting people to join a popular revolution. And when I have enough, to attack the royal palaces?"

"Try not to be absurd, Colonel. You will be flown into Saudi Arabia by private jet from the French Air Force. You will be chauffeur-driven to a small palace on the outskirts of Riyadh. And there you will meet the Saudi military commanders loyal to the Crown Prince, and there you will meet the terrorist commanders who mostly have ties to al-Qaeda. And there you will be briefed as to the size of your force and its assets.

"From then on, you will decide what you require. Transport. Armored vehicles. Maybe some artillery, which is currently being stored in the desert. Helicopters. Maybe tanks. Everything is available. But you will mastermind the entire operation. Communications and, above all, the attack on the King's palace. Anything you ask will be provided."

"And for all this I am to be paid ten million dollars, and five more when Prince Nasir takes over. And what then? Do I stay on in Riyadh?"

"No. You leave, probably within a few days. A French Air Force jet will be waiting to fly you directly home to Pau-Pyrenees Airport."

"And who's supposed to wipe out the King and his immediate family and advisers?"

"I think that is an honor we would leave to you. Because that way there will be no mistakes," said Savary. "Your reputation precedes you."

Jacques Gamoudi poured himself another cup of coffee. "How long would I be in Riyadh?"

"Several months. You would be attended at all times by personal bodyguards, with a staff of perhaps six former Saudi Army officers, handpicked men who know the country and love it, but are tired of the King and his entourage.

"You would move around locally with a driver, in a Saudi government car. There's dozens of them in Riyadh. Yours would be provided by the Crown Prince. For longer journeys you would be provided with a helicopter and a pilot. Royal Saudi Air Force, courtesy of Prince Nasir. You would get to know him well."

"And if I continue to refuse?"

"You won't, Colonel. This is your country sounding the bugle for battle. And you will, as you always have, answer that call."

"But there must be others? Younger officers. Men who have just as good qualifications."

"We have chosen you, Jacques. And we have informed two people only of our choice. The President of the French Republic, and the Foreign Minister of France."

"Oh, nothing serious," said Colonel Gamoudi. "It's nice to keep things on a low level, eh?"

"And the money?" asked the General.

"Well, of course, that's enough to tempt any man. I think of all I could do for my family. It would be beyond my dreams to be that rich. But why dollars, why not euros?"

"You mentioned dollars first, Jacques. You said *not for a million dollars*—and I stayed in that currency because ultimately you would be paid in dollars, by the Saudis, through us, for the good of France."

"Do I still have a choice? What if I do refuse?"

"I think that would be spectacularly unwise," said the General. "You are the man we have selected. This is the biggest operation for France since World War Two. It means more to us than any action by a French government since we joined the European Union. It will seal our prosperity for a hundred years."

"Yes, I suppose it would." And again Colonel Gamoudi

seemed overwhelmed by it all. He stood up and paced the room again, eventually turning around and asking, "But why me?"

"Because you are an experienced combat fighter. You understand command, and you understand a sudden and ruthless assault on an objective. You know how to deploy troops. You understand the critical path of any attack, you know what cannot be left undone. More importantly, you are an expert with high explosives.

"Even more importantly, you are a Muslim, and you are expert at working with Muslims, at home in their environment. With the massive military and financial backup of the French Republic and Saudi Arabia, there is an excellent probability that our mission will be accomplished."

Jacques Gamoudi stood still. And then he said, "How and when will I be paid?"

Gaston Savary took over. "You will receive five million dollars upon your verbal agreement to undertake the task. This will be wired into an account that will be opened in your name at the Bank of Boston at one-zero-four, Avenue des Champs Elysées. It will be an account controlled solely by you. Once the money is paid, no one can touch it save for you and your wife, unless you so specify. There will be irrevocable documents to that effect."

"And the second installment?"

"That will be wired into the same account forty-eight hours before your attack commences. And you will be in a position to check its arrival. Plainly, if it does not come you will not launch the attack." Gaston Savary looked quizzical. "Jacques," he said, "I assure you, your paltry sum of ten million dollars is the very least of the problems facing the French government and the incoming Saudi regime at this time."

"Am I obliged to keep the money in France? Perhaps to avoid taxes?" asked Colonel Gamoudi.

"Colonel," said General Jobert, "you will have a letter, signed by the President of France, absolving you from all French government taxes for the remainder of your lifetime, and that of Giselle."

Jacques Gamoudi whistled through his front teeth. "And my bonus?" he said.

"That will be presented in the form of a no-refund, no-recall cashier's check, to be held by Giselle. But dated for one month after the operation. She will be given the check at the precise time we pay the second five-million-dollar installment."

"And if the attack should fail?"

"Our emissaries will call at the house to retrieve the check."

"And if I should be killed in action?"

"Giselle will keep the check and deposit it to her account at the Bank of Boston."

"And am I free to move the money around if I wish? Perhaps to a different bank?"

"It is no business of ours what you do with the money," said Gaston Savary. "No business at all. Except for us to express our immense gratitude for what you will have done for your country. And to wish you the best of fortune and prosperity in the future."

"And what if the attacks from the sea should fail, and the Saudi oil industry is somehow saved?"

"If that happened the operation would be canceled. You keep the initial five million, and come home."

"And the second five million?"

"We are paying ten million for you to launch the attack and take Riyadh," said Savary flatly. "Clearly, we don't pay if you do not attack. And the attack would be impossible if the King remained in control of the Army, which he would, if the oil keeps flowing. Everything depends on the destruction of the oil industry."

"You make it very clear, and very tempting," said Jacques Gamoudi. "Giselle?"

"Well, I don't want you to die," she said. "And I did think we were past all this fighting and battles. I am very happy here, and you are happy. However, I cannot pretend that I would not wish to have all that money. How dangerous is this?"

"Very," said Gamoudi, without hesitation. "But we fight a weakened enemy. Maybe one with no stomach for the fight. I think your Saudi prince is correct—no army wants to fight for someone who may not pay them. It knocks the stuffing out of them. Soldiers too have wives and families, and I think the Saudi Army may feel they have no alternative but to join the new regime. That way they carry on getting paid.

"A popular rising by the people is often the easiest of military operations. Because there are too many reasons for their opponents not to fight—one of these is normally money, the second is usually more important; all soldiers have a natural distaste for turning their guns on their own people. They don't like it. And quite often they refuse to do it."

"If I agree, will you do it?" asked Giselle.

Before the ex–Foreign Legion commander could reply, Gaston Savary stood up and Michel Jobert gave a suggestion of a nod.

"Jacques," said Savary, "you and Giselle have much to discuss. We were thinking in terms of one week. I am going to give you two business cards: one is for me and my personal line, the other is for the General and his private number at COS headquarters. If you and Giselle decide to go ahead, you will call one of us, and say very simply that you wish to talk. Nothing more. You will then replace the telephone and wait.

"Meanwhile, remember, the only people in the whole of France who know anything of this are the President, the Foreign Minister, the four people in this room, and two Admirals of the French Navy. That's eight. I need hardly mention, you will say nothing to anyone. But of course we know you never would. We know your record."

And with that, the two callers from Paris stood up and shook hands warmly with the mountain guide and his wife. But before they left, Savary had one last question. "Jacques Gamoudi," he said. "Why Hooks? Such a strange name for a Frenchman to adopt."

Colonel Gamoudi laughed. "Oh," he said, "that was the

name of the U.S. Ambassador we successfully evacuated out of Brazzaville back in June, 1999. Fourteen U.S. citizens altogether. Ambassador Aubrey Hooks was a good and brave man."

Two months later, August 2009

It had been a long, somewhat intensive, road to Bab Tourma Street, in the old part of the city of Damascus. There had been a zillion contacts with Hezbollah, even more with the militant end of the Iranian government. There had been countless clandestine talks with contacts inside al-Qaeda, mostly orchestrated by Prince Nasir. And finally a succession of e-mail exchanges with the leaders of the most feared of all terrorist groups, Hamas.

But Gaston Savary and Gen. Michel Jobert had finally made it. The Syrian government staff car, containing two local bodyguards and the two Frenchmen, pulled smoothly to a halt outside the big house near the historic gate in the city wall. This was the secretive and well-guarded home of the Hamas Commander in Chief, Gen. Ravi Rashood, and his beautiful Palestinian wife, Shakira.

And Prince Nasir had been insistent. *We need this man. He will bring us military discipline, and he will bring with him heavily armed, experienced Arab freedom fighters. We can't destroy a military air base with a bunch of amateurs, and this Hamas C-in-C is the best they've ever had.*

And now Gaston Savary and General Jobert were about to meet him, on his own ground. But, nonetheless, as allies. France's roots in Syria go very deep, but the key to this forthcoming conversation rested in one simple fact—there could never be an Islamic nation that stretched from the Arabian Gulf to the Atlantic end of North Africa so long as Saudi Arabia operated with one foot in the United States of America. Every Islamic fundamentalist knew that, every Islamic fundamentalist understood that there was something treacherous, non-Arabian, about the way the Saudi King both ran with the fox and hunted with the hounds. Or whatever the desert equivalent of that saying may be.

And now these two Frenchmen were here, about to enter the lair of the greatest terrorist the world had ever known. And they were bringing with them, perhaps, a formula to change everything. Savary and Jobert would be made very welcome by General Rashood, the native Iranian who had once served as an SAS Commander in the British army.

The door was opened by a slim young Syrian dressed in the customary long white robe. He bowed his head slightly and said quietly, "General Rashood is awaiting you." They were led down a long, bright, stone-floored corridor to a tall pair of dark wood doors. The Syrian opened one of them and motioned the Frenchmen through. Their two bodyguards, provided by the government, took up positions outside.

The room was not large, and General Rashood was alone, as agreed. He sat at a wide antique desk with a green leather top. To his left was a silver tea service, which had been brought in as the government car arrived. To his right a service revolver was placed on the desk, symbolically next to a leather-bound copy of the Koran.

Ravi Rashood rose and walked around the desk to greet his visitors. A thick-set man, with short dark hair and an unmistakable spring to his step, he wore faded light blue jeans and a loose white shirt. *"Salaam alaykum,"* he said in the customary greeting of the desert. Peace be upon you.

The two Frenchmen offered a couple of sharp *"bonjours"* in response, and General Rashood poured them all tea into little glass cups in silver holders. "Welcome to my home," he said graciously. "But time is short. You should not linger here for many reasons. In Damascus the walls and the trees have ears, and eyes."

"It's not much different in Paris," said the French Secret Service Chief. "But Paris is bigger, and thus more confusing."

General Rashood smiled and offered his guests. sugar, saying quietly, "I have of course been briefed very carefully about your plan. I have studied it in all its aspects. And I believe every Arab of the Islamic faith would welcome it. The antics of the Saudi royal family really are too excessive, and as you know, there can be no real prospect for a great Islamic state so long as Riyadh allows itself to be ruled by Washington."

"We understand that only too well," said General Jobert. "And the months go by, and the situation grows worse. The King, it seems, will tolerate anything from the younger members of his family. I expect you read of that appalling accident involving the passenger liner off Monaco. The King simply refuses to discuss it. According to our sources, the Crown Prince, Nasir, is the only hope that country has of growing up and taking its place at the center of the Islamic world, where it belongs."

"Of course I have not been briefed about the precise requirements of your plan," said Rashood. "But I understand we are looking at the destruction of the oil industry, followed by a military attack on one of the Saudi military bases, and then the capture of Riyadh and the overthrow of the royal family."

"In the broadest terms, correct," said Michel Jobert. "The main thing is to take the oil industry off the map for maybe two years. Because as soon as that is achieved the King will automatically be weakened badly. In Riyadh the mob is almost at the gates right now. The looming bankruptcy of the nation should be sufficient for them to herald a new regime."

"I don't think we can attack one of those military cities," said General Rashood. "They are too big, too solidly built, and too well defended. Have you thought about the air bases?"

"Exactly so," replied General Jobert. "We think the King Khalid Air Base, at Khamis Mushayt, is the one for us. If we can hit and destroy the aircraft on the ground, and achieve the surrender of the base, I think we could launch a separate squad at the command headquarters of the main base and demand their surrender.

"Remember, they will already know we've hit and crippled the oil industry, and they'll know we've hit and destroyed a large part of the Saudi Air Force. I think they might be ready to surrender. And if Khamis Mushayt surrendered, that would probably cause a total cave-in of the Army, especially as the television station will by now be appealing for loyalty to the incoming new King."

"Yes, I think all that follows," said General Rashood. "But what precisely is it you wish me to do?"

"I would like you to train and command the force that will assault the bases at Khamis Mushayt. And we would like you to be in constant communication with the commander in charge of the attack in Riyadh, and to move in to assist him in the final stages of the coup d'état in the capital."

"And where do I get the force to attack Khamis Mushayt? I would need specialists."

"French Army Special Forces," said General Jobert. "Well-trained, experienced fighters with expert skills in critical areas. We would also expect you to bring perhaps a dozen of your most trusted men. Your guides inside Saudi Arabia will all be al-Qaeda, who will provide backup fighters if required."

"We'll need several months for training and coordination," said General Rashood. "Where will we train?"

"France. Inside the classified areas where we prepare all our Special Forces. Top secret," replied General Jobert. "Most of it inside the barracks of the First Marine Parachute Infantry."

"And then?"

"Final training will be at a secret camp in Djibouti. From there you move into Saudi Arabia."

"How?"

"We thought that would be a problem best left to your good self."

General Rashood nodded gravely. "I imagine there will be no budget restrictions."

"Absolutely not. What you need, you get."

"And for myself? Do you have a figure in mind for my services?"

"In such a patriotic mission for the Islamic cause, we wondered if you might consider doing this for nothing."

"Wrong."

"You wouldn't? Not for the ultimate creation of an Islamic state?"

"No."

"A shame, General. I was led to be believe you were an idealist."

"I am, in some ways. But if I manage to achieve our objectives, I imagine there will be literally billions of petrodollars flying around in favor of France. Otherwise you would not be here. You are not idealists. You are in it for gain. And I do not work as an unpaid executive for greedy Western states, although I appreciate the philanthropic nature of your request."

"Then do you have a figure in mind?"

"A figure on the value of my life? Yes, a lot."

"How much?" asked Savary.

"I would not get out of this chair to embark on such a mission for one cent under ten million dollars. And if it works I want a bonus."

General Jobert nodded. "I think that could be arranged."

"And, in addition, there would need to be a substantial payment to a Hamas account, since we need to pay perhaps twenty men perhaps a hundred thousand dollars each.

"What do you think Hamas would require?" asked Savary.

"For the loss of their Commander in Chief? For maybe six months? I'd think another ten million."

"That's a great deal of money," said General Jobert.

"Not to the Saudis," said General Rashood. "And don't bother telling me France is paying, because I know that could not be true."

General Jobert smiled, as if to confirm he might have known what to expect from this Middle Eastern hard man who had defected from the SAS to follow his heart back to the desert lands of his birth.

"And your bonus?"

"If we take the southern bases, and I successfully help

your commander in Riyadh, putting a new king on the throne of Saudi Arabia—I think another five million dollars would be fair."

"I think that, too, could be arranged," said General Jobert. "But this will take some months to put into practice . . . Perhaps you could make a very short trip to Paris in the next few weeks, to meet our Riyadh commander. You will be working closely together in the coming months."

"That would be my pleasure," said General Rashood. "But now you must go. We will continue to communicate through the Syrian embassy in Paris. And I will confirm the agreement of my masters in the Hamas council."

The Frenchmen shook hands with the General on the agreement. And they hurried from the house and into the waiting car, which would speed directly to the airport and the waiting French Air Force jet, bound for Paris.

Wednesday, August 26, 2009, 4:00 P.M.
Damascus International Airport
Syria

Daniel Mostel, age twenty-four, was one of a few thousand Jewish residents of Damascus. His well-connected parents, who ran a highly successful car hire company with excellent government contracts, preferred the relaxed religious mood of Syria's principal city, and had always resisted the temptation to immigrate to Israel.

Mostel worked in air traffic control and hoped one day to become a pilot. He spent most of his evenings studying to take the Air France examinations. On weekends he attended a pilot training school out at the other airport, Aleppo, east of the city.

The family had lived in Damascus for several generations. Indeed, Mostel's grandfather had worked as a flight engineer during the 1930s, when France effectively ruled the country. But it was his maternal grandfather, Benjamin Lerner, who had most influenced young Daniel. Benjamin had lived in Israel and had often regaled the young Daniel with stories of Israel's monumental bravery during the wars with the Arabs in 1967 and 1973.

The result was that Daniel Mostel was a member of the *sayanim*, that secret, worldwide Israeli brotherhood whose members would do *anything* to help the tough, beleaguered little nation that stood defiantly at the eastern end of the Mediterranean Sea, not so much surrounded as engulfed by Arab states.

Daniel Mostel was a fanatic for the cause of Israel. He had often considered leaving home and returning to the land of his forefathers. But his main contact in the Mossad knew he was of more value to Israel right there in the control tower of the Damascus International Airport, staying alert and watchful. Mostel had never breathed a word to his parents about his involvement with the *sayanim*. But he had told his grandfather before he died that he was fighting for the cause the best way he could.

And at this particular moment in the hot afternoon, he was greatly confused by an Air France jet airliner, a European Airbus, standing separately from all other aircraft, with no passengers, and nothing, so far as he could see, in the way of a flight plan.

Shortly after four o'clock he saw the air crew plus two flight attendants board the jet, and ten minutes later a black Syrian government car pulled up to the base of the steps up at the forward section. One single man stepped out of the rear door of the automobile and climbed nimbly up the wide embarkation staircase. He carried a small leather holdall and wore faded blue jeans with a white shirt and a light brown suede jacket.

Mostel saw the crew close the aircraft's main door immediately, and he watched the plane taxi out to the end of the runway. Two stations down from his own, he heard his boss say firmly, *"Air France zero-zero-one cleared for takeoff."*

Daniel Mostel had not the slightest idea who was aboard that aircraft. But he knew there was but one passenger. And it was a big plane to be carrying only one person.

It was out of the question that he should ask where it was going or whom it was carrying. It was plainly none of his business. And to make such an inquiry may very well have aroused suspicions about himself.

General Rashood had been most certainly correct about one thing—the walls and the trees had ears and eyes in Damascus.

Daniel Mostel took his break at 5 P.M. local time. He left the airport for ten minutes, driving out to a lonely part of the desert. And there, using his mobile cell phone, he called a very private number at the western end of the city, out on Palestine Avenue. And he reported the departure of the Air France flight. He gave the serial number painted on the fuselage, the zero-zero-one flight number, which was plainly invented, and the fact that a government car had delivered the plane's only passenger. Took off to the west, 1630.

Twenty minutes later Mossad agents were being alerted in Cairo, Tripoli, Baghdad, Tel Aviv, Rome, Nice, Paris, London, and Amsterdam. The Mossad, Israel's relentlessly efficient secret service, disliked anything clandestine being conducted by anyone in their territory. And this possessed the hallmarks of secrecy on an international scale. The signal to the agents was simple: find out who's onboard Air France zero-zero-one out of Damascus.

And since the brotherhood of the *sayanim* was active in just about every airport and flight check-point in Europe, it took about a half-hour to establish that the flight was on its way to Paris, where it was due to land at 7:30 P.M., a two-hour time gain on a five-hour flight.

Simon Baum, who waited up on the viewing deck at Charles de Gaulle Airport, was watching through binoculars with several other plane-spotters. But Simon was not just a member of the *sayanim*. He was the Bureau chief of the Mossad's entire Paris operation, located in the basement of the Israeli embassy.

He saw the Air France flight come in to land, right on time, and he guessed correctly that it would taxi somewhere close to the area in which a French government car was waiting, close to where the young "baggage handler" Jacob Fabre was standing behind a line of in-flight catering carts, hidden from view, holding an extremely expensive digital camera with a long-range lens built in.

Young Fabre had done this before. He too was a member of the *sayanim,* and he was well accustomed to trying to snatch pictures of incoming passengers who were apparently of interest to the Mossad. The camera belonged to Simon Baum, and there would be a cashier's check for €1,000 in the mail for him the following week.

He watched the aircraft taxi into position no more than forty yards from where he stood. The main cabin door opened, and a flight attendant stepped outside and waited at the top of the steps. Fabre aimed the camera straight at the door as the only passenger appeared . . . *click* . . . *click* . . . *click.* The passenger turned away to speak to the flight attendant. Then back toward the terminal building.

Click . . . Fabre caught him once more. Then twice as he came down the stairs. But then the man turned away, toward the waiting car. Fabre snapped the car for good measure. And then shot two more frames through the rear passenger window as it sped away toward the private entrance to the airport. Nine shots. In the next twenty minutes he would hand the camera back to Monsieur Baum, and hope that the pictures would develop satisfactorily.

The government car came through the guarded gates swiftly, and immediately a black Peugeot fell in behind and tracked its quarry all the way along the main road into the northern suburbs of Paris. From there the government car turned west and headed across the top of the city toward Taverny, where it moved fast down two quiet streets and swung into the guarded gates of COS.

The pursuing car did not follow into the final approach road, but swerved away to the south, back to the central part of the city and the Israeli embassy.

But the Mossad now knew two things. The mystery man from Damascus was ensconced in the Commandement des Opérations Speciales in Taverny. And secondly COS *really* did not wish anyone to know his whereabouts.

Simon Baum knew it would be extremely difficult to track

anyone in France whom the military did not wish to be tracked. If the mystery man from the desert was going anywhere internally, he would travel by military jet or helicopter.

Simon Baum would rely on the *sayanim*, and meanwhile he would send Jacob Fabre's photographs over the Internet to all of his main offices and agents in France, and something might break loose. He held out no real hope that the visitor was of any special interest to him or his organization, but the Mossad did not attain its fearsome reputation by not bothering. It had become the world's most notorious intelligence network because it missed nothing, left nothing to chance, and solved all problems to the best of its ability.

You might have a chance to get away from Britain's MI-6 and, indeed, since the Presidency of Bill Clinton, from the CIA. Generally speaking there was no chance whatsoever of escape from the Mossad.

And so young Fabre's photographs were circulated throughout the vast network of the Israeli Secret Service. And, curiously, the first coded e-mail signal came back from headquarters in Tel Aviv. It said simply: VISITOR TO PARIS, GEN. RAVI RASHOOD, C-IN-C HAMAS, AKA MAJ. RAY KERMAN OF BRITISH SAS. ELIMINATE.

Simon Baum stared at the name of the most wanted man in Israel, Maj. Ray Kerman, who had jumped ship in the Battle of Palestine Road, in the West Bank city of Hebron three years ago. Kerman, who had hit Israel's Nimrod jail and released every one of the most dangerous political prisoners in the entire country. Kerman, scourge of the U.S. West Coast, the most wanted man in the entire world. And here he was, having dinner in the Paris suburb of Taverny with French military chiefs, under strict government protection. Simon Baum could not believe his eyes at the name on the screen before him. But the Mossad does not make mistakes. If they said it was the Hamas C-in-C, then that's who it was.

But ELIMINATE? *Mon Dieu!* They must be joking. At any rate. Not this trip.

Simon Baum never slept that night. He remained in his

office, in the bowels of the Israeli embassy, sipping cognac poured into dark Turkish coffee—what Parisians call *café complet*. He constantly checked his e-mail.

But the night was quiet, and so was the new day. Baum worked restlessly, checking dozens of communications until the early afternoon, when he finally dozed off in his office. He was asleep at his desk when the long-range French Marine Commando helicopter, the SA 365-7 Dauphin 2, clattered into the sky above Taverny, bearing the COS director, Gen. Michel Jobert, and the Hamas General, Ravi Rashood, along the first miles of their long journey to the south.

They flew to the eastern side of Paris, well clear of the heavy air traffic around Charles de Gaulle Airport, and set a course due south. It would take them east of the city of Lyon, then down the long Rhone River valley, all the way to the delta in the glistening salt marshes of the Camargue. From there they would swing east along the coast, across the great bay of Marseille, and into the small landing area the Foreign Legion operated at Aubagne, fifteen miles east of France's second city.

It could scarcely have gone more smoothly. Except for one certain Moshe Benson, air traffic controller at the small regional airport near the village of Mions, which stood eight miles southwest of Lyon's main Saint-Exupéry Airport, and thus considerably closer to the flight path of the Marine Commando helicopter.

Benson picked the helicopter up on the airport radar as it clattered ten thousand feet above the vineyards of Beaujolais. He realized instantly that it was military, not transmitting, and not offering any call sign to this particular control point. This was slightly unusual, even though the military in France were apt to operate with a degree of independence.

Moshe Benson made a routine call to the control tower in Marseille to report formally that a fast, unidentified helicopter had just come charging through his air space, and that they might keep a watch for it. He told them he assumed it was French military.

Meanwhile, Simon Baum was awakened by one of his agents to learn that a Marine Commando Dauphin 2 helicopter had taken off one hour ago from the Taverny complex and appeared to be headed south. The Mossad chief immediately called four *sayanim* at various airports—Dijon, Limoges, Lyon, and Grenoble. The only one who could help was Moshe Benson.

Simon Baum knew that the range of the Dauphin was less than 500 miles and he knew that Marseille was 425 miles south of Paris. Unless it was going sightseeing along the Riviera, that particular helicopter was going into Marseille or, more likely, to the military base at Aubagne.

For some reason he was not quite able to explain, Baum badly wanted to know who was onboard that Dauphin. He had a gut feeling it might be the elusive terrorist commander Ravi Rashood. And his country wanted that man dead at any cost.

He called two of his top agents in Marseille and told them to get out to Aubagne on the double. He checked his man in the main city airport, Marseille-Provence, and put him on full alert, though he did not expect the Dauphin to fly in there.

Thus, by the time Generals Michel Jobert and Ravi Rashood touched down in Aubagne in the gathering dusk, there was a black Peugeot discreetly parked along the main road to Marseille, 200 yards beyond the main gates to the Foreign Legion garrison. Through powerful binoculars, Simon Baum's men had watched the Dauphin land, and now they were watching for an army staff car to exit the garrison bearing at least one and possibly two passengers.

They had only four minutes to wait. And when General Jobert's Citroën began its fifteen-mile journey into the city, there was a Mossad tail right behind, with two of Simon Baum's most lethal operators in the two front seats. They were not so much agents as hit men.

They drove directly into Marseille, and ran west down the wide, main boulevard of La Canebiere, toward the Old Port. With the busy harbor in front of them, they turned

right and made their way to the north side, to the Quai du
Port, and immediately turned away from the water, into the
labyrinth of streets that housed some of the best restaurants
in Marseille.

The army staff car came to a sudden halt outside the
world-renowned fish restaurant L'Union, and both General
Jobert and General Rashood disembarked and hurried up
the two front steps. They were inside, with the big ma-
hogany doors closed behind them, before the Mossad track-
ers had turned the corner.

But Simon Baum's men saw the car backing into a parking space not twenty yards from L'Union's main entrance,
and they guessed that the passengers had already made an
exit. Agent David Schwab jumped out and waited outside
the restaurant, while his colleague, Agent Robert Jazy,
parked the car and returned on foot.

Five minutes later both men went into the paneled bar
area of the big, noisy restaurant and identified General Rashood from Jacob Fabre's photographs, which they had received from Paris via the Internet. Neither of them could
identify General Jobert, and the third man, now speaking to
the two new arrivals from Paris, was unknown to them.

The Mossad agents did not know it, but they were watching a minor piece of secret history. This was the first meeting between General Rashood and Col. Jacques Gamoudi,
the two men who would command the military assault on
Saudi Arabia.

In two separate places, twenty-five feet apart at the long,
polished wooden bar, the five men sipped glasses of wine
from the vineyards of the Pyrenees, until, shortly after 7:30
P.M., General Jobert and his men walked out of the bar into
the main restaurant and were led to a wide, heavy oak table
covered with a bright red-and-white checkered tablecloth in
the corner of the room. Two flickering candles were
jammed jauntily into the necks of empty bottles of Chateau
Petrus, the most expensive Bordeaux in France.

The three men occupied three sides of the table; no one's
back was turned to the arched entrance across the room.
Colonel Gamoudi and General Rashood had already estab-

lished a mutual respect and were locked in conversation, mostly involving the armored vehicles necessary to storm Riyadh's main royal palace from the front. General Rashood favored a quiet, fraudulent entry against unsuspecting guards, who could then be taken by surprise, with an armored vehicle jamming the main gates open.

Jacques Gamoudi was inclined to hit those main gates with a tank, and have his infantry charge from behind that heavier armored vehicle, moving straight ahead, firing from the hip.

"My method is less likely to cause us casualties," said Rashood. "Because that way we'll call all the shots, with a huge element of surprise. A tank's damned noisy and likely to alert the entire place."

"It's also very scary," replied Colonel Gamoudi. "And may even cause a quick surrender of the palace guards."

At this point the waiter came, and all three of them decided to order the local speciality, bouillabaisse, a seafood stew with onion, white wine, and tomatoes flavored with fennel and saffron. One big steaming bowl for three. They ordered a bottle of white wine from Jurançon, and some Italian antipasto to start.

"I think one of our main problems will be getting the guys in for the hit on the King Khalid Air Base," said Rashood.

"Bouillabaisse—air base—it's all the same to us, heh?" laughed Gamoudi. "And the sea's the key to both operations."

Michel Jobert chuckled, and the conversation continued in a light-hearted manner until the main course arrived. The principal decisions had been made. Both Rashood and Gamoudi had accepted the money. The plan was to be executed as masterminded by Prince Nasir.

But they all understood that the sticking point was the entry into southwestern Saudi Arabia. "It's all very well for you, Jacques Gamoudi," said Rashood. "Your guys are in and ready, as soon as you arrive. I have to get my squad into the country, and it's not going to be easy. I don't know if the Saudis can fight, but there's a lot of them. And we have to be extremely careful."

"That's true, General," replied Colonel Gamoudi. "Because my operation depends entirely on the news from Khamis Mushayt. It's critical that the Saudi Army in Riyadh understand there has been a major surrender in the south. And critical that they know it before my opening attack."

Rashood nodded in agreement. At which point, agents David Schwab and Robert Jazy suddenly appeared in the waiting area of the main dining room. Now they each wore long, black leather coats, which they had not been wearing in the bar. They were standing in the slightly raised entranceway at the top of the two wooden steps that led down into the dining area, facing Jacques Gamoudi head-on, from a distance of around 100 feet. They stood to Rashood's left and General Jobert's right. Colonel Gamoudi was staring back at them, when, amazingly, he saw each of them swiftly drawing AK-47s from inside the front flaps of their coats. He watched the unmistakable shape of the short barrels being raised to shoulder height.

With the instincts of the lifetime combat soldier, he grasped the heavy table and hurled it forward, wine, bouillabaisse and God knows what else crashing to the floor. With his left hand he grabbed Rashood by the throat and with his right he grabbed the General, hurling them both down.

The opening burst from the AK-47s smashed a line of bullets clean down the middle of the hefty table top, which now acted as a barrier between Rashood, Gamoudi, and Jobert, and the flying lead from the Kalashnikovs. All three of them could hear the bullets whining around the room. Behind them, two waiters had gone down with blood pumping from their chests.

Crockery was shattered, bottles of wine were smashed, women were screaming, everyone was rushing for cover. Another ferocious burst of fire confirmed that the hit men were making their way across the restaurant. Jacques Gamoudi drew the only weapon he had, his big bear-hunting knife, and Ravi Rashood pulled his Browning 9mm from the wide leather belt near the small of his back.

Colonel Gamoudi snapped to Rashood, "It's you they're after, *mon ami*. I'll take one, and you shoot the other soon as you can see him. General Jobert, stay right there behind the table."

And with that, the iron-souled mountain guide crashed under the adjoining tables until he reached a heavy white column in the center of the room. The precise path of Jacques Gamoudi was obvious by the sheer volume of destruction he left behind him on the floor of the restaurant, overturned tables and chairs, magnificently cooked seafood, burning candles mostly extinguished by wine and the contents of ice buckets.

But it was impossible to shoot him as he dived beneath the tables, staying low, hammering his way forward. However, the Mossad men gave it their best shot, and bullets ricocheted in all directions.

Agent Jazy now hung back, at once looking for the charging Gamoudi and trying to provide cover for his partner, as David Schwab moved forward for the kill, advancing toward the upturned table, behind which his quarry was crouching.

But somehow Jacques Gamoudi got around behind Jazy. He leaped at him with a bound that would have made a mountain lion gasp, and plunged his knife right into the man's throat, ripping the windpipe and jugular. Jazy had no time to scream. He dropped his rifle and fell back, dying, in the mighty arms of Le Chasseur.

Agent Schwab turned around and swung his rifle straight at Gamoudi, who was using Jazy as a human shield. He hesitated for one split second, and Ravi Rashood, moving even faster than Gamoudi, dived horizontally out from behind the table and shot Schwab clean through the back of the head, twice. A line of bullets, hopelessly ripping across the timbered ceiling, was the Mossad man's only reply.

The entire room was now a bloodbath—or at least a blood-and-wine bath. Fifteen diners were injured, five of them seriously, four staff were dead, including the headwaiter, who had been caught in the opening crossfire. Such was the speed of the battle that no one had yet called either an ambulance or the police. Surviving staff members were either in shock or still taking cover.

Colonel Gamoudi and General Rashood hauled Michel Jobert back to his feet. They grabbed for the two fallen AK-47s, all three of them running for the exit.

Outside they could see a black Peugeot with a driver plainly awaiting the two hit men. To the amazement of his two companions General Jobert cut the driver down in cold blood, right behind the wheel, with a burst of fire that obliterated the windshield and riddled the driver's-side door, and the driver's left temple.

They piled into the backseat of their own car, and General Jobert snapped to their driver, "Aubagne! And step on it! Back roads. Stay off the highway."

And at high speed they headed out of Marseille; they were men who were above suspicion, two decorated French Army officers, one of them serving at the highest possible level, and an Arabian General called in to assist France in a highly classified operation, by presidential edict.

"Trouble, sir?" asked the driver.

"Not really, Maurice. Couple of amateurs made a rather silly misjudgment," said Michel Jobert. "Not a word, of course. We were nowhere near Marseille."

"Certainly not, sir. I know the rules."

Thursday, November 19, 2009
National Security Agency
Fort Meade, Maryland

LT. CDR. JIMMY Ramshawe, personal assistant to the director of the world's most sophisticated intelligence agency, was looking for the third time that fall at a sudden, sharply upward spike in the world's oil prices. He had noticed one in September, another in October, and here were West Texas Intermediate trading futures today at almost fifty-three dollars a barrel on Wall Street's NYMEX exchange.

It was the same story on the International Petroleum Exchange in London. Brent Crude had actually hit $55 there earlier that morning, before New York opened for trading. In mid-afternoon it fell back to $48.95. The pattern was not drastic, but it was steady.

Somewhere in the world, perhaps shielding behind international brokers and traders, there was a new player in the market. And as Jimmy Ramshawe put it, *the bastard's buying a whole lot of oil. And he's doing it on a damn regular basis . . . I wonder who the hell that is.*

Gas was now four dollars a gallon at the pumps in the United States, which was pleasing no one, especially the President. In England it had hit almost nine dollars. And so far as Jimmy could see, it was all caused by just one big player in the futures market, on both side of the Atlantic—buying, buying, buying, driving up the prices.

Lt. Commander Ramshawe could not fathom how the buyer had managed to keep it all so secret. The sheer volume of oil futures being purchased was of mammoth proportions. Someone who thought he needed an extra 1.5 million barrels a day, or almost 40 million barrels a month.

"Multiply that bastard by forty-two," muttered Ramshawe, "and you've got some bloody mongrel out there trying to buy one and a half billion gallons of gas every month. Christ! He must have a lot of cars."

The initial suspect, in the young Lt. Commander's opinion, had to be China. *A billion bloody cars and no oil resources. But then*, he thought, *they wouldn't do it like that. Not out there on the open market, buying high-priced futures. They'd cut some kind of a deal with Siberia or Russia or the Central Asians around the Baku fields. It can't be them.*

And it could scarcely be Russia, which now had all kinds of oil resources from the Baku fields. Great Britain? No, they still have their own North Sea fields. Japan? No. They had very cozy long-term contracts with the Saudis for both gasoline and propane. So who? Germany? France? Unlikely. Especially France, who for years has been reducing its oil requirements in favor of nuclear-powered electricity plants.

Nonetheless Lt. Commander Ramshawe reckoned it had to be one of them, because no one else could play on that scale. He keyed into the Internet and checked the energy status of France, which was not only the fifth largest economy in the world but also one of the largest producers of nuclear power.

Ramshawe read a pocket summary of the recent history of the French oil giant Total, merged with the Belgian company Petrofina in 1999. Then it merged again, with Elf Aquitaine, to create, unimaginatively, TotalFinaElf, the fourth largest publicly listed oil company in the world—right after ExxonMobil, Royal Dutch Shell, and BP.

The company had proven reserves of 10.8 billion barrels, and production of 2.1 million barrels a day. It owned more than 50 percent of all the refining capacity in France.

TotalFinaElf was the seventh largest refiner on earth. It was a major shareholder in the 1,100-mile pipeline out of Baku, through Georgia to Turkey's Mediterranean port of Ceyhan.

Christ! thought Jimmy. *They're big enough, but why? France uses only 1.9 million barrels a day, and if push came to shove their own oil company produces more than that. Beats the hell out of me, unless they're closing down their nuclear power plants and switching back to oil.*

So far as Ramshawe could see, this was a hugely unlikely scenario. France had reduced her oil usage in the past thirty years, from 68 percent of gross energy consumption to around 40 percent. But she still imported 1.85 million barrels a day, mostly for road, rail, and air transportation. As a nation she was totally reliant on imported oil, the vast bulk of it coming from Saudi Arabia, with some from Norway and a very small amount from other producers.

France generated 77 percent of her electricity from nuclear power, and she was the second largest exporter of electricity in Europe. *They're not going to close down the bloody nuclear plants, are they?*

The young Lieutenant Commander actually had other things to do right now, but he put in two routine calls, to the International Petroleum Exchange in London and to NYMEX in New York, leaving messages at both numbers to call back the National Security Agency in Fort Meade.

Ramshawe knew both men at those numbers, having talked with them during various oil crises before. He did not want this to be official. He just wanted someone to mark his card on who was the unexpected major buyer in the world oil market right now, the guy driving up the prices not to earth-shaking levels, but enough to cost a lot of people a great deal of money.

Lt. Commander Ramshawe knew there were always reasons for things. When someone was in any market, buying heavily, there was always a solid reason. Just as when someone was out there selling there was always a reason. And in Jimmy Ramshawe's global view, those reasons needed to be located and assessed. As his boss Adm. George Morris so often said, *Damned good intelligence officer, young Ramshawe.*

And it did not take him long to find his answers. Roger Smythson, a very senior oil broker in London, said he could not be certain, but the buyer who was unsettling the London market was undoubtedly European. He had already run a few traces, and it looked like France.

Orders, he said, were coming in from brokers based in Le Havre, France's biggest overseas trading port, which contains the largest of all the French refineries, Gonfreville l'Orcher. In Roger's view, the fingerprints of TotalFinaElf were all over some huge trades made from that area.

From New York, the suspicion was the same. Frank Carstairs, who worked almost exclusively as a dealer for Exxon, said flatly, "I don't know who it is, Jimmy, but I'd bet a lot of money it's France. The orders are all European, and there's a big broker down in the Marseille area who's been very busy these past couple of months."

"That's a major oil area, right?" said Ramshawe. "TotalFinaElf country, right?"

"Oh, sure," said Carstairs. "Marseille handles around one-third of all France's crude oil refining. Terminals at Fos-sur-Mer, that's us, Exxon. Berre, that's Shell, Le Mede, TotalFina, and Lavera, BP. They got a damned great methane terminal down there, and an underground LPG depot the size of Yankee Stadium."

"That's liquid petroleum gas, right, Frank?"

"You got it, Jimmy. Mostly from Saudi Arabia, like the majority of French oil products."

"Thanks, Frank. Don't wanna keep you. Just wondering what's going on, okay?"

Same day, 7:00 P.M.
Chevy Chase, Maryland

The big Colonial house that stood well back from the road, fronted by a vast lawn and a sweeping blacktop drive, was not an official embassy of the United States. Though no one would have guessed it.

There were two armed Special Agents, one just inside the wrought-iron gates, one in a black government automobile near the front door. There were surveillance cameras set into the gables of the house, laser beams, alarm bells, and God knows what else.

And the visitors were legion. In any one month, the agents at various times waved through cars from foreign embassies, cars from the Pentagon, cars from the National Security Agency, cars from the CIA, and cars from the White House.

When Adm. Arnold Morgan (Ret.) was in residence, there were a lot of people with a lot of problems who needed the advice of the old "Lion of the West Wing." And since many of those problems had a direct bearing on the health and well-being of the United States of America, the Admiral usually agreed to give people the time of day.

As retirements went, the autumn of the Admiral's life was full of bright colors. The former National Security Adviser to the President was still in action, unpaid, but still growling . . . *I wouldn't trust that sonofabitch one inch.* So much for the President of one of the richest states in the Middle East . . . *Who? That dumbwit couldn't fight his way out of a Lego box, never mind build a decent nuclear submarine.* So much for the science and research director of the world's fourth largest Navy.

Admiral Morgan was like a desert sheik dispensing wisdom and guidance to his flock at the weekly *Majlis.* Except the Admiral's flock was worldwide, with no racial boundaries. There were probably ten foreign armed services, allies of the United States, who preferred to check in with the Admiral before making any major decision. The same applied, often, to the President of the United States, Paul Bedford.

Most of the Admiral's guests came at their own request. But the guest tonight was there as an old friend, invited for dinner by Admiral and Mrs. Morgan, the beautiful Kathy, who had served as his secretary in the White House with the patience of Mary Magdalene.

Gen. David Gavron, the sixty-two-year-old Israeli ambassador to the United States, was unmarried, though there were at least two Washington hostesses who were nearly certain he might marry them. He loved dinner with Arnold and Kathy, and he always came alone. The three of them met quite often, occasionally at their favorite Georgetown restaurant, sometimes at the Israeli embassy, three miles north of the city, and sometimes here in Chevy Chase.

It was growing cold in Washington, and Admiral Morgan considered he was in the final couple of weeks of his outside barbecue season. On the grill were five gigantic lamb chops—which would be eaten with a couple of bottles of Comtesse Nicholais's 2002 Corton-Bressandes, a superb Grand Cru from her renowned Domaine Chandon de Briailles, in the heart of the Côte de Beaune.

Morgan was a devotee of the Comtesse's red burgundy, and considered lamb chops to be utterly incomplete without it. Which meant that the chops were incomplete about a dozen times a year, because Corton-Bressandes cost around fifty dollars a bottle, and Arnold considered that a touch extravagant on a day-to-day basis.

However, he had purchased a couple of cases of the 2002 several years ago, and he took great delight in serving it to special guests, like David Gavron, who had introduced him to the perfect, silky dessert wines of the old Rothschild vineyards fifteen miles southeast of Tel Aviv. Admiral Morgan's cellar was never without a case of that.

Tonight it was a very relaxed dinner. The wine was perfect and the chops were outstanding. Afterward they each had a slice of Chaume cheese and finished the Burgundy. By 11 P.M. they had retired to the fireside in the timbered book-lined study, and Kathy had served coffee—a dark, strong Turkish blend that Gavron himself had brought as a gift.

They were discussing their usual subject, terrorism and the sheer dimension of the pain-in-the-ass it caused all over the world, the cost and the inconvenience. Which was, after all, what the terrorists intended.

Quite suddenly, General Gavron asked, "Arnold, have

you heard anything more about our old friend Maj. Ray Kerman?"

"Plenty," replied the Admiral. "Too damned much. Volcanoes, power stations, and god knows what. But we never really got a smell of him. He's an elusive sonofabitch."

"We nearly had him, you know," said the General. "Damn nearly had him."

Morgan looked up sharply. "What do you mean, nearly had him?"

"Darned nearly took him out."

"You did? Where? When?"

"Couple of months ago. Marseille."

"Is that right? I never heard anything."

"I'm not surprised. But do you remember a major gangland killing in a restaurant? Bullets flying. Customers injured, staff dead?"

"Can't say I do."

"No. The French police covered it up pretty tight."

"You've lost me, David—what about Kerman?"

"The night before the killings, we picked up Kerman arriving in Paris. On an entirely empty Air France flight, big European Airbus-Boeing. Then we located him again at the French Foreign Legion training base at Aubagne, just east of Marseille. Remember, we want Kerman just as badly as you do."

"And then?"

"We sent two of our best agents in."

"Assassins?"

"Agents, with a . . . well . . . flexible agenda."

"And what happened?"

"They were both killed stone dead in some kind of a shootout. But of course no one knew who they were. The French police announced it was a gangland killing, involving drugs, tried to blame one of the dead waiters.

"We never even knew what was going on till we saw police pictures of two dead men being carried out of the restaurant. They were never even released, far less published, but one of our field officers saw them, and instantly identified one of the bodies on the stretcher, throat cut wide open."

"Christ!" said Morgan. "What about the other agent?"

"Also dead. Two bullets to the back of the head, fired from a semi-automatic Browning high-power pistol . . . nine millimeter. The SAS has used them for years, but not many other modern forces do."

"None of this was in the newspapers, right?"

"Certainly not. For some reason the police, or the French government, someone, wanted this thing played right down. We of course were not anxious to have the names of our dead agents plastered all over the place. And they carried no identification with them. We just decided to let it ride. And the French kept it quiet for us. The bodies apparently vanished. And no one ever heard anything more. But it was Kerman we were after. And Kerman, I believe, whose finger was on the trigger of his trusty Browning service revolver."

"You think he cut the other agent's throat?"

"No. That must have been his buddy, whoever that was."

"Jesus. Sounds like another SAS man," said Morgan.

"Doesn't it? But Hereford has reported no one else missing. Whoever it was, it was a very professional response. We have never before lost agents, armed to the teeth with AK-47s, to a couple of amateurs having dinner, armed only with a sheath knife and an old-fashioned pistol."

"You think Kerman's still in France?"

"I don't know. But he left from Damascus. That's where we logged on to him. But our people did not see him return. He could be anywhere."

General Gavron could not of course have known about the devious way General Rashood made his escape from France—the long car journey back to Paris; the first-class seats onboard a regular, crowded Air France flight to Syria; the French Secret Service steering the Hamas assault chief through security, complete with his Browning 9mm; the two accompanying bodyguards from the First Marine Parachute Regiment, all three wearing traditional Arab dress. It all looked too normal in Damascus Airport, way too normal to attract the attention of Daniel Mostel.

"Kerman," said Morgan. "He's like the goddamned Scarlet Pimpernel."

"Well, the trail's gone cold," replied the Israeli General.

"So we're back where we started," said Morgan. "He might be in Syria. But it could be Jordan, or Iran, or Libya. Or even Cairo. And now France."

"Yes. But that was a damn funny business in Marseille, Arnie," said the General. "I mean, what's Kerman doing in France in the first place? And what's he doing in Special Forces aircraft? Landing at a Foreign Legion base? And who was he dining with? And how come he has the obvious protection of the French police, not to mention the French Government?

"That restaurant was the scene of a colossal crime. And the police refused to release any information whatsoever. A lot of people were hurt, some killed, but they would not even name the dead. I mean my agents."

Admiral Morgan smiled. General Gavron still regarded himself as the head of the Mossad, even though he retired from that position several months before. *But I guess,* thought Arnold, *when you've fought a tank battle alongside Bren Adan in the Sinai, been wounded, decorated for valor, and literally laid down your life for Israel, you're apt to take even its minor problems very personally.*

He looked into the wide, tanned, open face of the Israeli. And he probed into those bright blue eyes for a sign of disquiet. And he found it. David Gavron was bitterly unhappy that one of Israel's greatest enemies might be planning another operation.

Morgan could see almost straight through the former Israeli battle commander, as if the unacceptable thought were reflected in those piercing eyes . . . *What the hell was Kerman doing in France, smuggled in, and probably out again, all with government protection?*

The following morning, Lt. Commander Ramshawe's phone rang before 0800. He recognized the voice instantly. "Morning, sir," he greeted the former director of the National Security Agency.

"Jimmy," said Admiral Morgan. "Do you remember a couple of months ago reading anything at all about a gang shooting, something to do with drugs, in Marseille?"

"No, sir. Doesn't ring a bell."

"It was pretty big. Like fifteen injured and maybe six dead in a real bloodbath in some restaurant near the waterfront."

"Still doesn't ring a bell, sir. But I'll get right on it, check it out. Do you have a more precise date?"

"It was in the last week of August. Restaurant called L'Union. Police apparently wanted it kept quiet. They released very little. But the Mossad lost two agents, both killed in the fight. One of them had his throat cut. They reckon the other one was shot by Major Ray Kerman."

"Jeez," said Jimmy Ramshawe. "Here he comes again."

"Precisely my thoughts. See what you can dig up. You and Jane want to come over for dinner later? We'd be glad to see you. And we're getting to the end of the grilling season. How about some New York sirloin steaks? Keep your strength up."

"Sounds great, sir. We'll be there. Second dogwatch. Three bells, right?"

"Perfect. 1930. See you then, kid."

Jimmy Ramshawe had absolutely no idea why, but whenever the Big Man came on the line, a ripple of excitement shot right through him. The unerring instinct of Admiral Morgan for real trouble was infectious. And so far as the young Lt. Commander could remember, the Admiral had never been wrong.

And another thing. What was it with this Marseille bullshit? He'd never even thought about the place for years on end. And now he'd heard it big time, twice, in twenty-four hours. *The bloody frogs are up to something,* he surmised. *The ol' Admiral doesn't come in with requests unless something's afoot.*

But the trouble with France was, he couldn't really read the language. What he needed was an English-speaking newspaper that might carry the story. He keyed into the Internet and whistled up the foreign pages of the *London Daily Telegraph.*

Result: one big fat zero. *Not a bloody line about a mass murder. Bloody oath, they're getting slack over there.*

James Ramshawe was born in America, but both his parents were Australian, and he still spoke with the pronounced accent of New South Wales. His fiancée, Jane Peacock, was the daughter of the Australian Ambassador in Washington. Both of them loved to have a go at the Brits for being incompetent and inept. And an unreported mass murder in the next-door country would do Jimmy fine for a few hours.

Bloody pom journalists. Wouldn't know a truly significant story if it bit 'em in the ass.

He actually knew that was not true. But it amused him to say it, even under his breath. Anyway, beaten by the system, he sent for a translator and keyed his Internet connection into the news pages of *Le Figaro*, last week in August.

The big French national daily was better than the *Telegraph*, but not by much. It reported a serious shoot-out at L'Union restaurant in Marseille, a French city historically known for its connection to crime, drugs, smuggling, and other nefarious activities. The newspaper claimed that fifteen people had been admitted to hospital and some of them had been released that night. It also believed that there were only TWO fatalities (Jimmy's caps in his report) when it was clear there were more. Because they named the dead waiters, but not the Mossad agents.

The whole drift of the story was an inter-gang battle involving drugs—professional villains—killing each other. It was of no significant interest to ordinary citizens. And the innocent bystanders caught in the cross fire? They would receive generous compensation from the restaurant's insurance company.

The headline in *Le Figaro* was over just one column, on page seven. It read: GANGLAND KILLING IN MARSEILLE; DINERS AT L'UNION RESTAURANT WOUNDED IN CROSS FIRE.

There was no follow-up on any of the next five days.

"Well, I guess that's the bloody end of that," said Ramshawe.

Well, nearly. Because the young intelligence officer, who enjoyed the ear of the mighty, had received this story from the mightiest of all, Admiral Morgan himself. *And the great man does not go real strong on half-measures,* Ramshawe thought. *He called me because he wants some bloody answers. And he wants 'em quick, like by dinner-time tonight. That's why we're going to his house, right?*

He immediately told his interpreter, a twenty-three-year-old civilian graduate named Jo, to get on the line to directory inquiries in France and get the number of L'Union restaurant in Marseille. He then told her to make the call and to put it on the speakerphone in the middle of his desk.

He listened with interest as the phone rang on the faraway south coast of France and was answered on the fourth ring.

"Préfecture de police, Marseille."

"Tell 'em you want the restaurant, not the bloody gendarmes," hissed Ramshawe.

Jo struggled boldly, but was told firmly, "The restaurant is closed. We have no information about its re-opening."

"Tell 'em you don't understand why a closed restaurant has its phone calls automatically diverted to the police station," hissed Ramshawe.

But again, Jo encountered a brick wall: "I have no information on that," replied the Marseille gendarme.

"Pull rank," said Ramshawe. "Tell 'em who we are. And then tell 'em we want to know precisely how many people were killed in the mass murder at L'Union because we believe at least one of them may have been a United States citizen."

Jo went right ahead, beginning, "Sir, this is the Director's office in the National Security Agency of the United States of America in Washington. You may call back to verify if you wish. But we want some answers, and if necessary we will go to presidential level to get them. Please bring someone of senior authority to the telephone."

"Un moment, s'il vous plaît."

"Beautiful, Jo. That's my girl." Lt. Commander Ramshawe grinned. And in the background they both heard a voice say, *"Sécurité Americaine."*

And then a new voice came on, speaking excellent English. "This is Chief Inspector Rochelle. How may I assist?"

Ramshawe took over. "Thank you for coming to the phone, Chief Inspector. My name is Lt. Cdr. James Ramshawe and I'm the assistant to the Director of the National Security Agency in Washington. I thought I was calling L'Union restaurant, but we came straight through to you. I would like to know exactly how many people died in that shooting in the restaurant two months ago. We have reason to believe one of them was an American citizen."

"Non, monsieur. That is not the case. There were two members of staff, one of them the headwaiter, both French, killed instantly. And then two more staff members died in hospital. They also were French, and both known to me. No member of the public injured in the shooting died later in the hospital. That's four people dead altogether, all French. The whole thing was drug related."

"I see," said Ramshawe. "And what about the men who came into the restaurant and carried out the shooting. Were they arrested?"

"Unfortunately not, sir. They all got away. Three of them. And our inquiries have led us to a drug gang in Algiers, where we are continuing the search. The perpetrators of the crime are known to us. And have been for several years. But these people are very elusive."

"Are you absolutely certain that no one else except members of staff were killed?" asked Ramshawe.

"Absolument," replied the Chief Inspector. "You see, only the staff were standing up. Everyone else was sitting down. The bullets hit the waiters."

"Do you think the Algerians got their man?" said Ramshawe.

"I think so. One of the waiters was very suspect to us. But I am not at liberty to name him, for obvious reasons. However, we think the assassins achieved their objective."

"Very well, Chief Inspector," said Ramshawe. "Thank you for being so helpful. I will make my report on the basis of the information you have given me."

He replaced the phone, saying under his breath, "That is one lying French bastard."

"I'm sorry, sir?" said Jo.

"Oh nothing, really. It's just that when you get told that a renowned international intelligence agency has just had two of its agents murdered on a certain day, at a certain time, in a certain place, there is an extremely high likelihood of that being true. When a French policeman then tells you it never happened, there is an extremely high probability of that being a fair dinkum whopper."

Jo laughed. "Well, the first man we spoke to was obviously in a defensive mode. But the Chief Inspector seemed relatively forthcoming."

"No doubt," replied Ramshawe. "But he was still telling a flagrant lie."

And then he said, "Jo, I've got a plan. You go and rustle up a couple of cups of coffee, and we'll see if we can get one of Langley's finest around to that restaurant."

Four minutes later he was outlining the story to the European desk of the CIA, who had a good man in Marseille. In fact they had two, both in residence. Sure, they'd get right on it, especially if the Big Man was interested. They'd do some snooping, see if anyone knew anything, maybe someone who was working on the refurbishing of L'Union.

Friday, November 20, 4:00 P.M. (LOCAL)
Rue de la Loge
Marseille

Tom Kelly, a Philadelphia-born newspaper reporter, was twenty-nine years old and preparing to marry a Bryn Mawr history teacher when he fell in love, helplessly, with one of her French students. She was Marie Le Clerc, aged twenty-one, from Marseille.

Kelly bagged his job, bagged the history teacher, and followed Marie home to France. There he married her, found himself a job as news editor on a local paper, and moved to head up the political desk of *Le Figaro* in Paris. From there he drifted into a close relationship with two CIA agents, mostly because he was a fountain of knowledge about politics in the capital city.

At which point the CIA requested he come to Washington, where he was cleared for security and then stationed back in Marseille with a very useful freelance contract from the *Washington Post*. Kelly was thirty-six now, and he and Marie had two children and lived close to her parents, in the western suburbs of the city.

Right now he was making his way along Rue de la Loge toward L'Union. He could see it about fifty yards ahead. There was a white truck outside, and two ladders were jutting out through the wide open front door of the restaurant. Men at work, he thought.

When he reached the entrance, he turned left, up the steps and into the main foyer. There was a strong smell of paint and a deafening screeching sound from the main dining room, where two men were "sanding" the oak floor. Up above him were two painters, on scaffolding, working on a beam, which he did not know had recently been decorated with a long line of bullets from an AK-47.

No one took a blind bit of notice as he strolled across the room inspecting the refurbishments. He did not look so far removed from being one of the workers. He wore dark blue trousers, a matching wool sweater, and a light brown leather jacket.

Eventually someone noticed him and came over, inquiring if he could help. Rene was his name, an electrician by trade.

Kelly's French was excellent, and he came straight to the point, identified himself, and told Rene that he was trying to find out how many people had been killed that August night, since his government believed one of them may have been an American citizen.

There seemed to be no one around in any authority, and Rene was glad of the break and happy to help. "I don't really know myself." He shrugged. "But Anton, up the ladder with the paintbrush, he may know. His brother was a friend of the waiter who died in hospital . . . let me call him down."

Anton descended from the ceiling by way of the scaffolding, and shook hands with Kelly. "There were six people died in here that night, including the two guys who came in with the Kalashnikovs. One was shot and one had his throat cut."

"Anton, how do you know that?"

"Because we all went to the funeral of Mario, and another guy who worked here saw the whole thing and he told us at the reception. He said the two guys who came in with the guns were both killed—he thought by the men they had come to assassinate. He said they weren't just crazies. They were professionals who had come to kill someone specific."

"And Mario was still alive when he they carried him out?" asked Kelly.

"Yes. Unconscious but still alive. But the guy at the funeral said there were six bodies carried out. He remembered because only four of them went in an ambulance. He said the other two were taken away in a police van."

Friday, November 20, 1300 (local)
National Security Agency

Tom Kelly's report came in from the CIA's European desk immediately after lunch. It confirmed what had been obvious to Lt. Commander Ramshawe from the start. There were not four people killed at L'Union. There were six. The French police had gone in and cleared out the bodies of the two Mossad agents and were saying nothing about it to anyone.

And, if they knew, they were most certainly saying nothing about the man the agents had come to kill. Admiral Morgan's man had been sure those two assassins had come for Major Kerman.

And if, thought Ramshawe, *it was straightforward, why hadn't the French authorities simply admitted there had been an attempt on the life of the ex-British SAS Major, which had failed, and somehow Major Kerman had made his escape?*

Only one answer to that, was Ramshawe's opinion. The bloody French knew darned well the Major was in that restaurant, and probably at their invitation, since they had taken very large steps to hush the whole thing up.

So why did France arrange a secret meeting with the most wanted terrorist in the world? That was a question to which there would be no answer. The French were not admitting Kerman was in the country, not admitting someone had tried to kill him, and very definitely not admitting he had more than likely killed one of the assassins.

This was, the Lt. Commander knew, the end of the line. The French were saying nothing. The two Mossad men were dead. And no one knew where Kerman was. Or the men he was having dinner with at L'Union restaurant. To pursue the matter further would be a monumental waste of time, especially since the Mossad would not wish to publicize the death of its agents.

Nonetheless, Ramshawe logged all of the information onto his private computer files and downloaded a copy of the CIA report to show Admiral Morgan at dinner that night.

Same day, 7:30 P.M.
Chevy Chase, Maryland

Lt. Commander Ramshawe and Jane Peacock were in luck tonight. Admiral Morgan was a friend of both their fathers, and he elected to push the boat out one more time with a couple more bottles of Comtesse Nicholais's Corton-Bressandes. Ramshawe's eyes lit up at the sight of the bottles warming gently by the log fire in the study.

He helped the Admiral barbecue the steaks, mostly by holding an umbrella over him in the chill late-November rain, then moving in to receive the steaks with the wide platter Kathy had kept in the warming oven.

The four of them knew one another well. Jane, who looked like a surf goddess right off Bondi Beach, loved to go shopping with Kathy in Georgetown because the Admiral's wife kept her on the straight and narrow fashion-wise, helping her choose items she knew would please Ambassador Peacock, dispenser of the allowance, financer of the ruinous college fees she annually required.

Don't be ridiculous, Jane, your father would have a fit if he saw you in that.

Kathy hated having live-in help and preferred to manage her own kitchen, and after dinner she and Jane tackled the clearing-up while the Admiral and Jimmy retired to the study.

They sat in front of the fire, and Arnold Morgan came swiftly to the point. "Okay, Jimmy, tell me what you found about the murders at L'Union restaurant."

"All calls to the restaurant are routed directly to the Marseille central gendarmerie. When you call, a policeman answers the phone. And when he does you are told nothing. No one knows anything. There's a Chief Inspector Rochelle who seems helpful, but is lying. He says there were four deaths that night. All French, all staff. Two died in the restaurant, the other two in hospital. There were not four deaths. There were six."

"How'd you find out?" asked Morgan.

"Well, I spoke to the Marseille cop myself. Then I had Langley put one of their guys on it in the city. And he did a damned thorough job. Got into the restaurant and interviewed one of the workmen painting the place. And the workman had met a member of the staff at the funeral of a waiter. This was a guy who was ducked behind the bar during the shooting. He told the CIA agent there were six dead men altogether. He saw four of them carried out to ambulances, and two others loaded into a police wagon. Anton, that's the workman, saw the whole scene. He says two guys came in with Kalashnikovs, started shooting, and were then both killed by the guys they had come for. I brought you a copy of the CIA report."

"Well, that fits in exactly with the story I was told originally," said Morgan. "And I'm afraid it's the end of the trail. The French are never going to say anything. And neither the Mossad, nor even the Israeli government, could possibly ask them."

"No, I suppose not," said Ramshawe in his rich Aussie brogue. " 'Oh, by the way Monsieurs, we just sent a couple of hit men into a crowded restaurant in the middle of Marseille, and after they'd shot half the staff and half the customers, they ended up dead themselves. Anyone know what happened to 'em?' "

Admiral Morgan chuckled. Young Ramshawe's keen, swift brain often gave way to a rough-edged Aussie humor. And it always amused him. But right now he was pondering a far, far bigger question.

"The thing is, Jimmy," he said, "we have to believe the Israelis when they say they located Kerman in France, and certainly the savage response to the Mossad hit men bears all the marks of that particular terrorist. But the main thing for us is to find out what he was doing in France. Who was he seeing and why?

"A guy like Kerman, or General Rashood—whatever the hell he calls himself—must understand the lethal nature of any kind of travel. He could be spotted by anyone. He's obviously better off skulking around the goddamned casbah or somewhere in the desert. But he made this journey. Apparently in an otherwise empty Air France passenger jet. A damned great Airbus all on his own. Someone at a very high level in France wanted to see him quite badly. And they are never going to admit it. Any inquiry from us would be like talking to the Eiffel Tower. We'll get nothing. And quite honestly, Jimmy, I think it's just a waste of time to pursue this further. Let's just file it, and watch out for the slightest sign of further developments."

"Guess we can't do much else, sir. But Christ, wouldn't you just love to know where that bastard is right now?"

"I dearly would, Jimmy. But I'd guess he's not in France anymore. Not after that uproar in Marseille."

At that precise moment, 11 P.M. on the night of November 20, Admiral Morgan was entirely correct. Less than three months later he would be wrong.

Tuesday, February 2, 2010, 2300
10,000 feet above the shore
Southern France

Gen. Ravi Rashood was in company with eight of his most trusted Hamas henchmen, three of them known al-Qaeda combat troops, plus three former Saudi Army officers. They were just crossing the Mediterranean coastline in a AS-532 Cougar Mk I French Army helicopter, a high performance heavily-gunned aircraft that had just made the 380-mile ocean crossing from Algeria.

The big Cougar had taken off from a remote corner of the small regional airport of Tebessa, which sits at the eastern end of the Atlas Mountains, where the high peaks begin to smooth their way down to the plains of Tunisia.

General Rashood and his team had made a deeply covert journey that day, from Damascus, in a private air charter flight, unmarked by any livery, straight along the north African coast to Tripoli. And there the Cougar Mk I had met them and flown the 250 miles to their first refueling point, at Tebessa.

Right now they were coming into Aubagne, the Foreign Legion base where the General had been six months before, on the day of the shootout at L'Union. Tonight, however, no one would disembark. The helicopter was immediately refueled for the flight north to Paris.

Under cover of darkness they would land at around 0300 at the French military's Special Ops base in Taverny, north of Paris. This would be their home for the next two weeks.

At this point, all of the Arabian freedom fighters accompanying the General were in Western civilian clothes, mostly blue jeans, T-shirts, and sweaters. But it was an intensely military journey. All of the men had maps and they were all studying the same thing, the huge King Khalid Air Base, beyond the Saudi Arabian military city of Khamis Mushayt.

The helicopter made a wide circular sweep around the west of Paris, crossing the Seine, and heading in to land across the foggy fields above the Oise Valley. They grabbed their bags the moment the helicopter touched down, and were shown immediately to a barracks not one hundred yards from where the Cougar had landed.

It was 0245, and Gen. Michel Jobert, the Commander in Chief of the entire base, was there in person. He smiled as he shook hands with General Rashood, to whom, in a sense, he may already have owed his life. They had not seen each other for six months.

They boarded an Army staff car and drove to the French commandant's residence, where the Hamas C-in-C would live during this period of intense training. In the morning they would meet for the first time the forty-eight highly trained combat troops of the First Marine Parachute Infantry Regiment, with whom they would fight in the forthcoming battle for the airfield at Khamis Mushayt.

Rashood and Michel Jobert sat before a log fire sipping a warming *café complet*, the thick dark French coffee with a dash of cognac. Each of them was amazed at the way the French government and indeed the police had kept the lid on the murders at the L'Union. And each of them understood only too clearly the dangers of General Rashood's traveling beyond the Arab world.

Rashood's journey from Damascus in August had been careful. But not careful enough. This time the journey was indeed untraceable. "It would be nice if we could avoid running into a couple of assassins trying to blow our heads off," said Michel Jobert. "Especially since Jacques Gamoudi is not due here until next week."

Rashood grinned. "He was very efficient that night, hah?" he said. "I think that character might have hit us, but for the table Jacques threw forward."

"Think? He *would* have hit us," said the General. "I never even saw them. And, *Mon Dieu*! Was Jacques ever handy with that damn great knife he carries."

"Saved us," said Rashood. "I'm glad he's on our side."

General Jobert, despite being the Special Forces mastermind behind the plan to topple the Saudi monarchy, could never accompany his men on the mission. Should he be captured or even killed, France's complicity in the operation would be blown forever.

As for the French troops who would take part, well, the First Marine Parachute Infantry Regiment would send them in without identification. They would conduct the operation within hours of arriving on Saudi soil and then leave immediately. Unlike Ravi Rashood, who would have to do rather more to earn his millions-of-dollars reward.

The following morning General Rashood and his eleven-man team from the desert gathered for a briefing before they met their forty-eight French comrades who would join them on the mission. They had breakfast together in a mess hall, and then reported to an underground ops room in which were arranged a number of chairs. At the front of the room were two tables, behind which were two large computer screens.

One showed the south shores of the Red Sea, with the old French colony of Djibouti to the west, and to the east, the mysterious desert kingdom of Yemen, the earliest known civilization in southern Arabia, a place that was active along the trade routes a thousand years before Christ. The other showed a much smaller-scale map of the Yemen border with Saudi Arabia, stretching along the eastern coastline of the Red Sea.

When the team was assembled, Generals Rashood and Jobert came in, accompanied by three French Special Forces commanders, all Majors in their early thirties: Etienne Marot, Paul Spanier, and Henri Gilbert. Today everyone, including the new arrivals from Arabia, was in work uniform: boots, combat trousers, khaki shirts, and wool sweaters, with black berets.

The eight Hamas/al-Qaeda men were seated in one row, three back, and while each of them had a smattering of French, directly behind them were two Arabic-speaking ex–Foreign Legion troops, who would act as interpreters.

The heavy wooden doors were closed behind them and two guards were on duty outside in the well-lit passage. Two more stood guard at the head of the short flight of stairs that led up to the corridor beyond the officers' mess.

General Jobert began the briefing, informing those assembled that this was not nearly so dangerous an operation as it may appear. Certainly they would need to be at their absolute best in combat, but by the time they launched their assault, Saudi Arabia would be in chaos—the lifeblood of the oil wells would have ceased to flow, the King would be under enormous pressure to abdicate, and the entire Saudi military would be in a state of mass confusion, unsure who they were working for.

Nonetheless, this was a room full of tension, as many young men prepared themselves to fight hundreds of miles from home, in a small group, in territory they had not seen before.

"I am sure," said General Jobert reassuringly, "the Saudis will be wondering who they are expected to fight for—the old regime, or the incoming one. And according to our principal source, the man who will become the new King of Saudi Arabia, the Army in Khamis Mushayt will be happy to surrender. No Arab soldier much enjoys being on the wrong side. That's a Middle Eastern characteristic."

He told them that in the broadest possible terms they were expected to attack and destroy the Arabian fighter-bombers parked at the King Khalid Air Base, five miles to the east of Khamis Mushayt. "A separate force is then expected to occupy the headquarters of the Army base and demand the surrender," he said. "This will almost certainly mean taking out the guard room, and possibly the senior commanding officers. General Rashood will personally lead this section of the operation."

The General then handed over to the most senior of the ex-Saudi officers—Col. Sa'ad Kabeer, a devout Muslim, descendant of ancient tribal chiefs from the north, and an implacable enemy of the Saudi royal family. Colonel Kabeer had commanded a tank battalion in Saudi Arabia's Eighth Armored Brigade in Khamis Mushayt. He would lead the opening diversionary assault on the air base.

Colonel Kabeer rose to his feet and nodded a greeting to the men before him. And then he told them, encouragingly, "The Saudi army has always suffered from a great shortage of man power. Thus there is always weakness. In addition, the head of the armed forces is a Prince of the royal family, as are numerous C-in-Cs and battalion commanders.

"We should remember that at the time of our opening assaults, every one of them will be terrified that their enormous stipends from the King are about to end. It would not greatly surprise me if several of them fled the country before we fired our opening shots. I am in complete agreement with Prince Nasir, the Crown Prince, that the Saudi Army will cave in the moment we attack. So we should conduct our operation with maximum confidence, knowing that right is on our side, and so is the incoming ruling government.

"I should like to begin by outlining the precise location and state of readiness of our target . . ." The Colonel stepped back and pointed to a spot on the second computer screen. "This is Khamis Mushayt. It is located in the mountainous southwest of the country, in the Azir region. This, by the way, was an independent kingdom until 1922, when Abdul Aziz captured it. The entire area still has very close ties to Yemen, from where we launch our assault.

"There is huge hostility to the Saudi King down here, because they believe he has abandoned his Bedouin roots and sold out to the West. In the totally unlikely event of failure, there will be no hostility to us locally, I am certain of that.

"Khamis Mushayt, right here, is a thriving market town with with a modern souk. There's a population of around thirty-five thousand and the town is situated twenty-two hundred meters above sea level. Except for March and August, when it rains like hell, it has a moderate climate, and there is a lot of agriculture and vegetation, should we need to hide.

"The Saudi Army's Field Artillery and Infantry Schools are both located at Khamis Mushayt. And it's also the headquarters of the Army's Southern Command. There are three brigades deployed here in the south to protect the region from any invasion from Yemen. The Saudis have, rightly, never trusted them. There's the Fourth Armored Brigade at Jirzan, on the west coast, the Tenth Mechanized Brigade at Najran, in the mountains, and the Eleventh at Sharujah to the east . . . right here on the edge of the Rub al-Khali—that, as you know, is the empty quarter.

"Now, you should all take a note of the GPS numbers for the King Khalid Air Base, in case anyone gets lost. It's precisely 18.18N 29.00°, and 042.48E 20.01°. The base controls all military air traffic in the area. There is, by the way, no commercial traffic. That all goes to Abha, twenty-five miles west.

"At King Khalid we're looking at two flying wings. One with McDonnell Douglas F-15s, the other with squadrons of British Tornado fighter bombers. In addition, there are elements of the Fourth (Southern) Air Defense Group to provide protection from air attack on the airfield. We probably should knock that out very quickly."

General Rashood, who would assume overall command of the three attacks, then stood up to discuss deployment. "As you can see," he began, "we have a sixty-strong squadron. Six of these will command a small headquarters, central to our communications with each other, and with Colonel Jacques Gamoudi in Riyadh, if necessary. There will be no direct communications with France under any circumstances whatsoever.

"The remainder of you will be split into three teams, each of eighteen men. Each team will arrive on station separately because it's far less risky.

"The first diversionary attack will be on the air base's main entrance and will be carried out by a group of al-Qaeda fighters, who will rendezvous with us when we arrive. They will provide our explosives, detonators, det-cord, and timing devices—all acquired locally. And when they launch their own attack at the gates, they will use small-arms grenades and handheld antitank rocket launchers.

"Meanwhile, Teams One and Two will cut their way through the wire and into the airbase on the far side. They will proceed to eliminate all the aircraft they can see, both on the ground and in the hangars. We already have excellent local charts and maps of the airfield, which will be distributed later. At the rear of the room you will see a large model that looks like a layout for model trains. It is in fact a very good scale model of the base.

"At the conclusion of the raid, which I anticipate will be conducted against only very light opposition, both airfield teams will move up to a secure point halfway between the base and Khamis Mushayt.

"Shortly before that, Team Three, led by me, will attack the main military compound. We will blast our way into the barracks and take the headquarters at all costs. We will inform anyone still standing that the King Khalid Air Base has fallen and that half the fighter planes in the Saudi Air Force have been destroyed—hopefully there will still be a fierce red glow in the sky, especially if we locate the fuel dump.

"And then we will demand surrender, before we blow the place to pieces. We'll force them to drive us immediately to the commanding General and his Deputy—that's two arrest parties of six each—and we'll hold them at gunpoint until the C-in-C broadcasts to the entire complex ordering a complete surrender. If they resist, we'll execute them. Which will terrify everyone else. But don't worry, they'll surrender. They're only toy soldiers.

"One thing of course to remember on a mission as highly classified as this: We leave no colleague on the battlefield. Anyone hit, injured, or dead will be brought out and returned with the squadron in France. That's one thing we can learn from the U.S. Navy SEALs. In all of their history, they have *never* left a man behind."

Already those with whom General Rashood would fight were beginning to smile and talk among themselves. For the first time, they were thinking they could pull this thing off. And perhaps the most important issue was the new concept of strong local support: The explosives coming from people in the town who hated the King. The readiness of the al-Qaeda fighters—Saudis, who would be joining them. And above all the feeling that they were representing the next King. This was not some terrorist attack on the innocent.

This was proper soldiering, with proper objectives, conducted under professional military commanders.

"Any idea how we'll get in there without anyone knowing?" asked a trooper.

"No, 'course not," replied Rashood sarcastically. "I thought we'd just hang around and see if there was a bus going our way. You have any spare Saudi *riyals*? We might need them for the fare."

The whole room fell about laughing. Despite the brutal reputation of the trained killer who stood before them, Ravi Rashood always knew how to speak to his team.

"Just checking," replied the trooper. "I'm used to coming in by parachute. And I didn't think you'd think much of that."

"Correct, soldier," said Rashood. "If it eases your mind, the answer to your question is, by sea."

"Not swimming, sir? The Red Sea's full of sharks."

"Not swimming," replied General Rashood smiling. "Something more dangerous than that. But with a much better chance of survival. We won't be dealing with that part of the plan until next week."

General Jobert formally thanked the Hamas Commander and then outlined the ground that would be covered over the next two days. "The first session this afternoon will be devoted to commands," he said. "Teams One and Two, both on the airfield and during preparation, will use only French since the majority of these specialist troops are from the First Marine Parachute Infantry Regiment.

"Team Three, commanded by General Rashood, will be made up mainly of Arabic-speaking personnel, with some French support from this base. All of them, however, speak English, which is the native tongue of the General himself. Therefore, we have decided that, throughout the mission, those under General Rashood's command will converse only in English.

"However, any communication back to your six-men headquarters must be in French, and for that reason Maj. Etienne Marot will serve as General Rashood's number two, with special responsibilities for communications. Do not, however, allow that to blind you to the real reason he is here. Major Marot commands the Army's Special Operation Light Aviation Detachment; that's a helicopter assault team. His business is to arrive in places when he is not expected."

There were a few chuckles around the room at that. And Major Marot himself, a tall, lean career officer from Normandy, permitted a wry smile beneath his wide black moustache.

"I wish then to deal with our fallback positions," continued General Jobert. "These are outlined on the maps you will be given shortly. By this I mean that should Team Three run into a five- thousand-strong Saudi Army guarding the barracks throughout the night, plainly we would not carry out our attack. But as you are aware, we do not build operations such as this without considering every possibility of entry, action, and escape.

"Before I hand over to your divisional commanders, I would just like to confirm that we expect the total surrender of Khamis Mushayt to lead to a general surrender of the entire Saudi military machine. But, remember, the actual assault on the royal palaces in Riyadh does not even begin until your mission is complete.

"This a just and proper war, born of the most terrible extravagances by just one family, to the utter detriment of the people. Everything depends on your work in Khamis Mushayt. That will be the military start of the chain of events that will bring a new enlightened reign to Saudi Arabia . . . a new King, who is already a great friend to France and indeed to all Islamic fundamentalists throughout the Middle East. You surely go with the blessings of your God."

General Jobert once again took his seat, and General Rashood introduced the next speaker, a distant relative of the royal family, who now commanded a battalion of al-Qaeda fighters based in Riyadh, Capt. Faisal Rahman.

Like everyone else, Captain Rahman was dressed in semi-combat gear. He rose to his feet and wished everyone "*As salaam alaykum*," the traditional Bedouin greeting, which he accompanied by another familiar gesture among desert Muslims, the right hand touching the forehead and the arm coming downward in a long, graceful arch.

"I should like to tell you of a vacation in Spain made in recent years by a King of Saudi Arabia," he said. "He arrived in a private Boeing 747 accompanied by an entourage of three hundred and fifty, and three more aircraft, one of which was kitted out as a hospital. His vast retinue swelled to over three thousand in a few days. There were more than fifty black Mercedes cars and an intensive-care unit and operating theater built into his woodland palace near Marbella. This building is a replica of the White House in Washington, where else?

"It cost fifteen hundred dollars a day in flowers! What with the King's water being flown in weekly from Mecca, his lamb, rice, and dates coming in from other places in Arabia, the King's bills were knocking hard at almost five million dollars a day. By the time the enormous court of Saudi Arabia left Spain, they had banged a hole in ninety million.

"The Spanish call any Saudi ruler by one simple name: King Midas. And there are those among us who think this entirely unnecessary—this lunatic expenditure, reckless extravagance, founded on wealth essentially bestowed upon us by Allah himself.

"It's not as if the King earned it or even won it. He was given it, at birth. In our view, he is the custodian and guardian of the nation's wealth. It's not his to fling around any way he wants. And it certainly ought not to be at the disposal of his thirty-five thousand relatives, who somehow believe they have the right to do anything they damn well please with it either.

"I don't know if you are aware of this, but every last member of the Saudi royal family travels free on the national airline, Saudia. Well, there's over thirty thousand of them now, and since it is customary for princes to have a minimum of forty sons, sometimes fifty, there may be sixty thousand of them before long. That's two hundred of them flying free every working day of the year. And since most of them fly at least twenty times a year, that's four thousand of 'em a day! Jumping in and out of aircraft free of charge. I have one question: is that in any way reasonable?"

The al-Qaeda commander paused. And before him he saw many heads shake, mostly in astonishment. There were also many nods of approval at his words. The numbers he quoted were indeed quite shocking. But there was a more shocking one to come.

"Twenty years ago," said Captain Rahman, "my country held cash reserves of a hundred twenty billion dollars. Today those reserves are down to less than twenty billion. Because of our close involvement with the United States, the government is paying 'protection money' to al-Qaeda. Hundreds of millions of dollars. Saudi Arabia was paying the Taliban to 'protect' Osama bin Laden.

"The battle we are about to fight in the hills of southwestern Saudi Arabia, and in the streets of Riyadh, is not revolution, nor even *jihad*. We are fighting to purify a country that has gone drastically wrong."

A young French soldier, deadly serious, called out, "And there really is a feeling in the country that will help us to achieve our victory?"

"Stronger than you will ever know," replied the Captain. "In the mosque schools all over the country they are turning out young men who have been taught to follow the old ways, the customs of the Bedouins, the ones who represent our roots. We are a natural people of the desert, but our enemies in neighboring countries are closing in around us. Almost the whole of Islam believes we have let down the Palestinians, failed to help them in the most terrible injustices committed against them by the Zionists.

"Other Arab leaders feel we have allowed Islam to be humiliated. And, in a sense, that is precisely what the government of Saudi Arabia has allowed to happen. We were all born to be a God-fearing nation, following the words of the Koran, the teachings of the Prophet, helping the poorer parts of our nation, not spending ninety million dollars on a vacation like King Midas."

At this point, General Rashood himself looked up. "Every Arab knows that the situation in Saudi Arabia cannot continue. There is too much education for that. I believe I read somewhere that two out of every three Ph.D.'s awarded in Saudi Arabia are for Islamic studies. The Saudi Arabian royal family's greatest threat is from within. The clerics are teaching truth. It's just a matter of time before the whole thing explodes."

"Just a matter of time," said Captain Rahman. "And I believe we will hasten that time. And the good Prince Nasir will come to power and make the changes we must have. I know this seems a very ruthless, reckless way of attaining our ends, but it is the only way. And the new Saudi ruler will owe a debt of gratitude to France that may never be repaid." The Captain hesitated before adding, with a smile, "But I understand he will most certainly try."

General Jobert stood up and announced, "I will now call out the members of each team. Your commanding officers have given this considerable thought. But the three teams of eighteen men have very different tasks, and the command headquarters situated in the hills close to the action also has a critical role to play.

"Please now, everyone pay attention while I make a roll call: *Team One, air base assault . . . commanding officer Major Paul Spanier . . .*

Sunday, February 7, 0830
Port Militaire
Brest

Two hundred and fifty miles to the west of Paris is the sprawling headquarters of the French Navy, around the estuary of Brest, where the Penfeld River runs into the bay. This is the western outpost of Brittany, home to France's main Atlantic base, where they keep the mighty 12,000-ton Triomphant-class ballistic-missile submarines. Not to mention the main Atlantic strike force and, from 2005, the French attack submarines, the hunter-killers.

Adm. Marc Romanet, Flag Officer Submarines, and Adm. Georges Pires, Commander of the French Navy's

Special Ops Division, were standing in a light drizzle wearing heavy Navy topcoats, right out at the end of the south jetty, beyond which France's submarines swung to port for entry into their home base.

They could see her now, way down in the bottleneck, over two miles to the west, on the surface, making six knots up the channel in twenty fathoms. Through the glasses Admiral Romanet could see three figures standing on the bridge. One of them he knew was the young commanding officer, Capt. Alain Roudy.

His submarine was called *Perle*, hull S606, right now the most important ship in the entire French fleet. This was the SSN that would attack the oil fields of Saudi Arabia, the lethal slug of war that would release four boatloads of frogmen to blast the great Gulf loading bays to smithereens. And then fire its missiles from the depths of the Persian Gulf, knocking out the huge oil complex of Abqaiq and slamming Pump Station Number One, halting the flow of the kingdom's lifeblood,

This was she. The 2,500-ton *Perle*, fresh from her refit in Toulon, now with a much smaller but no less powerful nuclear reactor, and her new, almost silent primary circulation system, which probably made the *Perle*'s propulsion unit the quietest in all of the undersea world.

She'd been down in France's Mediterranean Command Base for her major refit for almost six months. And she was a lot more important today than she was last May when she went in. At that time it had been assumed that the Saudi mission would be carried out by one of the brand-new boats scheduled to come out of Project Barracuda. But that program had been subject to mild but critical delay, and Prince Nasir could not wait.

He had been to see the President three times. And three times the President had insisted that the Navy move fast, in two oceans, and cripple the Saudi oil industry before the new year of 2010 was more than three months old.

The three men who had principally to deal with that request were the two Admirals who now stood at the end of the south jetty, plus their guest, who was currently sheltering from the rain in the Navy staff car parked beneath the

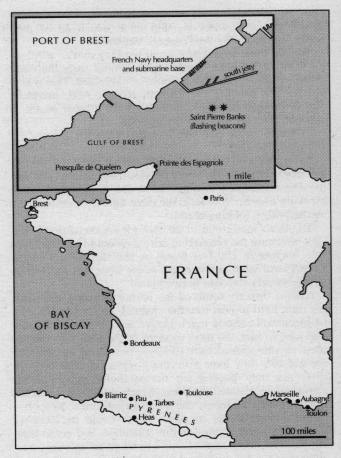

bright quick-flashing harbor warning light at the tip of the jetty, Gaston Savary, France's Secret Service Chief.

Admiral Pires had invited Savary to visit because he knew the pressure under which the President had placed him. He considered the least he could do was to show Savary the underwater warship upon which all of their hopes, and probably their careers, depended.

Tonight there would be a small working dinner at Admiral Romanet's home, where Savary would meet the commanding officer, and much would be explained. This was to be the first briefing for Captain Roudy. And, privately, Savary thought he would probably have a heart attack. It was not, after all, an everyday mission.

"Gaston, come out here!" called Georges Pires. *"I'll show you our ship!"*

Savary stepped out into the rain and accepted the binoculars handed to him. He stared out down the channel and saw the *Perle* sweeping through the water, a light bow wave breaking over her foredeck, the three figures in uniform, up on the bridge, looking ahead.

The three men stood in the rain for another fifteen minutes, watching the submarine drift wide out to her starboard side, staying in 100-feet water, as she skirted around the Saint-Pierre Bank, a rise in the ocean floor that shelved up to only twenty-five feet in two places.

Almost directly south of the harbor entrance she made her turn, hard to port into the channel, and headed in. Her jet black hull seemed much bigger now, and more sinister. She was, in fact, the most modern of the Rubis Améthyste class, commissioned back in 1993. But Naval warships do not get old, they have everything replaced. And now the *Perle* not only packed the normal hefty punch of her Aerospatiale Exocet missiles, which could be launched from her torpedo tubes, she also carried a new weapon—medium-range cruise missiles. These could be launched from underwater, using satellite guidance, and could literally thunder into a target several hundred miles away, traveling at Mach 0.9, just short of the speed of sound.

She looked a symbol of menace. And according to the rare communications she made with her base, while crossing the Bay of Biscay for home, she had performed perfectly. And above all, quietly.

The Toulon-based engineers at the Escadrille des Sous-

Marins Nucléaires d'Attaque (ESNA) had done their precision work superbly.

"That looks like a dangerous piece of equipment," said Gaston Savary, as the sub came sliding past the jetty without a sound.

"That is a very dangerous piece of equipment," replied Admiral Pires as he turned seaward to return the formal salute of Capt. Alain Roudy, high on the bridge.

Sunday, February 7, 2100
Official Residence
Flag Officer Submarines
Atlantic HQ, Brest

THERE WERE FIVE men, each of them sworn to secrecy, each of them in uniform, standing around the wrong end of Adm. Marc Romanet's long dining room table. The other end contained five place settings and two bottles of white Burgundy from the Meursault region.

But this was officially pre-dinner. And down there at the business end was spread a whole series of naval charts and photographs being studied carefully by the two Admirals, Romanet and Pires, plus Capt. Alain Roudy and Cdr. Louis Dreyfus, commanding officer of the *Améthyste*, the *Perle*'s sister ship.

These were the two submarines selected by the French Navy to cripple the economy of Saudi Arabia, and half the free world. Or, stated another way, to free up the wealth beneath the Saudi Arabian desert for the overall benefit of the Saudi nation. Or, alternatively, to return the Saudi government to the ways of Allah and to the purity of the Prophet's words. It all depended upon your point of view.

The fifth member of the group, Gaston Savary, was standing behind the Naval officers, sipping a glass of Burgundy and listening extremely carefully. He would be in front of the French Foreign Minister, Pierre St. Martin, in

Paris the following afternoon, for a debriefing. The decision of the four men with whom he was dining tonight would determine, finally, whether this mission was Go or Abort.

The issue being discussed was the Red Sea, the 1,500-mile stretch of ocean that was Saudi Arabia's western border. The Suez Canal formed the northern entrance, and the French submarines would, by necessity, make this transit on the surface.

They would travel separately, probably two weeks apart. Only the *Améthyste* would remain in this deep but almost landlocked ocean to carry out its tasks. The *Perle* would continue on and exit the Red Sea at the southern end, before proceeding up the Arabian Gulf and into the Strait of Hormuz, en route to its ops area, north of Bahrain.

The point was, could Captain Roudy make the southern exit underwater out of the range of prying satellites and American radar? Or would he need to come to periscope depth in order to move swiftly through the myriad islands that littered the ancient desert seaway before making his run out through the narrows and into the Gulf of Aden?

With the sandy wastes of Yemen to port, the *Perle* would pass to starboard the long coastline of Sudan, then the equally long shores of Eritrea, then Djibouti, before making the deepwater freedom of the Gulf of Aden. But the final 300 miles, past the Farasan Bank and Islands, follows a route where the water shelves up steeply on the Yemeni side, from 3,000 feet sometimes to 20 feet, which is precisely its depth off Kamaran Island.

The exit from the Red Sea is a long trench, narrowing all the way, with the island of Jabal Zubayr stuck right in the middle. Then there's Jabal Zuqar Island, and Abu Ali Island, both with bright flashing warning lights, which are totally useless to a submarine trying to crawl along the sandy depths of the 600-foot-deep channel. The rise of Hanish al Kubra is a navigator's nightmare, almost dead center in the channel, which is now only 300 feet deep and only about a mile wide.

However, there are two navigational channels there. One, with routes north and south, runs to the east of Jabal Zuqar, close to Yemen. It is shaped in the dogleg of the island's west coast. The other marked channel runs twenty-five miles to the southeast and skirts the western side of Hanish al Kubra. Essentially, it comprises two narrow seaways, north–south and fourteen miles apart, running alongside a series of rocks, sandbanks, and shoals. These are the trickiest parts because of the narrow channels, which skirt a couple of damned great sandbanks, one of them only sixty-five feet from the surface. However, this stretch, which does need the greatest navigational care, is the final black spot for the submariner.

Thereafter, both south routes converge into a forty-five-mile-long marked seaway, which suddenly shelves up again, to less than 150 feet, but has the advantage of being dead straight all the way to the southern strait, gently falling away again, to a depth of 600 feet.

In places it narrows to a few hundred yards, with a very shallow shoal to port, but it runs on into the Strait of Bab el Mandeb and then into the Gulf, into depths of 1,000 feet plus, right off Djibouti—and the U.S. base west of the Tadjoura Trough.

"Think you can handle that, Captain Roudy?" asked Admiral Romanet.

"Yessir. If those chart depths are accurate, we'll get through without being seen. Under seven knots in the shallow areas, but we'll be all right."

"The charts are accurate," said Admiral Romanet. "We sent a merchant ship through there a month ago using sounders all the way. We checked depth against chart depth from Suez to Bab el Mandeb. The charts are correct."

"Thank you, sir," said Captain Roudy. "Then the GPS will see us through the southern end. I'll run with the mast up."

"Very well," replied Marc Romanet, who was well aware of the tiny GPS system, positioned at the top of the periscope of the refitted Rubis. It was not much bigger than a regular handheld unit, and it would stick out of the water a matter of mere inches. The *Perle*'s CO had plenty of depth for that. And that minuscule system, splashing through the warm, usually calm waters of the Red Sea,

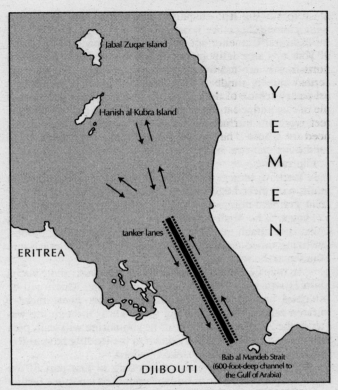

THE DEEP-WATER CHANNEL—SOUTHERN EXIT FROM THE RED SEA

would always put Alain Roudy within thirty feet of where he wanted to be.

"Before we dine I would like to go over the plan for the *Améthyste,* which will be following you through the Suez Canal almost three weeks later," said the Admiral. "Commander Dreyfus, you will, of course, run straight down the Gulf of Suez along the Sinai Peninsula and into the Red Sea at the Strait of Gubal. Have you done it before?"

"Nossir. But my executive officer has. And so has my navigation officer. We'll be fine."

Admiral Romanet nodded and looked back to his chart. "Your ops area is about halfway down the Red Sea, in waters mostly around five hundred meters deep. We have decided this is not a perfect area for an SDV (swimmer delivery vehicle), and anyway our Rubis submarines are not ideally equipped to carry one. Instead our SF will make the transit from the submarine in two Zodiac inflatables, six men to a boat. The outboard engines run very quietly, and the guys can row in the last few hundred yards for maximum silence.

"We have targets at Yanbu and Rabigh, enormous terminals, with these huge loading docks, in the picture here . . ." The Admiral pointed with the tip of his gold ballpoint pen. "They will be separate operations, ninety miles apart. The plan is to attach magnetic bombs to the supporting pylons, utilizing timed detonators, and then have the lot crash into the sea at the same time.

"At nineteen hundred, as soon as it's dark, the Special Forces will leave the submerged submarine, which will be stopped around five miles offshore. That gives them a fifteen-minute run-in, making thirty knots through the water in the Zodiacs. Two boats. The submarine will wait, pick them up, then travel quietly down to the loading bays at Rabigh, arriving at around o-two-hundred.

"There is no passive sonar listening in that part of the Red Sea, nothing before Jiddah, a hundred ten miles farther on, where the Saudi Navy has its western Navy HQ. That's a big dockyard, with vast family accommodation: mosques, schools, et cetera. But its only real muscle is three or four missile frigates, all French-built, bought directly from us. We're experts on what they can and cannot do. And anyway we're not going that far south.

"The chances of the Saudis' picking up a very quiet nuclear submarine running several miles offshore is zero. And even if they do, there's not much they can do about it. They have virtually no ASW capability. And even if they did send out a patrol boat, even a frigate, for whatever reason, we'd either hide easily or sink it."

Commander Dreyfus nodded. "Same procedures as Yanbu for the Special Forces? Send in two Zodiacs and wait?"

"Correct. Then you will move out to sea . . . you'll be around halfway between Yanbu and Jiddah . . . make your ops station somewhere here . . ." The Admiral pointed again to the chart. "Correlate your timing," he said, "with the bombs on the loading dock pylons. I want them all to go off *bang* at precisely the same time.

"So you will open fire simultaneously with the cruises, seven and a half minutes before H hour on the pylons. You will fire three pre-programmed batteries, four missiles in each. The first four straight at the Jiddah refinery, then four at the main refinery in Rabigh. And one into the refinery at Yanbu, right on the coast . . . here . . . directly north of your hold-area position."

"Fire and forget, sir?"

"*Absolument.* The moment the birds are away, steam southwest, out into the deepest water, then proceed south toward the Gulf of Aden. Stay submerged all the way. Then move into the Indian Ocean. Proceed south in open water, still submerged, to our base at La Reunion, three hundred miles off the west coast of Madagascar, and remain there until further notice."

"Sir."

"I think, gentlemen, we should dine now. And perhaps outline our plans for the Persian Gulf with Captain Roudy as we go along? *D'accord?*"

"*D'ac,*" said Georges Pires, jauntily using the French slang for "in agreement." "This kind of talk is apt to dry the mouth. I think a few swallows of that excellent Meursault up there would alleviate that perfectly."

"Spoken like a true French officer and gentleman," said Gaston Savary.

Admiral Romanet seated himself at the head of the table, with Georges Pires to his left and Savary to his right. The two submarine commanding officers held the other two flanks. Almost immediately a white-coated orderly arrived and served the classic French coquilles Saint-Jacques, scallops cooked with sliced mushrooms in white wine and lemon and served on a scallop half-shell with piped potato.

The orderly filled their glasses generously. For all four of the visitors it was much like dining at a top Paris restaurant. The main course, however, provided a sharp reminder that this was a French Naval warship base, where real men did not usually eat coquilles Saint-Jacques.

Admiral Romanet's man served pork sausages from Alsace, the former German region of France. There was none of the traditional Alsace sauerkraut, but the sausages came with onions and *pommes frites*. It was the kind of dinner that could set a man up, just prior to his blowing out the guts of one of the largest oil docks in the world.

The golden brown sausages were perfectly grilled, and they were followed by an excellent cheese board, containing a superb Pont l'Evêque and a whole Camembert . . . *les fromages,* one of the glories of France. And only then did the waiter bring each man a glass of red wine, a 2002 Beaune Premier Cru from the Maison Champney Estate, the oldest merchant in Burgundy.

Admiral Pires considered that, one way or another, the Submarine Flag Officer at the Atlantic Fleet Headquarters in Brest was a gastronomic cut above the hard men who lived and trained at his own headquarters, in Taverny. But Admiral Romanet, a tall, swarthy ex-missile director in a nuclear boat, was still concerned with the business of the evening. He had replaced the wine glass in his right hand by a folded chart of the Persian Gulf waters to the east of Saudi Arabia. And he now considered that he knew Captain Roudy sufficiently well to address him by his first name.

"Alain," he said, "I think we have established that your exit from the Red Sea can be conducted submerged. And, as you know, it's a two-thousand-mile run from there up to your ops areas in the Persian Gulf.

"As you know, it's also possible to enter the Gulf, via the Strait of Hormuz, underwater. The Americans run submarines in there all the time. However, it's not very deep, and some of the time you'll have a safety separation of only thirty-five meters in depth, which does not give you a lot of room, should you need to evade.

"However, I don't think anyone will notice you because they won't be looking. The Iranians on the north shore are so accustomed to ships of many nationalities coming through Hormuz, they are immune to visitors.

"Your real difficulties lie ahead . . . up here, north of Qatar. And that's your new ops area. You'll need to run north, straight past the Rennie Shoals . . . right here . . . marked on the chart. You'll leave them to starboard, but I don't think you should venture any closer inshore. You want to stay north, right around this damned great offshore oil field . . . what's it called? The Aba Sa'afah. There'll be some surveillance there, and it's marked as a restricted area, so you'll stay as deep as you can.

"Now, the main tanker route is right here . . . this long dogleg, about a mile to starboard. It's half a mile wide coming out, and about the same running in. It's deadly shallow, between twenty-five and thirty-five meters, which you don't need. And all around it, the deep water is starting to run out. This is a dredged tanker channel and it's the only way inshore if you want to stay submerged, at least at periscope depth.

"It would be nice to put yourself right here . . . in thirty-five meters of water, north of that sandbank. But it's too far off the Saudi shore—it would give the Special Forces team a near fourteen-kilometer run-in to this long jetty; that's this black line on the chart . . . the main loading dock, one mile offshore from the huge Ras al Ju'aymah oil complex. That's the biggest liquid petroleum terminal in the world. There's Japanese tankers as big as Versailles pulling in there night and day.

"And so, gentlemen, the *Perle* must make her run-in down the tanker route—that's about nine kilometers—and we'll have up-to-date data on how busy that route is at night. But the Saudi tanker docks are *always* busy, so we must assume a run south to our holding point will entail running between the VLCCs.

"You'll cut into the channel here . . . two thousand meters north of this flashing red light, marked number two. Then you'll cross the tanker route, watching carefully to starboard, heading straight toward this light on the Gharibah Bank . . . see it, Alain, right here?"

"Okay, sir. Six quick flashes and then the light, correct?"

"C'est ça. And then you run south down the ingoing channel for about five kilometers to your first drop-off point. Exactly here . . ."

"Do we leave the main channel to reach that point, sir?" asked Captain Roudy. "I mean when the Team One Special Forces departs the submarine?"

"I don't think so. It's too shallow beyond the marked sea-lanes. The lack of depth will drive you to the surface. And we cannot have that."

"You mean we let them out right in the main tanker channel?"

"No choice. But they have very speedy boats, and you'll wait for a break in the traffic, and then move fast. It's a two-boat mission. We're talking minutes here. Not half-hours."

"So Team One will be right in the middle of the main tanker route when they set off?" asked Alain Roudy, a shade doubtfully.

"Yes, they will. But it's well buoyed. Plenty of lights and warnings. Anyway those SF guys know what they're doing. But we will want two boats on that target. I think Georges thought four men in each?"

"I did think that, Admiral," replied Georges Pires. "Al-though we could probably achieve our mission with seven men in one boat. But that leaves no margin for error. We def-initely take two boats, just in case we have a problem, equip-ment failure or something. I'm talking rescue. We can't afford to leave anyone behind, no matter what happens."

"We cannot. You're absolutely correct there, Georges," replied Admiral Romanet.

"Anyway, as soon as Team One is gone, the submarine turns south and runs on down the ingoing right lane. You'll have to put a mast up from time to time for a visual. But, re-member, in these waters, you have no enemy. You are *le prédateur*, and there's no one to stop you. The issue here is that no one must know you exist, *n'est-ce pas?*"

"Nossir. So we don't wait around for the Special Forces at the first holding point? The one you've marked right here? I mean for them to return?"

"No, you leave them immediately. Proceed south for another five kilometers, to the very end of the tanker route. Then you cut through this narrow seaway between these shoals into an area that is, again, more than thirty meters deep, two miles northeast of the main tanker anchorage.

"Look . . . right here, Alain . . . at this point Team Two will be less than a mile from the enormous Sea Island Terminal, perhaps the most important part of this mission. As you know, we are going to blow it up. It's a massive loading structure, stands a little over one kilometer offshore from the biggest oil exporting complex in the world, Ras Tannurah. Sea Island is known as Platform Number Four, and it pumps over two million barrels a day into the waiting tankers.

"Now, at this second hold point, the Zodiacs have a very short run-in to the target. No more than eight hundred meters. We have been studying a progression of satellite pictures to see how light it is on that terminal. My own opinion is that the frogmen will have to swim the last three hundred meters. Just depends on the degree of darkness.

"But they will accomplish this very swiftly. There will be six swimmers carrying six bombs through the water. Each man fixes one bomb to one of the six principal pylons. It's a magnetic fix. Then he sets the timer and leaves, being very careful to keep the light blue wires as well hidden and as deep as possible.

"All this must be precisely coordinated with Louis's operation in the Red Sea. Because when they blow, they must blow absolutely together. It is essential that these huge explosions cripple the oil industry all at one time.

"So, the moment the timers are fixed, the frogmen head immediately back to where the Zodiacs are waiting. It should take them only two minutes to reach the submarine, climb aboard, and start back up the channel to the previous holding point, one hour north, and pick up Team One, which will be there by this time, after their much longer Zodiac journey."

"If that liquid petroleum terminal goes up," said Savary thoughtfully, "Prince Nasir will have lit a blowtorch from hell. It will probably light up the entire Middle East."

"The Sea Island Terminal would also have a fairly spectacular edge to it," said Captain Roudy. "Imagine a million barrels on fire out in the ocean? Ablaze. That would be quite a sight."

"But I am afraid you will not see it, Alain," said Admiral Romanet, smiling. "When Team Two is back inboard, you will have the *Perle* steaming away, straight back up the tanker route, directly to the missile launch point, right here . . . thirty-four kilometers east of the terminals.

"That's going to take you five hours at a tanker speed of ten knots. You'll need to be on your way by twenty-three-hundred, in order to launch the cruises at o-four-hundred. The bombs on the pylons probably want a seven-hour time delay. But you'll work that out."

"And, of course, we leave the datum immediately after firing the missiles?" asked Captain Roudy.

"Of course. You target the pipeline, the inland pumping station, and the Abqaiq complex. They will explode simultaneously with the pylon bombs. At which time you will be thirty-four kilometers away, heading quietly east, well below the surface. The Saudi oil industry will blow to smithereens within four minutes of your departure from holding point three, the firing area."

"Sir," said Captain Roudy, returning in his mind to the place that worried him most, "do we get the Zodiacs back inboard when the SF guys return?"

"No time. Scuttle all of the boats. Same for Commander Dreyfus. Get the frogmen back in, and take off, back up the tanker route."

"And then head east, through Hormuz and south to La Reunion, submerged all the way?" asked Captain Roudy.

"You have it, Captain. Then you have a vacation, and in a

few weeks, bring the *Perle* home, around the Cape of Good Hope."

"Well, sir. That sounds like a very good plan. And of course we do have a terrific element of surprise on our side. No one would ever dream a Western nation would be crazy enough to slam Saudi Arabian oil out of the market for two years."

"Correct," said Gaston Savary. "It would seem like that English proverb . . . er . . . cutting your nose to spite your face . . . but not in this case. I understand France's need for oil products has been taken care of. We do not need Saudi oil for several months. And when it comes back on stream, it will effectively be ours to market, worldwide, at whatever price we fix."

"What about OPEC?" asked Commander Dreyfus.

"I don't think Prince Nasir, the new King, will want to compromise his position with France, not to placate his fellow Arabian producers," replied Admiral Pires. "This is the most extraordinary military action. It could only have been created by a potential new King. It is also devilishly clever—a plan direct from *le diable*."

"Except that at the heart of it all lies an honorable objective," said Admiral Romanet. "To restore the best elements of the Saudi royal family and to give the people a new, enlightened ruler: our friend, the Crown Prince.

"Gentlemen," he said, "I think we should raise a glass to the takeover by Prince Nasir, and, of course, to the . . . er . . . prosperity of France."

Tuesday, February 23, 1030
French Foreign Legion Outpost
Gulf of Aden, Djibouti

The former SAS Major Ray Kerman had made his headquarters eighteen miles north of Moulhoule, close to the Eritrean border, on the northern Gulf Coast of Djibouti. He had chosen the semi-active Foreign Legion outpost of Fort Mousea, because the training of his fifty-four-strong assault squad would attract less attention there.

There, in one of the world's hottest climates, even in the cool season the temperature rarely dipped below ninety degrees. They were only eleven degrees north of the equator, and in summer the heat was around 106 degrees day after day. The entire country had only three square miles of arable land, and it hardly ever rained. Ray Kerman imagined he must have been in worse places than this tiny desert republic, but, offhand, he could not recall one.

His squad had been in hard training now for many weeks. The men had willingly driven themselves, pounding the pathways through the Taverny woods, fighting the Legion's obstacle courses down in Aubagne, and then hammering their bodies through the heat of the rough desert tracks around Fort Mousea.

To his men, he was known by his formal name, Gen. Ravi Rashood, Commander in Chief of Hamas. Even the more senior French officers now referred to him as General, and every day he joined them in their relentless military training. Some of them had served in the Foreign Legion and understood how hard life could be. But nothing, repeat nothing, prepares anyone for the regime of fitness required by a former SAS Major.

They were getting there now. Many of the assault team members possessed power that bordered on animal strength. They could run like cheetahs, fight like tigers. Even the Iron Man from the Pyrenees, Col. Jacques Gamoudi, who had visited for two days that week, was deeply impressed by the level of their fitness.

Out there on this burning shore they practiced every form of assault-troop warfare, building temporary "strongholds" designed to be attacked only by their own colleagues. All through the dark hours, they would watch, wait, study the stars and the cycles of the moon, slowly growing into their chosen roles as predators of the night.

They learned to cut wire, silently, within earshot of their own sentries, sharp but unheard. They learned to move quietly across rough ground, on their elbows, armed to the teeth. They learned to attack from behind with the combat knife. They learned priceless skills in near-silent communication one to the other. And they learned expertise in explosives. Some were just brushing up prior knowledge and training. Others were rookies at the combustion game. But not for long.

Above all, they learned to listen in the dark: to the soft breezes of the desert, to the approach of a distant vehicle—with the wind, and then against it, because the sound was different. They could recognize the snap of a breaking twig at forty yards, they could discern the sound of a footstep on the sand. By the end of February, General Rashood's men were supremely attuned to the rhythms of the night.

By day, they were trained physically, starting every morning at 0500, before the sun was up—jogging, sprinting, push-ups, and finishing with a four-mile run into the desert and back. There was a two-hour break, before a sumptuous lunch, the food flown in from France in a special refrigerated French Air Force jet. No group of combat soldiers was ever better fed. The French Republic had a very large investment in these men.

An entire barrack room block was converted into a kitchen. Cooks and orderlies were flown in from Taverny. There was beef, lamb, sausage, fish, chicken, and duck. If a man wanted a large fillet steak every day, he could have it. But the salad, spinach, cabbage, beans, brussels sprouts, and parsnips were compulsory throughout the week. There was also fresh French bread and milk, fruit from all around the Mediterranean. Gallons of fresh fruit juice, tea, coffee, and fresh cream.

The camp ran entirely on two large generators driven by diesel engines. Every afternoon, after the late two-mile run, there was a briefing before dinner, where General Rashood and the commanding officers would go over the plan of attack. Over and over.

The assault on Khamis Mushayt would begin on the night of March 25. And on this evening, February 23, at 1700, General Rashood was presiding, speaking in his native English, which all the Arab warriors understood, and most of the French. He outlined the various points of departure, informing them for the first time that they would make the 250-mile journey from Fort Mousea in seventy-foot-long Arab dhows, the traditional craft of the Red Sea, the one least likely to attract attention. Each man would be disguised as a Bedouin, dressed in traditional Arab tribal clothes.

The dhows' appearance was unique. They were lateen-rigged, with yardarms diagonal to the mast. Their single sails had propelled them on a million stately journeys through these waters for thousands of years; their high, peaked sails distinguished them from all other craft. As did their total unsuitability in rough water.

General Rashood's dhows would make this journey from Djibouti and run north, crossing one of the narrowest points of the Red Sea from west to east, and then sailing up the long coast of Yemen.

"These things make a fairly steady seven knots," said General Rashood. "In a light westerly breeze, that is, straight off the desert—which is what we usually get in these parts. The journey to the north coast of Yemen will take us less than two days, and we will leave in relays from here, beginning at first light tomorrow morning.

"The first convoy will be three dhows carrying my Team Three and the command staff of our headquarters. That's twenty-four passengers, eight per dhow. I do not want everyone concentrated together, in case of the unexpected. Each man will take his personal weapons, AK-47, service revolver, and ammunition, combat knife, and hand grenades. We will take food for seventeen days, plus water, radios, cell phones, bedding, and first-aid requirements. At no time will any dhow be out of sight of the other two.

"Teams One and Two will leave two days later, each of them in two dhows. That's two leaving around o-six-hundred, and two more at fourteen-hundred. All the dhows will land on a very lonely stretch of coastline in northern Yemen, each team in a separate location. Again I am trying to avoid a concentration of personnel and equipment. I am unworried about being attacked. I am worried only about being noticed. Your landing sites have all been selected after long study of reconnaissance photographs taken specially by French Air Force surveillance aircraft."

Everyone nodded in both understanding and agreement. There were even a couple of "*D'acs*" from the French officers. "And now," said General Rashood, "comes the bad news. I have racked my brains for a comfortable, unobtrusive way into southern Saudi Arabia from the coast of Yemen. But there is none. There're hardly any roads except the one along the coast, and that carries whatever traffic there is between the two countries. Which means it's busy. Which rules it out for us.

"We can't go by air, because the only landing places are Saudi controlled. We daren't risk helicopters because they're too noisy and may easily be located by military surveillance around Khamis Mushayt. And that means we'll have to walk."

"How far is it, sir?" called one of the Saudi troopers.

"Less than a hundred fifty miles, but more than a hundred thirty. Probably only a hundred and ten as the crow flies." General Rashood shook his head. "Sorry," he said. "We must walk through the mountains, and it will take us ten to twelve days. Anything we need we carry, and that means heavy bergan rucksacks, and there are not many armies that could do it.

"The terrain is awful, with steep gradients, and the heat's a bloody nightmare. But we are not ordinary forces. We're Special Forces. And we're about to find out how we got the word *special* next to our names. No one else could do it, except us."

Again the assembly of brutally trained men nodded in agreement. "Twelve miles a day does it, right, sir?" one of General Rashood's Hamas freedom fighters called out.

"Correct, Said," replied the General. "Sometimes it will be easier marching along the high ground. Other times it will be much more difficult. Maybe down to one mile an hour on the steep escarpments. But overall we'll aim for fourteen miles a day, and some days we'll cover perhaps twenty, and others only four. But we'll make it. We have to make it."

He waited for the interpreters to make clarifications, and there was no dissension. The General continued. "Each team will take a different route from the Yemeni coast through the mountains to our RV, which is four miles south of the King Khalid Air Base. There'll be al-Qaeda guides out in the mountains to bring us in. There is already a carefully selected "hide," and everyone will have a minimum of twenty-four hours to rest up before the attack. Most of us should get a little longer than that, but there will be recces throughout each night—around the air base and along the road that leads up to Khamis Mushayt.

"By the time you reach the RV, you may have used your food and water. Which is fine. There will be fresh everything awaiting us. The Foreign Legion brought the food and mineral water in through Abha Airfield, to the west of King Khalid. Al-Qaeda transported it by camel up through the foothills to our rendezvous point.

"There will also be local maps for each man, which I'll distribute in a moment. You will see there's a road leading up to the base, which we obviously ignore totally. We will come cross-country, to the village of al-Rosnah, then cross a secondary mountain track and into wild country above another village, called Elshar Mushayt.

"From there we look down through the hills and see in the distance the military base to the left and the airfield to the right. It's a perfect spot for us. And the people of both these little places probably know we're coming and will be ready to assist.

"Once we're in those hills we're more or less safe. Just so long as we shoot straight and hard on the night of March twenty-fifth."

The chefs had organized a superb farewell dinner and roasted a half of everything they had left, mostly duck, chicken, and veal. There was one large joint of lamb, and they even made a cassoulet. They had run out of potatoes and rice, but there was about a half-ton of spinach and salad. The cheeses that remained were plentiful, and the dinner was topped off with a massive chocolate pudding.

The commanding officers had even allowed a bottle of wine between four men, and by 10 P.M., when the troops retired to bed for a four-hour sleep, there was just enough left to feed the diminishing force for forty-eight hours. There was French bread, eggs, fish, and orange juice for Team Three's breakfast at 0400, one hour prior to departure.

The hours between 0200 and 0400 were spent breaking camp, with the twenty-four men packing their equipment and storing it in the most efficient manner: the processed food, water, ammunition, and bedding.

One hour before the sun rose above the Red Sea, to the east, they were driven down to the seaport on the north side of Moulhoule, where the three dhows awaited them. They had to walk the equipment out to the boats along the long jetties, and General Rashood himself supervised the seating and storing of supplies.

Each of the seventy-foot dhows was arranged for its eight passengers to rest up during the two-day voyage. Awnings were spread on poles to protect them from the pitiless sun out on the water. The moon was already setting as they pushed out into the offshore waters of the Bab el Mandeb Strait, running slowly north, sails high, in twenty fathoms and a light breeze.

The dhows sailed around four hundred yards apart, and by 0630, with the sun now just visible above the eastern horizon, they made their starboard turn, toward the blazing sky, each hidden man with a Kalashnikov inches from his hand, each man with a hand grenade in his belt.

To a passing ship, the three dhows could have been nothing but peaceful traders plying the old routes, probably carrying cargo of salt from Djibouti up to Jizan. They certainly appeared nothing like an assault force that would be attempting the capture of Saudi Arabia and the overthrow of the King.

But this was the unobtrusive start of a famous land attack: three Arab dhows, their cargo under awnings, elderly captains at the helm, sons and family tending the huge sails as they slipped through the wavelets on a hot, serene morning. It was a timeless, biblical scene in the Red Sea, one that could have been a thousand years old—not a semblance of menace, even in these dangerous times in the Middle East.

But General Rashood's instructions were clear . . . *any intruder gets within a hundred feet, civilian or Naval, eliminate the crew and sink the ship. Instantly.*

Thursday, March 4
Port Said
Egypt

They logged the French nuclear hunter-killer submarine *Perle* through the northern terminal of the Suez Canal shortly before midday. Captain Roudy would make most of the 105-mile journey on the bridge. But first he dealt with the formalities in Port Said, coming ashore and speaking personally to the customs officers and inspectors from the Egyptian Naval base situated beyond the vast commercial network that controlled the canal.

Egyptian officials rarely board a Naval vessel making the transit, largely because of objections by the Russians, who have always used the canal to transfer ships from the Black Sea and Mediterranean to the Arabian Gulf.

Captain Roudy watched one of the Egyptian Navy's *Shershen*-class fast-attack Russian gunboats move slowly by, heading south, and shook his head at the age of the craft. "Probably forty years," he told his XO. "I wonder if they've updated the old missile system—they used to be aimed manually like bows and arrows!"

Egypt had no interest in the French submarine, signed the papers, issued the permits, and informed the entire world by satellite that France had just sent a hunter-killer from the Med into the Red. There was nothing sinister about that. They did it by international agreement, like many other guardians of sensitive waterways around the world.

They were under way by 1230, and the *Perle* set off south on the surface toward the halfway point of Ismailia, at the top of Lake Timsah. By nightfall they were on their way down to the Great Bitter Lake, and at 0200 they came through Port Taufiq and ran into the Gulf of Suez. The water was still only 150 feet deep throughout this 160-mile seaway, but it was littered with rocky rises and a couple of wrecks, not to mention several sandbanks.

The seaway was narrow, about twelve miles wide, but the land on the portside, along the Sinai Peninsula, shelved out very gradually into the Gulf, and the left-hand side was thus no place for a submarine.

Captain Roudy kept the *Perle* on the surface until they had moved through the Strait of Gubal and into deep Red Sea waters. The seabed sloped sharply down there, to a depth of two thousand feet. And at 1709 on Friday afternoon, March 5, Alain Roudy ordered the French submarine dived, all hatches tight, main ballast blown.

Bow down ten . . . make your depth two hundred meters . . . speed twelve.

Aye, sir . . .

Until now, the speed, direction, and position of the *Perle* had been public knowledge. But shortly after 5 P.M. on that Sunday afternoon, this was no longer so. No one knew her speed any longer, or her direction or position in the water. And certainly not the intentions of her Captain.

Those watching the satellites may have assumed that she was headed south into the Gulf of Aden. But the important thing was, no one knew for certain. And no one ever would know either, since the *Perle* would not be seen or detected again; not this month.

Indeed she would not be seen until the second week in April, when she was scheduled to arrive in La Réunion. And by then, the world would be a very different place. Especially if you happened to be a member of the Saudi royal family, or indeed the President of France.

Five days later, as Captain Roudy worked his way south down the Red Sea, underwater, the *Perle*'s sister ship, the *Améthyste,* was ready to clear the submarine jetties in the Naval harbor of Brest, in western France.

It was 0500, not yet light, but there was a small crowd

gathered under the arc lights to see them off. Just families, the shore crew, a few engineers who had conducted her final tests, and, somewhat surprisingly, the head of the French Submarine Service, Adm. Marc Romanet.

They'd begun pulling the rods the previous evening to bring the *Améthyste*'s nuclear reactor slowly up to temperature and pressure. Commander Dreyfus had already finalized the next-of-kin-list, which detailed the names, addresses, and phone numbers of every crew member's nearest relatives, should the submarine, for any reason, not return. The NOK list was standard procedure for all submarine COs the world over.

Madame Janine Dreyfus, aged thirty-one, mother of Jerzy, four, and Marie-Christine, six, was at the top of the list. All three of them stood now, with the other families, in the pouring rain, under a wide golf umbrella, awaiting the departure—Janine watching her husband, and the children their father, who was standing with the officer-of-the-deck and the XO, high on the fin, speaking into his microphone.

At 0515 the order was issued to "Attend bells." Eight minutes later, Commander Dreyfus snapped to the engineers, "Answer bells." The XO ordered, "Lines away," and the tugs began to pull the *Améthyste* away from the pier.

The strong, gusting southwest wind off the Atlantic swept the rain almost sideways across the hull, and Commander Dreyfus, his greatcoat collar up, cap pulled down, waited for the tugs to clear before calling, "Ten knots speed!"

The great black hull swung to starboard in a light churning wash, and she moved silently forward in the rain, across the harbor, toward the outer point of the south jetty, then out into the main submarine roads of the French Navy.

She swept wide of the Saint Pierre Bank and then steered two-four-zero, southwest down the narrow waters of the Goulet, her lights just visible in the squally weather. Some wives of crew members stayed to see them finally disappear. Janine Dreyfus and her children were the last to leave.

Commander Dreyfus finally left the bridge as they approached the light off Point St. Mathieu, at the southwestern tip of the Brest headland. Then he ordered the ship deep, on a long swing to starboard beneath the turbulent waters of the outer Bay of Biscay, and then south to the endless coastlines of Portugal and Spain and the Straits of Gibraltar.

Friday, March 12, 1500
Northwestern Yemen

This was the hottest day so far. Gen. Ravi Rashood and his men were still walking. They had been going for almost ten days now up through the mountains, ever since the landing on the deserted beaches north of the Yemeni town of Midi, four miles from the Saudi border at Oreste Point.

Only the supreme fitness of the men had kept them going. The concentrated food bars they carried with them had kept their essential bodily requirements intact, but the last two days had seen some weight loss, and the General was anxious for them to reach the RV.

No one had complained as they trudged up the high escarpments, heads down, hats pulled forward, day in and day out, guided only by the General's compass and GPS. But when elite troops like these ask for rest, you give it to them immediately. And General Rashood noticed that these requests were now coming more often than before.

The temperature was constantly in the low nineties, and the army bergens the men carried on their backs were growing lighter as they devoured their food, but not sufficiently to make the march much easier.

Their weapons were slung across their backs, and each man carried a heavy belt of ammunition across his chest. In four-man groups, they took turns carrying for thirty minutes at a time two heavy machine guns set on leather grips. It would be incomprehensible for a normal person to grasp the strength and training of these men; to watch them walk, mile after mile, sweat pouring off them, uphill, then downhill, not pausing, even to take in water, only when it seemed someone might pass out.

General Rashood knew they had another four miles to cover before dark. Almost thirty miles behind him he knew

Team Two was moving slightly quicker under the command of the teak-hard former Legionnaire, Maj. Henri Gilbert. His own tireless number two, Maj. Etienne Marot, made a satellite communication with Henri every two hours.

The final group, Team One, commanded by the Corsica-born Maj. Paul Spanier, was twelve miles in arrears of Major Gilbert, and moving faster than all of them, along a different route. That was the nature of a march like this: everyone began to get slower.

The sun was just beginning to sink somewhere into the Red Sea, several miles to their left, when Team One saw two camels appear on the horizon. They were walking in a slow swaying rhythm, unchanged in thousands of years. And they were not on the track that General Rashood's men occupied. They were coming from the northeast, across rough, high desert sand littered with boulders and virtually no vegetation, leaving a dusty slipstream behind them. Sometimes the riders disappeared with the undulation of the ground, but their dust cloud never did.

General Rashood checked them out through binoculars. Both Bedouins were armed, rifles tucked into leather holsters in front of their saddles. The General ordered everyone off the track, to the right, down behind a line of rocks . . . weapons drawn . . . action stations.

Slowly the Arab riders advanced on their position, and made no attempt to conceal themselves. They drew right alongside the rocks and dismounted. The leader spoke softly. "General Rashood. I am Ahmed, your guide."

"Password?" snapped the Hamas commander.

"Death Squad," replied the Arab.

General Rashood advanced from behind his rock, right hand held out in greeting.

"As salaam alaykum," responded the Bedouin. "We have brought you water. There are only two miles left of your long journey."

"I am grateful, Ahmed," said the General. "My men are very tired and very thirsty. Our supplies are low."

"But ours are plentiful, and they are very close by now. Let your men drink . . . and then follow us in."

"Did you see us from far away?"

"We saw the dust, and we saw movement along the track from more than two miles away. But we never heard you, not until now. You move very softly, like Bedouins."

"Some of us are Bedouins," replied the General. "And we are grateful to see you."

Ahmed's companion, a young Saudi al-Qaeda fighter, had pulled two plastic three-gallon water containers from his camel and set them up on a low rock for the men to drink. That was two pints each, and there was not much left after ten minutes.

They picked up their burdens again, the two Arabs remounted, and they set off—as always moving north—and the ground began to fall away in front of them as they approached the "hide" the al-Qaeda men had built.

At first it was difficult to discern. Not until they were within a hundred yards could they make out its shape—a crescent of rocks guarding the rear and a solid rock face 150 feet to the south, overlooking a dusty valley. Beyond that were low hills, and in the far distance there was flat land, too far away to see the aircraft hangars on the King Khalid Base.

Inside the "hide" were wooden shelters about eight feet high, with just a back wall. The other three sides were open, with poles holding up palm-leaf roofs covered in bracken. One square earth-colored tent, again with bracken on the roof, plainly contained stores. Big cardboard containers could be seen through its open double doors.

Off to the left were several small primus stoves for cooking. There was no question of a fire out here, since its smoke would be seen in the crystal-clear blue skies from both the air base and the army base, nearly five miles away.

This rough "hide," set in the foothills of the Yemeni mountains, would be home to the French-Arabian assault force for thirteen days. It would be a time of intensive surveillance of the bases, checking every inch of the ground, studying the movements of the Air Force guards night after night, observing the movements in and out of the main gates, noting the lights that remained on all night.

When Captain Alain Roudy's missiles slammed into Abqaiq's Pumping Station Number One in the small hours of Monday morning, March 22, General Rashood's hit men would be ready.

Monday, March 15, 0900 (local)
Central Saudi Arabia

The main road leading to the ancient ruins of Dir'aiyah, twenty miles northeast of Riyadh, was closed. At the junction with al-Roubah Road, just beyond the Diplomatic Quarter, a Saudi military tank stood guard. Two armed soldiers were talking to three officers from the *matawwa*, the Saudi religious police, that fearsome squad of moral vigilantes who enforced the strictest interpretation of the Koran. Almost to a man the *matawwa* supported the creed of Prince Nasir. Above an official-looking sign read ROAD TO DIR'AIYAH CLOSED OWING TO RESTORATION.

Motorists who stopped and claimed to be going on farther than the famous ruins were informed that they could pass, and were given a permit to be handed in to the guards stationed two miles from the ancient buildings. No one would be allowed to leave their vehicles. And it was the same coming south from Unayzah.

When the highway reached Dir'aiyah there was a roadblock in both directions. Uniformed soldiers prevented anyone going down the track that led west from the main highway. They collected passes and politely told motorists that the reopening of the ruins would be announced in the *Arab News*. Of course, most drivers who arrived at that point did not care much when the ruins reopened; the tourists had already been stopped miles away, on the edge of the city.

Anyone who gave any thought to this might have been quizzical about the ironclad security that now surrounded the very first capital city of the al-Saud tribe. Dir'aiyah, the kingdom's most popular archaeological site, was under martial law. Not since the Turkish conqueror Ibrahim Pasha ransacked, burned, and destroyed the place almost two hundred years ago had a Saudi army seemed so intent on defending it.

In effect, Dir'aiyah was just a ghost town because, in 1818, Ibrahim Pasha had demanded that every door, wall, and roof be flattened. His marauding army pounded the walls with artillery, even wiped out every palm tree in the town, before they marched back to Egypt.

The palm trees grew again, but the Saudis never wanted to rebuild what was once their greatest city, and instead elected to start again with a new capital to the south, Riyadh. And for more than a 180 years Dir'aiyah was just the remnants of the old buildings—a mosque, the dwellings, the military watchtowers, the shapes of the streets—an entire cityscape, all open to the skies.

It was a place where life had become extinct, just a sandblown Atlantis, with the sounds of shifting feet, as the tourists with their cameras shuffled around one of the glories of Arabian history.

Until Col. Jacques Gamoudi showed up, that is.

He had arrived on a scheduled Air France flight from Paris to King Khalid International Airport on December 2 and been in residence in Riyadh ever since. His appearance in the Saudi capital was completely unobserved. He took a cab from the airport and checked into the busy Asian Hotel off al-Bathaa Street.

Not for two days did he meet with three emissaries from Prince Nasir, and that was in the Farah, a local restaurant on al-Bathaa Street resplendent with large red-and-white Arab lettering above the door, enhanced by a large picture of a cheeseburger. From then on things looked sharply up. That afternoon he moved into a beautiful house behind high white walls and a grove of stately palm trees.

He was given a communications officer, two maids, a cook, a driver, and two staff officers from the al-Qaeda organization, both Saudis, both natives of Riyadh. One of them was the brother of Ahmed, General Rashood's guide seven hundred miles away in the foothills above Khamis Mushayt.

And for two weeks they studied the maps, looking for an ideal spot to store armored military vehicles, several of them carrying antitank guns and possibly six M1A2 Abrams, the most advanced tank ever built in the United States. Saudi Arabia's armored brigades owned more than three hundred of these battlefield bludgeons, half of them parked in lines at Khamis Mushayt.

They also needed a place to stockpile light and heavy machine guns, for later distribution, and for handheld rocket and grenade launchers. Not to mention several tons of ammunition and regular grenades. Much of this arsenal was currently in storage in the military cities under the watchful gaze of Saudi Army personnel sympathetic to the cause of Prince Nasir.

The questions were, when could the cache be moved, and where could it go?

Jacques Gamoudi called staff meetings, sometimes attended by six, even eight, specially invited al-Qaeda revolutionaries. He conferred with his small specialist team, and he spoke encrypted to General Rashood in the south. There was no communication whatsoever with France.

One night there was a sudden visit from Prince Nasir himself, and Jacques Gamoudi expressed bewilderment at the principal problem: how to move the hardware out of the military stores and place it all under tight control, ready for the daytime attack on the reigning royal family and their palaces.

The Prince himself had masterminded the acquisition of the weapons, and he had called on his loyalists to store and protect them. Curiously that had not been difficult. All of it was essentially stolen from the Royal Saudi Land Forces, which, awash with money for many, many years, were apt to be relatively casual with ordnance.

For two years there had been the most remarkable nationwide operation of pure deception going on in Saudi Arabia. One by one, battle tanks had gone missing from the big southern base at Mushayt, driven out straight through the main gates, on massive tank transporters, and north to Assad Military City, at Al Kharj, sixty miles southeast of Riyadh, where the national armaments industry was also located.

No one bothered to inquire when the tank had been loaded on the transporter by regular soldiers. The sentries never even questioned the drivers as the huge trucks roared out through the gates. And certainly the guards at Assad never even blinked when a Saudi Army transporter, driven by serving Saudi soldiers, hauling a regular M1A2 Abrams tank bearing the insignia of the Saudi Army, drove up and banged on the horn. They naturally let them in.

The tanks were parked in a neat group out on the north side of the parade grounds, and everyone assumed someone else had issued the order. But you can only do that when half the population hates the King and all he stands for. And even then, only if they think there is a real chance of a change of regime.

No one ever said anything. Hardly anyone even noticed. And it was the same with hundreds and hundreds of weapons boxed, crated, and moved from base to base, always placed in a spot that everyone assumed had been designated by a senior officer. When, actually, those spots had been designated by no one.

Prince Nasir's secret arsenal was there for all to see. But no one really saw it. There were literally thousands of rounds of ammunition packed into the storage centers at Assad. Another huge cache of weapons had been driven to the southern warehouses in King Khalid Military City itself. But there was no paperwork. It was all just there, like everything else. And no one would miss it when it went, in the two weeks leading up to March 25.

There were even armored cars hidden quietly in various wadis and oases, all of them looking official, all of them occasionally visited by uniformed personnel from the armored brigades. Sometimes they were moved, sometimes left for another two or three days. But no one ever tampered with the well-paid Army in Saudi Arabia, and there were many officers and corporals already dedicated to the safety of the arsenal of the Crown Prince.

But now it was time to move. And the Prince and his advisers had each assumed, like the Saudi guards and quartermasters, that someone else had that under control. In fact, no one had it under control, even though it was the first question Colonel Gamoudi asked . . . *where's our base camp? . . . From where do we launch our attack? . . . Where's our command headquarters? . . . Does it have communications? . . . If so let's test them right away. You can't have a decent revolution if you can't talk to each other.*

From the very beginning the Saudi rebels had been bemused by the forthright military opinions and questions gritted out by the ex–French Special Forces commander.

And the trouble was, he could not solve the problem. It was the Saudis who knew the territory, they who knew the available strongholds and houses. It was they who were supposed to be telling Jacques where to make his headquarters, not Jacques telling them.

And by late February it was growing tense. Hiding boxes of ammunition and even cases of light machine guns was one thing. Disguising a damn great Abrams combat tank in someone's front yard, on the outskirts of Riyadh, prior to charging straight down the Jiddah Road with guns blazing on the morning of March 25 . . . well, that was rather a different matter.

Colonel Gamoudi had marked up various possibilities—big houses with big gardens behind high walls. But he did not like any of them. It was always in his mind . . . *One careless word from a servant, one sighting by an unsuspecting passerby, one friend of the family loyal to the Crown . . . that was all it would take.*

He told the Prince of his concerns. He told him he needed a base where the public could not go. It had to be near a main highway, and it needed to be absolutely impenetrable by prowlers or sightseers. That meant it needed to be a place that *could* be cordoned off, for an obvious reason, a place that would cause no consternation among the public.

"Sir, do you have the power to select somewhere, and have

the authorities deem it off limits until further notice? Somewhere we can start moving into, somewhere we can move
the ordnance . . . somewhere from which we can attack?"

Prince Nasir pondered for two hours. He paced the room
and sipped his coffee. He pored over the map of the city and
its environs. And at 2:30 A.M. he stood up and smiled.
"Yes," he said. "I have it. I am, after all, head of the National Guard, and I have many serving officers loyal to me.
The *matawwa* are also fiercely loyal to me. No one would
think twice about it if we closed an historical site for
restoration. I would not even need to tell anyone."

Which was why, on Monday, March 15, there were eight
M1A2 Abrams tanks parked bang in the middle of the ancient ruins of Dir'aiyah, and why the eighteenth-century
mosque had a new roof, made of camouflage canvas to shelter the hundreds of tons of materiel hidden behind its great
sandstone walls. . . . And of course why the ramparts of the
old city were again manned by heavily armed guards, hud-
dled behind high rock outposts, with searchlights front and
center, all powered from the electric cable that once fed
only the kiosk selling guidebooks, ice-creams, and cold
drinks to tourists.

Ibrahim Pasha would have needed to think twice about
an attack in the year 2010. Because any intruder caught un-
lawfully within a quarter-mile of Dir'aiyah was essentially
history.

Col. Jacques Gamoudi had a grudging admiration for the
thoroughness of Pasha's attack, but he was grateful for the
high section of the city wall left unharmed. He had a total
of twenty-five armored vehicles parked beneath it, on the
inside. And every hour, military vehicles arrived with more
and more ordnance.

Le Chasseur, working in a specially built wooden office,
logged and recorded every single delivery. The walls were
pinned with maps. He knew the location of the principal
palaces he must take. He knew where the radio station was.
He was briefing his drivers and, above all, his tank commanders. There would be casualties, he was certain of that,
and he was amazed at the volunteers who came forward to

pilot the tanks he wanted driven directly into the principal palace.

It seemed that whatever he asked for was provided. The Moroccan-born Colonel knew in his own mind he was ready to take the capital of Saudi Arabia.

Wednesday, March 17, 0100
25.50N 56.55E, Speed 12, Depth 50

Capt. Alain Roudy's submarine was steaming into the Strait of Hormuz, the great hairpin-bend gateway to the oil empires of the Middle East. The *Perle* ran fifty feet below the surface, holding course three-one-five, slightly to the Iranian side of the seaway. Right now they were not trying to evade or avoid anyone's radar or watchdogs.

They were leaving a very slight wake on the surface, but one that would have been discernible only to an expert. This did not include tanker captains or their afterguards, and there were no patrol boats in radar sight, either from the Iranian or Omani Navy.

There was a massive LPG tanker making ten knots, way up in front, and twenty minutes ago they had passed a 350,000-ton Liberian-registered VLCC heading south about four miles off their port beam. Alain Roudy knew the seaway would probably grow busier as they headed into the mainstream north-south tanker routes inside the Gulf, but for the moment, the *Perle* ran smoothly underwater in thirty fathoms, oblivious to wind, waves, and tide.

They would begin their turn to the left two hundred miles hence, to the northeast, west of Ras Qabr al Hindi, the jutting headland of the Musandam Peninsula, the northernmost point of the Arab sultanate of Oman, and a closed military zone. Captain Roudy would probably encounter Navy patrols off there, and he would accordingly slow right down, wiping that faint but telltale wake clean off the surface.

From there the submarine would head west, steering

course two-six-one, slowly, only seven knots, directly toward the Saudi oil fields. It was a 520-mile run, 170 miles a day, which would put them comfortably in their ops area in the late afternoon of Sunday, March 21—just west of the Abu Sa'afah oil field, that is, and five miles east of the world's busiest tanker route, the one that led down to Saudi Arabia's Sea Island Terminal.

On board the *Perle* were sixteen men from Commander Hubert's D'Action Sous Marine Commando (CASM)—underwater action commando. This was the French Navy's combat diver capability, and they were very good, right up there with the U.S. Navy SEALs and Britain's SBS. Twelve of these frogmen, the swimmers who would hit the oil platforms, came directly from CASM, Section B, Maritime Counterterrorism, which was a bit rich under the prevailing circumstances. The other four, expert boat drivers and communications personnel, had been seconded to the mission from Commander Hubert's specialist Second Company. They were the four best men in the critical fields of placing the Zodiacs inch-perfect in the right place, and staying in communication with the swimmers and the mother ship.

The hit men had been very within themselves on the journey out—quiet, thoughtful, and rarely seeking conversation with the crew. But everyone understood. These sixteen men represented the frontline muscle of the mission. Should they fail, or be hit by gunfire and wounded, or even killed, the result would be an absolute catastrophe for the Republic of France.

Everyone appreciated what these swimmers were scheduled to accomplish and also the dangers they faced. Of course most of the crew knew the precise identity of the target.

But submariners were apt to be extremely bright, and there was no one aboard the *Perle* who did not understand that the men from CASM were most definitely going to hit something hard. That was the critical path of the mission, the sharp end. Black ops men, in all the Special Forces in all the major Navies, were allergic to failure.

Commander Jules Ventura, a thirty-two-year-old bear of a man—swarthy, taciturn, half-Algerian, from Provence—would lead the divers to the probably more dangerous off-shore LPG Terminal at Ras al-Ju'aymah. The submariners who served with Ventura and talked to him were already treating him like a god. Which was the one thing that actually made Big Jules smile.

Thursday, March 18, 1630
25.40N 35.54E, Course one-four-zero, Speed 7, Depth 400

The *Améthyste* crept slowly through the warm waters of the Red Sea, 340 miles south southeast now from Port Said. There were almost 600 fathoms below her keel, and her new nuclear reactor was running sweetly. She made no sound in the water, and the biggest excitement so far on this journey was when they passed, briefly at PD, within five miles of the flashing light on the jagged El Akhawein Rock jutting up from the seabed at latitude 26.19.

Thirty-five miles ahead of them was their next marker, another craggy rock, Abu el Kizan, suddenly scything up from the seabed on the desolate sand-swept Egyptian side. They would pass within twenty miles, too far to see its light, even if they came to PD, 120 miles from the ops area.

They were in good time for the night of March 21, when they would blast the massive Red Sea oil terminal at Yanbu al-Bahr clean out of existence, a few minutes after their commanding officer, Louis Dreyfus, had fired a volley of cruise missiles straight at the Yanbu, Rabigh, and Jiddah refineries.

Generally speaking, the *Améthyste* was a more cheerful ship than the *Perle*. But her mission was infinitely less dangerous, since she was operating in deep open waters, in a lonely sea—at least, in terms of warships—against a country that had a weak Navy and was inexpert in the use of submarines.

Améthyste was the biggest fish in the tank, so long as there were no U.S. Navy submarines passing through. Thus

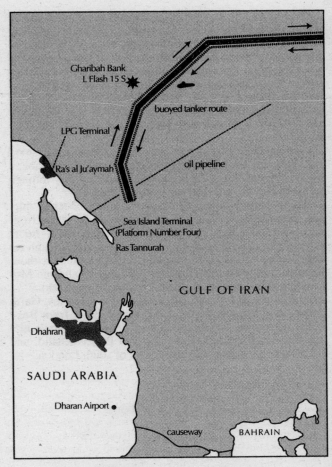

THE TANKER ROUTE LEADING TO
THE GREAT SAUDI ARABIAN OIL TERMINALS

she had no enemies as she crept through these international waters. And if Commander Dreyfus and his helmsmen held their nerve, they would never have any enemies, because no one would even see her for the next four or five weeks. And when they did—thousands of miles south in the hot western waters of the Indian Ocean—there would be no reason on earth to suspect that she had anything whatsoever to do with the night of stupendous combustion that destroyed Saudi Arabia's oil industry. That was surely, just "an Arab thing."

Commander Dreyfus and his senior officers understood this extremely well. That knife-edge element of real danger, always present in the *Perle* as she picked her way through the Gulf of Iran, was missing from the *Améthyste*.

Which was why the *Améthyste* was a very cheerful ship. And why the dark, lean, and droll commander of the frogmen, Garth Dupont, aged thirty-one, spent many hours playing bridge with his colleagues and the crew, though for stakes about twenty-six thousand times lower than those wagered by the late, great playboy Prince Khalid bin Mohammed al-Saud in the lush environs of Monte Carlo.

In fact the entire sum of the cash wagered by Garth Dupont and his pals on the 3,000-mile voyage from Brest added up to one—one thousandth of the money blown in a half hour in Monte Carlo by the late Prince Khalid, and HRH Princess Adele (deceased), late of south London.

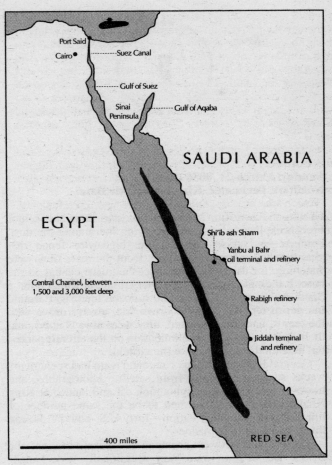

Port Said
Cairo
Suez Canal
Gulf of Suez
Sinai
Peninsula
Gulf of Aqaba

SAUDI ARABIA

EGYPT

Shi'ib ash Sharm
Yanbu al Bahr
oil terminal and refinery

Central Channel, between
1,500 and 3,000 feet deep

Rabigh refinery

Jiddah terminal
and refinery

400 miles

RED SEA

THE NORTHERN END OF THE RED SEA

5

Sunday, March 21, 0030 (local)
Northern Perimeter, King Khalid Air Base

GENERAL RASHOOD, MAJOR Marot, and their two senior French explosives experts were lying flat among the dust, bracken, and rocks, beyond the high-wire fence that guarded the air base from attack from the rear. They were watching, for the umpteenth time, the guard change in the base. It took place at this time every night, at which point a Saudi Air Force jeep drove half a dozen men right around the perimeter. They always drove fast, always drove with the jeep's main beams raised, they were always noisy, and their lights cast a useful illumination on the aircraft parked out here on the north side of the airfield.

General Rashood and his command team had spent many weeks studying the field from satellite photographs, and however many training flights took off and landed at King Khalid, there always seemed to be the same number of fighter-bombers on this station—forty U.S.-built F-15s, and thirty-two British Tornadoes.

The U.S. aircraft were arranged in five rows of eight, the British jets in four rows. Very occasionally wide hangar doors, two hundred yards away, were opened, and it was possible to see three more fighter aircraft in there. It may have been a service rotation, or just running repairs to active aircraft. General Rashood could never quite tell whether the aircraft were the same ones or not, because he saw them only every three days, and his view was head on to the identification numbers.

The attack was to begin four days from now, on Thursday, March 25th. And tonight's final recce was critical, to make certain none of the airfield routines were broken. The guard changed at the regular time, the aircrew in the brightly lit hangars and workshops stopped work at 1800, and the base was more or less asleep soon after midnight.

On Thursday night, the twelve top demolition men in Maj. Paul Spanier's Team One, operating in pairs, were going in there. Their task was to work their way down the lines of F-15s. Simultaneously, Maj. Henri Gilbert's Team Two demolition experts would be in among the Tornadoes, prior to the opening frontal attack on the two hangars, one of which they had never seen opened.

General Rashood had his own idea of sequence, which was for bombs to be set on the engines of the standing aircraft, with timers set for detonation at 0100 Friday. That was seventy-two explosions, which, given the jet fuel onboard, ought to create a blast similar to Hiroshima.

He was allowing a generous fifteen minutes per aircraft, which meant that each team had one hour and thirty minutes to set the explosives on six of them. In addition, Rashood allowed four minutes more on each aircraft for the teams to remove wrenches, screwdrivers, pliers, and bits of cut and spliced det-cord. That was almost two hours per team to take care of the fighter-bombers. Thus the frontal hit on the hangar doors would take place at 0100.

Tonight's first tasks were principally about time, checking that from the guard change at 0030 it would take exactly fourteen minutes for the jeep to speed out past the only spot among the parked aircraft where intruders could be seen.

Busy demolition men tend to get preoccupied, but on Thursday night each man would have a tiny beeping alarm on his watch that would sound at 0042, the signal for everyone to hit the deck, lying flat in the dark until the Saudi Air Force's final patrol was past and on its way back to the barracks.

Ten minutes earlier, the first moment that jeep had driven

by the hangars, General Rashood's two det-cord men would be at the great sliding doors and winding the high explosive around the locks. When the aircraft blew, the doors would blow too, and the spare men from Teams One and Two would be in there with bombs set for five minutes.

As the staff of the airfield charged out to witness the total demolition of the seventy-two aircraft on the field, they would see the hangar go up in a fireball. And then the fuel dump, which was situated on the eastern edge of the airfield and would probably provide the biggest explosion of all.

In the meantime, the al-Qaeda fighters who were scheduled to open up a diversionary fight at the gates at 0050, thus occupying many of the guards, would now be assisted by the spare men who had blown the hangars.

Their orders were to move fast through the airport buildings and return to the main gates with hand grenades to blast both guard rooms, thus trapping the Saudi defenders front and rear. At 0055, the al-Qaeda men were to fight their way inside the base, carrying two heavy machine guns, and to open fire on the accommodation block and communications rooms without drawing breath.

That, reasoned General Rashood, would effectively be the end of Saudi resistance: almost every aircraft on the base blown to pieces, the hangars destroyed, most of the guards dead or burned, buildings on fire. What was there left to defend? If it wasn't the end of Saudi resistance, something had gone drastically wrong.

Right now he was certain they had thought of everything. The charts of the airfield back in Taverny had been completely accurate, the scale model they had studied had been perfect. The surveillance photographs had been remarkably helpful, and the detailed plans of both the F-15s and the Tornado fighter jets, provided by Saudi sympathizers inside the base, were a priceless guide to the demolition men.

Nonetheless, General Rashood was still lying in the dirt outside the wire on the northern perimeter of the airfield. He felt that he knew the place better than his own home back in Damascus.

Through his binoculars he watched the jeep with the new

guard detail drive from the guardhouse to the gates. It
picked up the men coming off duty and drove them back to
the accommodation block. Six more guards then boarded
the jeep, and it swung around and headed out onto the airfield. It always drove down the main runway and then
picked up the narrow perimeter road and made a circuit of
the whole air station.

· Tonight the General was making a final decision as to
where to station two of his men lying flat, machine guns
ready, just in case it was necessary to eliminate the six
guards in the jeep. For a few days he had considered that the
best spot might be in the bracken, right inside the fence. But
upon reflection, watching the angle of the jeep's lights night
after night, he decided that there was perhaps a one in ten
chance the beams might pick up movement in the grass.
And then they'd have an uproar on their hands before the
aircraft demolition team had completed its work. The
Saudis might even have time to communicate and turn on
the airport floodlight system, maybe even send for help
from the military base, which would have helicopter gunships down there in about ten minutes.

The prostrate General shuddered at the thought. It could
all go wrong, right here on his patch. And he could not tolerate that. No, the two Hamas bodyguards protecting the
men in among the aircraft would take up position behind
the wheels of the aircraft nearest the perimeter path. That
way there was no possibility of their being seen, not in the
dark, and they would be only fifty feet from the jeep as it
passed.

Plainly, it would be slightly hairy for the two bodyguards
operating five feet below a ticking time bomb in the aircraft's engine. But these were professionals, and they would
be safe on the guard stations until 0055, when it was time to
run like hell, out under the wire with the twenty-four demo
guys and into a big Saudi army truck, which had been hidden in the desert for three weeks, and would be on station to
get them out and back to the "hide."

Rashood intended to put his main wire cutter on duty at
the fence at all times. Everyone would go in through a small

gap in the fence—three feet by four, two at a time—at 2300, and then the fence would be put back lightly to avoid any detection by the occupants of passing jeeps.

The moment the last jeep had sped past, almost certainly traveling too quickly for proper observation, the wire man would complete cutting a huge gap, ten feet wide by twelve feet, so the getaway truck could practically back in.

Now, as General Rashood lay there deep in thought, the lights of the jeep lit up the northern perimeter road. Rashood watched the range of its beam every inch of the way, and as it roared past, all of his instincts were confirmed. The bodyguards would take up station on Thursday night behind the landing wheels of the F-15s.

Between now and then, the surveillance team would switch their attention to the military base, five miles away. In General Rashood's mind, the airfield plan was complete. Now he had four days to refine his plan for the assault on the Khamis Mushayt army headquarters and the subsequent, vital surrender of that sprawling Saudi military base.

**Same Day, 1830
Dir'aiyah**

Jacques Gamoudi was more and more impressed by the Crown Prince of Saudi Arabia. In the past few days, Prince Nasir had arranged for a succession of heavy-duty construction hardware to arrive at the outer walls of the ancient ruins. There were a couple of bulldozers, two cement mixers, various trucks with commercial names printed in Arabic, three vans, a pile of scaffolding, and, since yesterday morning, a crane that looked like it could lift the Hanging Gardens of Babylon.

There could be no doubt there was serious restoration work afoot out here on the edge of the desert. No doubt whatsoever why the main road out of Riyadh should be closed to any vehicles not driving straight through the area.

Shortly after dark, the white-robed Prince himself arrived for a conference with his forward commander from the French Pyrenees.

"Ah, Jacques!" he greeted the French colonel. "Come and talk to me out beyond the ruins. Walk with me to the temporary home of a true Bedouin." He placed his arm around the shoulders of Jacques Gamoudi and together they walked out between the shattered buildings of the ancient city, continuing for perhaps a half-mile, where a three-sided tent had been erected, in front of which a gigantic Persian rug was spread upon the sand.

There were probably fifteen close friends in attendance, mostly political and religious advisers, and relatives of the prince. Colonel Gamoudi was at home among them. Above his regular combat gear, he now wore the customary red-and-white *ghutra* complete with the *aghal*, the double head cord traditionally worn on top of the Arabian headdress. He looked what he now was: a freedom fighter in the cause of Islamic fundamentalism.

Prince Nasir loved the desert. Those who knew him well talked often of his hatred of the gaudy palaces of the royal family. It was said that when he first saw his own new official residence, on the outskirts of Riyadh, he took one look at his sumptuously decorated bedroom and walked out of the door, marching along the upstairs corridor until he came to a small, almost bare, spare room. "I'm happier in here," said the great-great-grandson of Ibn Saud.

And even now, many years later, the fifty-six-year-old Prince still preferred the old ways to the new. And still, almost every night, his servants drove him out to the desert, where they pitched the great three-sided tent and sat out under the stars and told their stories and discussed the politics of the day and the coming revolution.

Behind the tent, Jacques could see the cooks at work over modern barbecue grills; he could see the line of Range Rovers parked nearby; he could smell the roasting lamb; and he could see the great bowls of dates and the tall glasses of iced camel's milk.

He sometimes had to give himself a reality check. And

this was one of them, as he stood next to a royal family of Bedouins, robed, speaking quietly, close to the timeless oasis of Dir'aiyah. It was a scene that had scarcely changed for thousands of years. Except for the Range Rovers.

He stared at the tall, bearded Prince of the blood who accompanied him, and he watched the deference bestowed upon him—the gentle bowing of heads, the graceful sweep of the right arm from the forehead, the murmured *"as salaam alaykum"* from the robed brotherhood.

Four days from now he was to try and capture their country for them, with tanks, high explosive, gunfire, and mayhem. *"Jésus,"* thought Jacques. "What could I have done to deserve all this?"

But the Prince was bidding him to be seated. And he was placed next to Nasir on the vast rug set upon the hot sands. Above them the sky was clear and the temperature was rising by the day in the central desert, now four weeks on from the cold nights of mid-February. Tonight it was around eighty-one degrees. A pale moon was rising above the endless shifting dunes to the southeast, and the great revolutionaries of the Saudi royal family were relaxed.

Which was a sight more than Jacques Gamoudi was. He had spent his weeks here scheming and planning a simultaneous attack on several targets. His advisers had promised him that he would have an army to help him. But he had never seen that army. He knew there were immense stores of small arms and ammunition in the city, and he of course could see the heavy artillery he had around him, the armored vehicles and tanks.

When the time for the attack came, Le Chasseur would make no mistakes. So long as he was obeyed, he would take Riyadh. But where the hell was his army? That's what he wanted to know. So far as he could tell, he had about twenty-four known fighting men, all Saudi, all al-Qaeda, most of whom he saw every day. The rest were a mystery.

And since he was probably going to take to the streets four days from now, he ventured to ask Prince Nasir whether he was absolutely sure the army would show up.

The Prince smiled while thoughtfully eating a couple of

dates. "Jacques," he said, "you will have an army of thousands, a great army that will sweep away everything in its path. And you will lead them, and explain to them the critical targets you have chosen. They will follow you and your chosen commanders, and you will be astounded at their bravery and determination.

"And remember, as you look around this very oasis, when Dir'aiyah fell to the army of the Ottoman Empire, in 1818, that was the *only time* in recorded history that the heartland of Saudi Arabia has been conquered by a foreign invader. And it's never happened since. My people, in time, conquered this land, they took almost the entire Arab Peninsula. We are warriors and we understand, to a man, that you will lead us in our fight this week."

Colonel Gamoudi actually thought that was all very well. And he was used to the flowery language of Arab military wannabes, which he privately thought the Prince was. He looked the Crown Prince of Saudi Arabia straight in the eye and said softly, in French, *"Où qu'ils soit,"* wherever they may be.

"Jacques," said the Prince, "as you know, we have been stockpiling arms in the city for many weeks. We have vast caches of weapons stored in two houses in the Makkah Road. We have them on Al Mather Street and Al Malek Saud Street. Our main ammunition dumps are in great houses on Olaya Street. I'm mostly discussing AK-47s and hand grenades. But we have handheld rocket and grenade launchers."

"Sir," said Colonel Gamoudi, "you will remember I had asked about the possibility of a suicide bomber aiming a plane straight at the main royal palace. I still think that's the quickest and most effective way of spreading instant chaos. And striking at the heart of the rulers. Is that likely to happen?"

"So far we have only 230 volunteers for perhaps the greatest act of martyrdom in our history. They are men who understand they will be saving their families, their friends, and their country. They are all *Wahaabis*, which is the true Islamic teaching of our nation. Any one of them would be proud to answer the call of the three trumpets before crossing the bridge into paradise."

Jacques brightened up considerably. "But, sir," he said, "when will our great army begin to muster? Remember, I've never even seen it."

"Jacques, I have observed you since you have been here, and I have observed the great importance you put upon communications. I have seen you demand the most expensive cell phones, radio, and satellite communications in the world . . . and I know you have briefed your commanding officers in the greatest detail.

"Each one of the men you speak to every day, the Saudi officers who will fight for us, the men who masterminded the acquisition of the arms, have an area of the city that they control. And many, many people understand that something is going to happen soon. On Wednesday night, after ten o'clock, the people will begin to gather their arms at our safe houses all over the city.

"Jacques, when you lead our convoy of tanks and armored vehicles down the main road and into the city, the people will come from every dwelling in Riyadh. They will come in the thousands, and they will flock behind your battle tanks, and they will march with you and your high command. And they will follow you into the mouth of hell.

"Oh yes, Jacques Gamoudi. They will come. They will most definitely come . . . *Bismillah*, in the name of God."

Colonel Gamoudi brightened up some more. But he said, "You mean I will never see this army until it falls into line behind our artillery?"

"No one will ever see this army until it falls into line behind your artillery. We must both have faith."

Right now Jacques understood why he was being paid a minimum of $10 million dollars to organize this people's revolution. It was Sunday evening, and he knew that on Tuesday morning there would be $5 million paid into his private account in the Bank of Boston in the Champs-Elysées. He also knew his bonus check of yet another $5 million was being handed to Giselle at their home in the Pyrenees.

She would instantly call and inform the Bank of Boston that her check had arrived. At 2 P.M., here in Saudi Arabia, given the three-hour time difference from Paris, Jacques would dial the bank's number on his cell phone and tell the operator, "Extension three-eight-seven."

The reply would be simple: "Three-eight-six." And he would cut the call off. *Three-eight-six* meant that his account showed a balance of $10 million, and they had heard from Madame Hooks that she now held an irrevocable cashier's check for $5 million, to be deposited on the day King Nasir assumed power.

Either that, or he, Jacques Gamoudi, was on the next plane out of King Khalid for Paris, $5 million richer, and no further obligations. The money from the French government, he knew, would be there.

"Your Highness," he said, "I have faith in you. And I have faith in the officers I have met here in Riyadh. I have been impressed by their planning, and their staff work. Each of them knows and understands our objectives. I am sure that on Friday morning they will confuse and demoralize our enemies, with their audacity and daring."

Prince Nasir smiled. "Then your opening attack will follow the master plan you have worked on?" he asked. "The military vehicles will leave here in convoy the moment we hear that Khamis Mushayt has fallen? Two combat tanks and eight vehicles will head cross-country, straight to the airport, and you head into the city, where Colonel Bandar's brigade will peel off and go directly for the principal television station?"

"Correct," replied the French Colonel. "It is essential that we control the airport, and hold power over all public communications. Major Majeed, who has become a wonderful friend to me, will take the airport by storm, and it will surrender easily. But I have instructed ten al-Qaeda commandos to go straight to the control tower and capture it with gunfire, if possible with no damage to the equipment.

"Colonel Bandar will take television channels one and two by force of arms, but hopefully without loss of life. If he drives that Abrams tank straight through the front door they'll put their hands up, believe me. Journalists die only by accident, not from choice."

"And the remainder of the convoy?" asked the Prince. "Will that advance into the city for three miles, as you suggested, as if in a military parade, right to the edge of the central area?"

"Yes, sir . . . while it gathers our followers. But then it will swing left, back onto Al Mather Street and return north, to join the four main battle tanks and the six armored vehicles we leave back at the junction of the Jiddah Road."

"Of course by then we shall have thousands of armed followers behind the tanks," added the Prince.

"And hopefully a substantial group from the Makkah Road," replied Colonel Gamoudi. "Men who will march to join us—maybe a thousand of them—under the command of our good friend Major Abdul Salaam."

"Good, very good. And then?"

"I lead the convoy to the east, straight around the diplomatic quarter, and into the area where the main palaces are located. Major Abdul Salaam's brigade immediately hits the Prince Miohd bin Abdul Aziz Palace, where the full-morning council meeting will be taking place before the King's arrival at 1300."

"And attempt to capture them, round them up?" asked the Prince, perhaps considering the fate of his several cousins and childhood friends, who would be attending that meeting.

"Absolutely not," replied Colonel Gamoudi. "That's our first objective. We go in hard, rockets, grenades, and gunfire. We take out every single person in the building and then knock as much of it down as we can. We cannot allow the officials inside to live, for fear of later uprisings, and we do not want the building. That palace and all of its occupants is on our critical hit list. To seize a ship of state, you first smash its rudder."

The Prince nodded. "And then?"

"We pass two more minor palaces as we go out to the

east, and we take them by force of arms. I do not expect many important people to be in them, whoever is, we wipe out—not women, or children, of course, but anyone who may later bear arms against us."

"Do we knock down the buildings?"

"No. We need those big buildings to set up our new command posts. And once we've taken them, we push right on to the King, who will be in the Al Salam royal palace. And as you know, this is a very large building. I will press the red button on my comms system, and the suicide bomber instantly takes off from the airport, which by now we control."

"Straight at the palace?"

"Straight at the upper levels of the palace. I'll take care of the lower levels, and the guards."

"And the King and his family?"

"The King dies. And so do any princes serving him. If the great man is as smart as I think he is, he'll have many of his family already evacuated. Probably within hours of the oil bombardment on Thursday morning."

"And the families, Jacques? The King's wives and many children . . . if any of them are still there?"

"Sir, if you had asked me to slaughter women and children, there would be a different commander sitting here with you. And I would be with my wife, Giselle, in the Pyrenees."

"Even for fifteen million?" asked Prince Nasir.

"Even for fifteen billion," said Colonel Gamoudi quietly. "I'm a soldier, not a murderer."

Prince Nasir again nodded his head gravely. "And when the palace falls?"

"I recall Maj. Abdul Salaam to organize a total occupation of the building. I have detailed six al-Qaeda staff officers to assist him in this. All prisoners will be marched to the smaller royal palace, a half-mile down the road, where they will be held under guard.

"I will then open a new communication center and Colonel Bandar will transport television crews there, and you, sir, will make your first broadcast to the nation, informing the populace that the King has fallen and the city is in the hands of the armed forces of Prince Nasir Ibn Mohammed al-Saud, the great-great-grandson of Ibn Saud. And you will address them with your message of hope, inspiration, and future prosperity."

"And you, Jacques, what further degradations do you have in mind for my country?" The Prince smiled.

"I will regroup my army, sir, hopefully with many more trucks and transports, and make my way to the southwest, to downtown Riyadh, where we take and occupy several places, no more firing unless there is serious resistance. And if there should be, I am afraid we must be utterly merciless."

"Which places?"

"Oh, the big shopping centers, the council building, King Fahd Medical Center, the post office, the bus station and railway station, Central Hospital, because there may be wounded."

"And the main Army? The ones in the other great military cities of Saudi Arabia?"

"That will all be taken care of by General Rashood. He will compel the Commander in Chief of Khamis Mushayt to speak to his opposite number in Tabuk, informing him that Khamis Mushayt has fallen to the troops of the Crown Prince.

"He will also tell him that the King has been removed and that his great friend Prince Nasir implores him and his men to change their allegiance immediately, particularly as the Prince is the only man in the world who can pay them and take care of the families. The King is dead. Long live the King."

Crown Prince Nasir remained slightly quizzical. "And you are not concerned that the opening action in this great saga is all concentrated around the east side of the city, while the central area scarcely knows what's going on?"

"Not with a man like General Rashood taking care of the rest of the Saudi armed forces, sir. To take any country, you must first cut off its head. That's the King. When he falls, everything starts to cave in. You will be the King of Saudi Arabia by Friday afternoon."

Prince Nasir rose and beckoned to Le Chasseur.

"Come, Jacques," he said, "it is almost eight o'clock. And I would like you to pray with us."

"Thank you, sir," replied the devout Muslim colonel from Morocco. "I would be greatly honored."

And the curious thing was, he meant it. And the great bond of Islam seemed to engulf him along, as he stood next to the Arab Prince, out there on the shifting sands around the oasis of Dir'aiyah.

Same Day, Sunday, March 21, 1900
24.10N 37.35E, Speed 5, Depth 100

The *Améthyste* moved slowly through the dark waters west of the jagged island of Shi'ib ash Sharm, guardian of the ten-mile-long deepwater bay along the coastline north of Yanbu al Bahr.

Shortly after 1900, with night settling heavily over the ocean, Commander Dreyfus ordered his ship to the surface, and the French nuclear hunter-killer came sliding up out of the depths of the flat, calm Red Sea to take up her ops station. Water cascaded off her hull as she shouldered aside the ocean, moving forward slowly, making as little surface commotion as possible for a 2,500-tonner.

Just ahead they could see the warning light on Sharm's rocky headland, flashing every few seconds and casting a white light on the glinting waters, mostly to warn tanker captains of the dangers inherent in not making a sharp landward turn.

Shi'ib ash Sharm sat five miles off shore, directly west of the loading platforms that serviced the world's biggest oil tankers at the far end of the seven-hundred-mile trans-Saudi pipeline. That was the one that ended at the port of Yanbu, having cleaved its way across the vast central desert and over the Aramah Mountains, all the way from Pump Station Number One, near Abqaiq.

To reach the main loading terminal at Yanbu, tankers had to make a hard turn, at either end of Sharm, from the north or south. For the SF insert tonight, Commander Dreyfus had chosen the northerly route, a three-mile-wide seaway between the island and a large shallow area that had to be avoided by the VLCCs and most certainly by the *Améthyste*.

The water was beautifully flat, and the rising moon to the east, from behind the mountains, was casting a pale light on the narrows. The submarine was just about invisible, its black hull casting no shadow on the surface. But inside there was a frenzy of activity.

Several hands were already hoisting and hauling the deflated twenty-two-foot Zodiacs up through the big hatch on the forecasing and manhandling them onto the deck, where the seamen had already brought out the electric air pumps.

The 175-horsepower Yamaha outboard engines that would power the two craft were coming up separately from the torpedo room, where they had been stored for the voyage. Within moments, six engineers were out on the casing, three of them bolting the heavy motors into position on the stern, expertly clipping on the fuel lines, and attaching the battery cables and ignition wires while the boat was still being inflated.

The engines were clipped into the upward-tilt position. Two other seamen filled the fuel tanks with diesel and loaded a four-and-a-half-gallon spare fuel tank inboard each boat. Also being loaded were assault rifles, ammunition, six grenades, just in case, and the comms transmitter, which would guide them home after the bombs were fixed.

There were also medical supplies, morphine, and bottles of water, mainly in case someone was badly injured and needed to drink. The two "attack boards" that contained the swimmers' watch and compass, both inbuilt, non-glare, were also placed onboard.

The lead frogmen would swim in with the boards out in front of them; they would especially need them if they had to exit the Zodiacs sooner than planned, for whatever reason—busy harbor, launch activity—anything the Zodiac captain considered might compromise the safety of the boats, if anything or anyone came too close.

When the first Zodiac was ready, they pushed it to the downward slope of the deck and allowed the hard-decked inflatable to slide down into the water, held secure by two lines attached to its bow, each one held by two brawny seamen.

Another two men attached and rolled a wooden-rung rope ladder down the side of the *Améthyste*, and the officer-of-the-deck signaled for the first six of the Special Forces assault group, led by Lt. Garth Dupont, to come up through the foredeck hatch and proceed to the head of the ladder.

Dupont was of course unrecognizable from the chuckling bridge player of the lower deck. He was dressed in his jet black wet suit, hood up, goggles above his face, which was coated in black camouflage cream. His big flippers were attached to his belt, and on his back, in a waterproof rucksack, he carried a massive sixty-pound "sticky bomb," which would clamp magnetically to one of the giant steel pylons supporting the loading dock in Yanbu. Also on his belt were his sheathed specially made Sabatine combat knife and a roll of det-cord and wires, with a twenty-four-hour timer.

His air system, the Draeger, also carried on his back, was a compact model, containing air for only ninety minutes, which was about twice what he would need. The system was a special non-bubble breather, which would betray nothing to a curious sentry staring down into the water. In any event, the Frenchmen would operate fifty feet below the surface, which would render them invisible from the platform.

Privately, all four of the frogmen hoped that there would be tankers on the docks, which would cast huge shadows and shield the men from anyone's eyes. They would work in the dark, unseen, somewhere down below the tankers' keels, which would, of course, suit them absolutely perfectly.

The four swimmers would work in pairs, and when the bombs were stuck hard to the pylons, the timer would be magnetically clamped to a third one, with wires running to the splice in the det-cord. When the timer reached 0400, it would send an impulse into the det-cord splice, which would ignite the explosive fuse.

This would streak at a rate of two miles a second, straight into the detonators fixed to the bombs, which would blast the pylons in half, probably blowing the deck on the platform into several pieces. Any ship on the dock would probably have its hull split asunder and sink to the floor of the harbor, all 300,000 tons of it, which, in time, might take quite a bit of removing.

Add to this the activity of the *Perle*'s cruise missiles, which were to hit the faraway pumping station at Abqaiq, and the great Red Sea port of Yanbu al Bahr was in dead trouble—starved of oil, its loading terminal obliterated, perhaps half a million tons of shipping jamming its jetties.

Garth Dupont climbed backward down the ladder, found his footing, and slipped over the rubber hull of the Zodiac, which was still held with fore and aft lines by the seamen on the submarine.

Then, one by one, his five-man team joined him, the three other swimmers, the boat driver, and the comms officer with his GPS receiver and mobile phone to communicate codes back to the submarine if necessary.

Seaman Raul Potier took the wheel and kicked the engine over; it started first time. If it hadn't, one of the engineers would probably have been keel-hauled. Potier untied both lines and expertly curled and then hurled them back onto the submarine's deck. He took the Zodiac quietly away from the hull, fifty feet out into the water, and waited.

The comms man pushed the buttons to dial the officer-of-the-deck up on the casing, checking that the phone was working. Then they reversed the process, ensuring they had two-way transmission. The second Zodiac was lowered into the water, and the second half of Team One went through the same checks. When they had checked the phones once more, one to another, they set off for Yanbu, the massive, 900,000-barrel-a-day oil colossus of the Red Sea.

The Zodiacs carried no running lights as they moved swiftly through the water at around half-speed, fifteen knots. Garth Dupont sat next to the driver, his night binoculars trained on the black ahead, but his vision was not improved by the rising moon.

A mile in front he picked up the lights of a tanker coming toward them, off his starboard bow, but he could see only her green running light and he guessed that she was leaving by the southern route around Sharm. Way ahead of that was another tanker, going his way, slowly into port, probably lining up to receive the last oil from Saudi Arabia for a very long while.

Within twelve minutes they could see the lights on the loading docks, now only a couple of miles ahead, across the bay, and it quickly became clear that this was a busy Sunday evening. Dupont could pick out two tankers he thought were on the jetties, with three waiting to come in, a mile offshore out to his port side.

One mile from the jetties he ordered Potier to slow right down to five knots, then to slip in very slowly. The Navy had no indication of sonar surveillance in these waters, but Dupont was taking no chances. By now it was clear that there was a great deal of light on the docks, shining from both the enormous tankers and the jetty itself. And those lights seemed to spill out for two, maybe three hundred yards into the main approaches to the Yanbu terminals.

Dupont ordered the engines cut back to idling speed, just enough to hold a position without drifting. He took one final look ahead and ordered the other swimmers to action stations. The four men sat down and pulled on their flippers, fixed goggles, and Draeger lines, and then slid softly over the side. The comms officer quietly passed the instruction to the second boat. There was no shouting in black ops.

The eight men in the water came together as two groups, two leaders and two followers in each. Garth ordered them deep with a silent thumbs-up gesture and they began to kick their way underwater, each of the "followers" swimming with their right hands on the left shoulder of their leader, in the pitch-black water twelve feet below the surface.

The leaders swam with flippers only, their attack boards held at arm's length out in front of them, like regular floatable kickboards, but these boards contained instruments that showed the precise time and direction, without the swimmer needing to pause to check either watch or compass.

The lead pair in each group had made the inshore journey in Garth Dupont's boat. This meant there was no need for instructions to be passed from one group to another. In any event, the plan was simple. Each four-man team was to head directly toward the tankers, Dupont's men to the one on the left, the others to the one on the right.

Given the complications of mooring lines, and propellers that could start at any time, the underwater leader had ordered them to take each tanker amidships, diving right down to the keel—forty feet on a loaded tanker but only thirty feet on these half-laden hulls.

There would be twenty feet of water under the keels, and once through and under the dock, the swimmers were to head to the far ends of the platform and place their bombs deep on the corner pylons, two men attending each objective.

And so they kicked in rhythmically through the water, one pressure stroke on the flippers every ten seconds . . . *KICK . . . one . . . two . . . three . . . four . . . KICK . . . one . . . two . . . three . . . four.* Kick and glide, conserving energy, all together. That way they arrived on the starboard sides of the tankers absolutely together. Using their hands on the hulls, they pushed their way under, and Dupont was relieved to find there was a long gap down to the harbor floor.

Nonetheless, it was nothing short of dead creepy down there in the pitch dark, like some hideous horror film. If they'd had time they would probably have shuddered. However, on the dock side of the tanker it was suddenly much brighter, which felt better, but was plainly more dangerous.

Both groups now made for the seaward pylons on the two corners, and both were irritated at the number of barnacles on the steel. They had to scrape them off with combat knives before the bombs would clamp on tightly. Of course, the time settings were all different in the countdown to H hour at 0400 hours.

For instance, at 1956, on the first pylon, the timer was set for eight hours and four minutes. On the landward corner pylon, which took longer to reach, it was set for seven hours and fifty-seven minutes.

They made their way under the platform to seek out the

next four pylons, the center supports below the gigantic platform pumping systems. And there the clamping and timing processes were repeated until all eight of the sixty-pounders were in place, clocks set, the final one for seven hours and eighteen minutes.

With their cumbersome loads now gone, the men headed back the way they had come, under the tankers, and back out to the waiting boats. On the way in, they had kicked approximately eighty times, each one carrying them ten feet, or three and a half meters. On the return journey, again twelve feet under the water, they counted the kicks again.

At the count of eighty they all surfaced, quite widely spread out. Dupont reached for his "bleeper" to signal their position to the Zodiacs. But, as his did so, his number-two man whacked his head on Potier's bow and had to suppress a yell of terror, because he thought he'd hit a shark. This caused a lot of chuckling, and all eight men were instantly hauled inboard, breathing their first fresh air for well over an hour.

The Zodiacs now turned away from the Yanbu docks and made a fast beeline for the waiting *Améthyste*, out there beyond the north end of the island. The comms men were both in contact with the mother ship, and within fifteen minutes they saw the quick-flashing light signal on the submarine's foredeck.

They came alongside, grabbed the lines, and began to disembark. The last men off-loaded the rifles, ammunition, and equipment into canvas bags, which were immediately hauled inboard. Then they took their Kaybar combat knives and slashed six wide holes in each of the pressure compartments in the Zodiacs' rubber hulls. And before the hit men had even pulled off their flippers and hoods, both Zodiacs were settled nicely in two hundred fathoms on the bed of the Red Sea.

Commander Dreyfus ordered all hatches closed, main ballast opened, and took the *Améthyste* to three hundred feet below the surface, running south at twelve knots, straight down to the next great Saudi loading dock in the oil port of Rabigh.

The Special Forces had dinner immediately they returned and settled down to two tables of bridge. Garth Dupont, flushed with what he believed was the total success of their first mission, opened the bidding in *les piques*, spades, in the first rubber; he ended up bidding six and making one.

Everyone fell about laughing and someone mentioned they hoped he could count a damned sight better underwater than he could on the surface. Dupont assured them he was challenging for the Underwater Bridge Championship of France when they returned.

In fact Dupont had been asleep for only three hours when they reached the calm waters off Rabigh just after 0100 on Thursday morning. Commander Dreyfus had made fast time all along the Saudi coast, where they found that the deep ocean was absolutely deserted both on and below the surface. They picked up only two small fishing boats on their passive sonar all the way from Yanbu.

It was still only 2345 when they came to periscope depth, confirmed their GPS fix, and found the quick-flashing warning light on the headland of Shi'b al Khamsa, a small deserted island directly in front of the fifteen-mile-long bay that protected the port of Rabigh.

Commander Dreyfus left the island to starboard and pressed on for another four miles, right into the gateway to the bay, another wide seaway, with a flashing light on the right-hand side but nothing on the left, where a coastal shoal rose up three hundred feet from the seabed to a level only about a hundred feet below the surface.

However, the well-chartered bay had depths of three hundred feet until quite close to the shore. And Commander Dreyfus elected to make a hard right turn, at PD, into the wide southern end of the bay. This was no cul-de-sac, well, not for surface ships, because there was a narrow fifty-foot channel at the end of Shi'b al Bayda, one of three islands that more or less blocked the bay to the south. However, the Bay of Rabigh was a cul-de-sac for a submarine.

Commander Dreyfus thus came quietly to the surface and made a 180-degree turn in this sheltered, "private" end of the bay. There was not a ship in sight, on radar or sonar, on or below the surface of the water. And it would take him mere moments to go deep and vanish, heading out of the bay any time he wanted.

Rabigh was not as busy as Yanbu, mainly because it had no major trans-Saudi pipeline coming in off the Aramah Mountains. Nonetheless, it could be full of tanker traffic in mid-week since it did have a very large refinery. And this took in crude from Yanbu and dispersed it in various forms of gasoline, petrochemicals, and LPG, taking the heat off the constantly overworked terminal ninety miles to the north.

Once more Garth Dupont led his team out of the submarine and into two Zodiacs, new ones of course, same procedures, all the way into the docks. But Rabigh was not so light as Yanbu, and he hoped to find an even closer holding point. However, off to the left, in a holding area about two miles away, Dupont could see one tanker making its way slowly inshore, but the jetties were Sunday-night empty.

Just one other tanker was within sight of the frogmen, a VLCC of unknown origin, making its way out of the bay about a half mile off their port beam. But the Zodiacs carried no running lights, and the sky was cloudy. The warm air that hung above the water seemed muggy, and there was no moonlight to cast even the remotest light on the surface.

Dead ahead the jetties looked quiet, and about 400 yards out Garth Dupont decided to summon the hit teams overboard and down into the depths en route to the loading platforms. That way the boat drivers could hang around in the dark well clear of the distant incoming tanker, which appeared to be going so slowly it might not make its mooring by Wednesday.

But that was the nature of these VLCCs. They took about four miles to stop at their regular running speed in excess of fifteen knots. At four knots, creeping into the jetties, it took them almost forty-five minutes from two miles out, because they actually covered the last 200 yards barely above drifting speed.

"You just be ready to leave as the tanker arrives," Dupont had stressed to his men, explaining the importance of staying deep, well under the keel of the ship, the moment it came to a halt. He told them he wanted no heroics trying to go underneath the 350,000-ton hulk while it was still moving. "We move when that thing stops," he said. "Unless we can get out before it arrives."

Thereafter they kicked their way in, just as they had done at Yanbu. They were not observed, in fact, from high above, no one even had a look over the side. There were no active guards on the jetties, and the shore crews had gone for a welcome cup of coffee before the new tanker arrived.

In perfect isolation, the French divers worked underwater beneath the towering platform, and within fifty minutes they had all eight bombs expertly set; times were synchronized precisely with those beneath the loading terminal at Yanbu. And the slow, ominous ticking of the sixteen detonator clocks, deep in the water, separated by ninety miles of ocean, could not be heard by anyone.

At precisely 0400 there would be two almighty explosions on the east coast of the Red Sea. Dupont wondered how long it would take the Saudi authorities to work out that there might be a connection.

By the time they reached the seaward front of the dock, the incoming tanker was moored, and they had to go deep under the hull before they broke free into clear water. They all hated that part. But again there was plenty of water below the keel, and they kicked their way to freedom up the starboard side of the colossal hull.

They swam twelve feet under the surface, all the way back to the Zodiacs, kicking and counting, kicking and counting. When they burst up into fresh night air, they were around fifty feet from the nearest of their inflatables. The ocean was deserted, and within twenty minutes they had reached the *Améthyste*.

Procedures were identical to those at Yanbu. They unloaded the gear, climbed on to the casing, scuttled both boats, and headed to their headquarters on the lower deck. Commander Dreyfus ordered the submarine deep, and they moved quietly out of the bay before Rabigh.

Once in open water they steered course one-five-zero

down the main deep-water seaway of the Red Sea, 400 feet below the surface. They would not see daylight again for two weeks, until they reached the French Navy Base on the tiny subtropical island of La Réunion in the Indian Ocean, 3,800 miles away.

And no one, on the entire Arabian peninsula, would ever know what they had done.

Same Evening, 1730
27.01N 50.24E, Course two-five-zero, Speed 7 Depth 20

Night comes crashing in over the Arabian desert and its shores far more suddenly than in more temperate northerly regions of the globe. However, on this particular night, twenty-five miles off Saudi Arabia's Gulf Coast, it was never going to be fast enough for Capt. Alain Roudy.

The forty-one-year-old commanding officer from Tours, in the Loire Valley, was for the first time in his naval career on the edge of his nerves, though he would not have betrayed that to anyone, even his much younger second wife, Anne Marie. Actually, especially not his much younger second wife.

Captain Roudy was a disciplinarian, a man cut in the mold of eighteenth-century French battle commanders. And while he understood he might have been under pressure to defeat Great Britain's ferocious Admiral Nelson and his veterans in 1805, he reckoned he would have fought Trafalgar a sight better than the somewhat defeatist Comte de Villeneuve, who lost his ship, was taken prisoner, and later committed suicide.

Alain Roudy, who still lived in his hometown of Tours, was currently boxed into an extremely tough time frame. Right now it was around 5:30 P.M., and the light was not fading over these waters, twenty miles west of the Abu Sa'afah oil field. The *Perle* was twenty feet below the surface without a mast up, moving slowly toward the main tanker lanes, which would lead him down toward the gigantic LPG terminal off Ras al Ju'aymah.

The trouble was, he needed to be in those lanes by 1815, and every time he risked a thirty-second glance through the periscope he was seeing more moving traffic than there was on the Champs-Elysées at this time on a Sunday evening.

It was supposed to be a restricted area, but he'd seen at least two patrol boats circling the oil fields, four aged freighters to the north, three big fishing dhows, a trawler, and a ninety-foot harbor launch, plus two helicopters heading out to the landing platform in the middle of the Abu Sa'afah field.

In only sixteen fathoms of water, he really should have been moving west with a continuous lookout through the periscope. But he could not risk running with a mast jutting out, which may very well have betrayed him, or even identified him. He knew the Saudis would not have a submarine in these waters, nor probably a warship, but the *Américains sont très furtifs.* Captain Roudy did not wish to see the Stars and Stripes represented around here in any form whatsoever, above or below the surface.

The governing factor in his operation was that he needed to be fifty miles from the datum, in the launch zone, by 0400 tomorrow morning, Monday. And that meant there would be all kinds of deadlines to observe . . . *must be away from the last pickup point by 2315 latest . . . must be away from the first pickup point by 2215 . . . must wait two and half hours at the second point for the divers to return.*

And it all meant being in there, with those tankers, running south almost in a convoy, like them, at ten knots, not later than 1815, forty-five minutes from now. Otherwise, much later tonight, he would have to unleash his missiles before he reached the launch area specified by Admirals Romanet and Pires. He could not slow down, or ask for more time, because Louis Dreyfus would be accomplishing his much easier task over in the Red Sea, and they needed to be identical.

"*Merde,*" said Roudy under his breath, glancing at his watch for the seventh time in the last twenty minutes. *If the slightest thing goes wrong, we're in real trouble.*

Fifteen more nail-biting minutes went by, and Captain Roudy called, "PERISCOPE!"

"Aye, sir."

And once more he heard the smoothest of machinery carrying the telescopic mast upward, to jut out of the water. He seized the handles long before they were at eye level and took an all-around look at the surface picture. The speed and grasp that had once made him leading student at the French Navy's Ecole de Sousmarin had not deserted him. No one could record a surface picture in his mind faster than young Roudy. And twenty years later, nothing had changed. Capt. Alain Roudy was still the master of his profession, in all of France.

DOWN PERISCOPE!

The careful surface check took him exactly thirty seconds. And for the first time in several miles he could see nothing in any direction. It was also, he noticed, at last growing dark.

The *Perle* ran on through the dark water. There was still a half hour's running time before he must be in those tanker lanes. But if he was even fifteen minutes late, that quarter-hour would come back to haunt him all night. Because any other ten-minute delay would mean almost a half-hour behind his schedule. And there were still four miles in front of him, before the flashing light on the Gharibah sandbank.

The waters in a five-mile radius around the submarine were palpably deserted. Alain Roudy ordered a two-knot increase in speed. That, he knew, would bring him down to the tanker throughway in good time.

Again he ordered the periscope up for as short a time as possible. And then again, even though he was still relying on passive sonar to warn him of any ship coming close aboard. And suddenly, dead ahead, were the Gharibah sandbank lights, fine on his starboard bow.

Come right four degrees . . . steer two-six-zero . . . make your speed six . . .

Aye, sir.

UP PERISCOPE!

Alain Roudy saw a green buoy a hundred meters coming up to starboard, and he knew they were almost in the *outgoing* tanker lane. He peered through the lenses and down the route and could just make out the running lights of a massive ship heading toward.

DOWN PERISCOPE!

Aye, sir.

The turbines thrust her forward, and the *Perle* accelerated across the outgoing mile-wide lane, traveling at about the same speed as the oncoming VLCC, a mighty 300,000-tonner riding empty, high out of the water.

No one even got a sniff of her as Captain Roudy pressed on, and then, five minutes later, took a final look at the incoming lane to the right. This was his direction and his runway. Captain Roudy wanted a couple of miles between his submarine, fore and aft, and any other ships running down to the LPG dock this eventful Sunday night.

If necessary, he would wait around to ensure he had it, but in fact the *Perle* crossed the outgoing tanker's line of approach with more than a half mile to spare, and the nearest ship to them on the dark waters of the far side was another VLCC, about a mile and a half ahead.

Captain Roudy ordered a forty-degree turn to port, and the *Perle* fell in, line astern.

Steer course two-two-zero . . . make your speed fifteen knots . . . stay at PD . . . mast down . . . ten kilometers to ops area.

Two decks below, Cdr. Jules Ventura now summoned his men to complete their checks—attack boards, Draegers, rifles, and ammunition to be loaded into the Zodiacs. Combat knives, flippers, det-cord, timers, detonators, wires, cutters, screwdrivers, bombs securely packed. All six of the men going in were now barefoot in their jet black wet suits, hoods down, goggles high on their foreheads, faces smeared with black camouflage cream.

Final preparations were made for the boats. The Zodiacs would be hoisted first, then the two black Yamaha outboard engines, tuned like racing cars by the engineers, just in case. The two inflatables could probably outrun the *QM2* over a short course, assuming of course that someone had by now extricated *Shades of Arabia* from her portside bow.

Three minutes later, Capt. Alain Roudy ordered the helmsman to make a hard turn . . . *ninety degrees to port . . . stop engines . . . blow main ballast . . . surface . . .*

The *Perle* made her turn and came driving up to the surface, water streaming off the casing. She righted herself, moving forward, then slowly came to a complete stop, showing no lights.

On the command of the Captain, Commander Ventura led his men up the unlit companionway and out onto the casing. It was strange, but this great, burly, taciturn Special Forces leader was talkative now for the first time since they left Brest.

Ventura was encouraging his men, shaking hands with crew members, thanking everyone for all they had done on the voyage, as he left the ship, to face the unknown in an open rubber-hull boat. Ventura was transformed now into the mortal enemy of the King of Saudi Arabia and his Navy.

The boat driver went aboard the Zodiac first, and Ventura followed him, helping with the lines. When they were set to leave, the Commander personally curled and threw the lines back up to the deck, then sat down and ordered the big inflatable away from the submarine's hull.

It was extraordinary how thoroughly invisible the Zodiac became on the black water. There was no rising moon yet, and this was a black boat, with a black engine, carrying men in black wet suits, with black hoods and black faces. Even from thirty feet they were impossible to see.

Even the submarine, now without even flashlights on the casing, had effectively vanished from sight. Certainly when the gigantic VLCC came rolling past over in the outward lane, no one onboard the twenty-one-story crude-oil leviathan had the slightest idea that there was a 2,500-ton hunter-killer within a mile, with men on the deck and a black ops team about to destroy the world's premier supply of oil.

The second Zodiac came away from the *Perle*'s hull and melted into the night. The *Perle* herself came away from her holding position and melted into the ocean, back to PD, in the down lane, about a mile in front of a new oncoming tanker, and still a couple of miles astern of their original leader. All of them were on the seven-mile run to the world's largest offshore oil terminal on the manmade Sea Island.

While Team Two finalized its preparation for the insert, less than one hour hence, under the command of twenty-six-year-old Lt. Reme Doumen, Jules Ventura and his men chugged steadily along at only five knots. They had a lot of explosives on board, and a lot of time to set them. The *Perle* would not be back to collect them for almost four hours.

It was five miles down to the LPG terminal, and Commander Ventura had all the time he needed to study the dock lights and find the darkest stretch of water to begin the mission. He checked his attack board watch and saw that it was 1915, and he wondered what his friend and colleague Lt. Garth Dupont was doing. Dupont, he knew, was leading the identical mission on the other side of the Arabian Peninsula . . . *he's probably doing the same as me, groping about in the dark with a bomb on his back*, thought Ventura.

The Zodiacs were now running over the wide shoal that guarded the eastern approaches to the great offshore terminal of Ras al Ju'aymah. At least it guarded it from submarines, since there were only six fathoms here, and the outboards ran across it very slowly. Jules Ventura and his men finally arrived a half mile north of the loading jetties around 2000 hours.

This was a very bright terminal, and Commander Ventura saw no reason to approach it head on, not when all the undisturbed darkness was north and south of the outer dock.

He could see now what he had seen on the chart for so many weeks. The long man-made bridge/causeway to the offshore jetties ran four and a half miles out from the land, and ended in a great V shape at the end. He presumed the liquid gas pipes ran under the causeway and ended in the huge pumping and valve control systems positioned on the jetty, and plainly visible to the satellite cameras.

There were two tankers in residence, one of them an 80,000-ton black-hulled gas carrier out of Houston, Texas. Jules picked out the name *Global Mustang* on her stern. But he needed light-sensitive night-vision glasses to do so. He checked out the bow of the tanker at the other end, but he could not make out the lettering there. Not even close. He thus formed a definite conclusion that the north end was darker.

"Take her in another seven hundred meters," he commanded. "Dead slow, minimum revs. We'll swim the last few hundred."

Commander Ventura was in fact more concerned by the traffic than the light. To the northwest of Ras al Ju'aymah, there were five oil pipelines traversing the ocean floor—there was the Qatif oil field, there was another large offshore oil rig, there was an anchorage area for waiting tankers—all in a vast restricted area. The place was literally humming with small craft. Big Jules could see green and red running lights all over the place, but he had none on his Zodiacs and no one could see him.

They chugged almost silently toward the jetties, and still the great shadow of the dock hung over the water, and to the north there were no reflected bright lights beyond a hundred feet. Ventura called his men to action stations, and five minutes later they all slipped over the side and began the swim-in, just as Garth Dupont's men had done an hour earlier, over in the Red Sea.

There was one principal difference in the two missions. In Yanbu and Rabigh, Dupont's men had been ordered merely to blow the terminal out of the water, all eight bombs on the supporting pylons. Here at Ras al Ju'aymah, there was more to it. Commander Ventura was required to blast the pumping and valve system, thus igniting the colossally volatile liquid gas.

The terminal itself was more fragile than the docks at Yanbu simply because it was a mere seaward structure miles from the land. Out here, the terminal would probably collapse with the explosions of two or three sixty-pound bombs. Six would make total collapse a certainty.

But Jules Ventura, and young seaman Vincent Lefevre, aged twenty-three, needed to climb the structure, inside, coming up directly beneath the boots and trucks of the LPG personnel. And then they had to attach the massive time bombs right below the pumps.

"If you're going to blow the damn thing up," Admiral Pires had instructed, "you better make sure that liquid gas blows out like a flamethrower. Our objects are twofold: to destroy and to frighten. Make sure the blowtorch at Ras al Ju'aymah ignites."

They had studied the layout of these jetties for weeks now, and each man knew intimately the supporting pylon he sought. With all eight men in the water, the boat drivers and comms operators headed farther out for a few hundred yards, with orders to make their way back inshore for the pickup in one hour.

The swim-in took just two or three minutes, and as instructed, they gathered underneath the structure to hear last-minute words from Ventura, who told them, "You all know what to do . . . go in pairs to the two pylons you have been allotted and fix the six bombs. Then wait below the surface at pylon number four on the chart. Lefevre will be right above you, working on the two high bombs.

"Don't, for Christ's sake, let anything go off early, or you'll kill us all—'specially me and Lefevre. We rendezvous again under pylon number four and return to the Zodiacs together."

And so they swam to their appointed stations and like Garth Dupont's men, found they had to scrape away the barnacles in the warm water for the magnetic bombs to clamp onto the steel.

As they expected, the tide was not yet high, and Ventura and Lefevre took off their flippers below the surface at number four. Then they unclipped the straps that held the Draegers, because though the state-of-the-art breathing apparatus was weightless in the water, it weighed thirty pounds out of water. Jules lashed the gear to the pylon, twenty feet below the surface, and they pulled on their waterlogged black Nike sneakers and kicked their way up into the fresh, but dank, oil-smelling air below the jetty.

The steel strut they wanted, jutting diagonally up to the next horizontal beam, was now two feet above their heads. Both men reached up with thick rubber-gloved hands to grab it. From there on, it was a simple forty-foot climb to the underside of the decking on the high central area of the jetty. Simple, that is, for trained Navy black ops forces. Quite sufficient to induce a heart attack in lesser men.

They reached the uppermost horizontal, which stretched for twenty feet, four feet below the decking. Pylon number four ended right there. It was about the diameter of a telegraph pole and freshly painted, rust red in color. There were of course no barnacles this far above the water.

Ventura sat astride the beam and unzipped the rubberized container that held his bomb. He gently scraped the magnetic surface with his knife and then held it to the pylon, then felt its pull as the magnets jammed it hard against the steel.

Vincent Lefevre passed to Ventura the timing device, which on this type of bomb screwed into the casing. It could be done by hand, but you got a much tighter fix if you used a screwdriver. Ventura turned the timer into place, and set it for seven hours and forty minutes. He held out his hand for the screwdriver and tightened the timer and the screws that held the det-cord detonator in place.

Then he and Lefevre began to edge along the horizontal beam, Lefevre playing out the det-cord. Halfway along, they paused while Ventura took a length of tape and wrapped it around the beam, holding the det-cord firm and invisible from any angle. Which was when he dropped the screwdriver. It fell from his grasp and hit two metal beams with a metallic clatter on its way down and then splashed into the water.

Ventura had no idea if anyone was directly above, but he instantly drew his silenced rifle from its waterproof holster on his back and, with his finger on the trigger, stared seaward at the hull of the liquid gas tanker moored to the dock.

To his utter horror he heard running footsteps above him, just one person heading to the edge. Ventura and Lefevre were no more than sixteen feet inward from that point when they heard a thump above them. An upside-down face appeared from above and then the beam of a flashlight.

Whoever it was—military guard, gas crew worker, tanker man—Jules had no idea, but the man was staring straight at him.

"Who's there?" The words seemed disembodied since the face was upside down. But they were serious, and Jules took the only option open to him. He blew that face clean off its head with his silenced AK-47. There was just a muffled clicking sound, nothing as noisy as the screwdriver.

The body slumped over the edge, a burst of just four bullets riddling the forehead, blood dripping forty feet down into the sea. Ventura went along that beam like a circus tightrope walker. With an outrageous display of strength, he grabbed the throat of the man and hauled him overboard, straight down into the sea below. And he just stood there, his heart thumping, in deadly silence, wondering how many more they'd have to kill before they could get away.

To the amazement of both the Commander and the Navy seaman, there was not another sound, neither from above nor from the tanker. Whoever had seen them had been alone. There were no more footsteps above, no shouting, nothing.

Jules Ventura ordered Lefevre back along the beam. And he followed him to the junction of five steel rafters that came together in one spot, right below the gas pumps. And there they clamped Lefevre's bomb, which needed no timer, having been specially primed to explode via the det-cord charge.

Ventura wound the cord around the bomb and one of the beams, finally jamming the det-cord into the hole normally used for the timed detonator wires. He tightened two screws and leaned back to admire his handiwork.

One thing was for certain: when that first high bomb blew at 0400, the second one would follow, a millisecond later. He motioned to Lefevre to begin the climb down, which took them eight minutes. And they crossed one horizontal beam just above the water, to pylon number four, and then dropped back into the Gulf to collect their flippers and Draegers.

As arranged, the team gathered at the pylon, where Commander Ventura's men were longing to know why he had found it necessary to shoot someone. They pointed out the body, which had already drifted under the structure on the rising tide twenty-five feet away.

Commander Ventura's orders were brisk. They took the spare det-cord and wound it around the body, a long double-thickness cord coming out from under each armpit. Two young seamen were told to drag the body under the surface, hauling it back to the Zodiacs, line astern. Ventura told them that he did not give a damn about the man he had shot, but he gave a huge damn about anyone's finding the body.

And so they set off, four of the divers helping to pull the corpse through the water. When they reached the Zodiacs, they took a longer line from inboard, secured it to the body, and towed the body back behind the rear inflatable, like a water-skier who'd fallen off.

At the submarine, they took the same towline and lashed the man to the Yamaha engine. He was wearing military uniform and had plainly been in the Royal Saudi Air Force, which had special responsibilities for guarding and protecting the country's obviously vulnerable oil pumping stations, processing and loading facilities, and oil platforms in the Gulf.

The young Arab sank with the two little inflatable boats, straight to the bottom, in a hundred feet of water, right at the end of the Saudi tanker lanes. Six hours from now, there would be many others joining him in death. But no one would ever know that there was anything special about the loss of the young loading dock guard.

They were all merely fallen martyrs, in the cause of the world's richest and most avaricious industry.

THE LAST TWO Zodiacs were heading east now, back toward
the tanker lanes. Lt. Reme Doumen was from the chic Atlantic seaport of La Rochelle, where his father, a greatly re-
spected local ferry owner, was mayor.

Generally speaking, Doumen had never been on the
wrong side of the law in his life. But now he sat in the stern
of the lead Zodiac and gazed back at the floodlit steel structure of the massive Sea Island Oil Terminal, and tried to accept what he, Reme, had just done.

He knew, in the strictest naval terms, the full dimension
of his mission. He had just led a team of highly trained hit
men into the heart of the enormous construction and organized the placing of high explosives sufficient to knock
down the Eiffel Tower.

Doumen stared at the distant lights and at the gigantic
U.S. tanker on the jetty. They were two miles away now, but
he would take to his grave the memory of that night—the
pitch-black water under the ship, Philippe's hand trembling
on his left shoulder as they kicked into the pylons, the knife
on the steel, the tiny spotlight they used for the close electronic work, the lethal det-cord, the wires, the magnetic tug
of the bomb, the way his hands shook as he spliced the det-
cord to Philippe's bomb on pylon number three.

Six hours and twenty-five minutes. They were numbers he would never forget. And now it was almost 2230. Only five and a half hours now, before the true measure of his team's work would be known, before the Sea Island Terminal was blown into a thousand hunks of useless metal.

Would he ever tell his father what he had done? His girlfriend, Annie? One day, his children? Tell them of the night he became, for a couple of hours, one of the world's most prominent *terroristes*?

Of course he never would. The code of the French Special Forces, like all Special Forces, was never broken. And Doumen knew he had to cast that word *terroriste* from his mind, forever. He was Lt. Reme Doumen, loyal French Naval officer, and he had just completed the most important mission entrusted to his country's Navy since . . . well . . . Trafalgar.

Reme Doumen shrugged and glanced across the water to the other Zodiac. He wondered if everyone was thinking the same, looking back at the mighty oil loading terminal, knowing it had fewer than six hours to live. And that they had actually committed, with relentless precision, the oncoming outrage.

Doumen had always been a very tough kid. At one point it was thought he might represent France at rugby football. He was a medium-size center three-quarter, a hard, fast runner in university, and wanted by the Toulouse Club. But the Navy had other uses for his unusual strength, and his father, who had started life working as a deckhand on the La Rochelle ferry, was enormously impressed by the thought of an Admiral for a son. The French Navy beat the French Rugby Football Union comfortably.

But a *terroriste*? *"Mon Dieu!"* muttered Reme, as they came in toward the waiting *Perle*. "I'd better avoid tomorrow's newspapers for the rest of my life!"

Yet he knew he'd get the same old feeling of burgeoning pride in his uniform, and in the fact that the Navy had selected him alone to lead the Special Forces into the staggering assault on the Sea Island Terminal. What's more, he knew he would do it again, if they asked him.

Even as he led his team up the rope ladder to the foredeck, he could feel the sense of urgency in the submarine. The CO himself was out on the casing, and twice Doumen heard Captain Roudy exclaim, *"Vite . . . vite . . . dépêche-toi!"*

Of course, everyone knew the sub was stopped in a dangerous place, in the middle of the central buoyed channel, in probably the narrowest part of the tanker route. On the bridge and on the bow, lookouts with high-powered night-vision binoculars were sweeping the sea, for'ard and aft, for any sign of an onrushing VLCC, its helmsman a hundred feet above them.

The night was cloudy and very dark, and the transfer from the boats was made in excellent time. The two Zodiacs were scuttled, but the *Perle* just beat them in the race to get under the surface, diving to periscope depth, in fifteen fathoms, leaving Alain Roudy to decide whether to risk going deeper.

Right now there was thirty feet below the keel, and the CO decided to stay at PD, but to take down the mast, moving nor'nor'east up the outgoing channel at ten knots. That way nothing would gain on him from behind, and he would gain nothing on any ship up ahead. The ten-knot speed limit, and requirement, was strictly observed along Saudi tanker routes.

It was five hours running time to H hour. Five hours to 0400. Five hours to the temporary end to civilization as they knew it in the free world. The end of cheap oil on the global market.

The crew of the *Perle* was not giving this much thought as they pushed on up the channel. But there was a growing tension down in the missile room, where most of the operators were soon to launch all twelve of their cruises, not at some phantom practice target, as usual, but this time with real warheads packed with TNT and aimed unerringly, with precision and absolute malice.

After eight miles Captain Roudy ordered a course change to the northeast . . . *come right . . . steer course zero-five-zero . . .*

And twelve miles later he elected to leave the tanker lanes completely. With the main channel about to run due east, the CO ordered the helmsman to cross the lanes and exit to the north, making a wide sweep in deeper water for twenty-five miles to the missile launch area he had been allotted: 27.06N 50.54E.

They arrived at 0340, still fifty feet below the surface of the water, unobserved by anyone since first they went deep in the Red Sea south of the Gulf of Suez.

Missile Director . . . Captain . . . final checks, s'il vous plaît.

And for the last time, Lt. Cdr. Albert Paul illuminated the computerized screen that showed the targets and their numbers: Abqaiq Complex—25.56N 49.32E; eastern pipeline—25.56N 49.34E. The third barrage of four missiles would be aimed at 26.31N 50.01E, the Qatif Junction manifold complex, at four slightly different locations, hoping to blast the one area where the pipeline was custom-made, and would take months and months to repair.

Basically, hitting pipelines was not a great idea, nor was hitting oil wells, because both could be capped and repaired with standard equipment, which Aramco had in abundance. The trick was to hit the loading docks, the pumping stations, and, on the Red Sea coast, the refineries.

Captain Roudy's targets had been supremely well selected. The Abqaiq station handled 70 percent of all the nation's oil. It not only pumped from the enormous Ghawar field, over the mountains to the entire Red Sea coast, it also fed the entire east coast. This included the loading docks at Sea Island, Ras al Ju'aymah, and Ras Tannurah, from which Sea Island was fed.

The pipeline out of Abqaiq was plainly critical, and Prince Nasir had selected it as the only pipeline to be targeted. Alain Roudy's final target, the Qatif Junction manifold complex, directed every last gallon of oil on the east coast.

Prepare tubes one to four . . .

Aye, sir.

Ten minutes later, o-three-fifty . . . *prepare to launch . . . tube ONE . . . TIREZ DE FUSIL . . . FIRE!!*

The first of the *Perle's* MBDA Stormcat cruise missiles came ripping out of the torpedo tube, its aft swerving left and right as it found its bearings. It flashed upward through the water, broke the surface with a thunderous roar, and lanced into the night sky, the numbers flashing through its "brain" as it steadied onto course two-four-zero, still climbing, a fiery tail crackling in its wake.

It hit its flying speed of Mach 0.9, two hundred feet above the water, at which point the gas turbines cut in and extinguished the flames in its wake. In the warm air at sea level over the Gulf, Mach 0.9 was the equivalent of more than six hundred miles per hour, which meant that the missile would blast into the Abqaiq complex ten minutes from launch.

Before it had traveled twenty miles, there were three more missiles dead astern. The lead missile crossed the narrow peninsula of Ras Tannurah and swerved over the Saudi coastline at 0357. It rocketed over the coastal highway and changed course, flashing through the dark skies above the desert straight at the Abqaiq complex. With ten miles to go it made its final course change, coming in from the northeast on a line of approach that took it marginally north of the main complex.

At precisely 0400.01 it smashed with stupendous force straight into the middle of Pump Station Number One, buried itself in the main engineering system, and detonated with monstrous force—360 pounds of TNT in a blinding flash of savagery that would have blown an aircraft carrier apart.

No one working anywhere on the station's night shift survived. All of the main machinery was obliterated by the explosion. Anyone standing a couple of miles away might have been staggered by the destruction and fires that began as soon as the oil ignited. But just a short distance from the remnants of the pumps, there was a fire to end all fires as Alain Roudy's second missile slammed into the central area of Abqaiq's petrochemical fractioning towers.

These huge steel cylinders, full of belting hot gases and liquids, were colossally flammable. And they did not just burn. They incinerated into a violet and orange inferno.

Dante would have called the fire department. Heavy fuel oil, gasoline, liquefied petroleum gas, sulphur, and God knows what else blasted into the sky. And the heat was so intense it caused a chain reaction among these refining towers, which exploded one by one in the face of the searing fire.

Everything the towers contained was totally combustible, and years later Abqaiq would still be considered the world's largest industrial calamity, greater even than the Texas City disaster in 1946, when a tanker full of ammonium nitrate blew up an entire south Texas town. Abqaiq now burned from end to end. Alain Roudy's four missiles had all struck home. And he was not finished yet.

The next four smashed into the eastern pipeline on its way to the Qatif Junction manifold complex. Then that too exploded in a fireball. And out to the west the flames could actually be seen in the sky from the obliterated Sea Island Terminal, which seemed to blow itself to pieces at 0403 with about a square mile of oil on fire all around it.

The most spectacular fire was off Ras al Ju'aymah, where Ventura's two high bombs had slammed the upper deck of the terminal a hundred feet into the air, blown to smithereens the valve system for the petroleum gas, and ignited the blowtorch from hell, as forecast six weeks previously by Gaston Savary. The fire was currently roaring across the water, an incinerating white gas flame two feet across at source and 150 feet long.

The actual jetty was in shreds in the water, but the causeway was more or less intact and the liquefied gas pipe was jutting at a ridiculous angle, forty-five degrees to the horizontal, feeding the giant flame with an unending rush of propane that no one could turn off.

Twenty minutes after the explosions had comprehensively destroyed the Saudi Arabian oil industry on the east coast, no one had yet connected them together. There was no one alive who had been working near any of the explosion sites. The administration blocks at Abqaiq and Qatif were flattened, and anyone who was awake even remotely close to the fires could only stand in awe of the gargantuan flames exploding into the sky every few minutes. Abqaiq was of course right in the middle of nowhere.

Indeed the first alarm was raised in the distant city of Yanbu al Bahr, where the loading jetties had been blown sky high by Garth Dupont's bombs. But those jetties were close to the shore, and the explosion scarcely harmed any of the main parts of the town. The missiles fired by Commander Dreyfus had just hit the refinery, which stood a couple of miles beyond the Yanbu perimeters. And this meant that the Police Chief and several duty officers in Aramco's high-security forces were definitely aware that something big had just blown up.

The Yanbu police phoned Rabigh, which was in much the same condition as they were—big flames, constant explosions from the burning refineries, jetties gone. In turn they both phoned Jiddah, which had, in the last few minutes, lost its own refinery, courtesy of another well-aimed cruise by Commander Dreyfus.

Everyone called the security headquarters in Riyadh, where they had now heard from the town of Ras al Ju'aymah that the LPG jetties four miles offshore had just blown up and taken a 200,000-ton tanker with them. It was not, however, until after 5 A.M. that Riyadh learned of the full catastrophe in Abqaiq, which quite literally ended all activity in the oil industry west of the Aramah Mountains, and most of the activity on the east coast.

Nearly all of the great loading jetties in the country were smashed beyond repair, the pumping system was history, and the Qatif manifold would take at least a year to repair. The Saudis had always known their oil industry was vulnerable, but this was too much to comprehend.

They had a lot of security in all of the complexes, and yet some kind of a marauding force appeared to have breached every last line of defense, and laid waste to the golden goose that had turned this arid desert kingdom into a modern-day nirvana for one of the richest ruling families on earth. All 35,000 of them.

If the goose was still laying, anywhere out in the desert, she was laying fried eggs. Many of the oil fires would not be extinguished for a week.

And in separate oceans, a thousand miles apart, two undetected submarines of the French Navy were making their way quietly home. Indeed, on board the *Perle,* running silently toward the Strait of Hormuz, a hundred feet below the surface, Big Jules Ventura, destroyer of the LPG terminal, had just bid an extremely modest two-no-trumps.

Monday, March 22, 8:00 A.M.
Western Suburbs, Riyadh

Prince Nasir heard the news before most people, mainly because he had observers placed in all the selected sites, each of them under instructions to call him immediately anything happened. This made him an extremely busy prince between 0400 and 0420.

And now he sat in his study with Colonel Jacques Gamoudi, sipping coffee and watching the Arab-language television stations to see how the disastrous news was playing out. Most commentators had put together a conspiracy theory that the oil industry had indeed been destroyed by persons unknown.

Of course al-Qaeda was an immediate suspect, but al-Qaeda was a shadowy organization without a titular head, without a headquarters, without known leadership. It was a seething internal mob, angry, determined, stateless, and malevolent to the rulers of the kingdom. And since it was funded as an organization mostly by Saudi Arabia, or at least Saudi Arabians, it was difficult to see why on earth al-Qaeda should have wanted to cut off the hand that fed it. Certainly the activities of the assault forces of the night had in half an hour brought the Saudi economy to its knees. The question was, who were the assault forces of the night? And why had they committed this apparently motiveless act of flagrant criminal aggression? Not to mention, what military genius had masterminded the assaults so brilliantly that they had treated the security forces as if they did not exist?

Prince Nasir and Colonel Gamoudi cheerfully watched the tortuous writhing of the commentators trying to find answers to questions that seemed unanswerable. Prince Nasir considered it a brilliant night's work. And already, on television, there were constant calls to the King to speak to his people, to give them assurances, to point the way forward, to rally the Saudi nation. But right now the King was in shock. As were his principal ministers, and his Generals.

And on some of the English-language channels, political journalists were forecasting the end of the rule of the al-Sauds. Indeed they were forecasting the end of the Saudi economy, the total collapse of the currency, and the complete inability of the government to finance anything, now that the oil had apparently stopped flowing.

There was no word from the King, which may have been shortsighted on his part, since the nation was in the process of going bust. In fact there was no official word from anyone, until 1 P.M., when the Channel 2 newscaster handed over to a spokesman for the Government, who spoke rather angrily, informing the populace that there had been an attack on the oil fields and loading docks. But he said no details were available. Channel 3, run by Aramco, was understandably circumspect, revealing very little.

By far the best source of information was from the English-language stations in Bahrain and Qatar, which spent the morning interviewing anyone they could contact from Aramco. Slowly they pieced together the shocking truth that someone had launched a spectacular assault on the Saudi oil industry, coordinating stupendous bomb attacks, all apparently to explode within ten minutes of each other.

These stations were in constant communication with the London media, and by 11 A.M. they had camera crews heading by helicopter to the fires still raging on Sea Island and, to the north, the LPG terminal blowtorch. By 1 P.M. there were pictures of various Saudi oil infernos on their way around the world.

At 2 P.M. the first riots began in the capital city of Riyadh.

Same Day, 5:00 A.M. (LOCAL)
Washington, D.C.

Lt. Cdr. Jimmy Ramshawe was very soundly asleep in his parents' luxurious apartment in the Watergate complex, which he used as his home base. He and his fiancée, Jane Peacock, had been out late with friends and he had dropped her off at the Australian embassy at 2 A.M.

He was due in his office at the National Security Agency at 7 A.M., which did not leave much time for the amount of sleep he most definitely required. In Ramshawe's opinion, midday would have been a better start time.

And when the phone rang at 5:01 A.M. he nearly jumped out of his pajamas. He jolted himself awake, instantly, like all naval officers, accustomed to the lunatic hours of the watch, and muttered, "Jesus, this better be bloody critical."

The duty officer at the NSA chuckled and said, "Morning, Lieutenant Commander. There's something come up I think you ought to know about right away."

"Shoot," said Ramshawe, copying the standard greeting of his great hero, the now retired Adm. Arnold Morgan.

"Sir, it appears that someone just blew up the entire Saudi Arabian oil industry."

"They WHAT?" gasped Ramshawe, struggling to clear his head.

"Sir, I expect you'll want to come in right away. I suggest you turn on the television right now and take a look at CNN. They seem to be on the case pretty sharply."

"Okay, Lieutenant. I'm on my way. Try to contact Admiral Morris, will you? I know he's on the West Coast, but he'll want to know."

"Right, sir. And by the way, it's the biggest goddamn fire I've ever seen."

Ramshawe hit the power button. The television was already on CNN, and on the screen he could see the blow-torch from hell, blasting into the sky above the top masts of an enormous tanker that was sunk amid the shattered remnants of a loading jetty.

"Jesus Christ," said Ramshawe.

But then the picture changed to an area where the sea was on fire. Then it changed again, to the huge Red Sea refineries, all of them ablaze, still exploding, and showing no signs, yet, of dying down. The biggest fires of all, at the Abqaiq complex, apparently had not been photographed so far.

Jimmy Ramshawe sat up in bed in total astonishment, thoughts cascading through his mind, as he tried to pay attention to what the CNN commentator was saying. So far as he could tell, bombs had gone off in almost all of the principal operational areas of the largest business on earth. Whoever had done it, had coordinated a truly sensational attack. The guy on CNN was surmising that everything had exploded shortly after 4 A.M. Saudi time. And so far as anyone could tell, it was an internal matter, a "purely Arab thing."

Jimmy Ramshawe knew of course, like everyone else, of the growing unrest in the kingdom, as currency reserves plummeted and each citizen's share of the wealth beneath the desert floor dwindled by the year. He'd often been told by CIA guys that the Saudis were about two jumps from having the mob at the gates.

He turned the television up full volume and tried to listen while he took a quick shower. And the only copper-bottomed truth to emerge, at least in the terms required by a high-ranking intelligence officer, was that no one had the slightest idea who was responsible, nor why they had done it, and certainly not how they had done it.

The CNN commentator was concentrating on the consequences rather than the causes: the minor consideration of what happened now, when someone had knocked 25 percent of the world's oil supply off the global market.

Ramshawe was not, at this stage, interested in the market. That, he thought, would ultimately come under the heading of "inevitable." What exercised him was, who had done this and why?

He dressed rapidly, grabbed his briefcase, switched off the television, and headed for the underground car garage. When he reached the basement he made for the only item on this earth he actually loved as much as he loved Jane Peacock.

And there it was, the gleaming thirteen-year-old black Jaguar his parents had given him for his twenty-first birthday. It had been four years old then, with only 12,000 miles on the clock, having been previously owned by some elderly diplomat friend of his dad's. Today it still showed only 42,000 on the clock, since Ramshawe took it out of Washington only two or three times a year.

He and Jane usually traveled in her car, a small, unpretentious, but brand-new Dodge Neon, which did thirty-eight miles to the gallon as opposed to the sixteen he got out of the Jaguar. He used the Jaguar mostly for work, gunning it along the highway from the Watergate complex out to Fort Meade every day. He loved the stubby stick shift and the surge of power of the engine, the way it hugged the corners.

And this morning he really put it through a hard training run. On near-deserted, dry roads and a mission of national importance. Jimmy hit ninety miles per hour on the highway and came barreling down the road to the main gates of the NSA like a rally driver, pulling up at the guardhouse with a squeal of well-maintained brakes.

The guard waved him through briskly, smiling cheerfully at the Aussie security officer, who drove like Michael Schumacher and sat at the right hand of the NSA Director himself, the veteran Adm. George Morris.

Jimmy drove straight to the main entrance of the OPS-2B building, with its massive one-way glass walls. Behind these, up on the eighth floor, was the world headquarters of the Admiral. Jimmy took advantage of a privilege he had, but rarely used, and hopped straight out of the Jag and signaled one of the guards to park it.

"Thanks, soldier," he called cheerfully.

"No trouble, Lieutenant Commander. Gotta put those oil fires out, right?"

Ramshawe grinned. It was unbelievable how news, rumor, and distortion whipped around this place. Here, behind the razor wire, guarded by seven hundred cops and a dozen SWAT teams, the 39,000 staff members knew approximately a hundred times more than anyone in America about what precisely was going on in the world. Jimmy Ramshawe had long suspected each one of the 39,000 personnel briefed at least one person every ten minutes. The Fort Meade grapevine had long vines.

He reached the eighth floor, hurried into his office, and turned on the news. It was 0650, ten minutes before 3 P.M. in Saudi Arabia, and the fires were still raging. The news channel had essentially dealt with the blown loading docks in the big tanker ports and was now starting to concentrate on the inferno at Abqaiq.

No one had yet shone a spotlight on the critical importance of the smashed Pump Station Number One, but CNN had received pictures of the gigantic fire in the middle of the desert, as the gasoline, crude oil, and petrochemical refining towers and storage area continued to blast themselves into the stratosphere. No one, beyond biblical times, had ever seen anything like this before.

The commentator was still concentrating on the possible perpetrators and announcing (guessing) that al-Qaeda was somewhere in the background. But, of course, you couldn't call up al-Qaeda and check with their press office. And there were numerous other groups of Islamic fundamentalists who might, possibly, have favored the destruction, then the rebuilding, of the world's richest oil nation.

Indeed Prince Nasir himself, the fifty-year-old Crown Prince, had recently expressed such alarm over the situation in Riyadh that he had granted an interview to the London *Financial Times*. And in this, he had alluded to the possibility that someone, somewhere, might actually consider the destruction of the Saudi oil industry a cheap price to pay for the removal of the profligate ruling family, and a cheap price to pay for the removal of the status quo.

He had made further allusion to the fact that whatever else, it had nothing to do with him. But his heart was bleeding for the future of his ancient land. Very definitely. And, as a loyal courtier and a man sympathetic to the plight of his fellow citizens, it pained him to mention these unpleasant truths.

Right now, along with all the world's media, CNN had not the slightest clue about what was going on. And as their reporters took flying leaps from one conclusion to the next, Lt. Cdr. Jimmy Ramshawe, who was, after all, paid to think not show off his knowledge on the television screen, switched on his big industrial-size computer and delved into his "Hold" file, the one that contained all the little unsolved puzzles that had intrigued him over the past couple of years.

He had no idea what he was looking for. So he just keyed in the word *oil* to see if there was anything significant. And out popped the memorandum he had written himself last November—the one about France buying oil futures and driving up the world price on the London Exchange, and indeed in New York.

The activities of France had more or less ceased during December, but nevertheless, Ramshawe had made notes from the observations of his two sources, both of whom had a well-gripped handle on world prices, and both of whom had expressed bewilderment as to why France was so anxious suddenly to acquire new and different oil supplies.

He located a website that elaborated on the Gallic energy anxiety but found little of interest there, save that France imported 1.8 million barrels of oil a day, mostly from Saudi Arabia. And by the look of the morning news, that was about to dry up in the foreseeable future.

"I wonder," mused Ramshawe, "if everyone in the industrial world is about to have bloody kittens over this, with one exception . . ." He was thinking of course about the country that had already made other arrangements, and no longer cared whether Saudi Arabia had oil or not. *Could the French have known what no one else knew?*

Lt. Commander Ramshawe logged that as a possibility,

but dismissed it on practical grounds as a bit too fanciful. *It's sure as hell too wild a theory to start ringing alarm bells. But it might be the only theory around . . . guess we'll find out.*

At 0800 he ordered some coffee and a couple of English muffins. He decided not to call Admiral Morris at 0500 on the West Coast, and elected instead to contact his pal Roger Smythson at the International Petroleum Exchange, in London.

Smythson answered his own phone from his office inside the Exchange, and with admirable British restraint, he told Ramshawe that so far as he could tell, the roof had just fallen in.

"Chaos, old boy," he said. "Absolute bloody chaos."

"You mean the buyers are driving the prices up?" said Ramshawe.

"Are you kidding?" replied Smythson. "By the time this place opened, every single person involved in the buying and selling of oil on the international market knew the Saudis were essentially out of the game.

"I mean, Christ, Jimmy! Have you seen the pictures? The loading docks are on fire, the terminals have been blown up, and the main pump station at Abqaiq has been destroyed. Even the manifold complex at Qatif Junction is smashed beyond repair. I'm telling you, whoever did this really knew what they were about."

"You mean an inside job, perpetrated by Saudis on the entire nation?"

"Well, that's the way it looks. And you can guess what the panic's like here. Because, to people working under this roof, the words *Abqaiq complex* and *pumping station,* the *Qatif Junction manifold, Sea Island, Yanbu, Rabigh,* and *Jiddah*—they're everyday currency to oil men. We know how important they are. We know if there's a problem with any one of them, the world's oil supply is in trouble. But Jesus! They're all destroyed, and the price of Saudi sweet crude just went to eighty-five dollars a barrel, from forty-six dollars last night."

"Has it stabilized?" asked Ramshawe.

"Let me check on the screen. No. It's eighty-six dollars."

"What's going to happen?"

"None of us knows that until the Saudis make some kind of a statement. So far, they have not said a thing."

"What about the King?"

"Not a squeak out of him. And nothing from the Saudi ambassador to Great Britain. No one knows what's happening, and that makes the market so much worse."

"Well, there's not much we can tell you either," said Ramshawe. "We were waiting for word from our embassy in Riyadh. But nothing's come through yet."

"Hey, there is just one thing," recalled Smythson. "You remember the last time we spoke—about the French buying up futures?"

"Sure I do."

"Well, I kept an eye on that. And it was France, definitely. And they bought nothing from Saudi Arabia. But they went in strongly on Abu Dhabi oil, and Bahrain. They bought some from Qatar, and a lot from the Baku field in Kazakhstan, which is more expensive.

"You can't help thinking, can you? Because that makes France the only player in the world market that does not care about this crisis. So far as we can tell, they scooped up around 600 million barrels over the next year or so, despite their longtime contracts with Aramco."

Jimmy Ramshawe hung up thoughtfully.

Monday, March 22, 3:00 P.M.
Riyadh

The first riots after the collapse of the oil industry began in the Diplomatic Quarter of the city. A crowd of possibly four hundred to five hundred advanced on the U.S. embassy compound and began to hurl rocks at the walls. It was not yet clear why the Americans were being blamed for the potential collapse of the Saudi economy.

U.S. Marine guards retreated and then spoke to the crowd, yelling through bullhorns for them to retreat or face a volley of gunfire. Saudi's religious police were called, but ran into a hail of rocks and missiles from the crowd. The police commanders, accustomed to cooperating with the U.S., requested the Marines drive back the crowd with gunfire, but only over the heads of the raging populace.

The first volley had its effect. Most of the crowd turned and ran for their lives, but they reformed and gathered in front of the British embassy, shouting and chanting, "*INFIDELS OUT . . . OUT! OUT! OUT!*"

By now the Saudi rioters had acquired a few guns for themselves, which they began firing into the air, and finally threw a hand grenade into the embassy grounds. No one was hurt, but the local guards answered with real gunfire, and four Arabs fell wounded in the street.

The religious police had now summoned the National Guard in force. This was the historically loyal army, dedicated to serving and protecting the King and his family. It operated entirely separately from the regular Saudi land forces, and it accompanied the monarch wherever he went.

In Riyadh, the National Guard's elite force was the Royal Guard Regiment, which once was autonomous, until it was incorporated into the Army in 1964. Nonetheless, it remained directly subordinate to the King and maintained its own communications network and a simple brief: to protect the King, loyally and at all times.

It was this small but well-trained force that arrived in central Riyadh with the religious police on that Monday evening. Armed with light weapons and armored vehicles, they advanced on the crowd and drove them back.

But now the rioting populace regrouped at the major downtown junction on Al Mather Street and began marching into the main commercial district. This was a fiery dragon unsure at what it should roar.

Ever since the early morning the dragon had been listening only to radio and television networks talking about the "national bankruptcy" of a nation with no resources for many years. The terror of abject poverty, the first they had ever known, had gripped every resident of Riyadh. And then, shortly after 3 P.M., a rumor swept through the city that the banks were closing, and may not open again that week.

The British Saudi Bank on the wide throughway of King Faisal Street was one of the biggest buildings in the city, and with its doors slammed shut, it was suddenly targeted by the mob. The rioters now rampaged into the street outside the bank, stopping traffic, firing guns, and surging toward the main entrance.

The Saudi police were not up to this. Because there were a thousand people ready to storm the bank. The police used their mobile phones to contact the guardroom at the royal palace of the King, requesting extra reinforcements from the Royal Guard Regiment.

But none came, and at 4:45, four young Saudi warriors drove a huge garbage truck straight through the main doors of the bank, setting off burglar alarms and smoke alarms, and ramming the vaults located behind a steel portcullis. The trauma to the bank's security system also activated a complete shutdown of the counter areas, with steel grills and ironclad door-locking systems turning on.

Inside the bank the crowd went wild, shooting their old-fashioned rifles and, regardless of their own safety, hurling grenades that had materialized from somewhere, probably from members of the military who a few days hence would fight for Prince Nasir.

From there the crowd turned its attention on automobiles parked in the street, heaving them over onto their roofs and then setting them on fire. By 6 P.M. the entire situation was turning very ugly, mainly because the mob had no real target upon which to vent their fury. All they knew was, someone had wrecked the only asset the kingdom had, and the King appeared to be powerless, had never even spoke to his people—almost as if the royal family had decided to batten down the hatches and wait until the crisis was over.

As night fell, a terrible rampage of looting began. Armed with sledgehammers and axes, the people stormed into some of the most expensive shops in the city, battering down the doors, oblivious to burglar alarms. They stole everything they could, then torched the shops. As darkness fell, Saudi Arabia's capital was literally falling apart.

It was not until 9 P.M. when the National Guard began to

get some control. Of course many of the crowd had drifted away, holding their loot, some of it extremely valuable, grabbed from the tourist shops. The police and small details of Guardsmen began making arrests, but they were principally concerned with protecting the big downtown hotels, which were now bolted and barred like fortresses, with all guests on the inside.

The Al Bathaa, Safari, and Asia Hotels looked like war zones, with armed sentries patrolling outside. And in the middle of all this, Col. Jacques Gamoudi, in company with three al-Qaeda bodyguards, all former officers in the Saudi Army, toured the city in a jeep, watching carefully, making notes, and observing the unfolding chaos.

Every half hour his cell phone would ring, and one of the five French Secret Service agents who were planted in the city purely to assist him with information would call to update him on the fluctuating situation. The Colonel was probably the best-informed person in Riyadh among either the loyalists or the rebels.

In the opinion of Colonel Gamoudi, this was progressing entirely too quickly. Prince Nasir had warned him many times that his people would take to the streets just as soon as they realized that every part of their lives was threatened; that in the immediate future, the rulers of Saudi Arabia would have no money to distribute to the population.

And of course the people most desperately affected by this unfortunate turn of events were the royal princes, thousands of them, people like the late Prince Khalid bin Mohammed al-Saud.

Over the years, as the outcry against the King's family's spending grew louder, the princes had found all kinds of novel ways to supplement their incomes—many of them taking kickbacks from big construction firms like bin Laden, which had been making colossal profits from government projects. This was plainly about to stop, and so were the kickbacks.

Other enterprising princes would use all of their influence to buy any profitable business, particularly restaurants. They would just walk in and announce that they were buying the place, offer a ludicrously low price, and move in. The proprietor knew that there was no choice if he wanted to remain a free man.

In addition to all of this, some diabolically corrupt moves had been made by princes who served inside the government, particularly in the area of property development in the biggest cities.

But, of course, the favorite way was just to keep borrowing from the bank and never paying the money back. Everyone in business in Saudi Arabia was in fear of the wrath of the ruler and his family advisers, because the King was all-powerful. He had all the money. And the armed forces were sworn to protect him. But now the banks were closed, and their future in the country was obviously questionable.

The King himself was the principal wheel in the economy, but the other critical aspect of the financial health of Saudi Arabia was of course the daily spending of the people. The Saudi population of possibly nine million—no one had an accurate figure—spent its annual per capita stipend of approximately $7,000 on consumer products. And that $63 billion kept the wheels of commerce moving in this overblown welfare state, with its free everything, health, education, interest-free loans for buying homes, unbelievably cheap, below-cost interior services like electricity, telephones, water, domestic air travel, and of course gasoline. And right now no one knew what was going to happen.

There was an instant run on the currency, as merchants, businessmen, and other shrewd operators attempted to withdraw their funds. Currency holdings fell dramatically in just a few hours. And by 3 P.M. the Saudi American Bank was forced to join the Saudi British Bank in closing its doors, not just in Riyadh but also in Jiddah and Taif.

And all of this meant that more and more princes were on the move. By the end of that Monday afternoon the first of the private jets were leaving King Khalid Airport. Various members of the royal family who worked in government and in the armed services took only a short time to realize the extent of the financial crisis that loomed.

Throughout that morning and into the early part of the

afternoon, vast sums of money were being wire-transferred to French, Swiss, and American banks. Entire families were preparing to leave, many of them driving toward the northwest borders, which led into Jordan and Syria.

And the real trouble had not even begun.

Colonel Gamoudi continued his tour of the city, sensing with every turn of the wheel the turmoil among the population. In his opinion, this situation could explode. There were alarm bells ringing not just in the shattered portals of the big banks but also in the mind of Jacques Gamoudi.

He could see two main threats to the operational plans of Prince Nasir: (1) the mob was about to burn down the entire city; and (2) if things did not improve rapidly the King would consider calling in the Army from the military cities to restore order. The Army was still loyal to the royal family. That would put Gamoudi's own operation completely out of the question. However many rebels, anarchists, and al-Qaeda fighters he had, his dozen or so tanks and brigade-strength armored vehicles would be no match for the entire Saudi Army and Air Force.

Jacques Gamoudi could not wait until Thursday or Friday to launch his attack. This was all happening far, far sooner than anyone had previously thought.

He ordered his driver back to the Dir'aiyah base and, once there, called a staff meeting for 2200. Meanwhile, he took his cell phone out beyond the ruins and into the desert. He walked for ten minutes, fast, along an ancient camel route. And when he was quite satisfied that there was not a sound coming from anywhere, he punched in the numbers to a private line in the heart of the Commandement des Opérations Speciales (COS) complex in Taverny, north of Paris.

He used the veiled speech they had agreed upon for an emergency: "I wish to speak to the curator, *s'il vous plaît.*"

"The curator speaking."

"This party has started early and it's getting out of control. I think we should get moving at least a day early, maybe two days early. Can I have your agreement to proceed as I think fit?"

"Affirmative. I'll leave our friends in the south to you."

At which point the twenty-second conversation ended abruptly. Gen. Michel Jobert replaced his receiver. And Jacques Gamoudi pushed the button to end the conversation and walked slowly back to the garrison in the desert ruins.

The phone call had been critical, vital to the operation, and tactically sound—it would govern the entire French-Saudi alliance for the next forty-eight hours.

But it was a mistake, as Jacques Gamoudi knew it could be when he took the risk.

Same Day, Same Time
Joint Services Signals Unit
Island of Cyprus

This was a very secret place. It was the United Kingdom's listening post in Cyprus (JSSU), located at a place called Ayios Nikolaos, up in the hills north of the military base in the UK sovereign territory of Dhekelia, southeast Cyprus.

Here at the crossroads of east and west, British Intelligence operated a hub from which they intercepted satellite messages, phone calls, and transmissions emanating from all over the Middle East. To the north lay Turkey; to the east Syria, Israel, and Iraq; to the southeast Jordan and Saudi Arabia; to the south Egypt.

JSSU was manned by the cream of British electronic interceptors from all three services, the majority from the Army. They maintained a constant watch, monitoring communications around the clock, every one of their operators a highly qualified linguist trained purely to make literal translations of intercepted messages and conversations as they were transmitted.

The satellite communications intercept ran the gamut—faxes, e-mails, coded messages in 100 languages—the majority of the data being recorded on a long-running tape for later analysis. Particularly interesting conversations, however, were written down by the listening operator as they were spoken, and then immediately translated.

The electronic outpost in southeastern Cyprus was regarded as a priceless asset by British Intelligence, and in turn by the National Security Agency in Fort Meade. Because JSSU was part of the fabled British Intelligence operation in Cheltenham, Gloucestershire, GCHQ (Government Communications Headquarters). If Cyprus was the jewel in the crown of GCHQ, in turn GCHQ was the jewel in the crown of Britain's espionage industry, which cost $1.5 billion a year to run.

It was from Cyprus that terrorists' combat communications were first breached, from tiny Nikolaos where they hacked into bin Laden and his henchmen in faraway Afghanistan. The U.S. National Security Agency willingly pooled all of its intelligence with Cheltenham, where the 4,000-strong workforce operated in blast-proof offices under an armor-plated roof. It was a huge new building, absolutely circular, with a round center courtyard. They called it the Doughnut.

That particular Monday had obviously been a pandemonic day, with the Saudi oil fields destroyed and a zillion cell phone calls being made all across the Middle East. In fact, it was probably the busiest day in the Cyprus listening post since the Egyptian Second Army rampaged across Israel's Bar-Lev line in 1973. Only now, as the evening abated and the riots died down and businesses and banks closed, did satellite communications begin to slow up. Cpl. Shane Collins, a twenty-eight-year-old signals expert from one of the British Army's tank regiments, was at his screen in the Nikolaos ops room checking the traffic, which was, naturally, mostly in Arabic. He was just having his first cup of coffee of the evening when he heard a message that absolutely caught his attention. He wrote down nothing, but listened carefully, knowing it was being automatically recorded on that specific frequency.

The voice was French. Very French. *Le Conservateur? La fête? En avance?* Corporal Collins pressed his Listen Again button and carefully wrote down the full transcript, noting the brevity, the lack of any personal greeting, or even recognition.

He knew some French but not sufficient to be sure. He punched the brief sentences into his computer and transmitted them to the translation section on the next floor. Within five minutes it was back:

This party has started early, and it's getting out of control. I think we should get going at least a day early, maybe two days early. Can I have your agreement to proceed as I think fit?

Affirmative. I'll leave our friends in the south to you.

It was all in French. Both ends. And while Corporal Collins could not activate a trace to establish where the phone call had emanated, he immediately called over his duty Captain and reported that he had had a conversation on the satellite that was plainly more than just a personal call.

The Captain agreed that the call was unusual. And he lost no time in passing the text straight back to GCHQ in Cheltenham for detailed analysis. It was 2130 in Riyadh, 2030 in Cyprus, and 1830 in Gloucestershire, England.

The Middle Eastern Desk, deep inside the Doughnut, put an immediate trace on the satellite, searching for the start point of the call. They established a line on the frequency, which stretched back from Cyprus, across the Lebanon coast, south of Damascus, through Jordan, and straight through Saudi Arabia, bisecting Riyadh and the central desert, and ending somewhere down in the Rhub al Khali, the Empty Quarter.

Somewhere along that line, a Frenchman had activated his cell phone to . . . someone. GCHQ then put out a tracer to other listening posts to try to locate a different "line" that would bisect their own, revealing the location of the French caller. No one was surprised when another listening post in northeast Africa came up with one. The lines bisected each other around twenty miles north of Riyadh.

The Cheltenham analysts asked their computerized system to make several trillion calculations in five minutes, and quickly established that this was not a code but, rather, veiled speech. "The curator" was and would remain unknown, but the experts were certain this had military overtones.

Corporal Collins had sensed it. The analysts inside the Doughnut agreed with him. No greeting, no good-bye. This was a signal, not a conversation. One piece of information—the party started early and might get out of control. One question—can we go early? One answer—yes.

But, go where? What party? Did this refer somehow to the uproar currently going on in Riyadh? If so, who wanted to get involved? Had the JSSU tapped into al-Qaeda's command headquarters?

The British Intelligence officers had been wrestling with this problem all day. Why al-Qaeda, an organization that had received sums of up to $500 million from Saudi sources in the past fifteen years? Al-Qaeda, which was comprised of Saudis, who made up the vast majority of the 9/11 hit men and were believed to be almost the entire terrorist population of Guantánamo Bay, the U.S. Naval base in Cuba. Why on earth would al-Qaeda wish to cripple the economy that fed them?

Well, if not al-Qaeda, then who? The analysts at GCHQ were baffled about motive and culprit, but they were not baffled by the innate importance of Corporal Collins's signal. And at 2200 they relayed it on to the National Security Agency in Fort Meade. It was 1700 in Washington.

The NSA ops room had been buzzing all day with a perfectly astounding lack of information about the Saudi oil crisis. No one had given serious importance to the theory of outside involvement. It still seemed a completely internal Arab matter. Someone, for whatever reason, had apparently planted a succession of bombs from one end of the Arabian Peninsula to the other, and simultaneously blown up the entire shebang.

If there was malice, it was directed principally toward the King and the ruling members of the royal family. No one, from the highest echelons of America's espionage organizations to the top brass at the Pentagon, had come up with one feasible idea as to why a foreign power should want to perpetrate such an action.

The most available oil in the world was Saudi, and to most countries it would be unthinkable to be without it. Saudi Arabia, for instance, provided twenty percent of the daily requirement for the United States. Without it, France's mighty traffic network would grind to a complete halt.

And yet . . . Lt. Cdr. Jimmy Ramshawe had an uneasy feeling. Nothing about this astounding attack sat correctly with him. He had spent much of the day pulling up data on the Saudi oil defenses, and there were a lot of them. Every one of those giant structures—the pump stations, the loading terminals, the refineries, the offshore jetties at Sea Island, and the LPG docks off Ras al Ju'aymah—were surrounded by heavily armed guards.

According to the Middle East Desks at the FBI and the CIA, you could not get anywhere near those places, certainly not by land. You simply could not reach them, not carrying the kind of explosives that would blast them to smithereens. It was downright impossible. However, it could perhaps have been done by sea, with frogmen coming in and planting explosive under the docks.

At least, the U.S. Navy SEALs could probably have done it, or the Royal Navy. Maybe Russia, not China, but possibly France. Certainly not Saudi Arabia, a country that did not even own a submarine and certainly possessed no underwater Special Forces capability.

No. Lt. Cdr. Jimmy Ramshawe could not figure it out. And, anyway, even if the Saudi Navy had suddenly risen up as traitors against the King, that did not explain how someone else had managed to hit the Abqaiq eastern pipeline amidships, then blow up the manifold at Qatif Junction, flatten Pump Station Number One, and set fire to the biggest oil processing complex in the Middle East—the one at Abqaiq, which was situated bang in the middle of nowhere and operated behind a steel cordon of armed guards.

If this was indeed a purely Saudi matter, he, Jimmy Ramshawe, considered it must have been the biggest inside job ever pulled. And there was no motive. Not even a suggestion of one. If the action was Saudi, it was committed by a bunch of fundamentalist Muslims trying to commit financial suicide.

And the Saudis, he knew, were not regarded as stupid. He scanned back on his computer screen and checked the strength of the Saudi National Guard, the independent force whose special brief was to guard those oil installations in the Eastern Province.

The Saudis were revealing no accurate numbers, but there were thousands of troops, deployed by their commanders along some 12,500 miles of pipeline, which reached fifty oil fields and several refineries and terminals.

The force worked in close cooperation with Aramco, with its strong American connections, financially, technologically, and militarily. These people, Ramshawe mused, cannot be taken lightly.

A bunch of hit men creeping past battalions of guards, laser beams, patrols, probably bloody attack dogs . . . then fixing bombs all over the place! Get outta here. That's just bloody ridiculous . . . especially since dozens of bombs, from one end of the bloody country to the other, went off bang within a few minutes of each other.

The Saudi National Guard was just too strong for that. The brass at Aramco would not have let that happen. *Jesus! These guys have bloody tanks, artillery, rockets, plus a bloody Air Force, fighter-bombers, gunships, and Christ knows what else! I don't buy it. And I'm not going to start buying it any time soon.*

The clincher, so far as Ramshawe was concerned, was simple: the sheer number of targets hit. *You're trying to tell me, of all the guards in all of those priceless oil installations, not one of them saw anything . . . not a single warning, not a single mistake, not a single alarm. Nothing. A bunch of blokes dressed in sheets flattened and burned 25 percent of the world's oil, and NO ONE suspected anything! Get out. This was military. Not terrorism.*

The clock ticked past 1730, and a duty officer from the international division tapped on Ramshawe's door and delivered copies of the very few coded signals from GCHQ in

Cheltenham, anything that might be worth his time. These were delivered twice a day, in hard copy at his request. Admiral Morris used computers, but looking at screens was not Ramshawe's first choice. He liked the signals "in black and white, right where I can see 'em."

Ramshawe looked at the top sheet. He knew the satellite intercepts were arranged in descending order of importance by the NSA staff. And at first sight, he could not see anything wildly exciting about this early party someone was planning to attend.

But then he looked at the notes from the British case officer, which pointed out the brevity of the message and the fact that it had all the hallmarks of the military. And that grabbed his attention. Then he saw that the signal had been sent on a cell phone situated nineteen miles north of Riyadh, and that really tweaked his interest.

On a day like this, *anything* that said "Riyadh" was interesting. But what made his hair stand on end was the final paragraph, which displayed the conversation as it was spoken—in French.

Lt. Cdr. Jimmy Ramshawe instantly put two and two together and made about 723. "There's something going on," he told the empty room. "There's something bloody going on. And who's this bloody curator? And who's this French bastard poncing about in the desert, sending military signals?"

Jimmy had read enough signals from all over the world to know military when he saw it. There was the recipient of the call, the curator! *No one just asks for the bloody curator. That's a pseudonym. And the question—your permission to proceed?—that's military. No one on earth talks like that except Army, Navy, Air Force. And the reply! Jesus! AFFIRMATIVE! He might as well have signed it General de Gaulle. It's all military. These clever bastards at GCHQ have hit something here. I'm right bloody sure of that.*

The problem was, Lt. Commander Ramshawe was not sure whom to talk to. Admiral Morris was in the Navy yards in San Diego, probably out on a carrier, definitely not wanting to be interrupted, especially not by a wild, if well considered, speculation.

The Lt. Commander pondered the situation for a half hour. Then he decided that there was only one person he would like to wrestle with the problem, and he was retired. But this was right up the Admiral's street. Jimmy Ramshawe picked up the telephone and dialed the private number of the old Lion of the West Wing, Adm. Arnold Morgan himself.

"Morgan. Speak."

"Hello, sir. Jimmy Ramshawe here. Have you got a couple of minutes?"

"Well, we're going out soon, so make it quick."

Jimmy's mind jumped two notches. He would either deliver a slam-dunk sentence to seize the Admiral's attention, right now, or risk a slow-burn introduction, during which the irascible former presidential Security Adviser might get bored and tell him to leave it for another time. Jimmy knew that the Admiral's boredom threshold was extremely low. Seriously bored, Arnold Morgan would sit there contemplating the possibility of ending his own life.

Jimmy went for the slam dunk. "Sir, I believe it is entirely possible that the Republic of France, for reasons best known to themselves, have just blown up the oil fields of Saudi Arabia."

The Admiral chuckled and went into military mode. "Degree of certainty, Lt. Commander?"

"About one percent," replied Jimmy, laughing.

"Oh, then we should probably nuke 'em, right, Jimmy? This week or next?"

It was a funny relationship. The young Lt. Commander had worked with the Admiral on several occasions, and indeed Arnold Morgan knew both Ramshawe's father and his fiancée Jane Peacock's father, the Australian ambassador to Washington, really well.

Ramshawe and Morgan shared a kind of wry sense of irony. But for several years now, the ex–National Security Adviser had understood that when the studious young Aussie came on with a theory, it was almost certainly worth listening to.

sured Ramshawe that her husband did not have the slightest idea what she was going to order.

"Righto, sir," he said, grinning.

"And for Christ's sake stop calling me sir," said the Admiral. "I'm a retired private citizen who was in the Navy a long time ago. I've known your father for years, and your future father-in-law even longer. I think it's time for you to call me 'Arnie,' like everyone else."

"Yessir," said Ramshawe, which caused Kathy to giggle, as she always did, sometimes secretly, when anyone had the temerity to defy the great Arnold Morgan.

"Sorry, Arnie," Ramshawe added. "But here I go: As you know, we heard last November that one of the European nations was suddenly, and for no reason, buying up a whole slew of oil futures on the world market. We were told it might very well be France, and over the past couple of months it has apparently emerged as definitely France.

"I found out today that the French purchased more than six hundred million barrels for delivery over the next year. Some from Abu Dhabi, some from Bahrain, and some from Qatar, with an extra supply from Kazakhstan. But, *NONE* from their old friends and regular oil suppliers, Saudi Arabia. And they bought enough to take care of their 1.8-million-barrels-a-day import requirement all over again.

"I ask, why? Anyone needs extra oil, you go to Saudi Arabia. They've got more than everyone else, and with a big national government contract, it's cheaper. But no, France goes everywhere else. And today, someone destroys the entire Saudi oil industry, and there's only one nation in the industrial world that doesn't give a damn: France. Because she has her supply well covered from elsewhere. In my view, France *MUST* have known this was coming. Coincidence is too great, the circumstances too strange."

Arnold Morgan nodded. Said nothing. Hit the Chateau Lafleur with renewed zest.

"And then," said Jimmy, "what else do we hear? The most wanted Middle Eastern terrorist in the world, the Commander in Chief of Hamas himself, Major Ray Kerman, is picked up by the Mossad at some kind of a secret meeting in Marseille, shipped in by the French government via Taverny, the headquarters of their Special Forces operation.

"He is also secretly smuggled out. Plainly with the cooperation of the French Secret Service, who proceed to tell a pack of lies the size of a grown wallaby. All about the happenings of that night, the deaths at the restaurant . . . in Marseille . . . France," he put heavy emphasis on the last word. "What's the great Middle Eastern hit man fundamentalist doing in bloody France anyway? He MUST have had their protection. Forget that, sir. He DID have their protection.

"Which brings me to my last point. Sometime today, the GCHQ listening station in Cyprus picks up this message. It's plainly military, as you will see when I show you in a minute. And it was transmitted by a bloody Frenchman from a spot in the desert nineteen miles north of Riyadh. It was also answered by a Frenchman.

"Now how about that? And what I want to know is this: *WHO PRECISELY* was our Major Kerman meeting in Marseille when the bullets started flying? And where is Major Kerman right now?

"And, anyway, does that not suggest to you that France is somehow mixed up in this Saudi oil bullshit—right up to the armpits?"

Arnold Morgan again sipped his wine thoughtfully. Kathy ordered Parma ham and melon followed by Dover sole, and all three of them fell about laughing.

But the Admiral was taking this seriously; the French connection, that is, not the Dover sole. "Jimmy, I have not heard one sentence from anyone that suggests the attacks on the Saudi oil fields were conducted by anyone other than Arabs, probably al-Qaeda but most definitely by Saudis."

"They could not have done it, Arnie. I've been studying the bloody semantics all day. They could not. Unless the whole country was in revolution, including the Army, the National Guard, the Navy, and the Air Force. Otherwise it could not have happened."

"Why not?" said the Admiral.

"Because it's impossible. The Saudi National Guard,

which exists to protect the oil fields and the King, is a force of thousands. And they're heavily armed and well paid. They also have tanks, armored vehicles, artillery, rockets, access to the Air Force. All of those big oil installations are strongly protected—alarms, laser beams, floodlights, patrols, probably attack dogs. The Saudis are not stupid. They know the value of their assets and they have protected them stringently. Trust me. I've checked it out."

Arnold nodded. "Keep going," he said.

"Well, there were ferocious attacks on two massive loading platforms in the Red Sea plus three huge refineries, all of them blown to pieces. On the east coast they obliterated the Sea Island Terminal, blew up the liquid gas terminal at Ras al Ju'aymah. They knocked out the Qatif Junction manifold—that's the station that directs all the oil in the eastern half of the country; they smashed Pump Station Number One, which sends every last gallon of crude right across the mountains to the Red Sea port of Yanbu; they blasted the pipeline from Abqaiq, which sits in the middle of the desert; and they set fire to the entire Abqaiq operation, the biggest oil complex in the world.

"It all happened within a few minutes. It was an absolute bloody precision operation. And it was not conducted by a bunch of towelheads running around the desert with bombs under their bloody togas or whatever they're called. This was military. Because not a single alarm went off, no one made a mistake, no one got caught.

"And what beats the hell out of me is, how could anyone have got anywhere near Abqaiq or Qatif or the pumping station? They're all in the middle of dead flat desert. There's no cover. They're swept by bloody radar and guarded by literally hundreds of soldiers. I do not know how it was done. But it was not done by some shifty little bastard with a bomb. This was a military operation."

"Or a naval one," replied the Admiral.

"Sir?" said Ramshawe, longing to hear the Admiral utter the words that would put the two of them, and not for the first time, on precisely the same wavelength.

"If I wanted to knock out those installations," said Morgan, "I'd send in the SEALs from submarines to time-bomb the seaward targets. Then, on the way home, I'd flatten the oil fields in the desert with cruise missiles, fired sub-surface."

"So would I, Arnie. So would I. But the Saudis don't have a submarine. So it must have been someone else. And I think that someone was France."

"If there was even a semblance of a motive, I'd say you may be right, Jimmy. But it beats me why anyone would want to do this. But there could be developments in the next few days."

"Damn right, boss," said Ramshawe. "Remember, the Frog in the Desert: he's going to the party early."

Tuesday Morning, March 23

THE WORLD OIL crisis hit home very hard. Immediately after the opening bell at the International Petroleum Exchange in London, Brent Crude, the world's pricing benchmark, hit eighty-seven dollars a barrel, up around forty dollars from the close last Friday afternoon. Even on the opening day of Saddam Hussein's war against Kuwait in 1990, Brent Crude never breached the seventy-dollar barrier.

And it was not going down. If anything, it was still rising, as the big players battled to buy futures at whatever price it took. All of the major corporations that relied on transport to survive—airlines, especially airlines, railroads, long-distance truck fleets, power generators, and, of course, refiners and petrochemical corporations from all over the world.

The London market actually opened at 10 A.M. with the first opening bell for natural gas futures. And the last sight most of the gas brokers had seen on their television screens before coming to work was the 150-foot-long blowtorch from hell, blasting from the wreckage of the LPG terminal offshore from Ras al Ju'aymah, courtesy of Cdr. Jules Ventura, French Navy.

To the brokers, that signaled the end of Saudi Arabia's ability to produce liquid petroleum gas in large quantities. And when that ten o'clock bell sounded, in the great tiered, hexagonal-shaped trading floor of the International Exchange, it simply ceased to be a trading floor. It had become a bear pit.

People were caught in the crush to the lower levels as brokers fought and struggled to be heard—bidding, shouting, yelling: *UP TWO! . . . UP FOUR! . . . UP SIX! . . .* Dollar amounts unheard of in the sedate and mostly unexciting world of oil futures. Those "up twos" were normally just cents, usually trading in a slowish band between twenty and thirty-five dollars. Today they were not cents; they were dollars—regular greenbacks—and the yells were so loud no one heard the second opening bell, which sounded at 10:02 A.M., signaling the start of crude oil trading.

But the brokers did not need to hear it. They knew the time, and the pandemonium doubled, with an army of men in red, yellow, blue, and green jackets surging forward, roaring out bids for Brent Crude futures.

Exchange officials waited in vain for the chaos to die down. But it did not subside at all. It grew worse. And at 11 A.M., for the first time in the history of the Exchange, the bell sounded long and hard to signify that trading was being suspended.

The chairman, Sir David Norris, addressed the floor, saying that he hoped everyone would agree that this uproar could not be allowed to continue. He pointed out, among other things, that it was grossly unfair to the female brokers and traders, who were less used to operating in the front row of a Rugby Union scrummage.

Sir David, who had been a considerable rugby player himself at Cambridge University, where he also won a cricket Blue, insisted that some form of order be returned to the floor. And he requested that the biggest buyers and sellers attend a private conference in his office immediately.

At least this gave the market time to recover its breath. But the underlying frenzy was ever present and the morning high of eighty-seven dollars never showed any sign of dropping. On London's television news bulletins that evening, Sir David made a personal appearance to announce that the

Exchange would not open on Wednesday morning. "Trading is temporarily suspended due to the situation in Saudi Arabia," he said.

Many people thought that the alacrity with which the New York market, NYMEX, immediately followed suit suggested that Sir David and the Prime Minister had been in direct contact with the White House in the past few hours.

It should be made clear that the International Exchange in London is not so much bigger or more important than NYMEX in New York. Indeed it is often smaller. But the five-hour time difference meant that London opened first and set the prices. New York had to sit and watch from 5 A.M. until 10 A.M. before they joined the daily battle for America's fuel requirements.

And, of course, the knock-on effect from a tumultuous day's trading, during which oil prices had tripled at source, was nothing less than shocking.

By that Tuesday evening, in the United States, gasoline was costing $8 a gallon, instead of $2.50. In London, petrol prices at the pumps had tripled to a similar amount in pounds sterling. It was the same all over Europe, except for France, where prices went up less than one euro, and then fell back.

Japan was in chaos. The country had no access to natural gas, and almost every household throughout the islands cooked with propane. That was LPG, the stuff still thundering out into the sea off the oil town of Ras al Ju'aymah. That was where Japan acquired a huge percentage of its daily cooking fuel.

Restaurant prices in Japan doubled, on the basis that soon no one would be cooking anything, except over a fire. There was a stupendous run on electric cookers, which would probably turn out to be a waste of time, since Japan's energy grid was totally reliant on oil and gas from the Middle East.

Right now there were twenty-four Japanese tankers, between 4 and 1,000 miles from the Saudi oil ports in the Gulf. All of them were either on the verge of returning home or were trying to make the journey to other terminals, in the Black Sea or in other Gulf states. There was no oil available in the Red Sea, where the two main loading jetties were in ruins.

Internationally, airfares doubled overnight, led by British Airways and American Airlines, which immediately canceled all cheap transatlantic flights. And no one could really blame them, since no one knew the price jet fuel would fetch on the market at the end of the week.

The London stock market shuddered, the FTSE dropping 1,000 points in two hours. By the end of the day's trading, the Dow Jones Industrial Average crashed 842 points, wiping billions of dollars off corporate values. Airline stocks caved in worldwide, no one much wanting shares in flying corporations that could not afford their own fuel.

Industries all over the world that were reliant on heavy road transportation for food, agriculture, and automotives warned the public of drastic price increases unless the market stabilized. Shares in General Motors, Ford, and Chrysler crashed around 20 percent.

The population slowly awakened to the fact that the United States still imported one gallon in five of its gasoline from Saudi Arabia. And that particular gallon was about to vanish.

The Democratic administration had its back to the wall. And, in a special night session of Congress, Republican Senators and Representatives railed against the lunatic left-wing protection of the virgin wilds of Alaska, where oil-drilling had been so restricted by the shrill lobbies of Friends of the Earth, American Indians, Eskimos, and assorted tree-huggers.

The dire warnings of the Republicans throughout the twenty-first century had just come true in a blazing inferno on the other side of the world. America was too reliant on Arab oil, and especially reliant on Saudi oil. A reduction of 5 percent of its daily consumption would have represented an economic crisis for Uncle Sam. Twenty percent was earth-shattering.

On that Tuesday, at 9 P.M., the President of the United States, Paul Bedford, a right-of-center Democrat and former naval officer, broadcast to the nation direct from the White House. He assured everyone that the United States was not entirely dependent on Saudi oil, and that U.S. consumption had been falling in recent years.

He said that in the great scheme of things, this was a mere glitch, although it most certainly highlighted the world's vulnerability to terrorism. He said that once more the mighty economy of America had been shaken by actions on the other side of the world.

But it was not life threatening. He appealed for calm at the pumps, restraint in driving, and sympathy for "our very great friends, the Saudi royal family." He said he was confident that the al-Sauds would turn once more to America in the great task of rebuilding its industry, which would mean profits and jobs in the U.S.

And he reiterated the observation of the British Prime Minister, who spoke on global television a few hours previously. "Saudi Arabia has not lost its oil," said President Bedford. "It all remains intact beneath the desert floor. The Saudis have suffered a temporary setback in the mining and refining of that oil.

"With our help," he added, "that will be corrected in the very near future. I spoke to the King a half hour ago, and he had to be awake very, very early to take my call. But he was calm and measured in his assessment of the damage.

"He does not know who could wish such harm to the peace-loving peoples of the Arabian Peninsula, and, quite frankly, neither do I. But the road back to prosperity is already being built. There will be American engineers in Riyadh with the King and his advisers before the end of this week.

"For the moment, we have lost twenty percent of our daily requirements of gasoline. And the Energy Secretary is working on a program of allocations that will see us through the coming months. A little restraint, common sense, and consideration—that's all we need in order to come through this.

"Right now we are opening up new markets, finding more suppliers in South America. And I intend to speak to the Russian President in the morning with regard to special contracts in the Baku fields in Kazakhstan.

"I have ordered representatives of all the big oil corporations to report to Washington in the next twenty-four hours, and I intend to ensure there will be no price-gouging in this country. You may expect prices at the pumps to fall back. And in the wider picture of the economy, there will be corporate priorities, particularly for the major truck fleets and airlines.

"My fellow Americans, it is doubtful if the Saudis will ever need to provide twenty percent of our oil, ever again. This has been a wake-up call to the U.S.A., and I intend to place before Congress an immediate bill to step up drilling in northern Alaska.

"I have made it my personal crusade to rid this country once and for all of its dependence on Middle Eastern oil. And on that note, I wish you good night, and may God bless America."

Which was a pretty good speech, for a Democrat in crisis. The problem was, no one took the slightest notice.

All through the night there were huge lines at the pumps right across the country, the oil companies were effectively charging anything they liked, and prices were spiraling upward like in some fourth-rate banana republic.

Under a dark March sky, the Four Horsemen of the Apocalypse rode again. As Grantland Rice once observed, "In dramatic lore, their names were Famine, Pestilence, Destruction, and Death. But these were only aliases." In the U.S. of A, 2010, their real names were Gasoline, Diesel, Propane, and Jet Fuel.

And despite the President's appeal for calm, there was an even greater force preparing to fan those flames of fear all over the world. Even as the President wished everyone good night, newsrooms all over the country were preparing for a bonanza of frightening news, the priceless commodity that puts newspaper circulations up and sends television ratings sky-high.

The papers were preparing to run thousands of extra

copies, print advertising rates were about to hit an all-time high, and television advertising on the networks would instantly go to levels normally associated only with a Super Bowl Sunday or a presidential election.

Right now, the media was in fat city. And the more scared people became as they faced a loss of mobility, the more the world's news editors and advertising execs liked it. This was the week to justify big salaries and colossal expense accounts.

Hang on to your hats, boys!

U.S. ECONOMY CRIPPLED BY SAUDI OIL FIRES

PRESIDENT POISED TO BAN PRIVATE DRIVING

SAUDI OIL BOMBS BLAST U.S. ECONOMY

OIL FIELDS ABLAZE; FED WARNS RAMPANT INFLATION

RECORD GAS PRICES IN U.S. AS SAUDI OIL BURNS

Things were calmer in Pompeii in A.D. 79.

Tuesday, March 23, 2100
Andrews Air Force Base, Maryland

The U.S. Marine jet bearing the considerable figure of Adm. George Morris from San Diego touched down a little heavily. It taxied to the parking area, where a helicopter awaited him, rotors spinning, in readiness for the short journey to Fort Meade.

The Director of the National Security Agency had different priorities from both the administration and the politicians. Admiral Morris was not concerned with inflation, prices, or the economy. He wanted to know just three things: (1) who had blown up the Saudi oilfields; (2) why; and (3) might they do something else? Also he hoped to God young Ramshawe was on the case.

The Admiral was in his office twenty-three minutes after landing at Andrews Air Force Base. And Lt. Commander Ramshawe was on his way along the corridor with a file containing a high volume of speculation but very few undisputable facts. He went over more or less the same ground he had covered with Arnold Morgan, at the end of which the Admiral had said, "Jimmy, that's all very well observed. And I'm sure you are onto something, but I don't know what. Because there appears to be no motive."

Admiral Morris sat still for a few minutes, ruminating, as he always did when a very grave problem stared him in the face. At length he said, "I do agree this was a military operation. But I can only imagine it was the Saudi military. No one else could possibly want to smash up the oil industry. To what end? It doesn't make sense."

"I tell you what, sir. It made sense to someone."

"Guess so. You had a chat with the Big Man yet?"

"Uh-huh. Had dinner with him and Kathy last night."

"And what does he say?"

"He thinks the wholesale devastation in Saudi Arabia could have been achieved only with submarines, SEALs, high explosives, and, in the end, missiles to hit the land targets."

"That is the only way," said the former Commander of a U.S. Carrier Battle Group. "Unless you bombed them, which plainly no one did. And you could not pull off something like that with amateurs planting bombs in the night."

"Well, sir," said Ramshawe, "since we both believe Admiral Morgan is right about ninety-eight percent of the time, maybe we should check out the submarine theory."

"We most certainly should," replied Admiral Morris. "Get Admiral Dickson at the Pentagon. Send him my best and ask him to check the boards for all world submarines for the past month. And perhaps he could do it real fast. I don't want Arnold on the line wondering if we checked before we have."

The Lt. Commander was glad his boss was back. He grinned and said, "Right away, sir. He'll have SUBLANT send 'em over on the link, I expect. I'll come along to your office soon as we get 'em."

It took only a half hour. The Lt. Commander downloaded the sheets right away and headed back along the corridor to the Director's office.

He was not required to knock. Admiral Morris, a genial, wily international operator, held no secrets from his assistant. He was on the phone when Ramshawe came in and sat down in front of the huge desk, once occupied by Admiral Morgan himself.

"Okay, sir," he said when George Morris had completed his conversation. "I'll run through the no-hopers first. Ignoring the China seas, the Russians had a couple of Kilos in sea trials north of Murmansk, and a nuclear boat exiting the GIUK gap heading south down the Atlantic. That was on March second, and the satellites caught it entering the Baltic, then the Navy yards in St. Petersburg, where it still is.

"The Brits have a Trident in the North Atlantic, south of Greenland, and two SSNs in the Barents Sea, close to the ice cap. Nothing in the Channel or to the south. The other European nations with submarines—that's Italy, Spain, Germany, and Sweden—do not have one at sea between them. As you know, the U.S. has two L.A.-class SSNs with CVBGs in the Gulf, the northern Arabian Sea and south of Diego Garcia.

"The French have a Triomphant-class SSBN out of Brest, the *Vigilant*, in the Atlantic, north of the Azores, but here's the key information: this month they sent two Rubis Améthyste–class SSNs through the Med to Port Said, and on through Suez into the Red Sea."

"Same day, Jimmy?"

"Nossir. The *Perle* went through Port Said just before midday on March fourth, and the *Améthyste* went through last Thursday afternoon, around fourteen hundred hours."

"Did they come back . . . into the Med, I mean?"

"Nossir. In fact no one's seen them since."

"You mean they went deep in the Red Sea?"

"Apparently so, sir. We have a satellite pass over the canal and the Gulf of Suez at around nineteen hundred, and by then they'd gone, both ships, on March fourth and eighteenth."

"How about the southern end, through the Strait, into the Gulf of Aden . . . what's it called? . . . the Bab el Mandeb, right?"

"Yessir. And that's a spot we watch very carefully. Every ship entering and exiting the Red Sea is monitored by us, using satellites, surface ships, and shore radar. Neither the *Perle* nor the *Améthyste* has left the Red Sea."

"At least not on the surface?"

"Correct, sir. And neither of them has gone back through the canal to Port Said."

"They could, however, have made the transit dived."

"You sure about that, sir?"

"As a matter of fact, I am. There's a wide seaway out of the Red Sea, and it's mostly two or three hundred feet deep. I think most submarine COs do come to the surface. There are a few islands down there, and you need to be careful to stay in the defined north–south lanes, and it can be quite busy. It's easier to make the transit on the surface; the water's usually pretty flat.

"But I know U.S. commanders who have made that transit dived, and they've done it more than once. The entrance to the Gulf of Aden is an interesting crossroad. Once you're through, and sub-surface, no one knows where the hell you're going—north, south or east. It's a great spot to get lost in."

"Well, the *Perle* and the *Améthyste* are certainly lost, sir. There's no sight or sound of either of 'em. And there are no other submarines in all the world anywhere near the Red Sea or the Gulf in the past month. Unless a couple of U.S. Commanders went berserk and decided to slam the towelheads with a few cruise missiles."

"Unlikely, Jimmy, wouldn't you say?"

"Impossible, sir. If the oil stuff was hit by sub-surface missiles, they came from either the *Perle* or the *Améthyste,* on the basis that there were no other submarines for thousands of miles."

"The snag of course, Jim, is we don't know where either the *Perle* or the *Améthyste* is, within thousands of miles."

"Five gets you twenty if one of 'em's not still in the Gulf of Iran," said Ramshawe. "And five gets you fifty if the other one's not still in the Red Sea."

"No, thanks," said the Admiral.

"What now?" said his assistant.

"Ask Admiral Dickson if SUBLANT can find out whether any French submarine in the past five years has apparently exited the Red Sea underwater."

"Right away, sir. That'd be interesting."

"Not proof, of course. But a little food for thought, eh?"

Lt. Commander Ramshawe headed back to his staggeringly untidy office and put in a call to the Pentagon, to Admiral Dickson, Chief of Naval Operations.

"I can't promise absolute one hundred percent accuracy on that one, Lt. Commander," said the CNO. "We watch that area carefully and we watch all submarines in and out of the Red Sea. We'll have computerized records of all French SSNs and any Triomphant-Class. I'll have SUBLANT give you a pretty good picture of French practices going into the Gulf of Aden."

"Thank you, sir. I'll wait to hear from you."

"'Bout an hour," said the CNO. "By the way, is this for the Big Man?"

"No, sir. It's for Admiral Morris."

"Same thing," said Alan Dickson. "Give him my best."

The giant shadow of Arnold Morgan, which had hung over the United States Defense Department for so many years, had not receded. And every senior naval officer in the country knew of Morgan's continued obsession with submarines and their activities.

The smallest inquiry from the National Security Agency involving submarines—anyone's submarines—usually prompted the question "This for the Big Man?" even though Arnold had been retired for several months. Even though he had not sat in the big chair at Fort Meade for several years. He had never quite left. And a lot of very senior people, including the President, wished to hell he'd come back.

One hour later, SUBLANT put Jimmy Ramshawe's information on the Net to Fort Meade. The French sent submarines through Suez and into the Red Sea about four times every six months. Four in ten returned the way they had arrived, back through the canal and on to either the Toulouse Navy yards, in the Mediterranean, or Submarine Fleet Headquarters, in Brest.

The other six always headed out into the Gulf of Aden and usually went south, to the French base at La Réunion. Occasionally a French underwater ship headed up into the Gulf of Iran, but not often.

The United States Navy had no record of any French submarine exiting Bab el Mandeb sub-surface. According to the analysts at SUBLANT, no one particularly liked making that voyage below the surface. And in five years, U.S. Navy surveillance had always picked up any French submarine heading south out of the Red Sea on the surface of the water; although they had three times recorded Rubis-Class ships at periscope depth on satellite pictures.

Jimmy Ramshawe hurried back to the Director's office, turning over in his mind the now unassailable truth that France had put two guided-missile submarines through Suez with ample time to creep quietly into position and lambaste the Saudi oil industry.

This did not of course mean that they had done so. *But that bloody Frog in the Desert was looking a lot more menacing right now.* At least that was the opinion of Lt. Cdr. James Ramshawe.

Four minutes later, Admiral Morris instructed Ramshawe to keep the Big Man informed, but above all, to find out what he thought.

**Tuesday, March 23, Midday
Khamis Mushayt Bazaar**

Mishari al Ardh, at the age of twenty-four, was a market trader with his father. Their stall was always busy, selling fresh dates and a mountain of local fruits and vegetables. The old town, which stood more than 6,000 feet above sea level, enjoyed afternoon rain in March and August, which put local producers way, way in front of their brethren in the hot sandy deserts to the north.

Today was especially hard work. It seemed the news from the oil fields was so bad that people had developed a siege mentality and were ordering more of everything, much more than their families required—the way it is all over the world when the normal rhythms of daily life seem threatened. The Khamis Mushayt marketplace was seething with activity, much like gas stations in the United States.

Mishari was trying to bring order to five wooden cases of dates when a friend of his, Ahmed, a local boy his age, came rushing through the narrow street and beckoned him to cross over and speak with him.

Both young men were freedom fighters for al-Qaeda. Mishari crossed the street and accepted the folded piece of paper Ahmed handed him, and the terse instruction "Get this to General Rashood, on the heights, now."

Mishari walked to his father and spoke to him briefly. Then he walked through an alleyway to a parking lot where the aged family flatbed truck was kept. He jumped aboard and gunned it out onto the main road, deeper into the hills, up toward the village of Osha Mushayt, which was situated a mile from the al-Qaeda "hide" where General Rashood and his men were preparing for the attack on the air base on Thursday night.

He left the road after three miles and headed straight down the old desert trail to Osha. When he arrived he kept going, straight through the town and out into some really rough desert. Five minutes later he pulled up to the guard post and was immediately waved through. He came up here most days, with fresh supplies and, usually, the morning newspaper.

Mishari parked to the north of the camp and walked through to speak to the tall Bedouin who commanded it. He explained that a message had been dictated through the al-Qaeda network in Riyadh, by phone to Ahmed, who had written it down and requested that it be shown to General Rashood as soon as possible.

The Bedouin thanked Mishari gracefully and went directly to the General, who unfolded the notepaper and read to himself: *Situation on streets here volatile. King might want his soldiers. Can't risk that. Essential you go tonight. We have clearance from the curator. I'll go first thing in the morning. Godspeed, Ravi. Le Chasseur.*

General Rashood walked to one of the barbecues where the cooks were preparing the midday meal for everyone, and he slipped the note through the iron grill and watched it curl up and then burst into flame, directly below a roasting leg of lamb.

Then he turned to the Bedouin and said softly, "Okay, my friend. Our work is done here. Call a staff meeting right now. We attack tonight. And may Allah go with us."

Same Day, 1400
Riyadh

Col. Jacques Gamoudi sat in the shaded tent that housed the Crown Prince out on the desert floor. They both knew the message to the General was now delivered. They could only wait to hear that the Khamis Mushayt Military City and Air Base had fallen, and then they would move, hard and fast.

They had possibly thirteen hours to wait, and Prince Nasir would have to retire to one of the city palaces in order to be on the spot when the news came through. It would not be necessary to wait until General Rashood made contact. The military networks would be much quicker.

But when the news did arrive, they had to launch their attack on the royal palace. And at the precise, correct time, Prince Nasir must make his broadcast, announcing the death of the King and the shining future that now awaited the country. They would rebuild their oil fortunes.

In accordance with our ancient laws, as Crown Prince, I have assumed leadership of our country. I have taken my vows with the elders of the Council. And I have sworn before God to uphold our laws, both secular and religious. I am both your humble servant and proud leader, King Nasir of Saudi Arabia.

With those words the lives of 30,000 Saudi princes would never be the same. And neither would there ever be such unashamed opulence associated with the ruler of the desert kingdom. In his own way, Prince Nasir intended to avenge the disgraceful grandeur of the recent kings of his nation.

Meanwhile, in the busy streets to the south of Dir'aiyah, the city of Riyadh was once more in the throes of self-destruction, vast mobs of citizens again rioting, hurling stones and bottles, overturning cars.

At 3 P.M. (local) the king ordered the Army to take up a position of high alert. Like everyone else, he feared some sort of invasion might be imminent. And still no one had the remotest idea who was responsible for the destruction of the oil industry.

In the military cities of Tabuk in the northwest, King Khalid in the northeast, and Khamis Mushayt in the south-west, troops deployed immediately into pre-planned defensive positions. However, there were so many deficiencies in manpower and equipment that only around 65 to 70 percent of the total force managed to muster.

The King ordered naval forces at sea to form a defensive line around the coast, and his Air Minister ordered surveillance flights. There were not enough ships to defend anything much bigger than Long Island on a calm day, and the surveillance flights reported nothing unusual.

Even the helicopter patrols that the National Guard had ordered to overfly the city reported nothing except civilian unrest, despite one of them making a detour almost as far to the north as the ruins of Dir'aiyah. The pilot presumably considered the remains of the ancient city largely a waste of time.

There was no sign of the Saudi Air Force. Its fleets of fighters and fighter-bombers remained grounded, for one critical reason. For many years the Air Force had been commanded by royal princes, many of whom had been sent to train in England. And now these particular scions of the al-Saud family were quietly on their way out of the country. Vital instructions were simply not being issued to the pilots by these royal chiefs.

There was an element of frustration, of course, because there was nothing visible for the fighter-bombers to attack, but there was also an element of cowardice. These minor royals had been brought up to a life of unimaginable luxury, and their principal concern was for their own safety.

But the Air Force had another Achilles' heel. The ground staff had no wish to become involved in a war in which they might conceivably be bombed during the course of some kind of internal power struggle. Flight technicians, air traffic controllers, and personnel concerned with fueling and arming the aircraft were just melting away into the vast deserts that surrounded the major Saudi bases.

The only real activity within the Air Force was at the Riyadh base, where Number One Squadron, Royal Flight, was located. This fleet contained several Boeing 737s and 747s, British Aerospace executive jets, and other chartered aircraft. All of them were busy ferrying senior members of the royal family to neighboring Arab countries, Jordan, Syria, and Egypt. In some cases they were flying as far afield as Morocco, Switzerland, Spain, and France.

Inside the blasted ramparts of Dir'aiyah, under heavy camouflage, Colonel Gamoudi was bringing his force to a high state of readiness. He had great faith in General Rashood, in the south, and as darkness fell his petroleum tanker teams worked on the tasks of refueling the tanks and armored vehicles and loading the trucks with weapons and ammunition. He had always planned to leave this part of the operation to the last minute. Even if anyone had observed the convoy of gas tankers moving through the dusk and into the ruins, it would be far, far too late to do anything about it.

Prince Nasir himself, now in combat uniform—desert boots, fatigues, camouflage jacket—with a red-and-white-checkered *ghutra*, remained at the heart of the preparations, staying close to Jacques Gamoudi, watching an outstanding professional soldier make ready to capture a city.

Tuesday, March 23, 1900
Yemeni Mountains, above Khamis Mushayt

Ravi Rashood and his men broke camp as dusk fell over the desert. His sixty-strong troop, including his own Hamas personnel, began the march behind the al-Qaeda militia. Each man's face was blacked with camouflage cream. They all carried high explosive and their own personal weapons, plus the two big machine guns between teams of four men.

They had considered making the journey to their three separate destinations using trucks, because it was so much quicker. But General Rashood had decided against this. The level of high alert at both the military base and the Air Force base was, he decided, too big a risk. "The only thing worse than failure is discovery," he told his men. And all the senior officers agreed.

And so they faced the five-mile walk, down to the loop road that crossed the river and ran past both bases before rejoining the road it originally left. They traveled in single file, marching cross-country, staying off the old Bedouin tracks, with two al-Qaeda outriders mounted on camels a mile in front of the leaders, checking for intruders.

At 2100 precisely, there would be a truck breakdown to their right, two miles south of the air base, blocking the only approach from the west. They would cross the road into the rough ground that surrounded the airfield, knowing there could be no danger on their right flank.

Rashood's men had watched this road every night since their arrival, and nothing had ever come down from the left, from the military base itself. The General supposed there must be an internal road between the Army and the Air Force, and he placed just two sentries with a big machine gun on the left flank beside the road. If any traffic approached, both the vehicle and its passengers would be eliminated instantly.

They reached the road on time, and said good-bye to the six-man command team, the men with the communications equipment that would be essentially their only lifeline if things went badly wrong. The six would take up position on high ground overlooking the air base about a half mile to the north, with the capability of communicating with the General, the al-Qaeda commander, and all three of the demolition force's team leaders. They could also call up reinforcements in the town of Khamis Mushayt if there were a rescue requirement. General Rashood considered this most unlikely.

The combat teams crossed the road in pitch dark in groups of four, making a run across the blacktop on the command of the leaders. It was 2125 when General Rashood finally crossed the road, the last man to leave the "safe" side of the track.

This was the point where the attacking forces broke up. Maj. Paul Spanier and Maj. Henri Gilbert separated their twelve-strong groups and moved east, for the long walk around the air base to the high bracken at the edge of the wire on the north fence. Ten men who would go in separately and head for the aircraft hangars, then help to fight for the main entrance, would move along behind them. The two wire-cutters marched in the lead with the two French Majors.

General Rashood led his troop to the west to take up position four and a half miles away, close to the main gates of the military base. The al-Qaeda fighters who would launch the diversionary attack at the gates to the air base were under orders to begin at 0055, five minutes before every aircraft on the base was blown to pieces.

Meanwhile, it was al-Qaeda's task to ensure that the troop carrier trucks were in position, well hidden in the desert, with drivers ready to come in and evacuate the aircraft demolition teams on the north side. The team that blew the hangars and then assisted the al-Qaeda fighters at the gates would ultimately leave through the hills on the north side of the road with the local forces.

Only General Rashood and his twelve-strong attack squadron would remain on the ground after the air base was wiped out. And they would be stationed before the gates of the military city.

The night was cloudy, but the terrain had dried out since

a prolonged afternoon rain shower. It was extraordinarily quiet, and General Rashood had scheduled a ten-minute break after the five-mile walk-in from the mountains, not because of the distance but because they had all carried heavy loads of explosives and arms over very uneven ground.

And at the end of this time, the General shook hands with Major Spanier and Major Gilbert and wished them luck. He said good-bye to the al-Qaeda freedom fighters and also to many of the combat troops with whom he had become well acquainted. It was unlikely he would ever meet any of them again.

Upon completion of the operation, the majority of his troops were being flown in three helicopters from the northern slopes of the mountains back into Yemen. The General had authorized this because the Saudis' surveillance capability in this part of the country would be nonoperational.

As no one had known of their arrival, no one would know of their departure. All of the French troops would return home by air, taking off from the Yemeni capital, San'a, which is situated deep in the interior. Air France flies once a week to this biblical city, said to have been built by Shem, the son of Noah. This week there would be two flights.

General Rashood himself would fly in a Saudi Air Force helicopter directly from the Khamis Mushayt base to Riyadh, where he would join General Gamoudi and Prince Nasir and assist them with the final capitulation of the city.

Meanwhile, there was a great deal of work to do in the southwest. Major Spanier and his team traversed the perimeter of the air base and were in position by 2235. They made contact with the al-Qaeda commander who had the getaway trucks in position. He was accompanied by four armed bodyguards, two of whom would drive the trucks, and they checked radio frequencies with the senior French officer in case there should be an emergency.

By 2250, the wire-cutter detail had clipped out an entry point in the fence. There were no lights on out here, on the remotest side of the air field, which General Rashood had considered to be absurd. But this was a very quiet place, and no one had ever even dreamed of attacking it before. Not even the Yemeni in their most virulent mood against the Saudis.

And so, in the pitch dark, Major Gilbert and his eleven men began to move through the wire, racing inward, away from the perimeter road, and then swerving right, into the dark part of the field where the thirty-two British-built Tornadoes were parked in four lines of eight.

The men split into six teams of two each and began their work. Four teams started at the far ends of the four lines. The other two teams concentrated on the eight remaining aircraft, the ones nearest the perimeter, the ones closest to the approaching headlights of the guard vehicles.

The teams on the Tornadoes actually had a far better view of the perimeter road. It was Major Spanier's group, working in among the F-15s, who were unsighted by the thirty-two Tornadoes and could not see clearly along the road that led back to the hangars.

Which was why General Rashood had two machine gunners right now prostrated behind the wheels of the two F-15s closest to the perimeter. From ground level they could provide cover for both groups. But the moment Maj. Henri Gilbert's men had completed their work on the first six aircraft, two of the saboteurs would swap their detcords, explosives, and screwdrivers for machine guns.

They would take up new positions, behind the aircraft wheels at the farthest point, down the perimeter road. No chances. High-explosives men, working on targets, tend to grow preoccupied with their tasks. They need guards.

And one by one they attacked the Saudis' fighter-bombers. They unscrewed the panels that protected the engines on the starboard side, clipped out a gap in the wires that ran across this side of the block, and clamped on the first of the magnetic bombs that would blast the entire engine asunder. The bomb was of sufficient force to split the engine into two pieces and also to blow out the cockpit and control panels. Under no circumstances would this fighter-bomber ever fly again.

The French Special Forces were never certain how much fuel was aboard each aircraft, but they were sure that some of them were fully fueled. Observing from the long bracken in the afternoons with General Rashood, they had noticed that some of the Tornadoes had moved straight to the take-off point without refueling at all. Thus there was the high probability that the ensuing fires, as a result of the initial blasts, would be extremely hot, and would very likely leave only burned-out hulks in their crackling-red wake.

The teams worked carefully, using hammers and sharp pointed steel "punches" to bang a hole through each panel through which to thread the det-cord. When the bomb was fixed and armed, they refixed the panels and ran the det-cord out to a point midway between four aircraft.

And there one of their senior high-explosives technicians spliced the four lines into one "pigtail" and screwed it tightly into a timing clock. They checked their own watches, and after the first aircraft were dealt with at 2315, they set the main timed fuse for one hour and forty-five minutes. Each set of four aircraft thereafter would have their detonation times adjusted for the 0100 blast.

And despite the certainty of their operation—the definite fact that these bombs would blow up at 0100—they still made sure that no bits of det-cord, screwdrivers, or any traces of the operation were left lying around.

Even if they had to abort the mission, run for cover, or even find themselves on the wrong end of a firefight, it remained essential that no one ever know the French Special Forces had worked on the airfield at Khamis Mushayt.

Two patrols came and went, neither one of them even pausing as they rushed past the parked Tornadoes and F-15s. Each time, the jeeps set off from the hangars, the lookout men spotted them, and everyone hit the ground. Each time, the jeeps never even slowed down as they came past the ops area of the French Majors.

At 0042 the tiny alarms went off on each man's watch, signaling the scheduled ETD of the last patrol. For the third time, everyone hit the ground, knowing that, fourteen minutes from now, the jeep, packed with its six armed guards, would drive by less than fifty feet from the demolition teams.

They also knew that as that jeep drove away from the big doors to the two massive aircraft hangars, almost a half mile from where they were working, their own team would be into the gigantic doors, winding the det-cord, setting the timers, and concealing themselves in a place where they could see the blast, before charging inside to do their worst.

As the minutes ticked by, the tension rose, not because any of them was afraid of a straight fight, which they knew they would win anyway, but because of the danger of discovery—of the one careless move that would alert the Saudi patrol that something was afoot, the one-minute give-away that might give the Saudis the split second they needed to report back to the military base that they may be under attack.

On came the jeep, and the men pressed their black faces into the ground down behind the aircraft wheels. Only the sentries kept their heads up, ready to machine-gun that jeep to oblivion should there be the slightest suspicion of discovery.

But the jeep came and went as it always did. Fast and unseeing. And at the hangar doors, the French explosives team was wrapping the det-cord around the locks, with one lookout on each of the field-side corners of the buildings just in case of a foot patrol.

There was, however, no danger of that. Tonight, this Air Force base was as inefficient as it had ever been. The defection of some of their senior officers, royal princes who apparently had matters to which they had to attend in Riyadh, had caused a shuddering effect on morale. The pilots were without proper leadership, and while the oil fields burned and the capital city collapsed into self-inflicted chaos, there was literally nothing for them to defend, never mind attack.

Air Forces need targets, and dozens of aircrew and indeed guard patrols had gone missing, heading for the Yemeni Mountains. The pilots, a more senior breed, had not deserted their posts or resigned their commissions or even left the area. But they were mostly asleep or just sitting around talking. They were not hired to guard and service fighter aircraft. They were hired to fly them, and there was at present nothing to fly them at.

And anyway, for how long would they have their highly paid jobs, with the King reportedly on the verge of bankruptcy? In Saudi Arabia, as in all Western countries, the media was truly expert at frightening the life out of the population, if at all possible.

Just as "journalists" had had half the world terrified that the midnight date change at the new millennium would cause total catastrophe when every computer on the planet crashed, so the Saudi Arabian newspapers and television networks had the middle-line commissioned officers of the desert military convinced that they would never work again.

The Frenchmen set the timers on the hangar doors for 0100, and then headed toward the north fence to hide out while the work of their colleagues was completed. At 0100, they would take out the entire contents of the hangars, and then move toward the main gate on the southern perimeter.

At 0055 the al-Qaeda freedom fighters launched their attack on that gate. Two hand grenades were hurled into the outer sentry station, blowing up and killing all four guards. Four young al-Qaeda braves flew across the road and hauled back the wrought-iron gates, which were not locked while the guards were on duty.

Immediately four rocket-propelled grenades were blasted in from the other side of the road, three of them straight through the windows of the inner guardhouse, which killed all six of the night-duty patrol. One of them already had the handset in his hand, trying to report the first explosion. He died with the handset still in his hand, which made the opening attack a close-run thing. But the young Saudi never had a chance to speak.

Light instantly began to go on in the guards' accommodation block, and this was two hundred yards away, out of range for the rocket grenades—out of range at least for any form of accuracy. And that was why General Rashood had insisted that the moment those gates were open six young al-Qaeda fighters race through, four of them with handheld grenades, the other two with submachine guns.

Simultaneously, two British-built GPMG machine guns were being hauled into position on the flat ground opposite the remains of the inner guardhouse. Occasionally criticized for its heavy twenty-four-pound weight—that was unloaded, on its tripod—this thing delivered devastatingly accurate firepower out to a quarter of a mile. The SAS never went anywhere without this tough, reliable weapon.

And now the young Saudis were running, straight at the aimed barrels of three guards who had burst from the accommodation block door to find out what was going on. The first of the boys hurled his grenade straight at them, but they saw him in the light from the fires at the gate and cut him down with small-arms fire. The three other boys swerved left and hurled their grenades through the windows of the accommodation block, which disintegrated in a huge explosion.

The big al-Qaeda machine guns opened up inside the gates and peppered the front of the building, killing all three of the Air Force guards who had initially stepped outside. The final two of the six al-Qaeda runners reached the burning building and sprayed the far-side windows with gunfire, thus discouraging any further interference.

It was one minute before 0100, and the al-Qaeda sprinters were running back to their fallen comrade, confident they had stopped any communication from the guards, but heartbroken at the almost certain death of their friend and, for one of them, brother.

They reached him safely under covering fire from the GPMGs, which was precisely when the opening explosions from the airfield detonated with savage force. The first four Tornado aircraft literally exploded like bombs, and since light travels a lot faster than sound, the silhouettes of the sobbing young Arabs could instantly be seen as they tried to drag their comrade to safety, tried to stop the blood, tried to save him from dying.

The deafening explosion that followed made a sound like another bomb. And then all the aircraft on the field blew to pieces, during a thunderous short period of perhaps twenty-five seconds maximum. The skies above the airfield lit up, with wide luminous flashes reaching out along the skyline. And each one was punctuated with a mighty *BOOOOOM* as the F-15s detonated, some of them loaded with jet fuel.

Flames reached a hundred feet into the air, and the glow in the sky was visible for miles. At the conclusion of the eighteenth massive blast, with the last set of four fighter jets exploding, there was for a few moments a calm, interrupted only by the crackling of the flames. And then the biggest blast of all absolutely shook the base to its foundations.

The hangar door blew outward, and six of the French Special Forces raced forward, firing M60 grenade launchers aimed at each of the three aircraft inside, two of them fueled at the completion of their service. Six rocket grenades thus struck almost simultaneously, and detonated in the midst of several hundred gallons of jet fuel.

The blast was sensational. It blew the hangar to shreds and obliterated the curved roof, which collapsed, allowing the flames to roar skyward. The next hangar contained two E-3A AWACS, radar surveillance aircraft. And when the rocket grenades went in there, it was the final devastation for the base.

With flames raging into the sky, and almost eighty aircraft destroyed, there was scarcely anything left to defend. And the final elements of the Fourth (Southern) Air Defense Group, whose duty it was to protect the base from air attack, quite simply fled. If there was an excuse for their incompetence it was perhaps that their two commanding officers, both members of the royal family, had fled twelve hours before them.

In the end, the coup de grace was delivered by Maj. Paul Spanier himself. He stayed behind as his men charged back through the huge hole now cut in the perimeter fence, and, accompanied by two troopers, jogged for 400 yards and blew up the fuel farm with four rocket grenades. One would have probably done it, because fuel farms are apt to blow themselves up once something is ignited. No Special Forces squadron had ever been able to resist exploding a fuel farm, and the one here at Khamis Mushayt proved no exception to the general rule.

It went up with a gigantic blast, lighting up the desert for several miles. Back in the barracks area of the air base, the running figures could be seen heading back to the main gate. This was the twelve-strong force that had destroyed the hangars and were now detailed to nail down the final surrender.

The trouble was there were no longer any Saudi Air Force guard personnel left alive, and certainly none on duty. So the Frenchmen and their al-Qaeda comrades joined forces and commandeered a couple of jeeps and headed directly to the airport's control tower, which was apparently undefended.

They ripped an antitank rocket through the downstairs door, and the al-Qaeda commander grabbed a bullhorn from the jeep and demanded, in Arabic, a peaceful surrender, which he quickly achieved. The four duty officers, working high in the tower, came out with their hands up and were swiftly handcuffed and told to walk in front of the jeep directly to the main office block.

This building stood next door to the flight officers' accommodation. The al-Qaeda troops hurled a couple of grenades through the downstairs window of the offices, and immediately the door opened and six men walked out into the night with their hands high, unarmed and unable to offer resistance.

As agreed, the al-Qaeda commander demanded to see the commanding officer of the air station, who was no longer, of course, in residence. There was scarcely a senior officer left. In fact there was only one, and at gunpoint he was made to return inside the building and communicate to the Khamis Mushayt Military City that the air base had surrendered unconditionally to an armed force of unknown nationality. The air base, he confirmed, was history. There was not an aircraft on the field that could fly.

At this precise time, hundreds of military personnel were

gazing to the east, where the entire sky seemed to be burning. An intense red glow reached high into the heavens, with flames raging along the horizon. The families of·the remaining senior officers were terrified, especially as their most senior Commanders, the royal princes, had already left.

In the main communications center a phone call confirmed what they already knew—that the air base had been obliterated, attacked and destroyed by an unknown force. And even as they stood, petrified at the wrath that was plainly to come, Gen. Ravi Rashood and his trusty fighters from the desert and France stormed the main gates of the Military City.

They actually rammed the gates with an elderly truck, on the basis that it could quickly be replaced by a new army vehicle. General Rashood personally leapt from the front passenger seat and threw two grenades straight through the glass windows of the guardhouse.

The two sentries on duty were cut down by small-arms fire from the back of the truck, which was now parked dead in the middle of the entranceway, a favored tactic of the Hamas C-in-C because it stopped anyone else coming in, and it stopped anyone either leaving or closing the gates.

And out swarmed Ravi Rashood's chosen men, firing from the hip and racing toward the barracks, where the residents were right now in the upstairs rooms staring at the inferno on the air base. General Rashood's men blew the locks with gunfire and kicked open the door. They fired several rounds into the guardhouse, on the lower floor, killing four men, and proceeded up the stairs, firing as they went.

But it was somewhat unnecessary. The residents of the barracks were in no mood to fight any kind of a battle and they stood on the upper landing, with their hands folded on their heads as instructed by General Rashood's senior officers. The Hamas Chief left four men to guard their captives, then turned his attention to the command headquarters.

And there they met no further resistance. The officers and soldiers on duty surrendered as soon as the doors were kicked open, and the duty officer, with his skeleton staff in the ops room, did the same. General Rashood demanded to know where the commanding General could be located and was told that he had left.

"Who commands this place?" said General Rashood. "There must be someone."

It turned out to be a veteran Colonel, a career officer from the old school who had served in the first Gulf War. Rashood had him brought in with his four senior staff members by a hastily convened arrest party of al-Qaeda troops. The General always endeavored to keep France and the French troops as far from contact with Arab officers as possible.

This particular Arab Colonel did not need much persuading. General Rashood talked to him for perhaps two minutes, outlining what his men had achieved thus far, and the Colonel was wise enough to accept that resistance was hopeless. He agreed to order his three subordinate brigades to withdraw to their barracks, a mile away, and to wait there until further orders were issued.

There was only one exception to the mass surrender, and that was the Fourth Armored Brigade at Jirzan, over which the Colonel presided. He knew there had been some harebrained scheme dreamed up at headquarters in Riyadh, that a tank brigade should be placed in a high state of readiness in order to proceed to Riyadh in the event of an attempt at a military coup against the King.

This was the nearest heavy armor to Riyadh, and one or two of the more cautious members of the King's defense committee had decided to instruct the Jirzan Commanders to prepare to advance on the capital by road. This would entail loading the tanks onto transporters and driving them up the coast road and then over the mountains through al Taif. It was a distance of 700 miles and would probably take a week.

It was just a hopeless, last-resort measure—completely impractical, too slow, and militarily absurd. General Rashood smiled and asked who was in command at the Jirzan HQ.

The Colonel named a Prince, who was in fact deputy commander, and Rashood instructed him to get His Highness on the phone and tell him not to waste his time. In fact it was the phone call that turned out to be a waste of time, since the young Prince had already fled to Jiddah, where he had collected his family and flown to safety in Switzerland.

"Bloody waster," muttered General Rashood. And then he issued his final command. "Colonel, you will call the Ministry of Defense in Riyadh and instruct them that the air base here has been destroyed, and that the Khamis Mushayt Military City has fallen to the same attacking force. You will tell them that further resistance is out of the question."

The Colonel was happy to comply. He was so shocked at the events of the night, so amazed at the final conclusion of his command, that he forgot even to ask the General who he was. He was so utterly relieved not to be dead, so thankful his family was safe here in the officers' quarters, he had not the slightest intention of asking anyone else to die.

The Colonel's plan was simple: to remain here, in position with his men, until they were issued instructions from the new rulers of Saudi Arabia. General Rashood told him to keep watching the television and to expect a force of 200 al-Qaeda fighters to arrive in trucks throughout the course of the night.

"Just to keep order, you understand?" he said. "We would not want a sudden military uprising here, and for that reason I will be destroying all communications, both in and out of the base. Transports will be confiscated by the al-Qaeda network, and of course there are no aircraft left."

And with that, General Rashood handed over command to the al-Qaeda senior officer, who shook his hand, and wished that Allah should go with him on the second leg of his journey, this time to Riyadh.

By this time, the least crowded of the getaway trucks had driven around the perimeter and was parked at the gates to the military city. General Rashood, in company with his initial team of eight Hamas henchmen, now said good-bye to six of them. The three known al-Qaeda fighters would assume command-level posts right here at Khamis Mushayt, his two Syrian bodyguards would return to Damascus, and the three former Saudi army officers who had defected to al-Qaeda three years ago would accompany him to the capital city.

Thus the two Hamas men climbed aboard the truck for the drive back into the mountains, to the "hide," where helicopters from Yemen were just arriving for the evacuation. All troops would be ferried to the airfield at San'a in Yemen's old Russian army troop-carrying helicopters, a remnant from the times when the Soviet Union was the biggest player on the southern tip of the peninsula, when two Yemeni Presidents were exiled in Moscow. The helicopters were big, old, but air-worthy. Just. And they would fly very low and not very fast over the mountains, just in case.

The only other inherent risk in this evacuation was the all-seeing eye of the U.S. satellites. But the urgency of removing the evidence of French Special Forces overrode this, and Ravi Rashood decided that the risk of American detection was worth taking. In any event no one could possibly have detected the nature of the copter's cargo.

In contrast, the helicopter that would fly Ravi Rashood and his three bodyguards to Riyadh was brand new and had been flown into the military city the previous day by a two-man Saudi Army crew loyal to Prince Nasir. When it landed in the capital, it would be in the grounds of the palace of the Crown Prince.

Wednesday, March 24, 0100 (local)
National Security Agency

The satellite pictures coming in on the link from surveillance were at once definite, but almost impossible to believe. The United States now had vivid pictures of all the oil installations ablaze in Saudi Arabia, but these new images were incredible.

They showed with immense clarity that the mighty Khamis Mushayt Air Base, home to almost eighty fighter-bombers, had effectively been taken off the map. The base, which sits five miles east of the military city, was on fire, the lines of aircraft blazing, the hangars collapsed with burning aircraft plainly still inside.

Lt. Commander Ramshawe, who had been in his office for seventeen hours, stared at the images and for the second time checked his map. No doubt about it, that was Khamis Mushayt okay, and it had been hit by an immensely powerful enemy.

Jimmy Ramshawe could compare it only to the Israeli drubbing of the Egyptian airfields in the 1967 war. It was simply not believable, right here in the year 2010, that some country, somewhere, could go to war with Saudi Arabia unknown to the rest of the world. It could not happen. But he, Ramshawe, was right now staring at the evidence.

"No," he said loudly. "No one could have done this, except the Saudis themselves. And that of course is bloody silly."

He called the duty officer at the CIA and spoke briefly to the Middle East desk. They were as bemused as he was. They were receiving reports from field agents in the Saudi capital that there was further unrest in the streets, but nothing to suggest a bombing raid in the south comparable to World War II Dresden.

Then he called Admiral Morris and awakened him with the words, "Sir, I think someone just declared war on Saudi Arabia. They started off by flattening one of the biggest air bases in the country. Took out eighty fighter-bombers at Khamis Mushayt."

"They did?" answered Admiral Morris a little sleepily. "And now I guess you're going to tell me French Combat Command sent in a squadron of Mirage 2000s and let 'em have it."

"Er . . . nossir," replied Ramshawe. "I thought their new 234 Rafale fighter jets were much more likely."

The Admiral chuckled, despite the seriousness of the subject. "Any intelligence anywhere on this? CIA got any clues?"

"None, sir. No one has. It just happened, apparently. Right out of the blue. But of course we need to link the destruction of the oil fields on Monday to the demolition of the air base on Tuesday."

"Whoever did it . . . well, it's the same guys, right?"

"Plainly, sir. But this is a helluva thing, sir. The CIA told me the Pentagon is recalling all the senior brass as we speak. President's in the Oval Office by o-two-hundred."

"Gimme a half hour, Ramshawe. I'll be right there."

The Lt. Commander replaced the telephone and looked again at the pictures. He wondered what was happening at the military base. According to the CIA latest on the Net, there was some evidence of a firefight inside the main entrance. But nothing to indicate a bombing raid on the air base.

He sat back and thought, as quietly and as carefully as he could. *If no one bombed anything and the Saudi Army is still in place, this must be an inside job. But we've just about established no one could possibly have blitzed the oil fields, except from a submarine. And the Saudis don't have one. Tonight's stuff was too precise for missiles, those lines of burning aircraft were sabotaged. Otherwise there'd be visible craters. And it only takes one man to blow up a fuel farm.*

No counterattack activity from the Khamis Mushayt military base . . . So far as I can see, this is an internal Saudi thing. But they're sure as hell working with someone else. And I think that someone is France.

There was of course a gigantic flaw in his reasoning. He knew only too well the military and political chiefs would demand a motive. And so far as he could tell there was no motive.

But that doesn't bloody mean there isn't one, he thought. *It doesn't bloody mean that at all. It just means there's no obvious motive. Obvious to us, that is. And that's entirely different.*

He picked up the phone and asked someone to bring coffee for two to the Director's office, not that there was any danger of anyone's falling asleep. *This was a huge situation in the Middle East. And Christ knew where it would end.*

Admiral Morris arrived and asked immediately to see any communication from the U.S. ambassador in Riyadh. But there was just a report about the unrest in the city, the mystery of the exploding oil fields, and reports of a military disaster in the south. Without U.S. satellite pictures, the ambassador knew less than they did.

Admiral Morris used a magnifying glass to stare at the photographs taken from 20,000 miles above the earth. "Clinical, eh?" he grunted. "All the parked aircraft, both main hangars, and what looks like the fuel farm. No bullshit, they only hit what mattered. And there's no sign of general mayhem on the field or the runways. This wasn't a battery of cruise missiles. Otherwise there'd be stuff all over the place."

"They're my thoughts," replied Ramshawe. "This attack was made on the ground. And no one, apparently, saw anyone coming. Which sounds impossible. Those Saudi air bases are well protected, and this one stands right next door to one of the biggest army bases in the country. We're talking thousands and thousands of armed men."

"Jimmy. We're not really getting anywhere . . . in this place you always have to work on the words of Sherlock Holmes . . ."

"When you have eliminated the impossible, only the truth remains," Ramshawe replied.

"Precisely. So why don't we spend five minutes eliminating the impossible?"

"Righto, sir . . . Number one, it was impossible for any attacking force to have blown up the oil installations in the middle of the desert. Number two, it was impossible for anyone to have blown out the tanker loading docks from the land. Number three, it was impossible for anyone to have obliterated the coastal refineries except with missiles."

"All correct," replied Admiral Morris. "How about number four? It was impossible to have bombed the Khamis Mushayt Air Base without being picked up on radar. And number five, it was definitely impossible for any invader to have reached that airfield with God knows how much explosives and blown every aircraft to pieces without a great deal of cooperation from forces inside the Saudi military. They must have had maps, diagrams, and time for recce."

"Correct, sir. And how about number six? Whoever

launched those missiles must have done so from deep water, otherwise they would have been detected. It's impossible for the Saudi Navy to have achieved that."

"So where does that leave us?" replied the Admiral, plainly not wishing to hear an answer. "It leaves us," he said, "with one absolute truth. Somewhere inside the Saudi military there is a network of mutiny against the armed forces. It leaves us with a possible leader of that network, who may wish to seize power in Saudi Arabia. And it leaves us with an outside country willing to help that leader seize that power. And that's gotta be a big enough country to own a Navy with a heavy submarine strike force."

"Especially since two of 'em just went missing," said Jimmy Ramshawe.

Wednesday, March 24, 5:00 A.M. (LOCAL)
The White House
Washington, D.C.

PRESIDENT PAUL BEDFORD had been in his office for most of the night, reading reports, talking to Admiral Morris, conferring with his defense staff, and wrestling with the burgeoning economic uproar the events in Saudi Arabia were causing the rest of the world.

The trouble was, no one, not even the Saudis, knew what was going on. Certainly not the United States Ambassador in Riyadh. But at five minutes past five, his personal assistant informed him that the King of Saudi Arabia was on the line. World leaders have no time frames. It's part of the job.

President Bedford took the call instantly, greeting the King warmly, even though they had never met.

"Mr. President," said the beleaguered desert monarch, an edge of humility in his voice, "I am afraid I am speaking to you under the most trying of circumstances."

"So I understand," said President Bedford. "And there seems to be a great deal of confusion about the culprits for these attacks in your country."

"It would seem so," replied the King. "But whoever may be behind this, we are suffering some very serious blows both economically and militarily. It is likely we will have no oil to export for a minimum of one year and possibly for two."

"I certainly understand the gravity of the situation," replied the President. "And it is difficult to know what to do, in the absence of a clearly defined enemy. Do you have any ideas who this might be?"

"Not exactly, although it would not be a great shock to find the leaders of some fundamentalist Islamic group at the back of it. However, I felt it wise to inform you that all of my senior advisers believe the main group must be receiving outside help from some other country. It simply would not be possible for all this damage to have been caused by an internal Arabian group. Equally it would have been impossible for an outside assailant to have inflicted the damage without internal assistance from the Saudi military."

"I see," said President Bedford. "That makes matters even more difficult, eh? A devil on the outside and another on the inside."

"Precisely so," said the King. "I therefore conclude that my throne is very severely threatened, and I am no longer certain whom I can trust."

"And that's why you have come to us?"

"The Bedouin way has always been to stay with tried and trusted friends," said the King. "Your country represents the best friends I have had since coming to the throne. And now I appeal to you to help me in my time of need, as I have so often helped you."

Paul Bedford knew the King referred to the several times the Saudis had pushed more oil on to the market when supplies seemed threatened by this or that problem in the Middle East and to the many times they had stabilized the markets when oil prices seemed to be rising too drastically. Saudi cooperation with the U.S.A. had worked well for more than three decades.

But he hesitated before answering. As a former naval officer, the right-wing-ish Democrat from Virginia understood the importance of clear-cut military objectives. It flashed through his mind immediately that he could not commit U.S. troops to fight some kind of a phantom.

He spoke to the King gently, and with genuine concern.

"I do of course see your point of view," he said. "And if you wished an enemy to be driven from your borders you could most certainly count on the United States to be your first ally. Indeed we have a Carrier Battle Group in the Gulf at present, and we would not hesitate to send it to your aid. . . . But it seems to me neither of us has anything to shoot at."

The King laughed, despite himself. "What you say is true," he said. "I cannot see my enemy. But I know he is there. And I am very fearful of the next few days, for I feel he will strike at my country again."

"And even if your enemy is Saudi, you have no idea of the capability of his foreign friends?"

"Indeed we do not," replied the King. "But we believe they were sufficiently powerful to have destroyed our oil industry. Not one of my advisers believes that much damage was done by a group of internal terrorists."

"No," said the President. "My people at the National Security Agency are of the same mind. And my chiefs at the Pentagon, who are more cautious in their assessments of military action, are coming around to a similar view."

"I have never before been in such a predicament," said the King. "I am threatened for my life, my country is threatened, and yet I do not know by whom. I badly want to call upon the help of my very powerful friends in the United States, but I am at a loss as to what they can do."

"Sir," said the President, uncertain what title to give the ruler of a desert kingdom. "I have in Washington a wise and experienced expert on foreign affairs. He was the National Security Adviser to the last Republican President. I will summon him to my office this morning and ask his advice and opinion. When we have discussed the matter in proper detail, I will return your phone call and give you the benefit of his knowledge."

"You must be referring to the Admiral, Mr. President. Admiral Arnold Morgan? A very fearsome man."

"Correct," replied President Bedford. "Await my call this afternoon."

It was the first and last time the two leaders ever spoke.

Same Day, 0630
Chevy Chase, Maryland

In the very early days of spring, Admiral Morgan indulged his hobby of harvesting daffodils. And as the first of the brilliantly yellow blossoms burst into life in the garden, he arose at an unearthly time and advanced with a long basket to harvest the first flowers from the 2,000 bulbs of varying specimens he had planted—or at least had had George, the gardener, plant—two and a half years previously.

And here they were, for the second year running, already forming the start of the wide yellow carpet he so admired. However, Morgan liked daffodils in the house more than he liked the garden to be a sea of golden daffodils.

He snapped them off with military precision and laid them side by side in his basket. Kathy said daffodils were the only flowers he ever picked because he liked the sharp, obedient *snap* and the way daffodils did not hang around requiring clippers or a second tug.

"They just happen to be Arnold's kind of flower," she told friends. "On parade in full uniform early in the morning, and *snap*! Into the basket. No bullshit."

The parody was so witheringly accurate everyone laughed when she recounted the once-a-year exploits of the family horticulturist. "By April he's had enough," Kathy would say. "But he does like daffodils all over the house for a month or so."

On this Wednesday morning, the Admiral was almost finished. He was on his way back, around the pool, with an enormous basket piled high with the magnificent blooms. As he entered the kitchen, the phone rang. He set the basket down, telling Kathy, "Splash these out right away." Most people would have said, "Perhaps these should be put in water." Morgan did not put flowers in water. He splashed 'em out. *God knows why,* Kathy thought.

He headed to the phone and groaned when it turned out to be "the goddamned factory" . . . *Just a moment, sir, the President would like to speak to you* . . .

Morgan, who had been speaking to Lt. Cdr. Jimmy

Ramshawe in the small hours, had been nearly certain this
call was coming. And essentially he had been keeping his
head down.

"Morning Arnie," said President Bedford. "How's retirement going?"

"Pretty good, sir. All things considered. Just been picking
a few daffodils."

"A few *what?*"

"Daffodils, Mr. President. Bright yellow guys. First coming of spring. You pick 'em at first light. You want me to
bring you some, brighten up that goddamned dungeon you
work in?"

President Bedford was momentarily stunned. The very
image of Morgan prancing around a flower garden with an
armful of golden yellow blossoms was just a little too much
for him to grasp. An armful of hand grenades, maybe, torpedoes, possibly. Det-cord or even bombs. But daffodils? That
didn't sit real straight with the Virginian in the Oval Office.

Anyway, he simply said, "Gee, Arnie, that'd be real nice."

"Now what can I do to help?" asked the Admiral, amused
at how easy it was to throw the Commander in Chief off his
stride. "As if I didn't know."

"You're right, Arnie. Can you come in and see me? I just
had the King of Saudi Arabia on the line. And, Jesus, I'm
telling you that's one worried guy."

"I'm not sure I can help, sir," replied Admiral Morgan.
"But since your outfit provides me with a car and driver, the
least I can do is come in and have a chat. See you in one hour."

"Thanks, old buddy," said Paul Bedford.

"No trouble, Mr. President," said the Admiral.

Earlier That Same Day (local)
Dir'aiyah, Riyadh

It was almost first light when Colonel Gamoudi's mobile
phone, direct from Prince Nasir's palace, rang out among
the ruins of Saudi Arabia's former capital.

"Jacques?"

"Sir."

"Everything's go. Both bases at Khamis Mushayt fell in the early hours of this morning. The airfield and all the aircraft were destroyed. The military city surrendered at around o-three-hundred."

"How about the other garrisons? Tabuk? King Khalid? Assad? Any word?"

"Yes. They have not surrendered. All three refused when the commanding General at Khamis contacted them and suggested this might be a good time to quit."

"Okay. And does the Air Force have fighter jets in the air? Any sign of gunships?"

"No. I'm told Air Force morale is very low. Many princes have fled."

"Any sign of significant troop movements from any of the other bases?"

"I am told absolutely not. They seem to have gone into ostrich mode."

"Well, sir, you're an expert on sand, so we'll take that as definite."

The Prince laughed. "You are very funny, Colonel, even at a time like this. But now I must ask you, when do we attack?"

"Right now, sir. This is it. I'll call you later."

The phone conversation had already been too long for guaranteed privacy. Jacques Gamoudi hit the disconnect button and strode out into the open space beyond the walls of the mosque. He called all five of his senior commanders together and told them to fire up the heavy armored division. "We pull out in twenty minutes," he said.

Even as he spoke, Prince Nasir was on the line to the loyalists in the city, where thousands of armed Saudi citizens were preparing to march on the principal royal palace, behind the tanks.

And for the first time since 1818, the great crumbling walls of Dir'aiyah trembled to the sound of ensuing battle, as Jacques Gamoudi's big M1A2 Abrams tanks thundered into life and began moving out toward the road, passing the dozens of armored trucks loaded to the gunwales with ordnance.

The noise was deafening as they started their engines and rumbled forward, in readiness to form the convoy that would take down the modern-day rulers of Saudi Arabia.

With only minutes to go before start-time, Colonel Gamoudi moved back inside the ruins of the mosque and pressed the buttons on his cell phone. This was his final check with a small detachment of French Secret Service operators who had gone into Riyadh three weeks previously to gather the final information Gamoudi needed for his assault plan. The Colonel trusted his Saudi intelligence, but not quite so well as he trusted French intelligence.

Michel Phillipes, leader of the detachment, had little to add, except that the King had ordered the National Guard to deploy from their barracks on the edge of the city, with tanks and armored personnel carriers. According to Phillipes, the Guardsmen had been tasked with protecting at all costs the Al Mather, Umm al Hamman, and Nasriya residential areas. These were the districts that contained the walled mansions and gleaming white palaces of high government officials and many royal princes.

But Phillipes reported that this had been a very half-hearted operation. A few units had deployed somewhat nervously, and immediately retreated behind the walled gardens. But other units had not deployed at all, many of their soldiers having disappeared quietly back to their homes.

He said that the early-morning city news had announced that the major banks would again be closed for the day. But so far as he could tell, the predictable rioting and looting had not materialized. In fact, all his team felt that Riyadh was unusually quiet for this time in the early morning, with the sun already glaring above the desert.

"Seems to us like the calm before the storm," said Phillipes. *"Un peu sinistre,"* he added. A bit ominous.

There was, however, nothing even remotely ominous going on at Dir'aiyah. This was an army moving in for the kill. Weapons were checked, shells stored onboard the tanks, the Abrams crews climbing aboard. Engines roared, small arms were primed and loaded, ammunition belts slung over combat fatigues.

Every armored vehicle was prepared to open fire at a moment's notice. The gloves were off here in Dir'aiyah, and at 0920, Jacques Gamoudi's army rumbled out onto the highway and swung right for the capital, moving slowly, tank after tank rumbling down the dusty tracks from the ruins, truck after truck laden with trained Saudi fighters and hauling its warriors out onto the road.

And in the lead tank, his head and shoulders jutting out from the forward hatch, submachine gun in his huge hands, stood the grim-faced, bearded figure of the Assault Commander.

Jacques Gamoudi, husband of Giselle, father of Jean-Pierre, thirteen, and Andre, eleven, was going back to war. In his wide-studded leather belt he still carried his sheathed bear-killing combat knife, just in case today's fight went to close quarters.

He had ordered a rigid convoy line of battle, three tanks moving slowly along the highway, line astern, followed by a formation of six armored vehicles moving two abreast . . . then three more tanks . . . then six more armored trucks . . . then three more tanks, followed by a dozen armored trucks.

The packed troop carriers came next, with a rear guard of one final M1A2 Abrams tank. This was not an easy convoy to attack. If anyone did feel so inclined, it was damned nearly impregnable from the front, rear, and either flank. It was bristling with heavy weapons, and all of them were loaded.

Before they had traveled three miles, Colonel Gamoudi's cell phone sounded. It was Michel Phillipes again, reporting an early-morning stampede to King Khalid International Airport. It was the same in faraway Jiddah Airport, which also had many flights direct to other countries. Expatriates and their families, executives and managers within the oil industry, even manual workers and women, servants, teachers, secretaries, and nurses were desperately attempting to leave the country.

Scores of personnel from the Eastern Province were streaming along the road that led to the causeway to the island of Bahrain. The much smaller airport in Dhahran was packed with people trying to buy outward flights.

Even the U.S. armed forces were effectively making a break for it. Personnel from training bases across the country were attempting to reach Al Kharj, which lay 60 miles south of Riyadh—that was the old Prince Sultan Air Base in the Gulf War, and the only runway on which the U.S. military could organize contingency plans to evacuate its troops.

Michel Phillipes had men at Kharj airfield, where they encountered dozens of British expatriates who had been working on defense contracts. They met others who worked in Saudi Arabia for British Aerospace, and they were all trying to get out.

Judging by all known intelligence, Jacques Gamoudi could not imagine any stiff military resistance that morning, except from the guards at the main royal palace. And the convoy rolled on toward the northern perimeter of Riyadh.

All along the way, the armed freedom fighters waved at any local people they saw, presenting the face of friendship to everyone who stood by and watched. The troops even threw candy to passing children, following Colonel Gamoudi's creed always to make a friend if you can, when you're about to invade.

In fact the people generally assumed that this was the official Army of Saudi Arabia they were seeing. Everyone was in uniform, the vehicles were painted in Saudi Army livery. What else could it be? If there was to be more trouble following the destruction of the oil fields, this was surely the defense force of the King moving into position.

The first group to peel off was that of Gamoudi's great friend Major Majeed, whose two tanks and four armored vehicles swung left cross-country for King Khalid Airport, an objective they were ordered to take by storm.

Colonel Gamoudi's convoy pressed on to the head of

Makkah Road, where a vast, somewhat unexpected throng awaited them, shouting and cheering, waving in the air the brand-new rifles Prince Nasir's commanders had stockpiled so carefully for so many weeks.

In mighty formation they marched on down King Khalid Road, to the junction of Al Mather Street, where Colonel Bandar's group peeled away and headed directly to the main television stations.

Colonel Gamoudi pushed on toward the Interior Ministry, with the crowd massing behind his tanks and the Saudi commander bellowing through bullhorns for everyone to hold their fire until orders were given.

They approached the great wide entrance to the Ministry, with its massive oak doors, hand-carved in the magnificent Iranian city of Esfahan. The doorman, nervous, like most people, took one look at the incoming convoy and retreated, banging the great doors behind him.

Colonel Gamoudi immediately opened fire, slamming two shells straight into those doors, left and right, like a short broadside in an eighteenth-century naval battle.

The doors flew inward and smashed down into the foyer, and Jacques Gamoudi unleashed the dogs of war. Twenty-six al-Qaeda commandos, trained in the camps in the Afghanistan Mountains, charged forward, the lead six hurling hand grenades straight through the lower windows.

The simultaneous blasts in the downstairs offices were nothing short of staggering. Office workers were blown apart, crashed into walls, furniture was splintered, at which point the commandos raced into the building, machine guns held hip-high, yelling, *"Get DOWN . . . everyone get DOWN!!"*

Two government Ministers rushed from the mezzanine floor committee rooms, leaning over the wrought-iron handrail and looking below, demanding to know what was happening. The al-Qaeda men cut them down with a burst of gunfire, and both officials toppled over the balustrade grotesquely and to their deaths on top of the flattened doors.

Six more commandos piled in through the entranceway

and headed up the stairs. Everyone knew the layout of the building by heart since they had acquired the engineers' plans as used twenty years earlier by the Bin Laden Construction Companies.

And now, in a sense, they were in there fighting for the Ministry, in the name of their elusive spiritual leader whose creed they followed: to destroy the wanton, Western-influenced ruler of their home country.

The commandos reached the second floor and waited close to the eastern wall, beneath a huge stone archway. Three seconds later there was a thunderous blast from above, as Le Chasseur opened fire on the third floor and two more tank shells ripped high into the building. Plaster and masonry cascaded down the central area between the staircases.

And now the commandos were set to take the Ministry. There were fifty of them inside now, and they marched from room to room, kicking open doors, firing into voids, inviting anyone inside to surrender.

They combed every room, swept the corridors, herded dozens of terrified workers into order in the downstairs foyer. Thirty-two minutes after Colonel Gamoudi's opening shells, the Saudi Arabian Ministry of the Interior, complete with its entire staff, was the first casualty of Prince Nasir's takeover.

Colonel Gamoudi ordered the building secured. He left behind five trained commandos plus a group of twenty armed men selected from the great throng that had followed him to the Ministry. He ordered phone lines cut and turned his tanks around in the wide courtyard. Then he headed back north, toward the Diplomatic Quarter and the royal palaces that lay beyond.

At this precise time, Colonel Bandar's men reached the main entrance to the television stations, Channels 1 and 2 in the same building. The doors were glass, but Colonel Bandar, a former regular officer in the Saudi Army, elected not to drive his tank straight through them. But he drove up, within ten feet, and hurled a hand grenade through the

open window of the downstairs mail room, which blasted
asunder, scattering viewers' e-mails and letters to the
desert winds. He ordered the commandos inside the building. They came through the doors behind four grenades
that blew the foyer to pieces, sending an eight-foot-high
portrait of the King deep into the plaster of the ceiling,
where it hung for a few seconds and then crashed into the
rubble below.

Fifteen members of the staff came out with their hands
high and were ordered into the street, where a guard detail
lined them up against the wall and ordered them not to
move. Thirty more commandos dismounted from the troop
carriers and stormed into the building. The first floor was
deemed secure, and now they headed to the transmission
room, two floors above.

They came bursting up the stairwell, ignoring the elevators. Two permanent guards stepped out to block their entry.
Jacques Gamoudi's commandos gunned them down in cold
blood. The leading detail of six men rammed a steel chair
into the newsroom door, and they thundered into the long
room with its sound studios at the back and newscasting
sets occupying almost the entire foreground.

At first no shots were fired, as two of the raiders traversed
the walls, ripping electric plugs and cables out of their
sockets and tearing apart any electrical connections that
were all over the floor.

At a table in the far corner, much like the newsroom in a
newspaper office, the editors and reporters were preparing
for the next broadcast. With the stations now quiet, Colonel
Bandar's men opened fire, the bullets flying high above the
heads of the staff.

At which point the Colonel himself, a direct descendant
of the elders of the Murragh tribesmen in the south, came
through the door and strode over to the news desk, telling
the staff to get up, get their headsets off, and pay attention.
Then he barked in Arabic, "Who's the chief station editor?"

Two of the nine men pointed to different executives, and
Colonel Bandar shot them both down with a burst from his
submachine gun. He asked again, and this time one man

stepped forward and said quietly, "I am the news editor of the station."

"*WRONG!*" yelled the Colonel. "You *used* to be the news editor of the station. Right now *I* am the news editor. You will now go with my men and have your entire staff parade in the front hall. The slightest sign of disobedience, you and any member of your staff will be executed instantly. The rest of you, hold your hands high and walk slowly downstairs, no elevators."

Colonel Bandar appointed a four-man detail to accompany the former news editor all through the building, routing out the television station executives and journalists and ordering them to the front hall, where they were searched and allowed to stand easy, under guard.

Twenty minutes later, the Colonel came downstairs and demanded that ten transmission technicians report back to the newsroom. Ten petrified electricians stepped forward and made their way back up the stairs flanked by the Colonel's guards, under orders to reconnect the broadcast units that the marauding force had been so careful to leave intact.

The rebel leader then made an announcement that the kingdom would very soon be under new rule, that of the Crown Prince, who would be broadcasting within a few hours. He asked which of the staff would be prepared to carry on as before, but working under a new fundamentalist regime, and which of them would prefer to announce their loyalty to the outgoing King and face immediate execution. Not necessarily on this day, but certainly by the end of the week.

The staff of both Channel 1 and 2 right away pledged undying loyalty to the incoming ruler and were permitted to return to their offices, under guard, but still on the payroll. Colonel Bandar told them to prepare an outside broadcast unit to attend the Prince's palace four hours from then, to make the historic first film of a nationwide address by their new proprietor.

The main television stations had been captured with as little damage as possible, considering the circumstances. They would be up and running, under different management, within two hours. And now a ring of 200 armed men was placed around the building, to await the arrival of a specially appointed public relations executive, from the Aramco organization.

The staff would soon discover that he was a young man in his early thirties, passionately loyal to Prince Nasir, and he would oversee every future word broadcast on the two main Saudi channels. His salary would be $250,000 a year, and he was not a member of the royal family.

By now Major Majeed's group was driving forward, straight at the gates of King Khalid Airport, his convoy led by two tanks, line abreast, followed by four armored vehicles and 100 highly trained commandos, the leaders al-Qaeda combat troops handpicked by Jacques Gamoudi, the rest ex–Saudi military.

To the amazement of the security staff, the tanks swung into the precincts of the busy airport and headed straight for the control tower, crushing the tall, white fence like matchwood. They drove on, straight at the tower. Stunned passengers boarding packed passenger jets suddenly saw an antitank crew launch four rockets directly at the all-around glass windows high above the runways.

Only one hit. Two of the other three crashed into the building's lower floor, and the fourth smashed into the huge radar installation above the ops room, which was a scene of devastation.

All the windows had blown, mercifully outward, but the blast had played havoc with the sensitive equipment. Computerized screens were caved in, alarms were sounding, all transmissions to incoming aircraft ceased abruptly, and fourteen staff were badly hit by shrapnel. Two of them died instantly.

The commandos stormed the tower, demanding the surrender of all personnel in air traffic control, but there were no key operatives who could surrender. That antitank rocket had caused total catastrophe, and Jacques Gamoudi was going to be displeased. He had warned them to use rockets only if they met stiff resistance.

And now the control tower was wrecked. And Major Majeed's men were swarming into the airport ordering passengers out of the terminal at gunpoint, telling them to return to their homes, to the city, by whatever means they could. Airport buses were commandeered, taxis were ordered to fill up with passengers and to get out.

A squad of six heavily armed al-Qaeda warriors charged through the downstairs baggage area, informing personnel to concentrate on outgoing flights. They informed staff that their jobs were safe, but their task was to get people out of the airport and swiftly onto departing flights.

The al-Qaeda fighters in the tower ordered electricians from the first-floor ops room to switch off the runway lights. Fueled aircraft ready for takeoff could leave, but fully laden passenger jets would not be permitted to land.

Major Majeed ordered the restaurants to stay open and keep serving, and he told the airport announcement system to keep ferrying passengers out to Riyadh, but on no account was any aircraft to land without special permission from the Major himself.

Abdul Majeed wanted to ensure that private corporate jets coming to pick up senior technology staff from Aramco and British Aerospace were given maximum cooperation. Prince Nasir was going to need these people in the very near future. One hour after his arrival, the Major called Jacques Gamoudi and informed him that the airport had fallen to his forces.

Back on King Khalid Road, Colonel Gamoudi's convoy was again heading north, back toward the junction with Makkah Road. There must have been 10,000 people swarming behind him. He ordered a halt to the convoy at that junction and ordered the now-returned Colonel Bandar to take command of another tank, one armored vehicle, plus four troop carriers and to head for Jubal Prison, on the outskirts of the city, where many al-Qaeda sympathizers were held, most without trial.

His orders were terse. "Blast your way in, and take it by force of arms. They're only prison guards, and they'll surrender. Then release everyone. And stay in touch." Colonel

Bandar was pleased at the prospect of driving a tank straight through a big doorway. It was an opportunity he had refrained from at the glass entrance to the television station.

And now, with the airport, the Ministry, and the broadcasting services under control, Colonel Gamoudi turned his attack toward the main objective—the palace of the forty-six-year-old King of Saudi Arabia.

But first he wanted to deal with the Prince Miohd Bin Abdul Aziz Palace, where Prince Nasir had said that a full morning council would be convened. Whether or not the royal princes in this family gathering were still there, Colonel Gamoudi did not know. But he knew this was the guiding council of the monarch. If there was ever going to be a future uprising, it was likely to emanate from men in that palace this morning.

In the lead tank, now sitting up on the hatch with his machine gun held across his chest, Gamoudi looked every inch the conqueror, a powerful, bearded man, ice cold in his expression, riding at the head of a formation of tanks and armored vehicles, troop carriers, and literally thousands of born-again desert warriors, marching along, not cheering, dead serious, as they moved to dethrone the King.

Their route took them deliberately through the Diplomatic Quarter, since Colonel Gamoudi wished to make it quite clear that all foreign governments understood the thoroughness of the takeover. Occasionally there were small crowds of embassy staff out on the sidewalk watching the passing army gravely, doubtless making a thousand mental notes for soon-to-be-written diplomatic reports on the battle for Riyadh.

There was a crowd outside the British embassy, no one outside the French embassy, and a large crowd outside the American embassy. Jacques Gamoudi did not want any of these people to be injured if his convoy met sudden resistance. And he shouted at them as they passed, *"GET BACK INSIDE! DO NOT COME ONTO THE STREETS! YOU WILL BE INFORMED OF GOVERNMENT CHANGES LATER!"*

No one, of course, had the slightest idea who he was. He spoke Arabic with an accent, and all the armored vehicles carried the insignia of the Saudi Arabian armed forces. But this was a sizable convoy and it was plainly headed somewhere. And despite the general savvy of the personnel at the embassies, who knew perfectly well something major was most definitely afoot, it was still extremely baffling.

But as Jacques Gamoudi's tanks rolled by, it was particularly baffling for one senior U.S. envoy, Charlie Brooks, who had served in many U.S. embassies in North and sub-Saharan Africa throughout a long and distinguished career in the Diplomatic Service. It was rumored that Charlie Brooks might be the next U.S. Ambassador to Iran, at the new Tehran embassy.

Brooks stared hard at the man on the tank who was yelling at him to get back inside. Brooks was not terribly used to being yelled at. He looked at the man hard. There was a flicker of recognition. Gamoudi was wearing a *ghutra*, and it was quite hard to get a clear picture of him. And yet . . . to Brooks there was something familiar about him.

His mind ranged back over his many postings, trying to think of anyone he may have met who looked similar. But he could not focus on an individual. At least not until the convoy was out of sight around the next corner.

And then Brooks's mind slipped back several years, to a blisteringly hot day in June 1999, in the Congo, the old French colony, when the U.S. embassy in Brazzaville had been under direct threat from revolutionary forces. He remembered the siege conditions behind the embassy walls, and he remembered the rescue. That was what he really remembered.

The helicopter clattering into the grounds, manned by French Special Forces, their leader running into the embassy ordering everyone to grab what they could, documents and possessions, and to get on board either the helicopter or the French army truck at the gates.

He remembered the leader—an amazingly tough-looking bearded character, brandishing a machine gun and barking orders. He remembered him on the embassy driveway, ordering the helicopter into the air. And he remembered him herding the remaining staff down to the truck, manhandling packing cases full of documents and then running and jumping aboard the truck at the last minute.

They had made it the few miles to Kinshasa Airport, where the same French military officer was in charge, leading everyone out to the apron at the edge of the runway where the MC-130 aircraft was waiting.

If he thought hard, he could recall Aubrey Hooks and his staff piling up the steps into the aircraft, carrying what suitcases they could. He could hear in his mind the shouts and commands of the bearded man with the machine gun as he urged them onto the plane.

And he recalled the team from Special Ops Command Europe, mostly survey and assessment personnel, also joining them, until the aircraft could take no more. There was room for everyone except the French troops who had made the evacuation possible. And they remained at Brazzaville. Charlie Brooks remembered sitting with the United States Ambassador as the MC-130 hurtled down the runway and banked out across the Congo River. The last sight he had of the Congo was of the little group of French Special Forces standing outside the airport buildings, waving to the flight as it left them. He did not think he would ever forget their bearded leader.

But now he was not *quite* so sure. He could almost swear the guy up on the lead tank was the same French combat soldier. He could even remember his name . . . well, nearly. He seemed to recall the French troops called their boss Major Chasser.

He just wished he could have heard him speak in his normal voice, then he would have been sure. The yell a few moments ago, *"GET BACK INSIDE!"* addressed to the Americans in English, did not do it. But he was still damn near certain that was Major Chasser up there on the tank.

And as a career diplomat, working closely with the CIA, he did have one overriding thought: what the hell was he doing up there on the tank anyway, reading the riot act to local citizens in the goddamned middle of the capital city of Saudi Arabia? It beat the hell out of Charlie Brooks.

Unless France was somehow attacking the country. But the tanks were Saudi. And no foreign nationals served in the Saudi Arabian armed forces. It didn't make sense. And after several minutes of serious thought, it still didn't make sense to Brooks. Maybe he was mistaken after all. The guy did look like an Arab. But then . . . so had Major Chasser.

The big lead M1A2 Abrams rumbled on through the Diplomatic Quarter, the marching army bringing up the rear looked even larger now than it had been fifteen minutes previously. Their next stop was the Prince Miohd Palace, with its high white walls gleaming in the sunlight, and from 200 yards out Colonel Gamoudi and the two tanks flanking him opened fire.

The shells went screaming into the walls, punching huge holes. Bricks and concrete flew everywhere. Four other shells smashed straight into the second floor of the palace. The guard post high on the outer walls crashed inwards, but this was an important place, and a detachment of twelve guards rushed out to defend their royal masters.

Again Jacques Gamoudi's tanks opened fire, this time not with their big artillery but with raking machine gun rounds, sweeping a steel curtain across the road and the palace gates as lethal as the German gunners on the Somme.

The twelve guards fell in the road, and Jacques Gamoudi's tanks rolled forward, straight at the gates, Colonel Gamoudi himself standing up forward, his fist raised high, and shouting, *"FOLLOW ME!"*

The big M1A2 Abrams rammed the iron gates, which buckled and then ripped off their hinges, flying inward, sparks flying as they grazed the concrete paving of the driveway. The Colonel leaned back and hurled two grenades straight through the windows to the left of the doorway, and the commander of the tank to his right hurled two more, all four of which detonated with diabolical force, instantly killing the staff in the guardroom and the secretary to the right of the foyer.

The doors were flung open, and another detachment of six guards rushed out, perhaps to surrender, perhaps not. They were heavily armed, but their weapons were not raised. Gamoudi cut them down where they stood, round after round spitting from his submachine gun. No questions asked.

And now his commandos were in, pouring out of the two troop carriers behind the lead tanks. The first four men up the steps to the building were crack ex–Saudi Special Forces, battle commanders in their own right, veterans of anti–al-Qaeda "black operations" in the opening years of the twenty-first century.

They opened fire on the empty foyer, spraying machine gun rounds every which way. And right behind them came six al-Qaeda fighters, heading immediately for the stairs.

Which was where the first serious problem began. The guards upstairs on duty in front of the main conference room had been given possibly two minutes to man their defenses. They had two heavy machine guns at the top of the stairs, and with the al-Qaeda troops fighting to get a foothold on that second floor, they opened fire and blew the invaders away, killing all six of them on the stairs.

By now Jacques Gamoudi was in the door, and he saw to his horror that the machine gun was now aimed at him alone. He hurled himself to the floor, sideways, away from the stairs, and somehow clawed his way through the rubble to the cover of the big reception desk, a hail of bullets riddling the wall behind him.

His other troops were under the stairs in a relatively safe position. And with no visible targets, the machine gun at the top of the stairs was temporarily silenced. Jacques Gamoudi edged his way out almost directly below the upper balcony.

Right now he thanked God he had learned in the Pyrenees to become something of a master at the great French pastime of *boules*, with its heavy biased metal balls and the requirement for devilish backspin in the long forward arching throw to the "jack."

Gamoudi had spent many cheerful hours in the late afternoon with the village men back home in Heas, playing in the grandly named Heas Boulodrome, a shady piece of rough, flat, sandy ground near the modest town square. It had often occurred to him that a *boule* was approximately the weight of a hand grenade. A bit heavier, but not much.

He ripped the pin out of his first grenade and tossed it over the balustrade, where his men lay dead halfway up the stairs. It fell just below them. There was silence now in the foyer, but immediately the machine guns above opened up straight at the stairs again, where the hand grenade was rattling around.

Gamoudi had only a split second, and he took one stride forward and hurled his second grenade, with a wicked top-spin twist, upward toward the balustrade. Because of its weight it did not have much spin, not like a cricket ball or a baseball. But it did have just enough, and it curled over the upper balustrade, detonating four seconds later, right after the one on the stairs.

How Jacques Gamoudi got back underneath that high balcony he never knew; he knew only that he took off from his left foot, twisted, and landed facedown on the floor, eight feet behind his throwing mark. The explosion blew the upper balustrade clean off its foundation, and it crashed down into the lower hall. If Gamoudi had still been standing there it would have killed him stone dead. He felt the ground shake as the balustrade hit the floor.

Upstairs was a scene of carnage. The palace guards were killed to a man, their two machine guns blown into tangled wreckage. Colonel Gamoudi regained his feet, and roared orders to the men waiting outside the door. Three of them came bursting out of the wreckage of the guardroom and followed him up the stairs, the other one called for a medical detail to recover the bodies of their fallen comrades, over whom Gamoudi and his men were clambering.

At the top of the stairs they paused before the big double doors. The Colonel booted the doors open and then stood back for three grenades to be hurled inside. Fifteen Saudi ministers, fourteen of them royal princes, were seated around the table. Only two of them survived the blast, having had the good sense to get under the table before the grenades came in. The two stood up at the far side of the table and made a gesture of surrender, but Colonel Gamoudi shot them dead in their tracks with two savage bursts from his machine gun.

By now his men were fighting their way up the stairs. There was no opposition, but it did look as if the entire second-floor balcony structure might collapse. With thirty men now on the upper floor, Colonel Gamoudi gave his final order to his forward commander in the Prince Miohd Palace . . . *secure the building . . . arrest anyone left in it . . . any opposition, shoot to kill . . . I'll leave a force of one hundred men outside.*

The question now was, where's the King? He plainly had not arrived for the council meeting. They would have found him, his huge entourage, and about seventeen Mercedes limousines if he had. But there was no sign of him. It was impossible he had not yet heard of the staggering events of the past two or three hours.

Colonel Gamoudi called together the senior staff officers still serving in the front line of the battle with him. He checked the road maps, pointing out the two minor palaces, situated approximately along the route to the Al Salam royal palace, where he expected to find the ruler.

Again his instructions to his commanders were terse. "There will be no one of any great importance in either of them," he said. "Take them both by force of arms, causing as little damage as possible. We want the buildings and we do not want blood and dead bodies all over the place.

"Tell the staff to remain in place—any royal princes, take prisoner . . . but I doubt there will be any. You'll want a force of maybe forty people for each palace. No more. The new King will make his opening broadcast to the people from one of them."

And with that Col. Jacques Gamoudi headed back to his tank for the one-mile journey to the residence of the King. They had not traveled more than 100 yards before the next serious problem appeared to be hovering overhead, one Saudi military helicopter, that was not on their own aircraft list. It appeared to be taking an unusually close look at the marching revolutionary army.

Jacques Gamoudi raised his binoculars and checked the clattering chopper, which was now flying low, about 300 feet above his tank. The numbers on its fuselage did not correspond to any of three choppers run by Prince Nasir. So far as Gamoudi could tell, it might be arriving to evacuate the King, and he could not tolerate that. But before he could call up two or three Stinger missiles and attempt to shoot it down, it flew off, straight toward the palace.

And then, before Gamoudi could finish cursing, two more Saudi Army helicopters came battering their way over the horizon, flying low above the buildings. Again Jacques Gamoudi raised his glasses, and this time he could see the insignia of the King's Royal Regiment painted clearly on the rear of both helicopters.

He assessed this as an operation to evacuate the King. And he was correct in that. The two helicopters, giant troop-carrying Chinooks, followed the first much smaller one directly along the road to the palace, and Gamoudi saw them hovering, preparing to land inside the walls that surrounded the royal residence.

This was an emergency. He ducked back inside the tank, seized the communications system, and shoved down the red button. And twenty-one miles away, at King Khalid International Airport, an aging Boeing 737, takeoff priority number one, began to roll down the main runway with two young al-Qaeda braves at the controls, making their last-ever journey, the one before the three trumpets sounded, summoning them across the bridge, into paradise and the arms of Allah.

The Boeing banked hard left, racing east across the northern approaches to the city. Laden with fuel, it came in low over the desert making 300 knots. Colonel Gamoudi halted his convoy 1,000 yards short of the palace, awaiting the arrival of the suicide bombers, whose task it was to slam into the building.

It was a four-minute journey from the airport. Everyone saw the empty silver-colored passenger aircraft flying straight toward them. It came in low, drawing a bead on the great curved dome of the central part of the building. Everyone held their breath as it screamed above them, losing height, its engines howling.

Inside the cockpit, the pilot sensed he was too high. He throttled back, and forced the nose down, increasing the revs on those mighty Pratt and Whitney engines. Too late. They were still too high. With 400 yards to go, the pilot hauled back on the throttle, cut the engines altogether, and the Boeing lurched into an all-engine stall.

The nose came up as the aircraft dropped fifty feet like a stone. And then it made a perfectly hideous belly-flop landing *bang* on top of the dome and burst into flames. The dome collapsed, killing anyone on the upper floor. The Boeing lurched left and then tipped right, landing on its wing, which spun it around hard.

It hit the ground with a mighty crash, leveled a grove of twenty-eight palm trees, and flattened five parked Mercedes-Benz staff cars. The eight-man guard detail at the rear of the palace was killed instantly, but the objective of the entire exercise—the King and his most trusted advisers—was unharmed, as they hurried out of the building toward the waiting helicopters.

There were eighteen of them, but no women or children, the King's family having escaped four hours after the military bases at Khamis Mushayt had fallen. But there was a substantial group, and space on the helicopters was tight. There were packing cases of priceless jewels and artifacts to be loaded before the passengers could board.

Colonel Gamoudi was quite certain of the Chinooks' mission. He urged his task force forward, heading for the palace gates. He could see the black smoke rising from the grounds in the rear of the palace, but even from this half-mile distance he knew the Boeing had not accomplished its allotted task.

And now his prize might be slipping away. The very last thing a brand-new King needs is a very-much-alive old one. Even the British drummed Edward VIII and his American divorcée girlfriend straight out of the country to France, once they had decided King George VI would become the rightful monarch back in 1936.

It would be the most awful blow to King Nasir if the deposed ruler was somehow living high on the hog in Switzerland, spending some of his multibillion-dollar fortune, while he, Nasir, struggled to put Saudi Arabia back on its feet. One way or another Jacques Gamoudi had to nail the departing monarch. And he had about ten minutes, maximum, to do it.

He could see the third helicopter circling, hovering, and then dropping down also to land behind the high walls, in the vast front garden before the palace. *"Merde,"* he muttered, frantically signaling to all drivers to make all speed to the gates of the King's residence.

Engines howled, but the palace was still three minutes away. And it was still one minute away when the air was split by two enormous explosions. Flames and black smoke rose into the air, but no one could see what had happened behind the walls.

They reached the gates and smashed their way through amid scattered gunfire from the remaining palace guards, who had taken refuge inside the downstairs floor of the palace. Colonel Gamoudi's men returned fire with heavy machine guns and quickly silenced the defenders, who appeared to have no further desire to stick their heads above the parapet.

But the scene in that front yard was one that Jacques Gamoudi would remember for the rest of his life. The two Chinooks were blasted beyond recognition, six dead robed Arabs lay on the ground, and off to the right, leaning somewhat casually on a palm tree, was the unmistakable figure of the former British SAS Maj. Ray Kerman, in company with one of his Hamas bodyguards. They were both holding antitank rocket launchers, still smoking.

"Afternoon, Jacques," said General Rashood. "I thought I'd better get rid of those two Chinooks for you. You don't mind, do you?"

Jacques Gamoudi was almost speechless. *"Jésus Christ!"*

he exclaimed. "Did you just get here in that third helicopter?"

"How the hell did you think I got here?" said the General, looking surprised. "On the bus?"

Gamoudi shook his head and laughed. But then the enormity of his problems came cascading back upon him, and he suddenly shouted, in a loud, involuntary voice, "*Jésus Christ*, Rashood! WHERE'S THE KING! WHERE THE HELL'S THE KING?"

"He's in there," replied the General, nodding toward the palace.

"*How do you know?*" said Gamoudi, his voice rising again.

"Mainly because I just saw him go in there," said Rashood. "With a group of five bodyguards. The King was carrying an AK-47."

"But what if he escapes? Out the back way or something?"

"He can't. I just sent three of my commandos to seal off the rear entrance. Anyway, I'd guess it was too bloody hot to get through the gardens. There is, I expect you noticed, a 200-seater Boeing 737 with about 400 tons of fuel on fire under the date palms."

"So we'll have to roust him out, right?"

"Yup. Do you guys want me to give you a hand?"

"*Mon Dieu!* Was General de Gaulle French?" Gamoudi replied. "You need a machine gun?"

"What d'you think I need, a bow and arrow?"

Gamoudi ignored the sardonic humor of the victor of the Battle for Khamis Mushayt and headed back to his waiting chiefs-of-staff. Someone fetched a machine gun and ammunition for General Rashood, and an al-Qaeda soldier turned up with a diagram of the royal palace, courtesy of Osama's organization, which had provided engineers' maps of buildings constructed by the bin Laden family business.

Jacques Gamoudi had seen the plan of the palace before, but he never thought he would need it. He had counted on the suicide bomber to inflict fatal damage on the huge hall of royal residence. He had assumed a final intervention by the forces of Prince Nasir would be strictly routine.

But things were now very different. The palace had some serious damage high up on the dome, and there was obviously going to be masonry all over the top floor. But the first two floors, which contained twenty-seven bedrooms, were probably unscathed, and it was likely the King's personal bodyguard, numbering at least twenty armed members of the Royal Regiment, would put up a desperate fight to protect their forty-six-year-old ruler.

They might even have a pre-planned hiding place, like the old "priest holes" in Catholic monasteries, where clergymen hid from the malevolence of Henry VIII in medieval England.

Colonel Gamoudi did not think much of the prospect of chasing the King up some chimney or into some dungeon. And neither, for that matter, did General Rashood. They studied the floor plans of the sprawling palace. It was a maze of corridors, great yawning state rooms, dining rooms of unimaginable luxury. And below were kitchens and storage rooms. There was a long arched walkway to one side of an interior courtyard. Jacques Gamoudi shook his head in frustration.

And what was the King doing right now? Was he on the phone, perhaps informing the world of his plight? Maybe he was telling his friend, the President of the United States, that his palace and his regime were under attack by a bunch of lunatics and that the United Nations must somehow save him? Worse yet was the possibility that the King's extremely shrewd army commanders were planning to hole up inside the vast building and make their escape under cover of darkness. Colonel Gamoudi and General Rashood had inflicted heavy damage and they had a popular uprising going their way, but the King was still staggeringly rich, owning and controlling tremendous military resources.

And those resources might well be capable of getting him out, and that would be appalling news for Prince Nasir. Both Gamoudi and Rashood could well imagine the King sitting in some palatial residence on Lake Geneva, not so far from his multibillion-dollar fortune, giving weekly "exclusive" interviews to the world's media.

There would be headlines pointing out the sheer tyranny, the wickedness, and the savage lowlife intentions of the armed thugs who drove the rightful King of the Saudis from his peaceful and prosperous kingdom. The fall of the best friend the West ever had. The media would love it, true or not, and it could very easily cause the United Nations to condemn Prince Nasir and all that he stood for.

"Rashood, we have to get him," said Jacques Gamoudi grimly.

"No need to tell me, old boy," replied the General, reverting to his natural Englishness while speaking to a Frenchman. "And we have to get him fast."

"Do we charge the front door with a tank and go in with all guns blazing?"

"Sounds better than ringing the doorbell," said Rashood. "Let's get a half-dozen guys with antitank rocket launchers aimed at the front of the palace. They can open fire on the second- and third-floor windows as soon as we've stormed the entrance."

"Right," said Gamoudi. "We don't want to drive these guys upward into that mess below the dome. There may be good cover up there, and we don't want to fight on a bomb site."

"Correct," said Rashood. "We better beef up that detail in the rear of the building, if it's cool enough. But we don't want a lot of guys in the open. For all we know the troops inside are mounting machine gun nests in the windows."

"We're going to have to fight for this on the inside," said Gamoudi.

"'Fraid so," said the General. "And we better be very quick. I'm not much looking forward to it either."

They selected sixteen Special Forces to come in behind the tank. In their rear were twenty al-Qaeda and Hamas fighters, all carrying submachine guns and grenades. Jacques Gamoudi would lead the troops inside, the first moment they breached the entrance. He would concentrate on the downstairs areas, going room by room.

General Rashood would lead his commandos up the main stairs to the second floor. As ever, the principal danger was to the assault force, the troops who had to make it happen. The King's guard could fight a solid rearguard action, protecting their man, no hurry, until darkness came. And then they had a huge advantage, on terrain they knew backward. There was also, of course, the truly uncomfortable fact that no one knew what extra resources the King could call upon, including overwhelming world opinion.

Gamoudi and Rashood had to nail him. And they had to nail him right now. The Hamas General, for good measure, quoted the only rules that mattered during any military coup: "Let's do it fast, Jacques, and let's do it right."

Colonel Gamoudi boarded the M1A2 Abrams. The opening assault brigades moved into formation, and the engines of the tank screamed as it rolled toward the palace doors, the French veterans moving behind it.

The Colonel ducked low as the iron horse slammed into the doors, smashing them inward. And as they did so, two savage bursts of heavy machine-gun fire riddled the steel casing of the tank. Nothing penetrated, but the guns had them pinned down, half in and half out of the entranceway, facing into the main hall.

Now it was Jacques Gamoudi who could not dare put his head above the parapet. He ordered the tank to reverse and the gun to be raised. At which point he blasted the upper balcony with four successive shells, which crashed into the walls behind the gallery, which in turn caved in and caused the total collapse of the third floor in that part of the building.

There was dust and concrete everywhere, and the guns were, for the moment, silenced. The room on the second floor behind the shattered wall was nonexistent. Anyone in there was no longer alive. But there was no sound, and Colonel Gamoudi assumed the danger up there had receded.

He signaled for General Rashood to lead his men into the devastated reception hall and to take the remainder of the second floor. He watched the Hamas C-in-C bounding up the stairs, his troops following, tightly grouped on the wide marble staircase. There was still no sound from that second-floor gallery where the King's initial machine gun nest had been located.

Gamoudi split his men into two groups, one left and one right. He took the left-hand corridor and, room by room, booted open the doors and hurled in hand grenades. There was one aspect of this type of warfare that made the task slightly easier: no one cared who was in the rooms or whether they lived or died, and no one cared what damage was inflicted on the palace. There was no need for restraint.

Everything went to plan for six rooms. At the seventh, Jacques Gamoudi kicked open the door, and from inside someone threw a hand grenade out. It hit the opposte wall and clattered to the floor. Gamoudi wheeled around and, with his arms outspread, crashed everyone to the floor, or at least everyone he could grab—six of the eight.

When the grenade detonated he lost two of his best men instantly. The rest of them climbed to their feet coated in dust, some of them cut and bruised. As they did so, a second grenade flew out of the seventh door and clattered to the floor.

Again Jacques Gamoudi saw it and again he spread his arms, this time hurling the whole scrum in through the door opposite, and slamming the heavy door closed, just as the grenade blasted the corridor to pieces.

Suddenly this was serious. The men seized a huge piece of furniture and rammed it against the door, just to buy them a few minutes. They were short of guns, four of them still lying in the rubble outside. They had no more grenades left, and there were six of them essentially trapped until someone could open one of the high windows eight feet above ground level.

They had no idea how many opponents they had in this remote interior passageway. They knew the palace was surrounded, and they knew that General Rashood was gutting the upper floor for the King's guard. But they themselves were trapped, with only two guns and not much ammunition.

They did not dare shout for assistance, because there seemed no need to alert the opposition as to where they were. Whichever way they looked at it, this was the hunter hunted. And Le Chasseur took a very moderate view of that.

The one useful aspect of this reception room was the wide serving area at the rear—a massive marble-and-granite slab behind which they could take cover, even under heavy fire. The trouble was it would be almost impossible to fire back against a determined enemy, since that would require them to stand up against a white-marble background.

Their only chance was to cower there until the guards moved in, then hope to take them in close-combat fighting. Everyone carried a combat knife, and they all knew how to use them.

They could hear the huge doors being shoved open, the massive chest of drawers being edged inward. Gamoudi ordered his men to the floor, behind the marble serving counter.

They awaited their fate, which was not long coming. When the door was open less than two feet, six men, five of them uniformed and all of them armed, slipped into the room and opened fire at the space above the granite slab.

No one moved, until the commander signaled them to fan out and advance down the eighty-foot-long room. In English he called out, "Come out, all of you, with your hands held high . . . *COME OUT! IN THE NAME OF THE KING!*"

No one moved, and then the commander spoke again. "Should you decide not to come out, my men will throw three grenades behind that counter. We will retreat out of the door, and you will die. ALL OF YOU! NOW COME OUT WITH YOUR HANDS HIGH!"

And then, much more quietly, he added, "The King wishes to see those who would be his enemies. I will count to ten before the grenades are tossed in among you."

There was absolute silence in the room. Privately, Jacques Gamoudi thought they might catch a couple of the grenades and hurl them back, but even he doubted they would be able to catch all three.

"ONE . . . TWO . . . THREE . . . FOUR . . ."

Suddenly there was a slight movement at the doorway,

and with one leap the terrifying figure of General Rashood entered, a black mask protecting his nose and mouth from the choking dust and cordite in the corridor, his machine gun spitting fire in a long sweep right across the line of palace guards. Rashood aimed high, as he always did, at their backs. No one had time to turn and see their executioner.

It was like a firing squad. Nothing less. And one by one the guards slumped to the floor, bullets riddling their heads and necks, blood seeping onto the white marble.

The air was clean in here, and the General pulled the mask down from his face. He walked to the line of men he had shot dead in cold blood. He ignored five of them and he walked straight to the man who wore no uniform, but who, like the others, was facedown on the floor, the back of his head blown away.

He kicked the man over and stared down, directly into the unseeing eyes of a familiar face. Prostrate at General Rashood's feet lay the body of the King of Saudi Arabia. He may have lived like a Pasha, but he had died like a Bedouin warrior, his machine gun primed, facing his enemies. Except for the one who had shot him in the back.

"*Jésus*," said Jacques Gamoudi, as he walked across the room. "Am I glad to see you."

"Yes, I expect so," replied Rashood, in that clipped British accent of his, honed in the portals of a distant Harrow School. "But I owe you one. And I'd never say you weren't damned useful in a French bistro. Me, I tend to excel in royal palaces."

And with that he hurled his arms around his fellow commander. Between them, they had, after all, just conquered the largest country on the Arabian Peninsula.

Same Day, 4:00 P.M.

Prince Nasir stood before the cameras and made his inaugural broadcast to the people of Saudia Arabia from one of the smaller palaces a mile from the former royal residence. He described the death of the King, which had occurred during the People's Revolution, which had been so long in coming.

And he stressed that the late King and his enormous family had done nothing but plunder and spend the vast treasure beneath the sands—the treasure that belonged to everyone, not just to members of one family.

He railed against the closeness of the King and his immediate family to the United States, and how it was so much more natural for Saudi Arabia to forge alliances with closer and more traditional allies like France.

He pointed out the long history of cooperation between the two countries, and told the nation that he was already speaking to the French President in order to formulate a plan to rebuild the oil industry, which he deeply regretted had been the first casualty of the popular uprising. It was indeed a consequence of years of reckless living and massive incompetence by the royal family.

Where was the King when our great industries came under attack? The Crown Prince spread his arms apart in a gesture of mock confusion.

But throughout the broadcast, Nasir gave a message of hope and optimism. He swore to help Saudi Arabia regain its former position of wealth and influence, with a fair share of that wealth for every Saudi family. Not just one family.

He at last came to the words that everyone wanted to hear: *In accordance with our ancient laws, as Crown Prince, I have assumed leadership of our country. I have taken my vows with the elders of the Council. And I have sworn before God to uphold our laws . . . I am both your humble servant and your proud leader, King Nasir of Saudi Arabia.*

Same Day, Wednesday, March 24, 7:45 A.M. (LOCAL) the White House

KATHY MORGAN, SITTING at the wheel of their new Hummer, swung the civilian version of the U.S. Army's fabled Humvee straight into the West Wing entrance to the White House. Next to her sat her husband, Admiral Morgan, whom the guards saluted. Whenever the great man visited Pennsylvania Avenue it was like General Eisenhower returning to the beaches of Normandy. No one caused quite the same ripple of admiration.

He said good-bye to Kathy, who was having breakfast with her mother at the Ritz-Carlton, and headed toward the main West Wing entrance. The Marine guard stared at the enormous bunch of daffodils, saluted Morgan, and held open the door to the West Wing, inside which the Secret Service detail, on direct orders from the President, dispensed with the requirement for a visitor's pass and escorted the Admiral straight to the Oval Office.

Admiral Morgan, as he had done for so many years, walked briskly past the President's secretary, tapped on the door, and walked straight in.

The President stood and gaped at the daffodils. "Morning, Arnie," he said, smiling. "Hey, you got the blossoms. And you're right on time, as ever."

"End of the morning watch, eh?" replied the Admiral, mindful of the fact that the former Lt. Paul Bedford was immensely proud of having once served as navigation officer in a U.S. Navy guided-missile frigate.

The President chuckled. But his smile did not last for long. He buzzed his secretary and asked her to find someone to put his daffodils in a vase.

Then he said, "Sit down, Arnie. I've sent for some coffee. You want anything to eat?"

"No, thanks, sir. Coffee's fine. Guess we're talking about this Saudi Arabian bullshit, right?"

"We sure are. Just this morning the goddamned phone has never stopped ringing. Things are moving real fast. You heard any of the latest news?"

"Not as much as you have," replied Morgan. "Last thing I picked up on the radio was extreme fighting at the Saudi military city of Khamis Mushayt, and that the people of Riyadh appeared to be marching on the royal palace."

"Both correct," said the President. "But I hear now that the Khamis Mushayt Air Base has fallen, and so has the big Air Force station right next to it."

"Anyone say to whom it fell?" asked the Admiral.

"Ask not to whom the base fell," quipped the President. "Because we don't know. And neither do they. But the sucker fell, all right. Our air attaché in Riyadh reckons they lost half the Saudi Air Force."

"We got one shred of evidence of an outside foe?" asked Morgan.

"Nothing," said Paul Bedford. "If this is some kind of a war, it's one of the most secretive ever conducted. No one has the remotest idea who's doing the attacking."

"Guess someone does," mused the Admiral.

"And whoever that might be," replied the President, "they sure as hell know what they're doing. I've been looking at the stats on Khamis Mushayt. It's a huge and remote place. And no one even knows what happened. But they all say one thing . . . it's a one hundred percent Arab matter . . . conducted from inside the country."

Morgan nodded. "It just may be a little more complicated than that," he said. "Any news from Riyadh? I heard on the radio the Saudi Army may have turned on the King."

"Well, there's some rumor the airport's fallen to an armed assault force," said the President.

"Do we know where the King is right now?"

"No one seems to know. But I have spoken to him. And he was not under attack at the time."

"Is he in the royal palace?"

"I don't know that. I guess he doesn't want anyone to know where he is."

"'Specially not the guys who just blew up his oil fields and his Air Force, eh?" replied Morgan.

"Right," agreed the President. "'Specially not them."

"Any sign of the King's Army mounting a defense? He's got a hell of an armed force, and a lot of very sophisticated equipment."

"This whole thing seems like a series of devastating attacks—fast, professional, and very ruthless. Very military." The President looked utterly perplexed.

It was a few minutes after 8 A.M. Just then his secretary pushed open the door and walked over to the television set, which she tuned to CNN *World News*. "Sir, General Scannell just called to say it looks like the King of Saudi Arabia is dead. And he says the new King is about to broadcast."

"Thank you, Sally," said the President, turning with the Admiral toward the screen, where the anchorman was formally announcing the death of the Saudi ruler.

"The new King is fifty-six-year-old Nasir Ibn Mohammed al-Saud, a devout Sunni Muslim and a cousin of the slain King. He has been Crown Prince, heir to the throne, for almost twenty years and, like most of the Saudi royal family, he is a direct descendant of the founder of the kingdom, the legendary desert warrior Abdul Aziz, known as 'Ibn Saud.'

"And now we'll go live to Riyadh, where King Nasir is making his first address to the nation, and hopefully we'll have some real information on how all this took place."

The screen flickered, and suddenly the picture was of a robed and bearded Arab, his dress white, a red-and-white–checkered *ghutra* on his head, speaking to the people of Saudi Arabia.

The President and Arnold Morgan watched together as

King Nasir announced his regret at the death of his cousin, but nonetheless confirmed that this had been a "people's revolution," launched by thousands of citizens who could no longer acquiesce to the profligate spending of their ruler.

He sent his message of hope for the future, but Arnold Morgan frowned when the new King pointed out that France was his nation of choice to help rebuild the Saudi oil industry on both the east and west coasts of the Kingdom.

It was well known that Prince Nasir had long been a reformer, a strict Muslim fundamentalist who would stand by the teachings of the Koran and most certainly would not tolerate the spectacular levels of spending achieved by the royal princes. He himself was a man of the desert, and he believed in the Bedouin way of life, not only for others but for himself. He was a man of prayer and abstinence, and he despised the godless and material ways of the Western civilizations. And above all he wanted the United States out of the Middle East, and with that an end to terrorism.

But first he wanted a legal, internationally recognized Palestinian State. It was clear that now, for the first time, the Palestinians had for an ally the most powerful nation on the Arabian Peninsula. And at the head of that nation stood a man who cared nothing for the United States, nor for Israel.

This was not good for the man behind the desk in the Oval Office. And it was not good for the United States, where gasoline was currently commanding nearly ten dollars a gallon at the pumps. And the President said so.

"Seems to me there's only two parties doing well out of this," commented Morgan. "France and that goddamned towelhead up there with his goddamned self-satisfied smile."

"And his goddamned fleet of limousines, private jets, and servants," added the President, smiling.

"Yeah, but he says he has no interest in all of that," said Morgan.

"I know. But total power gets awfully addictive. And you cannot fault the lifestyle. He'll get to like it."

"Well, I really hope you're right, Mr. President. Because if you're not, and he really is a man of the desert, we're in real trouble."

"You mean no more Saudi oil?"

"Well, that. But also because Saudi Arabia has always been the missing piece in the jigsaw puzzle of the Muslim republics in the Middle East. Apart from the very small nations, we have always had Yemen, Iraq, Jordan, Syria, Kuwait, the Arab Emirates, Iran, Egypt, Libya, and most of North Africa. And, basically, you know where you are with all of them. They form one huge block of Islamic nations.

"But in the middle of them stands Saudi Arabia, which in modern times has always been neither one thing nor the other. No longer a fundamentalist Muslim nation, always a serious friend of the West, a group of devout Muslim princes, who own, literally, a fleet of the most expensive yachts in the world. Young men who profess devotion to the word of the Koran but live like Riviera playboys, at the King's expense.

"Saudi Arabia, our friend and ally, has always been the one huge thorn in the side of the Muslim republics. The one nation that is always out of step, the royal family that plays both hands against the middle. In short, the Saudis are a pariah to those who wish for a great Islamic Empire stretching from the Red Sea to Morocco.

"And some very influential Muslims have long hated the sight of them—guys like old bin Laden, even Saddam, the Hamas leadership, Hezbollah, all the supporters of the *jihad*. They hate Saudi Arabia for its endless wealth, its willingness to work with the West, and above all, its refusal to back any Arab action against the nation of Israel.

"Mr. President," continued Arnold Morgan, "that all ended about ten minutes ago. This Nasir character just placed the last piece into that Muslim jigsaw."

Paul Bedford stood up and walked the length of the Oval Office. "But what about the oil crisis, Arnie? What the hell's going to happen about that?"

"Mr. President, you are going to get the blame for that."

"ME?" exclaimed the Chief Executive. "What in the name of God has it got to do with me?"

"Everything. The American people are going to put up

with a ten-dollar-a-gallon gas crisis—for a little while. And then you're going to start hearing . . . *well, what the hell's the President doing about it? Why doesn't he negotiate with King Nasir? Why can't he be like other Presidents, stay friends with Saudi Arabia?"*

"I guess other Presidents have coped with that."

"Not quite," said Morgan. "Because this one is going to smash the world economy. It won't smash us, but it'll go damn close. Inflation will run amok, corporations will go bust, and the stock market will cave in. There'll be a run on the dollar, and our trading partners all over the world will be unable to pay us. This is a global financial crisis.

"And you, Mr. President, are going to be swept away in the torrent . . . a reviled figure in history . . . the President who let it happen . . . unless you do something about it. And damn fast."

"But what can I do? Right here we're dealing with a guy dressed in a sheet who wants to live in a tent in the desert. And he plainly wants nothing to do with us. And the fucking oil belongs to him." The President was just beginning to get rattled.

Admiral Morgan climbed to his feet. He stared across the room at the loneliest man in the world, who was standing, hesitantly, beneath a portrait of George Washington.

Morgan clenched his fist, gritting out the words: *"LEADERSHIP, Paul. You gotta raise your sights. Never mind the goddamned towelhead and his oil. You gotta stand up and say, I'M NOT HAVING IT. NOT AT ANY PRICE. NO ONE HAS THE RIGHT TO SMASH THE WORLD'S ECONOMY. AND HE'LL EITHER NEGOTIATE WITH ME, OR I'LL KICK HIS FUCKING ASS!"*

The President stared. But Morgan was not quite finished. He returned to his chair and said quietly, "And then, if we have to, we'll take his oil away and send the tribal bastard back into the wilderness. Because any other course of action is ultimately unacceptable, to the world, that is. Not just us."

"Arnie, are you saying I must be prepared to go to war with Saudi Arabia?"

"Sir, we don't go to war in the Middle East. We merely crash down an iron fist. It might be on some desert chieftain who thinks he can murder hundreds of thousands of people. It might be on a guy who has too many military ambitions and too many weapons. Or it might just be a guy we happen to think is unstable and dangerous to his neighbors. Either way, because of the effect of oil on the world's economy, we just cannot let some things go unchecked.

"And when some crazy prick under a palm tree thinks he can blithely wreck the economy of dozens of countries, just because he happens to have been born on some sand hill on top of a geological phenomenon . . . well, that's when the oil becomes a *world* asset rather than a national asset. And that's when we deem his stewardship of that oil has become remiss, and that's when we move to stabilize the world once more."

"Arnie, you should be sitting in this chair."

"No, thanks, Paul. I've got my own."

The President smiled. And there was one thought within him: *When this old warrior walks out of this office in a minute, I don't quite know if I can cope with this.*

Arnold Morgan read his mind. "Paul," he said, "it's all a matter a getting your thoughts straight. And you must be guided by a point of principle: If this Nasir character thinks he can screw up the world just because he feels like it, he's wrong."

The President nodded. "I sometimes think you forget I am the leader of a political party that stands to the left, and believes in freedom, help, and education for all the downtrodden peoples of this earth, including some of our own. It is not in our nature to go around crushing those who may seem to stand in our way."

Morgan looked up and glared. "The left has never been right about anything," he grunted. "Not about economy, not about the military, not about business, not about the rights of people, especially criminals, and not about geopolitics. The left and its useless ideals is why the Soviet Union and half of Europe just about went bankrupt. The left also brought China to its knees, and crippled Africa. The creeds of the left are not anything I'd have on my mind right now, if I were you."

President Bedford smiled and shook his head. He knew what to expect when he asked Admiral Morgan to come in and talk; Attila the Hun with a bunch of daffodils. "I'm not at all sure what I should have on my mind right now," he said.

"Personally, I think you should prepare yourself for the attacks on you, which are waiting to happen. And in my considered opinion, you're about one week away from an onslaught against your policies in the Middle East. Paul, they're gonna blame you for this oil crisis. Of course they'll know you did not instigate it. But they'll still blame you for not fixing it."

"Arnie, we still have not examined how bad it will be."

"Well, I'll tell you. With one-fifth of the world's oil suddenly gone missing, you'll have to start finding enough for the United States to operate normally. You'll go to Central America and South America and Kazakhstan for that. Then you have to open up some new and heavy drilling in Alaska. That way you look like a man who at least has a grip."

"I do have a grip."

"Okay. But there's more to it. This Saudi Arabia business is going to rumble on. And that may mean some countries are taken right to the brink—Japan, India, and Germany being three of them. And then, when the Saudis begin to put their oil industry together, there will be a rising swell among nations looking once more for that cheap, plentiful product. And right now I see us at the back of the line."

"You mean if this Nasir guy can sell it without us, he will?"

"Precisely. And that means you have to take a very aggressive stance right now."

"Meaning . . . ?"

"You have to do some serious ranting and raving. Whatever happened in Saudi Arabia, it was planned, planned very seriously. And whoever the hell planned it understood the consequences to the rest of the world."

"Do you think it was this Nasir character?"

"I think he was right in the thick of it. I think he knew it was happening, although I cannot be certain he was the precise culprit. Still, in general terms, the prime suspect in any murder is always the person who stands to benefit most from the crime. And that's surely our man Nasir."

"Well, Arnie, he's never going to admit that, and we're never going to ask him."

"No. But someone helped him. Some outside agent."

"As I recall, that was the King's view when I spoke to him a few hours before he died."

"Did he give any indication who that outside power might be?" asked Morgan.

"No, he did not. But I remarked that it sounded like a devil on the outside and another on the inside."

"How did he react to that?"

"He seemed almost resigned. Told me he was no longer certain whom he could trust."

"Since he's now dead, that was a rather prophetic remark."

"It surely was, Arnie. But how do you propose I proceed in this aggressive stance you wish me to take?"

"Sir, you must locate the country that made possible the overthrow of the Saudi royal family, which precipitated this crisis. That way we have a target, a political whipping boy, someone we can rail at, even attack. All of which will demonstrate that, in Paul Bedford, the United States has a President who will not put up with this subversive bullshit, which does so much harm to so many millions of people.

"We are often accused of being the world's policeman. And a lot of people do not like that. But when someone commits a massive crime, on an international level, everyone waits for the policeman to arrive. And they wait for him to deal with it."

"You mean I have to deal with this—find out what happened, on behalf of the dead King?"

"That way, all criticism of you will evaporate. You'll deflect it to the guys who committed the crime. And if you're smart, they'll take the rap for everything. We'll just look like the good guys, the victims who went in search of truth and, afterwards, perhaps revenge."

"Jesus. I like it, Arnie. I like it very much. By the way, do you have any idea which country was Prince Nasir's partner in crime?"

"I don't know. But if I had to put my last dollar on anyone, it would be France."

"FRANCE!"

Admiral Morgan revealed his suspicions and the suspicions of the National Security Agency. He talked about the missing submarines and the likelihood that the Saudi oil installations had been slammed by cruise missiles delivered from below the surface of the ocean. And he talked of the apparently inspired decision by the French to divest itself of reliance on Saudi oil several months before.

He reminded the President of the sheer impossibility of a successful attack on well-defended mainland oil fields in the desert kingdom. And he concluded, "Only from the sea, Mr. President, only from the sea."

"And they could not be Saudi Navy submarines or missile ships?"

"The Saudi Navy does not have submarines."

"But when I left the U.S. Navy, twenty-something years ago," replied Paul Bedford, "they were just getting brand-new ones from the Brits, weren't they?"

"They were. But it all fell apart . . . mainly because they had no expertise in these ships . . . and much of their coast is surrounded by shallow water, especially on the Gulf side. Anyway, it never happened. But the NSA is certain that whoever fired the missiles at the oil fields fired 'em from underwater. But it was not from a Saudi ship."

"Even so, Arnie, that's pretty scanty evidence. Okay, the French changed their oil-buying policy just in time. But that does not make them guilty of a crime against mankind."

"No, of course not. But getting out of Saudi oil was a very fortuitous and unusual thing to do. And I admit we have no proof it was French submarines that fired the missiles. But there were two French Rubis-class ships in the area, and they have both disappeared. Either of them, or even both, could have done it. And there was no other submarine within thousands of miles with the same capability. Except our own. And I happen to know we're innocent."

"You sure you're not still working here somewhere, Arnie?"

"Sometimes feels like it, I'll say that."

"Why don't you consider coming back and working with me?"

"For about ten thousand reasons, the main one being the likelihood of my beautiful wife leaving me."

"Well, if you ever change your mind . . ."

"No chance, Paul. But I quite like hovering on the outside, lending a hand and an opinion where I can."

"Do you have any further opinion on French involvement in this latest catastrophe?"

"Yes, sir. Yes, I do. The NSA is working on a very curious satellite signal they picked up emanating from an area north of Riyadh, the night before the battle for Khamis Mushayt. Some kind of coded message the Brits picked up at that hotshot little listening station they maintain in Cyprus."

"Why is that significant?"

"Because the transmission was in French. Coded French."

"Yeah? I didn't hear about that."

"I don't suppose you will until they crack it. The intelligence community, as you know, does not make a habit of boring the President to death with half-assed information. But I know they're on the case."

"Doubtless your young Australian buddy, Lt. Commander Ramshawe?"

"He's the one, sir. Shouldn't be surprised if someday he made the youngest NSA Director ever."

"What does he think—about the overall situation regarding France?"

"He is absolutely certain the French helped the rebel Saudis. And there's another part to this conundrum. Last August, two hit men from the Mossad made a valiant attempt to take out the Commander in Chief of Hamas, failed, and were both killed."

"Is that significant to us?"

"Yessir. It is. Because they made their attempt in the French city of Marseille."

"So? Where's the connection?"

"Sir, Lt. Cdr. Jimmy Ramshawe wants to know what the C-in-C of Hamas was doing in a French city, plainly under the protection of the French government, six months before a bunch of towel-headed brigands took control of Saudi Arabia."

"You mean, Arnie, in conjunction with the oil situation, France getting out of Saudi product? And the submarine possibility? And the French coded signal from Riyadh a few hours before the battle? Was the Hamas Chief involved in the command of the assault team? All that?"

"Now, sir, you're beginning to think like an intelligence officer." Admiral Morgan smiled. "And remember this point, above all else: when something absolutely shocking happens on a global scale, the solution is never down to one thing. It's always down to everything.

"And Lt. Commander Ramshawe, personal assistant to our esteemed NSA leader, George Morris, believes he is building a very powerful case against France. And if he can nail 'em, that's your way out of this whole goddamned mess. Because then you'll attack the French verbally, shouting and yelling about their unfailing selfishness, their total disregard for anyone else.

"And you tell the world how they helped bring down the Saudi King entirely for their own profit. Never mind half the world falling into a blackout, never mind hospitals and schools closing down because of power shortages. Never mind stock market crashes, highways coming to a halt, the world's airlines grounded through lack of fuel.

"They—the great, imperious, and haughty French, *la grande civilisation*—must go their own way, steering their own course along the road to prosperity. Gallic pricks. And you will step up to the plate and demand, with all the wrath and righteous indignation of the United States, that France be hauled before the United Nations to explain their conduct.

"You will once more look like the leader of the world.

But trust me. You cannot sit here and hope to Christ this stuff goes away. Because it's not going to.

"And if the French have really done this, sir—effectively taken Saudi oil off the world market, for their own ends—they deserve every last kick in the ass we can give 'em."

"Yes," said the President. "That they do."

Same Day, Same Time
National Security Agency

Lt. Cdr. Jimmy Ramshawe would have been pacing his office, except the floor was such a complete mess with piles of paper he would probably have killed himself. As it was, he sat staring at transcripts of messages and wondering why he was drawing a complete blank on every lead he had on the shattering events in Saudi Arabia.

The two French submarines were still missing. And for the umpteenth time Ramshawe counted the hours since the missiles must have been fired—0100 local on Monday morning . . . *that's sixty-five hours, and all that time the two missing Rubis, the Perle and the Améthyste, were moving away from the datum, probably at a dead-silent seven knots.*

Ramshawe took his dividers and assessed where on the chart the submarine in the Gulf had fired her missiles, calculating that they had also landed and retrieved a team of frogmen . . . *somewhere up here, northeast of the Abu Sa'afah oil field . . . must have been somewhere up here, because they couldn't make a getaway straight through the bloody oil field . . . they must have gone north.*

He hit the buttons on his calculator, multiplying sixty-five hours by seven knots . . . *455 nautical miles . . . that puts him somewhere here, through the Strait of Hormuz, and about 120 miles southeast running down the Gulf of Oman. One more day, and she's free and clear, steaming down the Arabian Sea in deep water—straight to the French naval base at La Réunion, unless I'm very much mistaken.*

Ramshawe adjusted his dividers to appreciate distances in the Red Sea . . . *the second submarine fired at the same time, somewhere off Jiddah . . . and they also ran away making seven knots . . . 455 nautical miles . . . that puts them in the narrowing part of the Red Sea, off this long coastline of Eritrea and Ethiopia . . . one more day and they're through the Strait of Bab al Mandeb, home free, running out of the Gulf of Aden . . . straight to La Réunion.*

Ramshawe considered this was essentially a blind alley. The French would admit nothing, probably would not even reply to an inquiry from the United States. And yet he could not stay away from the possible routes of the *Perle* and the *Améthyste*.

"I just wish to hell one of the other leads would come up," he muttered. "Maybe a little more on the Frog in the Desert. Maybe a fix on where his message went. If we could just find out who dined with Major Kerman that night in Marseille. Anything would help. And what about the new Saudi King confirming that the French were getting the cream of the rebuilding programs in the oil fields?"

Ramshawe felt he was on the right track. He was certain this was all to do with France. But like many another detective before him, he was just waiting for a break, just a tiny chink of light in some obscure corner that might one day illuminate the whole picture.

"Doesn't seem much to ask," he stated to the empty room. "Just one small break for Jim, one giant leap for the industrial world."

At 1100 local time, right there in the National Security Agency, he got it.

The CIA were just beginning to push through the system the firsthand reports from their own people in Riyadh. That included several field officers working for Aramco, several informants who worked for the agency out of local businesses, banks and construction corporations, and, of course, the serious professional operators inside the U.S. embassy.

Most of them were Americans, and all of them were passing back their accounts of the events in the capital city as it fell to the "forces of the people." And there was little in dispute, since almost everyone described the military convoy led by the big M1A2 Abrams tanks trundling through the city, taking the ministry, taking the television stations, taking the airport and then the royal palaces.

There was of course the hair-raising account of the suicide bomber crashing into the King's palace, and there were hazy accounts of the sporadic firefights inside the walls of the palace, and the burning of the two Chinooks that many people had seen fly over the Diplomatic Quarter. But it was the firsthand report from the veteran U.S. diplomat Charlie Brooks that instantly caught the eye of Lt. Commander Ramshawe. Because this was a man who had served the United States in many parts of the world, and understood the stakes. And what Brooks had written, from his vantage point along the direct route of the convoy, was nothing short of riveting. At least it was to Jimmy Ramshawe.

"All of the armored vehicles carried the insignia of the Royal Saudi Land Forces, and it was assumed we were watching a military exercise, except of course the presence of the Abrams tanks was unusual. However, I was struck by the presence of the commander who was standing up in the turret of the leading tank. He was a heavyset bearded guy wearing combat gear and a red-and-white Arab ghutra on his head. Like all of the other soldiers he was carrying a submachine gun and an ammunition belt across his chest.

"I was certain I recognized him, and of course I had to consider the fact I may have encountered him at any number of Saudi diplomatic receptions. It is perfectly usual that we meet serving Saudi military officers. And this man was most definitely an Arab in appearance.

"However, it took me a few minutes to place him. And I am now certain where I first met him. He was the leader of the French Special Forces team that rescued the staff of the U.S. embassy in the Congo, back in June 1999. I refer to the embassy of U.S. Ambassador Aubrey Hooks, in Brazzaville, where I served for several months.

"The forward commander on that leading tank was the

*same man. He had carried my bags into the French Army
truck outside the Congo embassy. I stood with him while he
loaded the packing cases full of documents, and I shook his
hand when we boarded the aircraft for Kinshasa. He was
definitely French. His men called him, I think, Major Chasser . . ."*

Jimmy Ramshawe almost choked on his stone-cold coffee.

He read the communication over and over, digesting the
stick of dynamite Charlie Brooks had sent by encrypted
e-mail direct to the CIA sometime during the past couple of
hours. And essentially his question was the same as Brooks's:
what the hell was this French Special Forces officer doing
leading an armored convoy to attack the palace of the King of
Saudi Arabia in the middle of the capital city of Riyadh?

He realized of course the explanation could have been
very simple. Many Middle Eastern defense ministries had,
over the years, employed retired Special Forces combat soldiers to help train their own armies. It was not unusual to
find SAS men helping the Israelis. Indeed Maj. Ray Kerman had served in just such a role.

And certainly the Saudis had employed many Army, Air
Force, and even Naval special advisers from Great Britain,
the United States, and, less often, France. The officer in the
leading tank may well have been hired by the Saudis after
he had retired from the French Special Forces.

But, according to Charlie Brooks, this guy was not serving in the capacity of a "special adviser." This guy, a foreign
national, was commanding the entire Saudi assault force,
the one that took down the King.

Lt. Commander Ramshawe understood something of
those desert people, and he had read often of the fierce
pride of the Bedouin. Ramshawe loved the writing of the
great Arabist Wilfred Thesiger. And he knew one thing for
sure: even if this was a rebel Arabian army, somehow split
from the main Saudi military machine, it was impossible it
was being led by a "bloody Frenchman."

Thoughts flooded through Ramshawe's mind. *Was this the
Frog in the Desert? Was this assault force in the Saudi capital half-French? Who the hell else was in those tanks? Was*

this a partnership between the new King Nasir and France? Or was Major Chasser just a bloke who'd emigrated to Saudi Arabia and somehow taken over the Saudi Army?

"Bloody oath!" muttered Ramshawe. "This Charlie Brooks has sure as hell lit up my little investigation . . . I don't know where to start . . . except I have to run this Chasser character to ground in a real hurry."

He picked up the report and headed along the corridor to see Admiral Morris, hoping to hell he was free to have a talk, and hoping to hell he had some hot coffee. Jimmy Ramshawe shuddered with anticipation at both prospects.

The Admiral was available, but his coffee was colder than Ramshawe's. George Morris read the report from Charlie Brooks and looked up sharply. "Two priorities, Lt. Commander: One, we gotta find out about this Chasser guy. Two, have a quick word with the Big Man before you start."

"Three," added Ramshawe, "will I get us some hot coffee?"

"Four, thank Christ you asked," replied the Admiral.

There was always a knowing repartee between these two that was unexpected—the lugubrious, wise, rigidly disciplined ex–Carrier Battle Group Commander, and the free-wheeling U.S.-born Aussie who operated on instinct and intellect, brilliance rather than structure.

"I'll call the Big Man while we're waiting," added Ramshawe.

He walked briskly back to his office, ordered coffee for the Director's office, and dialed Admiral Morgan's number in Chevy Chase. No reply. On the off chance, he hit the secure line to the White House and inquired whether Admiral Morgan was there.

"Who would the Admiral be visiting?" asked the operator.

"Couldn't tell you that," replied the Lt. Commander. "But I'd start with the President."

A few moments later, the President's secretary came on the line and said politely, "Lt. Commander, Admiral Morgan is in with the President right now. Would you like me to tell him you are on the line?"

"Please," said Ramshawe.

Within ten seconds the rasping tones of Admiral Morgan came down the White House line to the National Security Agency, as they had done so many hundreds of times before.

"Hey, Jimmy. This urgent?"

"Yessir. One of our guys in the Riyadh embassy just filed a report identifying a former French Special Forces officer in command of the leading tank that attacked the Saudi King's palace this morning."

"Jesus Christ! Is that right? Tell you what, stay where you are. I'll come out to Fort Meade and we'll go over this whole French bullshit right away."

Morgan replaced the telephone. He looked up at President Bedford and said, "I'd better go. We may have the breakthrough that will nail France to the wall. Can you get me a car?"

A car! At that particular moment, President Bedford would have wrapped up Air Force One in Christmas paper and given it to Arnold Morgan with love and gratitude.

A half hour later the Admiral was back in his old domain at Fort Meade, sitting in George Morris's chair—where else?—reading the report from Charlie Brooks and complaining about the quality, and especially the temperature, of the National Security Agency's coffee.

Nothing much had changed since Arnold Morgan first sat in that same chair a dozen years ago. He remained the glowering intelligence genius he always was—impatient, mercurial, bombastic, rude, and, according to his wife, Kathy, adorable. Just so long as you always remembered that his bite was one hell of a lot worse than his bark.

"I'll send for a fresh pot," said Jimmy Ramshawe, picking up the phone.

"Hot, Jimmy. For Christ's sake tell 'em to make it hot. Lukewarm coffee makes lukewarm people, right?"

Ramshawe was not absolutely sure he got that. But he still snapped, "Aye, sir." That was the response Admiral Morgan expected, and in Ramshawe's opinion it was a small price to pay for the presence of his hero.

"Jesus, we're damn lucky this Charlie Brooks was on the case," said Morgan. "And, of course, we have just one main objective, aside from the goddamned coffee: we must find out the precise identity of Major Chasser. Get Charlie Brooks on the line."

"Right away, sir," answered Ramshawe, lifting up the telephone and asking the operator to connect him to Mr. Charles Brooks at the U.S. embassy in Riyadh, Saudi Arabia.

That took only three minutes. In every U.S. embassy around the world, everyone hops to it when the National Security Agency is on the line.

"Brooks here. I've been expecting you guys for the last hour . . ."

"Morning, Charlie," said Ramshawe. "This is Lt. Commander Ramshawe here, assistant to the Director. I believe we've spoken a couple of times before?"

"Yes, we have, Jimmy. Guess you called about my report."

"I did. Very interesting. 'Specially that bit about the commander on the leading tank."

"That was him, I'm absolutely sure of that. Sorry I don't know his correct name, but they kept referring to Major Chasser. I spoke to him several times in Brazzaville, and he was definitely French, but he looked like an Arab."

"You're spelling that C-H-A-S-S-E-R?"

"Well, I am. But I'm only guessing. That's what they called him: Chasser, like Nasser."

"Charlie, we may want to pursue this further. If we do, can you give us some guidance, from back in Brazzaville, where we might dig up some detail?"

"Well, I'd have to look that up. You see, I only saw him during that one day, the day we all got out. But I may have some stuff still on my computer, you know, a few names of contacts who might know more."

"Okay, Charlie. We'd all be grateful. Maybe if I call in a couple of hours?"

"Don't bother, Jimmy. I'll e-mail the information."

"That would be great. Just one more thing . . . did you have the impression this Chasser was definitely in charge of the assault convoy?"

"Oh, there was no doubt about that at all. His tank, the big Abrams, was out in front. He was calling the shots, both to passing civilians and to the rest of the force to the rear of his armored vehicles. I walked farther up the street, behind the convoy, and I saw Chasser's vehicle slam straight into the gates of the royal palace. And he wasn't asking anyone's permission. Trust me."

"Okay, Charlie. You've been a real help. We may talk later."

"So long, Jimmy."

The Lt. Commander replaced the telephone and looked over to the big desk where Arnold Morgan and George Morris were talking. "He's very definite," said Ramshawe. "The guy was called Chasser, like Nasser. Spelled C-h-a-s-s-e-r."

"And right there we got a real problem," said Admiral Morgan, a little grandly. "The French do not have the sound e-r . . . like we say Chasser or Nasser. E-r on the end of a word in French, any word, is pronounced *ay*. If this guy's name was Chasser, the French would say, Cha-ssay."

"Well, Charlie said he heard Chasser, like Nasser. And he repeated it. He was certain how it sounded."

"But he's uncertain of what he spelled," said Morgan. "It's elementary. The sound does not exist in French."

Now, Ramshawe thought, for a bloke whose French accent sounds like Jackie Gleason trying to imitate Maurice Chevalier, the Admiral is being pretty dogmatic. So he pressed forward.

"Okay, sir. What's the nearest sound the French do have for E-R, and how do they spell it?"

"Well, they have e-u-r. As in *professeur,* professor. Sounds much the same. But that's how they spell it."

"How about Chasseur . . . is that possible? What does it mean?"

"How the hell should I know?" replied Morgan. "We got a French-English dictionary around here?"

"Probably not," replied Admiral Morris. "But I can get one sent down in about one minute."

At that moment the fresh coffee arrived with, miraculously, a blue tube of Morgan's preferred "buckshot," the little white sweeteners that tasted like the sugar both his doctor and his wife had banned. Word had already hit the kitchens: the Big Man was in residence. It was just like old times.

Admiral Morris poured, Morgan stirred, and a slightly breathless young secretary from the Western European language department came through the door with the required dictionary.

"Let me have that, kiddo," said Morgan, sipping gratefully. He skimmed through the first section, French–English, for the elusive word *Chasseur*.

And on page seventy-four he found it—*chasser,* the French verb "to hunt," or "to drive away." Pronounced, obviously *chass-ay*. Right below it was the word, *chasseur,* the French noun "hunter" or "fighter." The dictionary added *chasseurs alpins*, meaning "mountain infantry." The feminine was *la chasseuse*. But Arnold Morgan had it. Le Chasseur. The hunter. That was plainly their man.

"And a goddamned good nickname that is," he said. "For a tough sonofabitch French mercenary. Question is, who the hell is Le Chasseur. Better call Charlie back, Jimmy. Ask him if he thinks it's possible that Chasseur was his nickname rather than his correct name?"

"Aye, sir."

"That you, Charlie? Jimmy here again. We just wondered whether you thought Chasser could be a nickname rather than a real name?"

"Sure it could. I heard it more than once, but it could have been just the name he was usually called. Like Eisenhower was 'Ike,' Ronnie Reagan was 'Dutch,' John Wayne was 'Duke.' Sure, it might easily be a nickname."

Ramshawe confirmed the conversation. Morgan stood up to leave. "Keep at it, guys," he said. "Watch for the submarines, and keep checking the Brits for more on that message from the Frog in the Desert. Sounds to me like Le Chasseur might *be* the Frog in the Desert. Stay in touch."

And with that he was gone, and neither Admiral Morris nor Lt. Commander Ramshawe had the slightest doubt what they needed to accomplish next.

"Jimmy," said Admiral Morris, "we have to establish that this Chasseur guy is a French citizen, and/or a French resident, with a French home and possibly a French wife. If we can't establish those things, we have nothing. Not enough to point the finger at France."

"You mean the ol' *J'accuse*," said Ramshawe, in his Aussie accent, utilizing one of the only three French phrases he knew—along with *Je ne sais quoi* and *Arrivederci, Roma*, which he readily accepted could turn out to be Italian.

Admiral Morris shook his head. "Exactly," he said. "We must have sufficient evidence before we point the finger. And if this Chasseur in the front tank is really French, coupled with all the other stuff, we've probably got 'em."

"What do we do? Get the CIA on the case?"

"Right now," said Morris. "And they start in Brazzaville, where the Chasseur held high command in French Special Forces ten years ago. There must be people who remember him. There's still a major French embassy in that city. I'd say the guys could identify him with a proper name in less than a couple of days."

"I'll call Langley right away," replied Ramshawe.

Same Day, 0600 (local)
Brazzaville, Congo, West Africa

Ray Sharpe had been stationed in the former capital of French Equatorial Africa for two years. Here in this swelteringly hot city on the north bank of the Congo River he had held the fort for the U.S.A. in one of the least desirable foreign postings Langley had to offer.

But Brazzaville was an intensely busy port, a hub between the Central African Republic and Cameroon to the north, the former Zaire to the east (now the Democratic Republic of Congo), and Gabon to the west. The mile-wide Congo was the longest navigable river in the whole of Africa, providing a freeway for enormous quantities of wood, rubber, and agricultural products. And an enormous amount of skulduggery. Ray Sharpe was well tuned in to the buzz of the African underworld. Sometimes he thought there was more underworld than overworld.

But today he was not stressed. For a start, it was lashing down with rain—warm rain here at the back end of the season but, nonetheless, sheeting, soaking squalls that rendered several highways impassable. Drainage right here was not precisely top of the line. But, for Africa, it was almost adequate.

He was sitting on the wide, shady veranda of the French Colonial house he rented. For a change, he was not pouring sweat—thanks to the cooling rain clouds—and he was taking a man-sized suck at his first cold beer of the evening.

Sharpe was a native of New England, south Boston, a devoted fan of the Red Sox and the Patriots. A burly blackhaired Irish-American of forty-three, he had volunteered for Brazzaville mainly to escape a particularly messy divorce. All right, he probably drank too much, and his work took him away from his wife for much of the year, but he could not for the life of him understand why Melissa had to run off with some goddamned hairdresser named Marc—with a *c*, he always added contemptuously.

And he was always baffled by the fact that Melissa, without mercy, had skinned him alive financially. Christ! They'd been at Boston College together, where she'd been a cheerleader, and he'd been a star tight end. Their families dated back to the same county in Ireland, Limerick. And she'd tried to nail him to the wall.

All of which conspired to turn Sharpe into a classic expatriate colonial resident—stuck out here at the ass-end of West Africa, still drinking too much, missing home, but too short of serious cash, too disillusioned, and rapidly becoming too idle to return. He had learned to speak French, and he had friends in Brazzaville, but most of them were much like himself, with big expense accounts and nowhere much to spend the money, except at restaurants and bars.

Still, great fortunes were made in places like Brazzaville—importing, exporting, buying dirt cheap, selling back to the

U.S.A. or Europe. He'd seen it, he'd had opportunities, and there'd be more. But somehow he had never gotten around to making a commercial move himself. Not yet, anyway. But he'd get to it soon. Definitely.

Sharpe was just reaching into the cooler for a fresh beer when the phone rang. Who the hell was that? The beautiful chocolate-colored French waitress, Matilda, from La Brasserie in the Stanley Hotel up the street? Or maybe even Melissa, now without her faggot boyfriend, calling for more money.

"Jeez," he muttered, walking inside to pick up the telephone. "Sharpe," he said, inwardly groaning at the all-too-familiar *Good evening Mr. Sharpe, Langley here, West African Desk . . . just a minute for the Chief.*

Five minutes later he was back in his big swinging couch, staring at his notes. *French Special Forces Commander, June 1999. Evacuated the U.S. embassy. Envoy Brooks and Ambassador Aubrey Hooks. Believed nicknamed the Chasseur. Please trace—get real name, background, and current residence if possible. Urgent FYEO. Soonest please.*

For your eyes only. Sharpe's eyes were a tad bloodshot, and it was still raining like hell, but he drained his beer, grabbed his light mackintosh, and headed his Ford Mustang out through the tree-lined boulevards of the biggest city in this old French colony, toward the modern-day French embassy on Rue Alfassa. Of course, he knew the resident secretariat extremely well—like every diplomat, spy, and journalist.

His route took him straight through the central area of Brazzaville, which was still dominated by the Elf Oil tower jutting above the skyline, a symbol of French industrial power. He never gave it much of a thought, of course, and he would probably never know how significant that building was to his evening mission.

As luck would have it, most of the French embassy staff had gone home for the evening, leaving only the famously ill-tempered Monsieur Claude Chopin on duty. Aged about ninety-four and claiming direct bloodlines with the great composer—who was, anyway, Polish—Monsieur Chopin was a stern French patriot. The Republic's tricolor hung above his desk, next to a large portrait of General Charles de Gaulle. Old Chopin had worked here for about thirty-five years, and had spent most of those years sipping wine and griping and moaning.

He looked up and, seeing that his visitor was the American Ray Sharpe, issued what he thought was a smile but turned out to be a suppressed sneer. *"Bonsoir, Sharpe,"* he said. *"Qu'est-ce que vous voulez?"*

Which was only a marginally polite way of asking what the hell the CIA man wanted.

"C'mon, Claude, what's eating you, old buddy? I'm here on a simple mission. The smallest piece of information, that's all I want. You'll probably know it off the top of your head."

"Possiblement," replied Chopin, lapsing into his customary combination of broken English and pure French. "But whether I tell it to you is a matter *différente.*"

"Claude, I have come over to see you because it is a rainy evening and I was just relaxing, having a beer, when I was interrupted by a phone call of such insignificance it made my hair curl . . ."

"It's already *frisé*," growled Chopin, who was very bald and thought Sharpe's mop of curly hair made him look like a pop star.

Sharpe grinned. "Seriously, old pal, you can end my problems very easily . . . you remember when the gallant French Special Forces liberated the besieged Americans in the embassy right here in Brazzaville in 1999?"

"Who could forget?" Chopin shrugged, his mind roaming back to those terrifying days in the 1990s when armed gangs drove around the city with their victims' severed heads stuck on their car antennae. "Of course I remember."

"Well, I'm trying to remember the proper name of the Special Forces leader . . . they called him Le Chasseur . . . the hunter. Did you know him?"

"Of course I knew him. He was stationed here for several

months. He stayed up the street, at the Stanley, for a few weeks—all those French officers stayed up there."

"And Le Chasseur . . . you remember his name?"

"Why do you want to know?"

"Well, I've just been told there is to be a new presidential award for foreign nationals who have helped the United States beyond the call of duty." Ray Sharpe was a think-on-your feet liar of outstanding talent—like most spies.

"We would like to bring them to Washington, with their wives and families, and decorate them for their bravery. President Bedford insists on conducting the ceremonies personally."

"Very commendable," said Chopin. "And they picked Le Chasseur after all these years?"

"It sometimes takes a new President to recognize a debt of honor," replied Sharpe.

"Well, I can't help you much," said Chopin. "I heard he'd retired from the military. But his name was Jacques Gamoudi. Maj. Jacques Gamoudi. Everyone called him Le Chasseur, the hunter. He was a tremendous soldier, and a true hero, as I expect your American diplomats would confirm. Someone did tell me he'd made Colonel."

"Thanks, Claude. That's all we need. Washington will take it from there."

Five minutes later Ray Sharpe was back on the line to the West African Desk in Langley. Three minutes after that, the phone rang in Lt. Commander Ramshawe's office and a voice told him, "Jimmy, your man is Colonel Jacques Gamoudi, but he's retired from the military. And you're right about his nickname. He's Le Chasseur, the hunter."

Langley also told Ramshawe that their man in Brazzaville was still on the case and would call as soon as possible with anything more he could find. And this was not long in coming. Matilda's boss, behind the long wooden bar in La Brasserie at the Stanley Hotel, had been there for years and knew Jacques Gamoudi.

The barman was not full of precise detail, but he remembered the Major as he then was—a light-skinned French North African, originally from Morocco.

"Was he married?" asked Ray Sharpe.

"Yes. Yes, he was," replied the barman. "But she never came here. I saw a photograph of her, though. Her name was . . . er . . . wait a minute . . . she was Giselle . . . and either her parents or his . . . they lived somewhere up in the Pyrenees. I remember that."

"How come?"

"Well, he always talked of the mountains. He said he liked the solitude. I think his father was some kind of a guide. But anyway he often told me that when he retired he would like to find employment as a mountain guide, and he always mentioned the cool air near his wife's parents' home. I think the terrible heat and humidity here in Africa can really get to you after a few years. Anyway, Jacques dreamed of the mountains—somewhere cold, I know that."

Ray Sharpe got straight back on the phone to Langley, and finally returned to his beer cooler and swinging seat on the veranda of his Brazzaville home. It was still raining like hell, and he was comprehensively soaked. So he just sat steaming and sipping, wondering how the Red Sox were doing back home in spring training.

Lt. Commander Ramshawe studied his notes. He walked along to see Admiral Morris, and wondered, "Have we got enough to find him?"

"No trouble, Jimmy. I'll have a quick word with our military attaché in the Paris embassy and then we'll hand it back to the CIA guys in France to finish the job."

In the next two hours CIA agents in France made probably fifty phone calls, and one of them came up trumps. Their top man in the French city of Toulouse, Andy Campese, was especially friendly with his opposite number in the French Secret Service. And DGSE Agent Yves Zilber, knowing absolutely nothing of the highly classified nature of the work of Le Chasseur, was cheerfully forthcoming to an old friend.

"Jacques Gamoudi. Oh sure. He and I worked together for a couple of years. I haven't spoken to him recently, but he retired from the military and went to live somewhere up in the Pyrenees, near his wife's family.

"As I recall, he became a mountain guide up on the Cirque de Troumouse—that's a massive range up near the Spanish border, in the snow. You can only get up there about four months of the year, but I think Jacques is one of the top mountaineers in the area. He lives somewhere near a little place called Gedre."

Just before the CIA man rang off, however, the French Secret Service agent remembered one further piece of helpful information.

"Andre," he said, "Jacques changed his name, you know. A lot of guys retired from the service do. I might even do the same myself one day. Anyhow, he suddenly decided to call himself and his family Hooks. I once asked him why he picked such a curious name, and he said he once had a friend of that name, out in Africa."

Andy Campese rang off with much gratitude. But twenty minutes later, Agent Zilber had second thoughts about what he had said. What was a CIA man doing inquiring about a retired French Secret Service officer? It was probably nothing, but he wanted to clear himself.

Agent Zilber always reported directly to Paris, and he put in a phone call to 128 Boulevard Montier, over in Caserne des Tourelles, in the outpost of the twentieth arrondissement, way to the west of the city center of Paris. He spoke briefly to the duty officer and, somewhat to his surprise, was asked to wait. Then a new voice came on the line and said, "*Bonsoir*, Agent Zilber. This is Gaston Savary, and I would like to hear your report."

Agent Zilber was momentarily surprised at being put through to the head of the entire French Secret Service. This was very much a case of *WOW! Gaston Savary! Mon Dieu! The head of the DGSE. What have I said? Or, worse yet, done?*

"Well, sir. A short while ago I received a phone call from an acquaintance of mine, Andy Campese—works for U.S. intelligence. And he wanted to know a few details about an old colleague of ours, just a retired officer. No one important. And I just gave him a clue as to how to locate the man. It wasn't much. You know how we often swap information with the American agents. Andre Campese has always been very helpful to us."

"Of course," replied Gaston Savary smoothly. "What was the name of the officer in whom he was interested?"

"Col. Jacques Gamoudi, sir."

Gaston Savary froze. His whole system shuddered, his heart missed about six beats, his pulse packed up altogether, and his brain turned to stone. At least that's what it felt like to Savary. But he was trained to accept shock. And after a three-second pause, he spoke again. "And for which branch of American intelligence does Mr. Campese work?" he asked.

"He's CIA, sir."

Gaston Savary, a thin, sallow-complexioned man, turned instantly a whiter shade of pale. He was so stunned he gently put the phone down without making one further inquiry. And before him stood a vision of France being outlawed from the international community.

And it was his own department, the glorious Direction Generale de la Sécurité Exterieure (DGSE), successor to the sinister SPECE, that had sprung the leak.

Gaston Savary held his face in his hands and tried to breathe normally. He took an iron grip on himself and his emotions. But, in truth, he could have wept.

Thursday, March 25, 9:00 A.M. (local)
The Pyrenees

They'd been driving all night, fighting their way by car up the mountains from Toulouse, the temperature dropping, and the weather worsening all the way as they climbed into the rugged high country. The 220-mile trek had taken almost seven hours, two of those hours spent on the final forty miles running southward and upward along the winding, treeless road from the town of Tarbes to Gedre.

The easiest part was finding the address of Le Chasseur.

Even the local milkman, delivering early on the south side of Gedre, had known of the near-legendary mountain guide Monsieur Jacques Hooks.

In short order, Andy Campese and his colleague, a twenty-eight-year-old French-born American, Guy Roland, hit the village of Heas, entered the village store and bakery at 7:30 A.M., bought takeout coffee, a fresh warm *baguette,* and a few slices of ham.

Almost as an afterthought, Andy reached the door and called back, "Monsieur Hooks . . . straight on?"

"Four houses up the street on the left. Number eight."

Andy Campese considered he had done a very cool night's work. And it was cool—about 34 degrees Fahrenheit. They walked up to the house, which had lights on, but then decided to go back to the car, have breakfast and keep a firm watch on number eight until 8:30.

And at that point he and Roland opened the gate and walked up the pathway to the white stone house. They'd been quick and thorough, ever since Yves Zilber had put them on the right track.

But they had been nothing like as quick as the men who worked for Gaston Savary, the men who had arrived by helicopter and evacuated Giselle Gamoudi, and her sons, Andre and Jean-Pierre, three hours previously.

When the doorbell was answered, Andy Campese and Guy Roland faced a Frenchman who was most definitely not Colonel Gamoudi. He was about thirty years old and he wore a black leather jacket over a dark blue polo-neck sweater. His hair was cut in a short military style and he looked like a combat soldier from the First Marine Parachute Infantry Regiment, which indeed he had been until six months previously.

"No," he said in English, almost as if he knew their native language, "Monsieur Hooks is away on business."

"And Mrs. Hooks?"

"She and the boys are visiting her mother."

"Can you tell us where?"

"Somewhere near Pau, I think. But I have no way of contacting her."

"And you? Can we know who you are?"

"Just a friend."

"Any idea when they might return?"

"Sorry."

"Do you work with him up here in the mountains?"

"Not really. He's just a friend."

"Just one thing more . . . does Monsieur Hooks own this house?"

"I believe so. But I could not be certain."

"Okay, sorry to have disturbed you."

"Good-bye."

Andy Campese was a very experienced CIA operator. And he knew for absolute certain when he had encountered one of his own kind. The French Secret Service were parked in Jacques Gamoudi's house, there was no doubt of that. And no doubt in Campese's mind that wherever the Colonel was, it was very, very secret indeed.

He made one more stop at the village shop and inquired whether Madame Hooks had been in residence the previous day. He was told, "She was here yesterday afternoon. I saw her meet the boys off the school bus. But I noticed they did not catch the bus this morning."

"And Jacques?" he asked.

"Oh, we have not seen him for several months. He's supposed to be on some kind of mountain expedition . . . but who knows? Maybe he doesn't come back."

Andy called Langley on his cell phone, and at 3:45 A.M. in Washington, he dictated a short report, detailing the fact that he was 100 percent certain Colonel Gamoudi's residence was now under the strict control of France's DGSE. He said he believed the family had been moved out in the middle of the night, probably in response to his own call to Yves Zilber.

"And they must have moved damned fast," he said. "We drove straight up here from Toulouse, and they were long gone. Jacques Gamoudi himself has not been seen in the village for months. For the record, he lives at number eight Rue St. Martin, Heas, near Gedre, Pyrenees. Postcode 65113.

"The phone is listed in the book under Hooks—05-62-

92-50-66. I didn't try it because it's probably tapped, and there didn't seem to be much point. I don't even know if it's connected. Giselle Hooks and the children were definitely here yesterday afternoon."

While Andy and Guy Roland set off briskly down the mountains back to Toulouse, the French agent in number 8 was moving with equal speed. He hit the buttons from the house to the DGSE HQ on the outskirts of Paris and reported directly to Monsieur Gaston Savary.

"Sir," he said. "They were here . . . at o-eight-thirty this morning. Two CIA agents inquiring about Colonel Gamoudi and his family. They were polite, not particularly persistent. If I had to guess, I'd say they were just trying to establish his residence here. They demanded no details, except who I was."

"Which of course you did not tell them?"

"Of course not, sir."

Gaston Savary stood up and walked around his office. There was, he knew, only one solution to a burgeoning problem. He tossed it around in his mind for a half hour and the facts never varied . . . and neither did the answer.

If the Americans know that Colonel Gamoudi was the assault commander in Riyadh, they probably also know a few other pointers to our involvement . . . that Hamas thug from Damascus is not a problem—he's probably gone home already, with his troops, and will never be found, not in Syria.

The submarines are beyond detection, and anyway the French Navy does not answer to the Pentagon. I expect the U.S. government is aware of our activities in the oil market, but that's mere coincidence.

It's Gamoudi who's our problem. He's French. They have his address. And he's plainly been identified, somehow, as the leader of the Saudi revolutionary forces.

If they catch him, he may very well be forced to admit everything.

Gaston Savary glanced at his watch. It was just before 9 A.M. He picked up the telephone, direct line to the Foreign Office on the Quai d'Orsay, and he spoke very briefly to Monsieur Pierre St. Martin, saying, briskly that he was coming to see him on a matter of grave urgency.

Savary was so locked into his own thoughts he ordered a driver to take him. This was most unusual. The Secret Service Chief always drove himself, but this time he sat in the back-seat churning over in his mind the very few options he had.

When he finally walked into Monsieur St. Martin's office, his mind was made up. He accepted a cup of coffee, served by the butler, and waited for the man to leave. He then faced the French Foreign Minister and said icily, "Pierre, I am afraid we must eliminate Jacques Gamoudi."

Thursday, March 25, 0500
National Security Agency

LT. COMMANDER RAMSHAWE was on the encrypted line to
Charlie Brooks in Riyadh. It was the final check required
before Admiral Morris reported to the President that the
NSA was 100 percent certain the Saudi Arabian mutiny had
been led by a former French Special Forces officer from the
Pyrenees, thus implicating France, right up to its *pantalons*.

And once more the wily U.S. envoy had brought home
the bacon. He had spent the night in the basement of the
Riyadh embassy combing through the yards of film shot by
the security cameras mounted on the high walls of the embassy. The ones at the gate were too narrow in focus and did
not cover the entire width of the road. But the wide-angle
rotating camera, set just below the roof, covered the whole
scene. Brooks had in his hand a blowup print of the convoy
coming toward, then moving away. And clearly pictured
was the bearded figure of Col. Jacques Gamoudi, machine
gun ready, standing up in the for'ard hatch, the lead officer
in the lead tank.

The embassy camera had even shot pictures of the Colonel in an unmistakable gesture of urgency, beckoning to the
vehicles in the rear. Above him could be seen a lone helicopter, the one that circled before the Chinooks, the one
bearing General Rashood. Unhappily for the United States,
the camera could not see inside that copter.

Charlie Brooks told Ramshawe the photographs were on their way via the National Surveillance Office, and there was no question in his mind: the assault commander was the same man who had liberated the U.S. embassy in Brazzaville—Le Chasseur.

"Hey, Charlie," said Ramshawe, "I was just going to call you anyway. We got a name for your guy. Does Maj. Jacques Gamoudi mean anything to you?"

"Gamoudi," said Brooks. "Give me a minute . . ." He tried to remember those final hours in Brazzaville, the final days when the city was almost destroyed. The scene of chaos and terror was still real to him. He could still hear in his mind the gunshots, and if he thought hard, he could still smell the burning rubber of the upturned cars in the street. He had seen the severed heads on the antennae, watched the fury of the mob from behind the embassy walls.

He tried to recall the first time he ever saw Le Chasseur, the morning the French Special Forces came bursting through the embassy gates. There was gunfire outside, but the lunatic bloodlust of the revolutionaries was no match for the steady, trained fire of the French troops who drove them off.

But then he remembered: one of the French combat soldiers, the one driving the evacuation truck, had been hit as he climbed down from the cab. Brooks could see it in his mind—the man lurching in through the gates, blood pouring from a wound in his leg. Somehow, after eleven years, he had cast that image from his subconscious. But now he remembered the French trooper going down, falling, and then getting up again. He'd been standing two yards from him. And most of all he remembered the one single bellowing cry the man gave: "JACQUES!" He mentioned this to Ramshawe.

"You got him," said Brooks. "Le Chasseur's name was Jacques. You can take that to the bank. And the pictures will show you he was the assault commander in the force that stormed the Saudi royal palace."

"And now his Pyrenean home is under the special protection of the French Secret Service," muttered Ramshawe. And then he thanked Charlie Brooks for all he had done. Lt. Commander Ramshawe had quite sufficient data to send Admiral Morris directly to the President. After, of course, a quick check with the Big Man.

He walked back along the corridor to the office of the Director, where he knew Admiral Morris had been for most of the night. He tapped lightly and walked in, carrying his dossier of information.

"Hi, Jimmy," said George Morris. "Have we nailed it down?"

"Definitely, sir. Just spoke to Charlie Brooks in Riyadh, and he confirms he heard Colonel Gamoudi called Jacques, very loudly by one of his troops injured in the fighting. Better yet, he's been through the film on the embassy surveillance cameras on the outside walls. A few of the frames show the convoy and clear photographs of Gamoudi leading the operation. He's the forward commander in the lead tank. It's him all right.

"Back in the Pyrenees, the CIA guys ran him to ground. Found his house. But the French Secret Service were already in there. No sign of Jacques, of course, but there wouldn't be, would there? He's in Riyadh helping King Nasir. The CIA agent reckoned it was a race between him and the French Secret Service to get to Madame Gamoudi.

"The French won, and by the time our guys reached Jacques Gamoudi's village, at o-eight-hundred this morning, the Gamoudi family had been evacuated in the night. Now, I ask you, would the French have gone to all this trouble if Gamoudi had been an innocent mountain guide? Of course they bloody wouldn't."

"And this was definitely Gamoudi's house?"

"Dead right it was, sir. The CIA guys checked in the village, and the French agent in the house said it was probably owned by Gamoudi, but he did not know for sure. He was probably telling the truth."

"That'll do for us," said Admiral George Morris. "Now

all we gotta do is find Colonel Gamoudi, and somehow get him right back here to the U.S.A. That way we'll hang the French Government out to dry."

"You want me to run this past the Big Man?"

"Yes, I think that would be a good idea. Meanwhile, I'm going in to talk to the President."

Ramshawe drove his black Jaguar up to the door of the house in Chevy Chase at 0900. Two Secret Service agents escorted him through the front door to see Admiral Morgan, who was sitting by the fire in his study, growling at the *Washington Post* and the *New York Times,* in that order.

The *Post* was banging on about A FAILURE OF U.S. DIPLO-MACY IN SAUDI ARABIA, and the *Times* was carping about U.S. FAILURE TO UNDERSTAND THE ISLAMIC MIND, both of which, according to Morgan, showed the usual sad, naive, total lack of comprehension he associated with both publications.

"Liberal assholes," he said. "Fucking dimwits could learn more from two hours with young Ramshawe than they'll ever know." Then he looked up and saw his visitor. "Hi, Jimmy," he said. "Just thinking about you. What's hot?"

"Plenty. We just ran the ol' Chasser to ground."

"Chass-eur, Jimmy. Chass-eur," replied Morgan, still sounding precisely like Jackie Gleason doing his Maurice Chevalier. But he grinned. He refrained from hurling the newspapers into the fire, which he felt like doing, and set them down on a small coffee table next to him. Then he yelled "COFFEE!" at the top of his lungs—in a bold attempt to attract the attention of the sainted Kathy, in the kitchen—and chuckled at his own appallingness. Then he settled back and said, "Right, Lt. Commander, lay it on me."

"Well, sir, the CIA got after him in Brazzaville . . ."

"BRAZZAVILLE . . . that's some goddamned dung heap in the middle of the Congo River. How the hell did he get down there? I thought he was in Riyadh."

"He is, sir," said Ramshawe, chuckling.

"And will you, for Christ's sake, stop calling me sir? I'm retired. I've been a friend of your father's for years. Call me Arnie, like everyone else."

"Yessir," said Ramshawe, as they each knew he would, both of them being absolute suckers for the easy punch line. "Right, Arnie. The CIA went to work on him in Brazzaville because that's where we know he served for several months a decade ago. Remember we only had Le Chasseur, nothing else."

Morgan nodded. "No name, right?"

"No name. But we put the local man on it, and he came up with one almost immediately: Colonel Jacques Gamoudi, a Moroccan, always known as Le Chasseur."

"Nice accent," said Morgan.

"Thank you," replied Ramshawe. "Then the CIA gave the entire French staff the task of actually tracing him. And they located his family home, wife, children—the lot—in a tiny village up in the Pyrenees where he works as a mountain guide. And guess what?"

"The French Secret Service were in that house when they got there."

"How d'you know that?"

"Put yourself in their place: They've handpicked this superb Special Forces officer to mastermind their friend Nasir's takeover of the country. He's been out there training his troops for several months. He's probably served in the French Secret Service himself. Everyone knows him. Then, suddenly, up pops a U.S. agent, from the CIA, in the middle of France, wanting to know who and where he is. Plainly the French will deny all knowledge of him and his whereabouts. But they know Madame Chasseur is up in the Pyrenees with her children. And they know the CIA is hot on the trail of this Frenchman who is smashing up the world's economy. What would you do, young Ramshawe?"

"I'd get up the bloody mountains real quick and get Jacques Gamoudi's family out of there."

"Precisely, Ramshawe. And then what would you do?"

"Dunno."

"In my judgment, you would have little choice. You'd have to assassinate Jacques Gamoudi, and probably his wife as well. Because those two alone could tell the whole world what you had done."

"But I imagine Gamoudi was very highly paid by the French government to do no such bloody thing?"

"Yes, I suppose so, Jimmy. And I expect the government's secrets would be safe with him. But what if we got a hold of him? What if we threatened him with crimes against humanity or something. What if we got him to tell us what happened?"

"Well, in that case the Frogs might want him dead."

"Exactly. And if they somehow assassinated him, they'd have to assassinate his wife, too. Because wives who know their husbands have been murdered are likely to have a lot to say."

"Christ, Arnie. You're saying the French might right now be in pursuit of the Colonel?"

"I should think very definitely. If we want him, you'd better tell George to look sharp about it."

Just then the radiant Kathy came in with coffee. She greeted Ramshawe warmly and asked Morgan if he'd like her to buy him a bullhorn, just in case she was ever out of range.

The Admiral stood up and put his arm around her, saying to Ramshawe, "I can't imagine how she puts up with me, can you?"

The Lt. Commander decided this was not a question he need answer, but quipped anyway, "I'm afraid that's the lifelong problem the lower deck has when they're dealing with an Admiral."

"You'll find a lifelong problem dealing with an Admiral's wife if you're not careful." Kathy laughed as she swept off the quarter deck and went back to the kitchen. "By the way, are you staying for lunch?" she called back.

"'Fraid not, Kathy. I've got to get back, and it'll take me an hour in the traffic."

The Admiral sat back in his big chair by the fire. For a few moments he said nothing, apparently lost in thought. But then he did speak. "You know, Jimmy, this is a terrible thing France has done. I guess this Nasir character has told them they'll have the inside track on Saudi oil once it's up and running, maybe even an exclusive agency. And they've always bought a lot of military hardware from the French.

"But you think about it: Can you imagine the United States doing something like that? Or Great Britain? Or the Aussies? For pure personal gain, to let the rest of the world go to hell for two years? Wiping the world's most plentiful and best-priced oil right off the map? Bankrupting little nations? Damn near closing down Japan? Hurting just about everyone? And not caring? Jesus Christ. That takes a damn special nation."

"Arnie, are you certain in your own mind—I mean as certain as I am—that France is at the bottom of all this?"

"I am certain that a group of rebel Saudis could not possibly have done this themselves. I am certain they had outside help, and I am certain that outside help came from France."

"Is that sufficiently certain to start taking action?"

"Jimmy, I'm not the President. I'm not even an official government adviser. But if I were the President, I could not just sit back and see the industrial world go to hell while France sat back eating *escargots* and getting richer and richer off the Saudi oil industry. No. I could not do that."

Meanwhile, over at the White House, Admiral Morris was walking the President through the entire French scenario, explaining in detail how Le Chasseur was run to the ground.

When he was finished, the President looked extremely worried—for all the reasons Admiral Morgan had pointed out to him. He was going to be blamed for the financial collapse in the United States, and on a global basis, he would probably bear the responsibility for the collapse of the free world's economy, and some of the Third World's.

Generally speaking, through no fault of his own, President Paul Bedford stood on the verge of making a special kind of history.

"You have any suggestions, George? I mean, what I might do? Since you and your assistant seem to be the only people in the country who understand what's actually happening?"

"Sir, I'm not a trained politician. And I'm not that good at thinking like one. My task is to find out what the hell's happening, and then to try and interpret what might happen next. But if I were sitting in that chair of yours, I'd most certainly touch base with Admiral Morgan. He's the best I've ever met at this type of thing. Especially if there's a chance we may have to kick someone in the ass."

The President smiled. Five minutes later, just after Lt. Commander Ramshawe had left, the phone rang in the big house in Chevy Chase. One hour later, Admiral Morgan was back in the Oval Office, discussing with Paul Bedford another catastrophic collapse on the Nikkei, the Japanese stock exchange. In the four days since Saudi oil and gas stopped flowing, Japan's energy analysts had been able to forecast their oncoming power grid shortfalls, and diminishing reserves of natural gas.

It looked like a six-week problem. Which meant that on around May 10, the lights would go out in one of the biggest economies in the world. Japan's reliance on Saudi oil had long bothered these analysts, and now they could see a gigantic coop of chickens coming home to roost.

It would not be much different in the seething industrial hub of Taiwan. Nor on the west coasts of India and Pakistan, which stood directly opposite the main source of all their energy, the Strait of Hormuz, entrance to the Gulf.

China seemed to have some supplies flowing continuously from Kazakhstan, but the People's Republic was an enormous importer of Saudi oil, and right now Beijing was bracing itself for severe shortages of automobile fuel and electric power.

Indonesia had some oil of its own, but it was still reliant on Saudi product. Canada was much the same. But Europe was in trouble. The Old World had hardly any energy resources, except for some high-producing coal mines in the east and a small amount of oil left in the North Sea. Which put Great Britain in a real spot. As bad as America's.

Russia was smiling, and so were some of her former satellites along the coast of the Black Sea. And South

America could probably manage without the Saudis. But the interlinked global economies of the big players threatened everyone.

As the *Wall Street Journal* observed that morning: *"The ramifications of the crisis in the Saudi oil fields are very nearly boundless. The world's leading stock markets have already shuddered, as millions of dollars have been wiped off share prices in Europe, the Far East, and the United States.*

"And the stark fact remains, this planet cannot function properly without a normal supply of oil. And for the next twelve months, there is not going to be a normal supply of oil. On a global scale, that means, the only thing it can mean—bankruptcies, both large and small, market collapses, blackouts, and the failure of banks and power companies all over the globe."

The *Journal* did its best with some illustrations of potential disasters—the big banks carrying a huge debt from an airline that cannot refuel its aircraft? The major automobile manufacturers who can no longer sell product to a market that's run dry? The food industry struggling for energy to freeze and refrigerate its product? The national supermarket chains whose cold-storage facilities keep shutting down? The gas stations, the trucking corporations, oil tankers themselves?

"What happens when the industrial world starts to shut down? No one knows the answer to that. The human race is unfailingly resilient and always resourceful. But, short of war, the human race has never faced anything quite like this. And some of the most powerful industrialists in the world are surely preparing for an extremely difficult time."

Both the President and Admiral Morgan had read the article. But their reactions were diametrically opposed. Paul Bedford went into defensive mode, wondering how he could distance himself from, and at the same time cope with, the crisis. Arnold Morgan's mind raced ahead, to the time when the Saudi oil would come back on stream, and where the United States would stand at that time. He knew the solution to the problem rested right here in the present. Not next year.

He sensed that now was the time for action. And before him stood the specter of France. Because no one could really blame some robed religious fanatic from the desert for wanting his country free of American influence. That was unfortunate but understandable.

But France! What France had done was unforgivable. For, as sure as Arnold Morgan was sitting right here in the Oval Office, the French government had deliberately plunged the world into despair, entirely for her own gain and to the detriment of almost everyone else.

The French government would naturally deny everything. But Arnold Morgan knew the President's only chance was to come out fighting. And to accept that Saudi Arabia's oil had become a world asset, not an Arab one. And that the industrial nations were right now waiting for the world's policeman to draw his nightstick.

The President understood that millions of Americans had not forgiven France for her dogmatic stand against the United States during the run-up to the crushing of the murderous dictator Saddam, in Iraq in 2003. Nor had they forgotten the demands France had made to be given a share of the rebuilding contracts.

Seven years later, there were still restaurants in the United States that refused to serve French wine, even wine importers and wholesalers who refused to touch French products.

And here again was the world's most self-centered nation—this time perhaps having overstepped itself in terms of pure national interest—casting itself into the role of international pariah . . . assuming that someone, somewhere, felt they could prove French compliance in the takeover of Saudi Arabia.

Arnold Morgan was sure he could prove 100 percent French involvement. And he said to the President, "Sir, I am going to lay this right on the line for you. France was the nation that agreed to help Prince Nasir. Those oil installations were hit by French missiles fired from French submarines. Those oil-loading platforms were blown with time bombs fixed by French underwater commandos. Those military bases at Khamis Mushayt were attacked by a brigade of French Special Forces, and that street rabble was marshaled into a fighting force by a former French Army officer who led the assault on Riyadh on behalf of the new King.

"During the course of the next twelve months, you are going to see France move into the jockey seat in the marketing of all Saudi oil. It is entirely a matter for you whether we get left behind in the coming stampede to join the line for Saudi oil and gas."

"Arnold, do we have sufficient evidence to accuse the French absolutely of this treachery?"

"Damn right we do."

"What about the submarines, the *Améthyste* and the *Perle*? Where the hell are they?"

"One of them is heading into the Arabian Sea, the other into the Indian Ocean."

"And what if they don't turn up at La Réunion, as you and the NSA expect?"

"Doesn't matter a damn whether they turn up or not. There were only two hunter-killer submarines in all the world that could have fired those missiles. And they were French, in the area, and now they're missing, having behaved most unusually."

"Who has to speak to the French?"

"I suppose you do. Or your Secretary of State. Not that it will do any good. The French will just say they have no idea what you are talking about."

"So how can we hang 'em out to dry?"

"We have to capture Le Chasseur and make him talk."

"Is that likely to be difficult?"

"Extremely so. Especially if the French manage to assassinate him first."

"You think they might?"

"I would."

President Bedford stood up and walked to the other side

of the room. Once more he stood beneath the portrait of General Washington. "Arnold," he said, "I am asking you to come back here as my special adviser for a few months. You can name your salary."

"Sir, I'm not good at advice. I give orders and they have to be carried out. I will not offer my views for a bunch of half-assed Democrats to sit around wondering whether to do something else."

"How about I make you Supreme Commander of this operation, with powers to order the military into action?"

"Do you and your advisers have a veto on my decisions?"

"I would need to have that."

"Then it's time for me to go home. If you put yourself in my hands, you also put yourself in the hands of your most senior commanders in the Pentagon. And I will not order anyone to do anything without their agreement. I work *with* the Pentagon, not against it."

President Bedford ruminated. "Are you suggesting I give you supreme authority to take this nation to war?"

"Of course not. I am suggesting you give me supreme authority to kick a little ass with no questions asked. That way you'll save your presidency and we'll get back to where we want to be, dealing with the Saudis."

"Arnold, I am putting myself into a precarious position where you essentially tell me what is going to happen? Is that more or less correct?"

"Yes it is. Because I'm not having anything to do with this, unless you give me the authority to act and act fast. If you don't trust me, don't do it. But if you do trust me, I should decide pretty damn quickly if I were you. Because this bullshit with the oil could get right out of hand."

"Where do you want your office?"

"Right next to yours. And I speak only to you. I attend no Cabinet meetings, or any other meetings. I brief you, and you take your cue from that."

"Arnold, I would not think of doing this with any other person except you."

"Neither would I, sir."

"Salary?"

"Forget it. Just all the backup I need."

"Well, I guess that's a deal then. I appoint you Supreme Commander of Operation . . . what? Desert Fuel?"

"How about Towelhead Treason?"

"Jesus, Arnold." The President laughed. "I think something less inflammatory."

"Okay, let's make it Operation Tanker."

"No problem. Operation Tanker. When do you start?"

"'Bout ten minutes ago. Make sure my new quarters have a sizable anteroom for Kathy, and she'll need a deputy secretary."

"No problem. You speaking to France today?"

"Probably not. I'm concentrating our inquiries on the land battles, and I probably won't stick a firecracker up the ass of the French until we get a sight of those submarines. Then I can act as if we know rather more than we do."

"Uh-huh," said President Bedford. "And then what?"

"Oh, I don't think we'll get anywhere. The French will just do a lot of shrugging and say they have no idea what happened in Saudi Arabia. It is none of their business, *n'est-ce pas?*"

"Then what?"

"We find them guilty in the courtroom of Uncle Sam. And then, as they say in the Pentagon, we'll try to appreciate the situation."

"Do we say anything to the media?"

"Christ no, sir. Nothing. NO announcements. NO press conferences."

"And what about when someone notices you are ensconced in the White House right next to the President?"

"You have someone say that Admiral Morgan and the President are assessing a possible problem to the United States. They are working together as two former naval officers. Admiral Morgan is an acting, unpaid adviser on a purely temporary basis."

"Right before you have the SEALs blow up the Eiffel Tower or something?"

"More or less," replied Morgan. "But to set your mind at rest, we're not blowing up anything on land. But equally, we are not anxious that France should carry on as normal, running tankers in and out of their ports with oil from Abu Dhabi . . . while the rest of us starve."

"Oh, Christ," said President Bedford. "This is going to be interesting."

"For the final time, sir. Your only chance is to get aggressive, show your outrage, be absolutely fearless in your contempt for what France has done. Get the focus of blame right away from yourself. Shock and surprise the world as necessary. But look like the victim, and make a lot of noise. Above all, turn France into the enemy of the Free World. That way you cannot possibly lose."

"I'm listening, Arnie. And I know you're right. It's just that I have nothing to do with this. And I find myself in the middle of everything."

"Other Presidents in other times have felt precisely the same," replied Morgan. "We gotta bite the bullet and turn this thing around. And we have to somehow turn it to America's advantage. And that's going to cost France plenty."

One Week Later, Thursday, April 1, 11:00 A.M.
Diplomatic Quarter, Riyadh

Col. Jacques Gamoudi and Gen. Ravi Rashood had been keeping their heads well down while the dust of war settled. The city of Riyadh had been quiet since the new King took over, and the entire Saudi armed services had agreed to serve King Nasir.

He had already announced, to a thunder of national applause, an end to the massive annual stipends to the thousands and thousands of royal princes. He further announced that those royal princes who were left in the country—not many—faced a wide confiscation of their property, except for primary residences.

He advised those who could leave to do so, and immediately froze any assets of more than a half-million dollars kept by any prince in any Saudi bank. He ruthlessly passed these laws in retrospect, meaning there were a lot of casinos, hotels, and boat marinas all over the Riviera that were left holding large debts incurred by the former golden boys of the kingdom.

"Frankly," said King Nasir, in imitation of his great hero Clark Gable, "I don't give a damn."

The King's view was simple. These princes had had their day. And if any of them had debts that they expected the King of Saudi Arabia to pay . . . well, those days were over. They'd have to get a job and start paying them off. Either that or go live somewhere else and hide from their former dissolute habits.

He further announced that the only members of the royal family who would in future be paid anything were those who buckled down and found a way to serve a useful purpose in the kingdom. He made it illegal for any member of the vast former royal family to transfer money from Saudi Arabia to another country.

As for the armed services, he appealed to the land forces, the Royal Saudi Air Force, and the Navy to remain loyal to the Crown. He announced that the salaries of all serving members of those services would be paid as a matter of priority from Saudi Arabia's currency reserves. He told them he had allocated the sum of $3 billion for this purpose in the first year.

Thus King Nasir, at two strokes, had rid himself of a $200 billion a year "obligation to the princes," and gained himself a fabulously loyal national fighting force at a net "profit" of $197 billion.

As the Saudi soldiers, sailors, and airmen owed him a huge debt of honor and allegiance, so King Nasir felt toward Colonel Gamoudi and General Rashood. They were both ensconced in the big white house he had personally made available to the Colonel, and their every wish was his profound pleasure to grant.

They had servants, limousines, helicopters on call, a facility at every restaurant in the city to dine at the King's expense, endless invitations to attend the palace, and if they wished to dine with the King in the desert.

King Nasir was especially fond of his comrade-in-arms

Colonel Gamoudi, and he was growing to like equally well his forward commander in the battle for Khamis Mushayt. If the two leaders of the revolution so wished, they were free to remain and make their homes in Riyadh as permanent guests of the King for the rest of their days. They were the nearest thing to the most privileged of princes, ever since the former King went down in a hail of bullets from Rashood's machine gun the previous week.

The King had also moved forward on his promises to France. He had allocated $10 billion to the rebuilding of Pump Station Number One, the Abqaiq complex, the Qatif Junction manifold, the Sea Island Terminal loading platforms, the LPG Terminal off Ras al Ju'aymah, and the Red Sea refineries.

At present, there was of course a vast amount of incoming dollars still owed to Saudi Arabia, and while the King intended to increase the personal state allowances to all citizens to $14,000 a year, he did not feel able to commit billions to the rebuilding of the oil loading platforms at Yanbu al Bahr, Rabigh, and Jiddah. He would begin that work as soon as some oil began to flow.

But, true to his word, he immediately awarded all the major contracts to French construction corporations, with a gigantic sum of money for advice, consultation, and planning services to the giant French TotalFinaElf oil conglomerate.

All of this was done in secrecy and it would be many weeks before the full scale of Saudi Arabia's apparent debt to France was uncovered. Meanwhile, millions and millions of dollars' worth of hardware, oil pipeline, pumping systems, excavation equipment, trucks, and bulldozers were making their way systematically through the Mediterranean, from French ports to the Suez Canal.

It was boom time in the heartland of industrial France. Just as the French President knew it would be, almost a year ago when Prince Nasir had first come to call.

Meanwhile, the sun shone brightly on the Diplomatic Quarter in Riyadh. General Rashood and Colonel Gamoudi had elected to dine at one of the best Italian restaurants in the desert city, Da Pino in the Al Khozama Center, next to the Al Khozama Hotel on Olaya Street. It was a great favorite of Saudi Arabia's ruling class, who had formerly all belonged to one family, but now Da Pino was hitting very hard times, and it was easier to book a table than it had ever been. Of course, if General Rashood and Colonel Gamoudi had wished, the King would have bought it for them.

However, they only wanted a good dinner of pasta and chicken or veal, with fruit juice to drink, both being devout Muslims and unable to drink alcohol in this country anyway.

Their chauffeur drove them into the city from the Diplomatic Quarter. General Rashood caught his first glimpse of a black Citroën driving behind them before they were out of King Khalid Road. He could just see it through the passenger-side mirror, and while he was not particularly curious, he did notice that the vehicle was driving up close and had once refused to allow a white van to drift in between them. There was a loud blowing of horns. Rashood turned to see the van driver waving his fist. They turned left onto Makkah Road, and, routinely, Rashood checked to see if the Citroën was still behind them.

It was, but these were two of the busiest streets in Riyadh, so there was nothing unusual in that. However, when they made their turn onto Al Amir Soltan Street, Rashood saw the Citroën once again follow them closely. They sped under the big overhead junction with King Fahd Road and took the third left onto the wide boulevard of Olaya Street.

They pulled up on the right-hand side, where there was ample parking space. The chauffeur said he would be waiting right there when they had finished dinner. Both men climbed out on the right side, and Rashood watched the Citroën drive past and make a slow right onto Al Amir Mohammed Road. He never gave the car another thought.

Dinner was outstanding and the chef came out and talked to them. At the next table was Colonel Bandar, liberator of the Riyadh television stations, dining with his family. He and Jacques Gamoudi silently toasted each other with fruit juice, and introductions were made.

They all left, more or less together, just after 10 P.M., and Rashood and Gamoudi walked quickly through the precincts of the Khozama Hotel and out into the fresh night air. The chauffeur waved to them from across the street, and they stood chatting on the sidewalk while the stream of traffic passed.

Finally it was clear, and they stepped out into the street, with the traffic approaching from the left. Still chatting, they set off across the boulevard, when Rashood heard the squeal of tires on blacktop, from the left, no more than 100 yards away. He stopped instinctively, but Jacques Gamoudi kept going.

Rashood turned to see an approaching vehicle that might have made zero to sixty in four seconds. Through his mind flashed the thought *black Citroën*. He could see it bearing down on them traveling absolutely foot to the boards.

He jumped two steps forward and, with an outrageous display of strength, twisted, wrapped his left forearm around the throat of Le Chasseur, and hurled him backward. Jacques Gamoudi's head hit the ground first, followed by his shoulder blades.

For a split-second the ex–French Foreign Legion soldier thought he was dead. Another half-second and he would have been. The front wheels of the Citroën literally brushed the soles of his feet as it roared past.

Rashood leapt back onto his own feet. He heard the brakes of the Citroën shriek as it skidded to a standstill. For a moment he thought the driver was slamming the gears into reverse, and was coming back for them. They were sitting targets, almost in the middle of the road, with Jacques Gamoudi still supine, trying to clear his head from the wallop he had taken when he hit the road.

But no. The Citroën was stopped dead, but the rear door on the right side was opening. Rashood could see the tip of a rifle, then he saw their assailant's face: a dark, hard-eyed, unshaven thug. Ravi Rashood, the master unarmed combat soldier from the SAS, did not hesitate.

He raced toward the car and, with a thunderous right-footed kick that would not have disgraced a French Rugby Union fullback, he almost took the man's head off, snapped his neck, and broke his jaw in seven places. The rifle, a primed AK-47, clattered to the ground, and Rashood had time to grab it before the driver of the vehicle was out of the left front door and around the car aiming an identical weapon.

Rashood had no time to aim or fire his own weapon, but he did have time to ram the gun's butt into the man's face. It was a vicious, high, stabbing blow delivered like a harpooner within reach of his whale.

The blow smashed the bone in the center of the assassin's forehead. But he was still standing, still holding the AK-47. But now it was too late. Rashood was on him. He sidestepped the rifle and came over the top, planting the fingers of his left hand deep into the man's long curly hair. Simultaneously, he rammed the butt of his right palm with inhuman force into the base of the hooked Gallic nose that had briefly helped its owner look so menacing.

Rashood's blow had traveled more than a foot. And it packed unbelievable power as it exploded into the man's nostrils. It killed him stone-dead, driving the nose bone into the brain, the classic combat blow of the British-trained Special Forces soldier.

Jacques Gamoudi sat up groggily, just in time to see his colleague kill the second of their attackers. It was, in a sense, the street fight to end all street fights. One kick, one hit, one uppercut. One dead, one dying. All in the middle of the traffic.

"Not too bad," said Colonel Gamoudi, shaking his head and grinning at the same time, "for a guy who prefers fighting in royal palaces."

Rashood, who was already beckoning for the chauffeur to come and get them out of there, just said, "Christ, Jacques. That was obviously no accident. Someone out there is trying to kill us. And I have a feeling they want you more than they want me. You probably noticed the French car, French license plate, and that second little bastard smelled like a fucking garlic vat."

"Try not to impugn my adopted nationality with those English public school prejudices," replied Gamoudi. "Yes, we use a little *ail* for the flavor, but that does not make us *malodorants*."

"Silence, Gamoudi," said Rashood, as he hauled the French officer to his feet. "Otherwise I'll make you salute me every time I save your life. That's the second time in a week."

"Mon Dieu!" replied Gamoudi, in mock exasperation. "Where would I be without you?"

"At a guess, I'd say dead behind that serving counter in the royal palace," chuckled General Rashood. "Now try to shut up and get in the back of that car, will you—and don't get blood all over the seat rest or the King will be very cross . . . Ahmed, give me some of those tissues, the Colonel has whacked his head."

"I don't think his head hurts so bad as those two," said the chauffeur, passing the tissues and nodding at the two stricken assassins, one of whom was still breathing just inside the rear door. The other was lying dead below the Citroën's trunk.

"Probably not," agreed General Rashood.

Ahmed took off, speeding back to the big white house at the edge of the Diplomatic Quarter. And there they sat on the wide rear veranda, sipping fruit juice and deciding that Riyadh was no longer the place for either of them. Tomorrow morning they would both suggest that their tasks for King Nasir were over and that they must return to their own homes.

The trouble was, Jacques Gamoudi was now certain the French government was trying to kill him, and General Rashood agreed. They had to leave Riyadh, but the question was, where was Colonel Gamoudi to take refuge? And how was he going to get there without the French Secret Service hunting him down? It was not a role to which Le Chasseur was accustomed.

**The Following Day, Friday, April 2, 1800
National Security Agency**

"Right on time," said Jimmy Ramshawe, as he stared at the new pictures arriving online from the National Surveillance

Office. The shots showed the Navy base at France's old Indian Ocean colony of La Réunion. And there, tucked neatly into the submarine pens, was the newly arrived Rubis-class hull number S605, the *Améthyste*. Out of sight for three weeks since it dived just south of the Gulf of Suez, but rarely out of mind. At least, not Jimmy Ramshawe's.

He had calculated that the submarine had come through the Bab el Mandeb sometime in the midafternoon of Thursday last week. And he'd marked his chart at a spot right off the Horn of Africa, the jutting headland of Somalia, where he'd assessed the *Améthyste* would be last Friday at midnight.

It was 390 miles across the Gulf of Aden—and at twelve knots that was a thirty-two-hour journey, he told himself. Which left them a straight 2,400-mile run down the deep and lonely Indian Ocean, probably making around fifteen knots for six and a half days. On his chart Ramshawe had written, *looking for the Améthyste in La Réunion sometime in the late evening of Friday April 2.*

"Actually, the bastard's a few hours early," he muttered. "Must have been speeding . . . cheeky fucker."

And now, he wondered, *how about her mate?* Unseen since she was logged through Port Said on March 4, the *Perle* had a longer journey home, through the Gulf. Ramshawe's assessment had put hull number S606 well through the Strait of Hormuz last Wednesday. So she should have reached the Horn of Africa by Sunday, March 28.

"She's got six and a half days in front of her, so I'm looking at an ETA La Réunion sometime tomorrow evening, or early Sunday morning," he pondered. "Jesus, if that French bastard shows up on time, for me it's game, set, and match. Where the hell else has she been? And why did they both go deep in the Red Sea and stay there? None of the other French submarines making that journey *ever* do that. *Arnie, baby, we got 'em,* he thought.

He stared once more at the incontrovertible evidence of the all-seeing eye of the U.S. satellite. There she was right there in the dockyard of La Réunion, the *Améthyste*, moored alongside her jetty, under the command of Cdr. Louis Dreyfus, according to the records at Port Said.

It seemed incredible just to try and understand what she had done: obliterated the entire Saudi oil facilities in the Red Sea. But Lt. Commander Ramshawe knew what she had done, and in his candid opinion, the U.S. Navy would be justified in going right out there and sinking her—no bullshit.

But those decisions would be made by the Big Man now, and Ramshawe greatly looked forward to hearing his reaction after the weekend, when it would become clear that the two prime suspects in this still baffling case were sitting in the French dockyard a couple of thousand miles south of the datum.

They'll be there, he told himself. *I bloody know they'll both be there.*

He downloaded the prints and walked slowly along the corridor to see Admiral Morris, still staring at the satellite shots that in his opinion proved the absolute guilt of the French in this worldwide financial horror story.

Admiral Morris studied the prints and nodded sagely. "It's all starting to fit together, eh, Jim? When's the *Perle* due in?"

"Tomorrow evening, or early Sunday morning."

"Okay, let's not make a report to Admiral Morgan until she arrives. Seems to me a double on Sunday lunchtime is a whole lot better than a single right now at dinnertime on Friday night."

"We're going to get it, too," added Ramshawe. "It's all starting to make sense."

Saturday, April 3, Midday
King Nasir's Palace
Riyadh

The King listened gravely to the account of the attempt on Colonel Gamoudi's life on Olaya Street last Thursday night. General Rashood and Gamoudi had planned to keep quiet about the entire matter and make their way carefully out of the country in a few days. But the police had caused the most ridiculous fuss, some passerby had taken the number of their car, and Ahmed must have told about 7,000 people what had happened, because the King called Colonel Gamoudi on Saturday morning and suggested he and the General come in for a chat.

It quickly became apparent that he had no interest in the rights and wrongs of the killings. Two of his most trusted friends had been attacked in the streets of Riyadh, and he was extremely glad things had worked out as they had.

What the King wanted to know was who had attempted to kill his friends. But when he heard the story, as recounted by Rashood, he was inclined to agree with the General. The culprits may have been acting on behalf of the French government. And he did not approve of that. Not one bit.

Like them, he knew it would be pointless for him to check with the French President. No one would admit to an assassination attempt. But the reality of the incident remained. If the French had decided to take out Le Chasseur, they were now up against an extremely powerful enemy.

For King Nasir harbored all of that inbred Bedouin creed of loyalty, honed over thousands of year in the desert. Arabs do not easily abandon their friends. Indeed the Saudis' record of loyalty, even to their employees, was absolutely rigid. If they hired anyone into a position of trust, and that trust was not broken, it would not matter if they had hired a total incompetent. They would never abandon him. They would assume that their own judgment might have been awry, but that ought not to reflect upon the character of any person they had appointed. If he was not up to the job, then they would hire someone to help him. But they would never, ever fire him.

Perhaps the finest example of this friends-are-forever mentality happened in the emirate of Dubai, many years ago, when the legendary Sheik Rashid bin Said al-Maktoum, the ruler, gathered in the desert with his council to discuss the possibility of building the largest desalinization plant in the world. Eventually it came down to a short list of two—an excellent German corporation and the British engineers Weirs, of Glasgow, Scotland. The Germans had three advantages: they were more experienced, cheaper, and likely to be quicker. Sheik Rashid knew there were problems in Scotland. And he knew there were thousands of jobs on the line. But he had many, many friends in Great Britain, and indeed owed the existence of his entire country to Her Majesty's Government.

Finally he made his decision: "I have decided to award this contract to the British," said Sheik Rashid.

The Council was astonished. It was a full meeting, and they were sitting on a great carpet on the floor of the desert. His advisers immediately reminded Sheik Rashid of the price. This was a grandiose scheme, costing millions and millions of dollars. *Why will you not appoint the Germans?*

There was a quizzical smile on the face of Sheik Rashid when he replied gently, "Because I like the British more." And that was an end to it. The Scottish corporation successfully built Dubai's massive first desalinization plant.

And so it was with General Rashood and Colonel Gamoudi. They had put their lives on the line for King Nasir, and now they had become his friends. And to him this made them unique in all the world. He would hear no word against them, and he would protect them forever—with his life if necessary.

The French might have been wise to find this out about the new King of Saudi Arabia.

And here in his palace, the King pledged his support for the two warriors who had spearheaded his revolution. He told Jacques Gamoudi he must plan an escape and begin, somewhere, a new life. He, King Nasir, would give him every possible assistance, including a private jet to fly out, to take him wherever he wished.

Colonel Gamoudi was deeply touched. He took the King's hand and thanked him profoundly.

And King Nasir responded with the traditional hard eye-to-eye contact of the desert tribes. "Always remember, Jacques," he said, "I am a Bedouin."

Sunday, April 4, 1945
National Security Agency

Capt. Alain Roudy had made good time to La Réunion. And Lt. Commander Ramshawe was now looking at photographs of two Rubis-class hunter-killers moored alongside the submarine jetties in that tiny island.

"There you are, you little bastard," breathed Ramshawe, staring at the closeup shot of the newly arrived *Perle*. "Right where I bloody knew you'd be."

He called Admiral Morris, who in turn called Admiral Morgan, and the Supreme Commander Operation Tanker convened a planning meeting at the White House for first thing Monday morning.

It was now plain to everyone that France was behind the overthrow of the Saudi royal family. And Ramshawe knew this was probably it. Arnold Morgan was about to take action against the French. But this was a rare occasion when young Ramshawe could not work out which way the Admiral would jump.

"One thing's for certain," he decided. "He's not going to sit back and allow the French to get rich, not while half the world's struggling to keep the lights switched on."

It was with a heightened sense of anticipation that he arrived at the White House at 0900 on Monday morning. He and Admiral Morris arrived separately, and reported to Morgan's new quarters, where the Chief of Naval Operations, Adm. Alan Dickson, was already in conference, staring at a huge computerized map of France on a wall screen.

Arnold Morgan greeted the men from NSA both warmly and grimly. "I've briefed Admiral Dickson," he said. "And I think he agrees with me, that for the President's sake, we have to take some action. In the modern world it is simply impossible for anyone to act with total disregard for the plight of other nations. Especially on this scale.

"Now, we are not going to get either an admission or an apology from the French government. I plan to speak to the

French President, but I expect him to deny any knowledge of anything.

"Thus, so far as I can see, we have several missions. One, to ensure they can't just sit back and laugh at everyone else's problems. Two, to expose and then humiliate them in front of the United Nations. Three, to teach them a damn hard lesson."

Alan Dickson looked as if he were not sure about this. And Morgan instantly caught the doubtful look on his face.

"Alan," he said, "we have a very good man in the Oval Office. He loves the Navy, he trusts us, and he never allows anyone to tamper with our budgets. Through no fault of his own he is caught up in a global uproar that could finish him, if he doesn't move, move, move . . .

"I think we owe him our loyalty, our brains, and the muscle of the United States Navy. Because that's the only way he'll survive. He must be seen to be furious, he must be seen to identify the culprit, and above all, he must be seen to punish the perpetrator of this evil."

Admiral Morris right away mentioned the financial problems afflicting all the big Western stock markets, and, of course, the Japanese Nikkei. There had been a major statement issued from the International Monetary Fund, which was holding an emergency meeting in Switzerland later today.

And all over the United States, families with strong positions in the blue chip components that made up the Dow Jones Average were taking savage losses, which may not be recovered for two years, until the Saudi oil came back on stream.

"From this moment, I am going to deem the Saudi oil a global asset," said Admiral Morgan. "I am going to treat the French as if they have committed a crime against humanity. And, quite frankly, I don't actually give a rat's ass what any other country thinks. I am not having the well-being of the United States of America jeopardized by any other nation. *AND THAT'S FINAL*."

It was sure as hell final in that particular White House office. All three of Admiral Morgan's visitors nodded in agreement—even Admiral Dickson, whose patriotism had just been given a sharp wakeup call.

They waited for Arnold Morgan's next jackhammer blow. And each of them stood prepared for some kind of onslaught. But when the Supreme Commander Operation Tanker spoke, he spoke quietly, and thoughtfully.

"I am proposing to deploy a U.S. Navy blockade outside every French port that imports foreign oil. That's Le Havre, which is located at the mouth of the Seine River in Normandy. It contains the largest oil refinery in France, at Gonfreville l'Orcher.

"Marseille, in the south, handles thirty percent of France's crude-oil refining. There's a big terminal at Fossur-Mer; a Shell refinery at Berre; TotalFinaElf is in a place called La Mède; BP operates in Lavera; and Exxon uses Fos. Marseille imports a vast amount of methane, and close to the port there's a massive underground storage facility for liquid petroleum gas; a lot of it used to be from Ras al Ju'aymah, but the French have, of course, now made other arrangements.

"We also have to look closely at the six oil terminals in Bordeaux along the Gironde Estuary, at Pauillac and Ambes—that's a major plant for liquid chemicals.

"The final spot is Brest, which, as we all know, is a long harbor containing the main French Navy base. But there's also a considerable oil terminal in there, which takes both crude and LPG.

"Gentlemen, I intend to place United States warships at the entrances to all four of these seaways. I realize of course this will work only in the short term, because France will arrange overland supplies through Luxembourg and Germany. The Belgians will also help them out since they are considerable partners in the TotalFinaElf conglomerate.

"Nonetheless, the short term will be very miserable for them. Starve those ports of oil, and the place will swiftly run dry. In the long term, they'll overcome it. But right now I care only for the short term."

"Arnie," said Admiral Dickson, "I realize this is purely academic, but France has a very dangerous Navy, with a lot of ships in both Brest and Marseille. Have you considered the possibility they may come out and attack our ships?"

"No I haven't," rasped the Admiral. "They wouldn't dare."

"What if they did?"

"Sink 'em, of course. Remember, we are acting as the world's policemen, and the world is going to give its approval for us to do anything we damn well please. By the time the President has made a statement outlining the disgraceful role played by France in the current crisis, there won't be a nation on earth that disapproves of our actions."

"I agree. Attacks on policemen are generally frowned upon by law-abiding citizens. But I wonder whether we might not overplay our hand if we actually opened fire on a French warship?" Admiral Dickson was slipping into an extremely practical mode.

"I would not be concerned about that. Because we would immediately issue a detailed statement about the goddamned mayhem France perpetrated on the Saudi oil installations. Our drift would be, they asked for all they're getting."

Lt. Commander Ramshawe spoke next. "Sir," he said, "do you have any plans to act immediately, rather than wait for the slow-burn of the blockade?"

"Funny you should mention that," replied the Admiral. "Because as a matter of fact I do. But first I would like to brief you on the situation on the Riviera. For years France has been rolling in Saudi cash all along that coastline. Dozens of those young princes have kept huge motor yachts at places like Cannes, Nice, and Monte Carlo. It's been nothing short of a gravy train for the French. And in turn they, of course, are swift to point out that only the French seaports can provide the level of civilized living the royal princes require.

"I thought perhaps we might humiliate France in front of the whole world, by blowing up the entire contents of those harbors."

"Christ," said Ramshawe. "There'd be hell to pay in reparations and God knows what else."

"Not if no one had the slightest idea who'd done what to whom," replied Morgan.

"Are you talking U.S. Navy SEALs?" asked Admiral Morris.

"Yes, George, I am. Those blasts on the big pleasure yachts might be the only shots fired in this little war, but they'll cause more embarrassment to France than any other course of action we could possibly take. I also plan to check out the Gulf of St. Malo, in the north. But it's only interesting if there are a lot of big foreign boats in there.

"Either way, there will be huge claims for compensation from the yacht owners. And France will have to pay for a long time before the claims reach Lloyds of London, if indeed there is any coverage to protect people from an act of war."

"By that time, the President will naturally have broadcast and blamed France for the events in Saudi Arabia?" asked Admiral Morris.

"Correct," replied Morgan. "And the hatred against the French will be so great among so many countries that no one will know which nation committed the atrocities in the French harbors."

"I guess some of them will suspect the U.S.A."

"So they might," said Admiral Morgan. "But no one will know, and we'll admit nothing. And I'll tell you something else . . . most people will think it serves 'em right."

"Presumably you intend the SEALs to come in from the ocean and set timed bombing devices on several huge foreign-owned yachts, which will mysteriously explode long after our submarines are clear of the datum?"

"Yeah," said Morgan. "Pretty much the same techniques the French frogmen must have used when they hit the Saudi oil loading platforms."

"Well, there's a great belief in the desert of the old biblical maxim 'an eye for an eye,'" said Alan Dickson. "I guess France has it coming."

"Well, I would like to put this operation and the blockade

on the fast track. And while that all begins to unfold, I want to assess the possibilities of finding our friend Major Gamoudi."

"Could I just ask what we're going to do if and when we find him?" asked George Morris.

"Sure," said Morgan. "We're going to kidnap him."

"Kidnap him!"

"Well, he sure as hell won't want to show up of his own accord and tell us all he knows, will he?"

"Probably not. But we can't just snatch him, can we?"

"Why the hell not? We're probably looking at the man who murdered our great friend the King of Saudi Arabia. He'd be one of the most wanted men in the world. But we don't care what he's done. We want him to stand right up there in front of the United Nations Assembly and admit that France paid him to overthrow the King."

"You think he'll do that?"

"I don't think he has much choice. Plainly he's a man who could be charged with anything, and we know he stormed the royal palace in Riyadh. Charlie Brooks sent us a fucking photograph of him in the leading tank.

"What I'm hoping is, the French make an attempt on his life, as I'm certain they will. And then we can rush in and get to him first. That way he'll be damn glad to shop his treacherous employers, and save his own skin by rowing in with us."

"Well," said Admiral Morris, "he won't be able to return to France, will he?"

"Not likely," replied Morgan. "Which means we also have to get his wife and family out of the goddamn Pyrenees where they live, because if we don't, they'll be as good as hostages. And Jacques, being the kind of man he is, may prefer to die to save her and the kids from the malevolence of his own government."

"I wonder how the hell we'll ever know if France has attempted to assassinate him," muttered Jimmy Ramshawe. "Tell the truth, we don't even know where he is at the moment. He was in Riyadh a week ago, but a week's a long time in the assassination game."

Just then, Morgan's assistant secretary tapped and looked around the door. "Sir, there's an urgent call for Lt. Commander Ramshawe from one of our envoys in Saudi Arabia . . . would he like to take it in the outside office?"

The Lt. Commander climbed to his feet, nodding in agreement, and stepped out of Admiral Morgan's new White House headquarters. He sat at a spare desk in the outer room and said, "Ramshawe, who's speaking?"

"Jimmy, it's Charlie Brooks. I'm on the encrypted line, but I'm calling because I think something very interesting happened here last Thursday night. A couple of French hit men got wiped out in the middle of Olaya Street. They were both dead when the police arrived, one of 'em half in the car, which was a big Citroën. Paris registered. The other guy was lying behind it. They both carried Kalashnikovs, and witnesses say they were killed by the man they were after."

"Oh yeah? Go on, Charlie."

"Well, we have a few contacts in the Saudi police, and for a couple of days they carried out a regular investigation, just like it was a normal double murder. And then, according to our man Said, the investigation was stopped on the direct orders of the King. Apparently the car that drove the killer away from the scene was registered to King Nasir. And the police say that one of the men inside that car was Colonel Jacques Gamoudi. But there were a few reliable eyewitnesses, from whom the police took statements. They all say the same thing: the Citroën tried to run down two men at high speed, but it missed and stopped dead. There was some kind of a fight after that. And both the would-be murderers were killed by some terrible guy, obviously an expert in unarmed combat. One of 'em choked to death because of a broken neck, and the other had his nose somehow rammed into his brain."

"Fuck me," said Jimmy Ramshawe.

"And there's more. One of the eyewitnesses was a well-known ex–Saudi officer named Colonel Bandar, a fanatical loyalist to the new King. I've seen his statement. He says he served under one of the men, Col. Jacques Gamoudi, during the siege of Riyadh. The other was the Commander of King

Nasir's assault team in the south, the guy who took Khamis Mushayt. They'd all had dinner at Da Pino. But he did not know the name of the second commander."

Jimmy Ramshawe said, "This is a very important call, Charlie. And it's great you made it. Do you have copies of the witness statements to the Saudi police?"

"Yes. I guess I can fax 'em. And there's not much room for doubt. Someone just tried to kill Gamoudi, and I would guess he's now under the direct protection of the King. That's going to make it very difficult for us to locate him."

"As for his mate, I suppose that's out of the question?"

"They don't have a name for him, and I sense the police have become real sensitive. Just an hour ago, they would tell me nothing. They acted kinda scared. I guess Nasir's men are flexing a little muscle."

"I guess so, Charlie. Stay in touch, will you? This is very important."

Ramshawe made his way back to the office on a jaunty stride. "Gentlemen," he said, "we just got a real break. Last Thursday night there was an attempt on the life of Col. Jacques Gamoudi in the middle of the city of Riyadh. Someone drove a Paris-registered Citroën at high speed straight at him on Olaya Street."

"Presumably they missed," said Morgan.

"They did. And both men in the Citroën were subsequently killed, either by Gamoudi or his companion, who the police say was King Nasir's forward Commander in the battle for Khamis Mushayt. Identified by a Saudi Colonel loyal to Nasir."

"I told you so," said Morgan. "The French are trying to get him. And that's good news, so long as they don't succeed."

"Sir," said Ramshawe, "there's just one other thing. Both these assassins carried Kalashnikovs, and both of them were cut down before they could fire, by a guy who broke one of their necks and rammed the other guy's nose into his brain . . . that got a familiar ring to you?"

"You mean our old friend Maj. Ray Kerman, who specializes in such methods?"

"Our old friend Ray Kerman, sir, who flew into Paris last

August and was hunted down by the Mossad to a restaurant in Marseille that is now under the protection of the local gendarmes."

"That's the guy, Jimmy. You think we just found who he was dining with that night?"

"Absolutely, sir. One dollar gets you one hundred Ray Kerman and Jacques Gamoudi shared a bowl of that French fish soup *buoybase* that night . . . It's the specialty dish of Marseille, sir," he added knowledgeably.

"Which is all the more reason why you should avoid making it sound like a submarine anchorage," replied Morgan. *"BOUILLABAISSE, BOY! BOUILLABAISSE!"*

He still sounded like Jackie Gleason doing his Chevalier, but both Arnold Morgan and Jimmy Ramshawe knew that right now the noose was tightening around the throat of the French government.

Monday, April 5, 0900
The White House

ADM. ALAN DICKSON, the fifty-six-year-old former Commander in Chief of the U.S. Navy's Atlantic Fleet, was not wildly looking forward to the next ten minutes. As the current Chief of Naval Operations, he was about to inform Arnold Morgan that he considered it too dangerous a mission to try and blockade the five major French seaports at Le Havre, Cherbourg, Brest, Bordeaux, and Marseille.

First of all, it would take half the U.S. Atlantic Fleet of submarines to be in any way effective. Second, the French Navy might elect to come out and fight a sea battle. Third, it would cost more money than World War II.

Admiral Dickson felt like Lew Grade, the legendary London movie mogul who made the catastrophic money-losing film *Raise the Titanic!* and who afterward commented with characteristic self-deprecation, "I could have lowered the Atlantic for less!"

Nonetheless, Admiral Morgan was not going to love this.

There was a chill early-spring wind outside, cutting through the nation's capital, and Admiral Dickson, a heavy-set former destroyer CO in the Gulf War, still had his hands in the pockets of his greatcoat. One of them clutched the little notebook he carried everywhere, with its minute details of U.S. Navy fleet deployments, written in his tiny, near-calligraphic writing.

The frown that creased his forehead seemed kind of stark on skin the color of varnished leather. But Alan Dickson was an old sea dog, a man of strict, disciplined method from the New England city of Hartford. And he knew that Arnold Morgan, in this instance, was whistling Dixie. Okay. Right now Admiral Morgan had the power to do anything he damn well pleased . . . but not in this man's Navy.

Alan Dickson could see war on the horizon. And while he most certainly wanted to ram an American hard boot straight up the ass of the pompous, arrogant French, he did not savor the prospect of the U.S. Navy's being hit back by probably the most efficient Navy in Europe.

Admiral Dickson knew all about the fighting capacity of the French, their hotshot modern guided-missile frigates and destroyers, their powerful fleet of submarines, and their two fast and well-equipped carriers. And he had no intention of tangling with them.

He also knew he was one of the few people in this world to whom Admiral Morgan would listen. He further knew that the Admiral was not a dogmatic man, but if you wished him to change course a few degrees, you better be heavily armed with facts, facts, and more facts. Alan Dickson was certain he had 'em.

"Please go through now," said Kathy Morgan's secretary. "I assume you would like coffee with the Admiral?"

"Thank you," replied Admiral Dickson as he began the short walk toward Arnold Morgan's gun deck.

"Morning, Alan," said the office's occupant without looking up from a chart of the approaches to the Port of Le Havre, on the northern shore of the Seine River estuary. "Worries the hell out of me, Alan," Morgan said. "No goddamn deep water for twenty miles outside the main shipping channel—at least not deep enough to hide a submarine. It's gonna be hard. But we'll find a way."

"Sorry, Arnold. I didn't quite catch that. Which port are you looking at?"

"Oh, yeah, Le Havre . . . right here on the coast of Normandy . . . in a sense, this is the big one for us . . . this is where Gonfreville l'Orcher is located, the biggest oil refinery in France. "See it . . . right here, Alan . . . on this peninsula between these two canals. Sonofabitch must be two miles wide . . . look at this . . . gasoline all along the north shore, this huge petrochemical complex on the south side. Starve that of crude for a few weeks, you got one dry-hole country." Arnold Morgan had never quite thrown off his south Texas roots.

Admiral Dickson shifted his weight from his right foot to his left. He was grateful when Kathy Morgan drifted through the door carrying the coffee tray—one silver pot, two mugs, sugar, cream, and a blue tube of buckshot.

"Hello, Alan," she said. "Nice to see you. Black, as usual?"

"Thanks, Kathy."

She poured two mugs of incineratingly hot coffee, the way Morgan liked it, fired two bullets into Morgan's mug—the one on the left, which sported an inscription in black letters that read SILENCE! GENIUS AT WORK—and retreated to the outer office.

"Sir," said Admiral Dickson, seizing the bull by the horns, or at least the genius by the tail, "it is my considered opinion that a blockade on the big French ports would be too difficult, too dangerous, and too expensive."

Right now Morgan was somewhere along the buoyed channel, ten miles west of Le Havre, trying to maintain periscope depth. "Uh-huh," he responded, half listening, half blowing all kingstons. Then the shock of the CNO's words seemed to hit home. And for a moment he was speechless. He looked up. "Did you just say what I thought you just said?" he grated.

"Yessir."

"Well, what the hell are you talking about? I thought we all agreed our plan of action—for the President to come out and accuse France of treachery and then to blockade her, while we're still safe in the protection of solid world opinion. Isn't that right?"

"Yessir. But I thought about it some more. A lot more. And in my view it's a very shaky plan."

"Alan, you and I have known each other for a lot of years. Don't tell me you're losing your nerve?"

"Nossir. I'm not at all. But when you finish looking at these charts, like I've been doing for most of the night, you're going to see problems turning up every which way. You've already located one of them. The vast expanse of shallow water that surrounds the port of Le Havre. I presume you would like to maintain an element of secrecy, rather than charging into the attack on the surface like Captain Hornblower?"

"Alan, I want you to stand there and methodically, logically, destroy my plan. That way, if I agree with you, we can get going and start again. I don't want to hear it in a disjointed way. You said, I think, 'too difficult, too dangerous, and too expensive.' Lay it on me in that order. And for Christ's sake stop calling me sir."

Admiral Dickson could take an order as sharply as he could issue one. "Arnie," he said, "each of the seaports involves a wide, sprawling target. It's impossible, as you well know, to blockade with just one ship, even if it is a submarine. I admit you could do it, if you went right ahead and sank something immediately, thus frightening the bejesus out of everyone. But I think we should avoid that kind of first-strike violence in French waters.

"So we'd probably want two submarines at each place— Le Havre, Cherbourg, Bordeaux, Brest, and Marseille. That's ten Los Angeles–class SSNs from the Atlantic Fleet, most of them stationed well offshore because of the depth. We would need backup on the surface, mainly so the French could see we meant business. That would probably mean five frigates and five destroyers from our bases on the east coast. Plus two or three fleet oilers if we want them to work for several weeks. And even then the operation would only work off Cherbourg and Le Havre. There's a substantial French Navy presence in the port of Brest, and there are always French warships off the coast of Marseille. Bordeaux is probably worse, because the biggest French Navy firing ranges are positioned all along that stretch of Atlantic coast, and there are French warships all over the place almost all of the time. We'd certainly need at the very minimum, say, six surface ships off those three places, if we want an intimidating presence.

"Arnie, in case you hadn't noticed . . . that's more than twenty-five U.S. warships . . ."

"It's twenty-nine. And I had, asshole."

Alan Dickson laughed. But he pressed on. "My next point is the danger element," he said lightly. "And, again, in case you hadn't noticed, the French have a very formidable, very modern, well-trained Navy."

"I had, supreme asshole."

"Well, Arnie," continued the CNO, "consulting my little black book here, I would like you to consider the following facts: The French Navy runs two carriers, one for fixed-wing aircraft, one for helicopters."

"Right now they're both in Brest," replied Admiral Morgan. "The *Charles de Gaulle,* with twenty Super Etendards boarded, and the *Jeanne d'Arc,* with a lot of helicopters."

"Excellent," said Admiral Dickson. "Which brings me to the submarine force. The French run twelve of them, all very efficiently. There are six Rubis-class attack submarines currently operational, plus two strategic missile ships, and four Triomphant-class SSBNs.

"They also have thirteen operational destroyers, all of them armed with heavy arsenals of guided missiles. The latest Exocets. They run twenty guided-missile frigates stuffed with Exocets, some of them carrying the new extended-range missile, the MM40 Block 3, which is probably the world's foremost anti-ship missile."

"Is that the one with the new air-breathing turbojets instead of the old rocket motors?" asked Morgan.

"That's right," said Admiral Dickson. "Damn thing flies a hundred nautical miles"

"And at high speed, I read," replied Morgan. "Just subsonic, but fast. Can we take it out?"

"Maybe. But it's capable of complex flight profiles. And good enough for land attack."

"Damn thing. I guess we don't want to fool with it, unless we have to."

"No, Arnie. We don't want to do that. And in my view it's not necessary."

Admiral Morgan nodded, unsmiling. "Are we ready to talk expense?"

"No. Not quite. I just wanted to throw in a couple of points about the French military philosophy. As you know, they have always retained total independence. They build their own ships, missiles, and fighter aircraft. They always have. For them it's always France. Nothing else. And they're pretty damned good at it.

"It is my opinion that if we sank a French warship right off their own coast, they would fight back, probably with that damned missile. And it would not be the greatest shock in the world if they hit and destroyed a couple of our own frigates. And what do you want to do then? Bomb the Arc de Triomphe?"

"No," said Morgan. "No, I really don't."

"Well, then I guess we have to think again. Because to my mind it's just too reckless for us to blockade France and start sinking ships. They're just a little too strong for that."

"And ain't that a goddamn lesson for the left-wing assholes in our own precious Congress," growled Morgan. "In serious international discussion, even we, a hundred times stronger than almost all the other nations put together, do not much want to mix it with the French. And why? Because we know they have the capacity to hit back a little too hard. And what's more, they are proud enough to do it. And we do not want to get involved with such an operation. That's the precise philosophy that's kept this nation safe from foreign invasion for so long. No one wants to tangle with our military. We're just too tough."

"I agree with you," said Admiral Dickson. "Which still leaves us with the problem of how to deal with the French. And it's not easy. Because once President Bedford has made his speech, and hopefully lined up the rest of the world on our side, someone needs to do something."

"You got any suggestions?" asked Morgan. "I know you would not have come in here on a purely destructive mission."

"Arnie, I think we gotta hit the French oil industry at source."

"You do?"

"Sure, I do. As we know, they have replaced most of their Saudi crude oil and LPG contracts with ones from other Gulf States. And that's their Achilles' heel. That stretch of coastline is where the really big reserves are found—Abu Dhabi has an oil economy like Saudi Arabia; Kuwait has the second largest crude reserves on earth; and Qatar's north gas field is the biggest LPG source in the world.

"And that's where the French have gone. And that means French-owned VLCCs moving very swiftly through the Strait of Hormuz. In my opinion, Arnie, we should take out one French VLCC right there in the southern part of the strait. Smack it hard with a torpedo. No one will know what the hell's happened."

"Then what?" asked Morgan.

"We park a submarine at the south end of the Red Sea and wait for one of those big gas carriers to come steaming in from Qatar, en route back to Marseille, and we whack that one as well. Then the French will know they're in trouble. But they will not be certain who their enemy is."

"Then what?" asked Morgan.

"Well, I'd guess the French will get very haughty about the entire thing, but will say nothing. Not with the whole world ranged against them. But the next French VLCC to come trundling out through the Strait of Hormuz will be escorted by one of those brand-new Horizon-class destroyers that, as we speak, is with a French flotilla exercising out in the northern Arabian Sea . . ."

"Interesting," said Arnie. "Outstanding research. I like it already. Then what?"

"We slam the escort with a torpedo. You know, a new heat-seeking ADCAP. It'll go straight for the props. Probably blow off the stern. Put her on the bottom."

"Beautiful," replied Morgan. "Then what?"

"In deference to world opinion on ocean pollution, we sink the tanker with a battery of Harpoon missiles. That way we'll set her on fire, and the oil will burn instead of making a huge slick all over the goddamn strait."

"Yeah. I like it," said Morgan. "The assassin with a heart, right?"

"Yes. That's us. And that'll do it. The French will have been hit by an unseen enemy. The world will laugh. And there'll be a dozen suspects as to who committed the crime. But the French will not try again to bring oil out of the Gulf, because they will know what's likely to happen. And they will not want to lose another of their magnificent Horizons. So they'll just have to forget imported oil from the Gulf for a bit. Much like the rest of us.

"And, in the meantime, Arnie, we have to get a hold of Colonel Gamoudi and his family, and get 'em out of harm's way. Then we can hang the French out to dry in front of the United Nations."

Admiral Morgan stood up. "You win, old buddy," he said. "You're correct on all fronts. My damn plan was exactly what you say—too difficult, too dangerous, and too expensive."

"Don't beat up on yourself, Arnie." Alan Dickson grinned. "Every plan has to start somewhere. And you made everyone think . . . get world opinion straight, then slam the Frogs. It's just that much better to do it fast, do it hard, and do it in secret. That way we answer to no one."

Admiral Morgan grinned what he described on others as a "shit-eating grin," and said silkily, "We have no idea who hit the French tankers, or their destroyer, but there sure are a lot of suspects . . . heh, heh, heh."

"If it's okay with you," said the CNO, "I'd like to get back to the Pentagon. We got two CVBGs in the area, one off Kuwait, another in the northern Arabia Sea. I'll have the two SSNs come down the Gulf and take up station way down the Strait of Hormuz. The second group can make its way south to Diego Garcia, and the SSNs can peel off into the Gulf of Aden."

"You okay leaving the carrier without SSN escort?"

"Just for a few days. We'll send two more back in there from DG. That group's on station for another three months."

"Okay. Sounds pretty damn good to me, Alan. So you may as well get outta here, and on the way out tell Kathy to have Lt. Commander Ramshawe come over right away."

The CNO nodded and turned toward the door. As he opened it, Admiral Morgan looked up and said suddenly, "Hey, Alan." Admiral Dickson turned around. And Arnold Morgan just said, "Thanks for that. I'm grateful."

And all the way along the corridor to the West Wing entrance, the Admiral pondered the man in the new office. *In some ways he's the easiest man in the world to get along with—never misjudges real logic—never minds backing down. I suppose he's just not threatened. Doesn't mind being wrong. He's too damn big to care.*

Twenty minutes later, Arnold Morgan roared through the solid-wood door, *"KATHY! WHERE THE HELL'S RAMSHAWE?"*

Kathy Morgan entered the office. "I should think he's just leaving the Beltway," she said. "But since I am not currently employed as a State Trooper, I have no way of knowing the precise location of his Jaguar. But he is on his way. I spoke to him within two minutes of your last instruction."

"Too slow," said Morgan. "Empires have fallen on delays like that."

"So have marriages," she replied, stalking out of the room and leaving her husband guffawing into his chart of the Strait of Hormuz.

Ten minutes later, a slightly disheveled Lt. Commander Ramshawe hurried into the office. "Morning, sir," he said, dumping a pile of papers onto the large table at the end of the room.

"Where the hell have you been?" replied Morgan.

"Mostly making around eighty miles per hour around the Beltway," said the Lt. Commander.

"Not fast enough."

"The speed limit is sixty, sir," said Ramshawe.

"Not for us, kiddo. We have no limits—either speed, finance, bravery, or daring."

"What if a traffic cop stopped me?"

"Firing squad," said Morgan. "Soon as we locate his next of kin."

"Yessir."

"Right. Now come over here and gimme the items in order of importance that we want the President to stress tonight—the stuff that makes France look bad."

"Okay, sir. Mind if I start in sequential order first? Then you can decide importance."

"Eighty miles an hour is a high speed to attend a debate. Facts, James. Facts. Lay 'em right on me."

"Right, sir. August twenty-seventh. The Mossad tries to take out Major Kerman in Marseille. Question: what's the world's most-wanted Arab terrorist doing in France under government protection?

"Mid-November. We notice France apparently getting out of her Saudi oil contracts, driving up the price of oil futures, as if they knew what was going to happen.

"March. The submarines, coming through Suez and disappearing. The only submarines that could have hit the Saudi oil installations.

"March twenty-second. The Brits pick up the signal from northern Riyadh transmitted in French, requesting permission 'to go to the party early.'

"Late March. We receive photographs of the ex–French Special Forces Commander Colonel Gamoudi leading the attack on the royal palace in Riyadh, in which the King is murdered. We trace Gamoudi to his home in the Pyrenees. He's a French national, living permanently in France, with a French wife and French children.

"Same time. The French attempt to assassinate him in Riyadh, when he's with the same Major Kerman, who we now believe led the attack on the Saudi military base in Khamis Mushayt.

"Last week. The new King awards all rebuilding contracts to France.

"Same time. The submarines arrive back in the French

base at La Réunion. All mileages, times, and distances tally with the fact that they opened fire on the Saudi coastline. No other suspects."

Arnold Morgan looked up from his notes. "Perfect, Jimmy. I actually think it's better for the President to go in sequential order. Makes it easier to follow, and adds a certain amount of tension to the unfolding mystery."

"I'm with you on that," said Ramshawe.

"Okay. Now you sit there, and I'll write the speech in longhand. I'll want you there at all times as I come upon difficult bits, all right?"

"Okay, sir. I'll get the documents in order so I'm ready to front up, on demand. No bullshit, right?"

"No bullshit," Morgan responded. "But go out and tell Kathy to inform the President he will broadcast live at seven P.M."

"Right away, sir. How about the speechwriters, sir? Do we need anything from them?"

"Frustrated poets," said Morgan, gruffly. "Tell 'em to send in a computer typist in two hours."

**Monday, April 5, 7:00 P.M.
Briefing Room, the White House**

They were prowling now, the pack of newshounds Marlin Fitzwater always referred to as "The Lions." The White House press corps was gathered at a time that was irritating for the missed-the-edition afternoon newspaper crowd, but frenzy-making for the network television teams, and pressurized for the daily newspapermen with deadlines to meet, questions to ask, and stories to write.

The Briefing Room was seething. It was three minutes after seven o'clock. And the sixty-odd Lions believed it was long past their feeding time. You could hear their growling out in the West Wing corridors.

To a man, the newspaper Lions believed in their own importance as purveyors of the news that their organizations sold for a few cents a shot. The television reporters settled for the unquestioning general belief in Televisionland that they were indeed the gods of the airwaves.

And right now they all wanted to know why the hell the President was late. Didn't he understand that their time was precious? When he kept them waiting, he kept the whole goddamned nation waiting, right?

They guessed the subject would be something to do with Saudi Arabia, since for several days the newspapers had been filled with the repercussions of the military coup in Riyadh. And this afternoon there had been yet another precipitous fall in the Dow and the Nasdaq, and news from the international stock markets was, if anything, worse. Gasoline continued at an all-time high at the pumps, especially in the Midwest.

Suddenly, however, the door behind the dais opened and the President himself walked through, accompanied only by the scowling figure of Admiral Morgan, who glared across the room, as if spoiling for a fight if anyone stepped out of line.

His reputation was enormous. He rarely, if ever, deigned to speak to any member of the media, and he was quick to bite off the head of any offending journalist. And he did not give a damn what they wrote or said about him. President Bedford had insisted Morgan accompany him into the Briefing Room, from where he would broadcast tonight live.

He had been briefed by Morgan, and Morgan alone. And his instructions were clear: *You will say only what's on these sheets of paper. You will answer nothing from the floor. There will be no questions afterward.*

As Admiral Morgan had himself put it, "I just want to avoid someone yelling out, *DO YOU THINK THE PRESIDENT OF FRANCE IS A FAT-ASSED COMMUNIST?* And you reply jokingly, 'I don't entirely disagree with that sentiment.' And the headline screams, *PRESIDENT CALLS FRENCH LEADER A FAT-ASSED COMMUNIST.*"

At this point the President conferred briefly with the Admiral, and then he stepped up to the dais, and the cameras whirred. He faced a phalanx of microphones and a sea of eager but cynical faces, belonging to men and women who were ready to pounce, however limited their knowledge of the subject.

Lions are like that. If they're hungry enough, they'll go for any kill, even if the odds are stacked against them. Members of their breed call it courage with high moral intent. Arnold Morgan had a more graphic, profane description meaning . . . well, not terribly smart.

"Good evening," said the President. "I expect many of you will have guessed I am speaking tonight on a matter of national emergency. I refer of course to the recent events in Saudi Arabia, which have been responsible for such far-reaching economic issues for most of the Free World.

"Now, the Saudi royal family has for many years operated a system of government that was not our idea of democracy. But that burning desert land is situated far away from our own, and has deep tribal traditions and cultures that we cannot hope to understand.

"They are a kingdom, and a Muslim one at that, and they are not so many generations away from their ancient Bedouin roots. Their ways are not our ways, but they deserve our respect, and I can only say that in various times of international strife, the Saudis have been the first to come to our aid.

"Nonetheless, we were aware that all was not well domestically for them, and it was not really a great surprise to students of the region when an armed uprising broke out, the royal family as we knew it was swept from power, and a new King installed.

"For them the issue was a fairer system of government, with a fairer share of the wealth beneath the desert going to the people, rather than just to one family. The revolution that many of us expected has finally happened. In the long run, I for one believe it might very well be for the best.

"But tonight I am here to discuss the short run, and the crisis each and every one of us faces at the gas pumps, the severe inflation that is already happening here, in terms of air fares and all forms of travel, and the spiraling costs in electricity.

"I assure you this government is doing everything possible to get that under control. And in the coming weeks we will have it under control, as I promised you last week. However, tonight my talk to you has another purpose.

"I wish to inform not just citizens of the United States but citizens all over the world that the Saudi rebellion could not possibly have happened without the compliance of a heavily armed, militarily savvy Western country. And right here, right now, I point the finger at the Republic of France, which has acted in a way many of you may find unforgivable.

"The Saudi Arabian uprising was masterminded by France, executed by France, and led by France. The new King was backed by France. The old King was murdered by France. And all to seize an advantage in the international oil markets when Saudi oil came back on stream.

"I look at France, and I say again, I ACCUSE! Or, if they understand it better, J'ACCUSE!

"My fellow Americans, France did this. And you will no doubt have heard the new King Nasir of Saudi Arabia, in his opening speech, announce that France would receive all of the billion-dollar rebuilding contracts for the Saudi oil installations."

President Bedford hesitated, and took a sip of water. He stared out at the furiously scribbling journalists, knowing that many of them were dying to get through to their offices—but they were forbidden under White House protocol from moving or speaking until his address to the nation was over.

"In order that everyone understand thoroughly how we arrived at our conclusions, I will take you through the sequence of events that led irrevocably to the culprit.

"And the first thing I would like to mention is the level of the Saudi defenses around their oil fields and refining complexes. It's heavy. Military. Highly trained. Essentially, the Saudis have one principal asset, and that's oil. And they are far from stupid, and they know how to protect that asset.

"The only weapon that could hit those installations is a cruise missile, and it would need to be fired from a submerged submarine, not from the surface or from an aircraft. They would have spotted those. But they would not have spotted a submerged launch. And that's what happened. And the Saudis do not own one.

"Whenever anything is hit by a missile apparently fired from nowhere, you always seek an underwater launch. And it always turns out to be the case. No exceptions.

"And the United States Navy has a handle on every single submarine in this world—where it is, what it's doing, who owns it, and where it's been.

"My fellow Americans, there were only two submarines anywhere near the Saudi shores at the crucial time. And they were both French. We have their hull numbers. We logged 'em both through the Suez Canal, and we saw them go deep in the Red Sea. But we never saw them again—not till they turned up in the French base right on time, having fired their missiles at the Saudi oilfields. WE KNOW WHAT THEY DID.

"And we watched the French buying oil futures last November. We watched them getting out of their Saudi contracts. WE KNOW WHAT THEY DID.

"And we took photographs of the French Special Forces Commander who led the attack on the royal palace in Riyadh. We've been to his home in France. We know his name. WE KNOW WHAT HE DID.

"We know the French Government harbored and then hired the most dangerous military commander in the Arab terrorist world. We know the date and the French city where they hired him to lead the land attack on the big Saudi military bases at Khamis Mushayt. We know his name. WE KNOW WHAT HE DID.

"We heard the last military signal from the Riyadh commander to his French base; our good friends in the British Army intercepted it and passed it to us within a half hour. We know what it said. And we know who said it. WE KNOW WHAT HE DID."

The President paused to let his jackhammer words, drafted and honed by Arnold Morgan, ring around the room, and indeed around the world.

"As many of you know, this is not the first time the French have stepped out of line with the rest of mankind.

Not so long ago they tried everything they knew to stop a United States President remove from power one of the most villainous tyrants of our time from Iraq.

"This was a man whose hands dripped with blood, the blood of his own people. He was a man who started off as some kind of a tribal murderer and who ended up a full-fledged psychopath, who slaughtered an estimated three hundred thousand of his own people, some with chemical weapons. He was a man who had fired guided missiles at innocent Israeli families, tried to conquer Kuwait. And the French tried to protect him because of their commercial ties to Iraq.

"Perhaps it's because we saved them in World War Two, perhaps it's because their pride has never recovered from their government's cowardice and their army's lack of leadership. But it seems there are no lengths to which they will not go to remain solidly anti-American. And this time they have gone too far. They have brought the Western world to its knees financially. But only temporarily. We'll get up.

"Meanwhile my advisers are considering our position with regard to the French action. Right now we are about ready to declare Saudi oil a global asset. It may be that we, and our principal allies, consider the Saudis no longer competent to act as custodians of that asset. But we expect no cooperation from the French in any form.

"My fellow Americans, I am certain of our ground. I am certain of the very great wrong that has been perpetrated upon the nations of the earth. And I make no apologies for any sentence I have uttered tonight.

"I will take no questions. But I say again to the President and the government of the Republic of France, WE KNOW WHAT YOU HAVE DONE. AND I ACCUSE . . . I ACCUSE . . . I ACCUSE."

And with that, the Virginian Democrat, Paul Bedford, the forty-fifth President of the United States of America, turned on his heel and walked from the dais, leaving Admiral Morgan to answer any questions there might be.

However, the room was in such total uproar there was nothing that could have been heard, never mind asked and answered. The wire service reporters had stampeded to the back of the room, and within seconds were yelling down their cell phones. The time was 7:20 P.M., a critical time in many newspaper offices. The network television reporters were dying to fire in a question that would portray them on air as focused, wise, and farsighted political observers.

Trouble was they all went for immortality at the same time, and the result was absurd. Nothing short of bedlam. Admiral Morgan shook his head and growled into one of the microphones, "Either you guys get your goddamn act together and stop behaving like children, or I am leaving."

That statement was not broadcast on any network. And finally the din subsided and someone called out, "Sir, does the French President know what our President has just said?"

Admiral Morgan said, "For all I know the French President is in the sack, since it's after midnight in Paris. But if he's sitting up in bed watching CNN or something, I guess he's heard. We announced President Bedford's prime-time address several hours ago."

"Sir, do you expect to hear from the French President either tonight or tomorrow?"

"No. Not directly. But I expect the Prime Minister of France to make a statement on behalf of his government, denying any and all involvement in the recent events in Saudi Arabia. I expect him to denounce the United States as perpetrators of a gigantic lie against the French Republic, and to call upon the United Nations to reprimand our UN Ambassador in the strongest possible terms."

"What do we do then?"

"Shut up, Tommy, will ya? Haven't you got enough of a great story without standing there saying, 'And then what?' over and over. Jesus, do you guys actually get paid to go through this bullshit?"

That part was not broadcast either, on any network. But it made the reporters laugh, and no one much minded when the Admiral shook his head and said, "I'm outta this zoo. Go write your stuff."

Admiral Morgan left the West Wing immediately. Kathy was waiting at the wheel of his beloved Hummer, and they made the journey back to Chevy Chase together.

The fire in the study had been prepared, and all Morgan needed to do was light it and turn on the television. Mrs. Newgate, their new housekeeper, employed as soon as the Morgans returned to the White House, announced that dinner would be ready at 8:45, and would the Admiral like her to open a bottle of wine.

Morgan replied that the way he felt, a case would probably be more appropriate, but he would settle for a bottle of Château de l'Hospital 2000, a pricey red Bordeaux. "And you'd better pour it into a decanter," said Morgan. "Might as well drink it in style. Alan Dickson and I just decided not to blow the place up."

Mrs. Newgate's somewhat bewildered reply was lost in the thunder of Morgan's next words. *"JESUS H. CHRIST! THAT WAS FAST!"*

At which point, Mrs. Newgate, who hardly knew the Admiral personally, had not moved, and for a split second she thought he was being sarcastic. But then she noticed he was riveted to the television screen, where a man in a dark suit and a maroon striped tie was speaking in rapid French while a CNN interpreter turned his words into English.

"*. . . and France cannot understand the accusations of the American President . . . our government is completely unaware of any of the actions he attributes to us . . . we know of no French commanders in Saudi Arabia, our submarines make the Suez Canal transit every month . . . there is no mystery . . . we conduct exercises in the Arabian Sea and the Indian Ocean, as they do . . . our base is at La Réunion, theirs is at Diego Garcia . . . there's no difference.*

"*And what is this crazy signal from Riyadh they speak of? What signal? Was it in French? Who says so? And where are these photographs they claim to have? We have never been shown . . . it is absolutely preposterous that the President of the United States should level against us accusations of this nature.*

"*And I assure every citizen of this nation we shall take this matter before the United Nations in New York, and we will demand satisfaction. We will demand an apology. These charges are unfounded, and we deny them most vigorously. I am sure the Americans, with their innate jealousy of France and its civilized standards, would like them to be true. But I am afraid not, Mr. President. They are lies. And I end my address as President Bedford ended his. With a repetition, n'est-ce pas? NON! NON! And NON! again."*

"You go for it, pal," muttered Arnold Morgan. "You lying frog-eating bastard."

At this point, Kathy came into the study bearing a weak, tall Scotch-and-soda for her husband, the way he liked it. No ice. She glanced at the television and heard the commentator saying: *"And so, the United States stands accused tonight of slandering the Republic of France, and will probably have to face the censure of the Security Council of the United Nations.*

"A UN spokesman said a few minutes ago that President Bedford had made many allegations that would be difficult to prove. He added that the Secretary-General was most surprised that as a Permanent Member of the Security Council, the United States would choose to abuse another Permanent Member in this way."

At this point, the anchorman began to turn the newscast over to CNN's United Nations correspondent, who was standing outside the great building with the myriad national flags fluttering behind him in the rain.

"Thank you, Joe."

"You're very welcome, Fred. Perhaps you'd give an outline of the procedures we may expect against the United States . . ."

"Be happy to, Joe . . . and I should start by saying these are very grave accusations, and I understand France has already filed a request for an emergency meeting of the Security Council, which, under the charter, must now meet inside the next twenty-four hours.

"The Security Council is the most powerful body within the United Nations and contains five permanent members—China, France, the Russian Federation, the United Kingdom, and the United States of America. There are also ten nonpermanent members, and for a censure motion to go through, I am advised that a straight majority of nine votes would be required. We may assume that the United States and Great Britain will vote no to the French motion, and we may have one or two other supporters.

"However, informed opinion here at UN Headquarters suggests the United States will lose the vote and very probably will be hauled before the General Assembly, and be very publicly censured for making unsubstantiated allegations against a founding Member State."

"How about we substantiate them, asshole?" muttered Arnold Morgan.

Kathy made her biannual objection to his language, saying, "I do wish you would not use that disgusting word so often . . ."

"What word? France?" asked the Admiral.

"No."

"Well, what word?"

"I will not repeat it."

"Well, how am I to repent and promise to be better if I am kept in the dark about the entire basis of my crime?"

"You are, of course, impossible . . ." began Kathy.

"Hold it, darling . . . just for a moment . . . please . . . I want to hear what this asshole is trying to say."

Kathy, as ever, could not help laughing at him, and she walked back to the kitchen with the words of an apparent asshole in her ears. ". . . *Make no mistake . . . this is very serious trouble for this administration.*"

The Following Morning
The Pentagon
Arlington, Virginia

They were gathered in the fourth-floor office of Admiral Alan Dickson—Arnold Morgan, Admiral Frank Doran (C-in-C Atlantic Fleet), who had flown up from the Norfolk Naval Yards, and the Chairman of the Joint Chiefs, General

Tim Scannell, who had accepted an invitation to sit in on the meeting, even though this was, at present, strictly a Navy issue. In the opinion of Admiral Morgan, the least number of people who knew about this the better. As Supreme Commander of Operation Tanker, he took the seat at the head of the table. "Now I guess we've all seen the newspapers and listened to the television broadcasts, and understand that the U.S.A. is about to come under world-wide attack inside the United Nations. I should tell you that I planned that, because what we are about to do has a good chance of being judged so shocking that no one would dream we were the culprits, since we're in so much trouble already."

General Scannell and Admiral Doran both tried to suppress chuckles. But failed.

Morgan proceeded. "Gentlemen, we're not in any trouble. France, whatever that Prime Minister says, did take down the Saudi King and it did plunge the world economy into crisis. And we are going to do something about it."

He outlined the plan that Admiral Dickson had masterminded. The quick hit on the first tanker carrying French crude oil to come out of the Gulf. Then another hit on the first French tanker to enter the Red Sea through the Bab el Mandeb.

"That should slow them down some," said Morgan. "But the French are proud and arrogant. Admiral Dickson and I think the next French tanker will enter the Strait of Hormuz under escort. And that's when we cause a total uproar. We hit the escort first, with a torpedo. Then we hit tanker number three. And that will wrap it right up for France. They will not try to exit the Gulf with fuel oil again until we're good and ready to allow it."

"Arnie, is this a public operation . . . like we hit and we don't care who knows it?" General Scannell, the Chairman of the Joint Chiefs, looked concerned.

"Not at this stage," replied Morgan. "We'll launch from submarines, way under the surface, and we will not admit to anyone what we've done. We'll just let 'em all have a guessing game."

"Torpedoes?" asked the CJC.

"Yes. Fired from several miles out. But not in the case of the last tanker. We'll hit that with three or four Harpoons, set the oil on fire, save a lot of pollution."

"Do you intend to let anyone know it was the U.S. of A. that sank the ships?"

"No."

"I realize this is a kind of naive question to ask in a room full of sailors," said General Scannell, "but how do we know if a tanker is full of French oil or not? I thought they were all registered in Liberia or Panama or somewhere. They must all look the same."

"In a sense, they do, Tim," replied Admiral Dickson. "But we've been checking on both the VLCCs and the UL-CCs which service France . . ."

"What's a ULCC?"

"Same as a VLCC, that's a very large crude carrier. A ULCC is an ultra-large crude carrier, maybe up to four-hundred thousand tons."

"We gonna hit one of those?"

"Maybe," said Admiral Dickson. "But to answer your question about identifying the correct target, we've been re-searching the TotalFinaElf conglomerate and the methods it uses to move large quantities of oil. And much of it is done by a highly reputable corporation based in Luxembourg. It's called TRANSEURO, and they've run a fleet of maybe fourteen or fifteen tankers for years, under long-term char-ter to Total, mostly in the two-hundred-fifty– to three-hundred-thousand–ton range.

"In the trade they call it French Flag Tonnage. But these tankers ply their trade back and forth from the Gulf to Mar-seille, Brest, and the other French oil ports. They can carry either crude oil or liquid natural gas. And we can identify them with no trouble, even if they choose to fly a flag of convenience."

"We got submarines somewhere close?" asked General Scannell.

"Very close," said Admiral Dickson. "In fact we got two of the best submarines in the fleet out there right now.

They're in the Arabian Sea with the *Ronald Reagan* CVBG. The two newest Virginia-class SSNs, *Hawaii* and *North Carolina* . . . really great boats, seventy-eight-hundred-ton submerged-launch Tomahawk cruise missiles and thirty-eight Mark 8 ADCAP torpedoes.

"If we need four more, which I think we do, the *Cheyenne* and the *Santa Fe*—coupl'a L.A.-class attack submarines with the *Constellation* Group—are on station in the Gulf, off Kuwait. And we got *Toledo* and *Charlotte* ready to clear Diego Garcia any time we need 'em. Just so *Connie* ain't hanging around with no underwater backup."

"You don't see surface ships being needed?" said General Scannell.

"Well, we don't want to announce our presence, and I don't see a need for us to do so. This is a very simple sub-surface operation. But we got a couple of Arleigh Burke guided-missile destroyers within two hundred miles."

Arnold Morgan knew Dickson was referring to the *Decatur* and the *Higgins*—9,000-tonners, both built in Maine—two of the most lethal warships afloat. Both armed with short-range deadly accurate McDonnell Douglas Harpoons, with their ship-killing 227-kilogram warheads, plus fifty-six Tomahawk ship-launch cruises. A thin smile crossed the face of the Chief of Operation Tanker.

"I may be slightly at a loss here," said Admiral Doran. "But can someone tell me what precisely we hope to gain from this? What good will it do us to sink French tankers?"

"Well, in part it's a point of principle," said Arnold Morgan. "The current financial crisis is going to get worse. There'll be shocking repercussions for people all over the world. And the basis for our actions is to hang France from the highest tree in front of the international community. That way we'll save President Bedford. If we do nothing, he'll end up getting the blame, because that's the way the world works.

"The U.S. economy goes down the gurgler. The press and indeed the people will round on the President of the day and ask why he did nothing while Wall Street burned. But they can't hardly do that if we got us a real live culprit out there swinging in the wind."

Admiral Dickson interjected. "And the humiliation of France may well pave the way for the U.S.A. to move back into Saudi Arabia and take charge of the global distribution of the oil. We'll still pay the Saudis, same as they've always been paid, but we may just have to get into control and make darned sure this does not happen again." Like all service chiefs, the Admiral saw a major role for the U.S. Navy right here, and he was not about to let the opportunity slip by. "As I see it," he continued, "we gotta make France seem like too big an embarrassment for the Saudis, or anyone else in the oil game, to deal with."

"Correct," said Admiral Morgan. "I also intend to inflict some heavy damage in some of their harbors. I thought we might get Admiral Bergstrom's boys to take out a few luxury yachts along the Riviera. That will further alienate the Middle Eastern oil states against France. They all keep their damn great private ships in French ports, or Monte Carlo.

"Essentially, we're working to a master plan, and you'll find the pieces all fall into place very quickly. There is, however, one missing piece, and we must find it."

"What is it?" asked General Scannell.

"We have to find the French Colonel who led the attack in Riyadh. He's Jacques Gamoudi, and we need to kidnap his wife and children, and then grab him and get them all to America. And we gotta do it before the French assassinate him, which they've already tried to do once."

"Jesus," said the Boston Irishman Frank Doran. "This is like working for the Mafia."

Everyone chuckled at that. But Arnold Morgan agreed with him. "Sometimes," he said, "contrary to the policies of a certain Democrat of the nineties, you gotta get down and dirty."

"The first two options are easy—the sinkings and the blastings," said Admiral Dickson, "but how do you think we'll get along in the kidnapping business?"

"Right now we have the CIA and the FBI working in Riyadh," replied Morgan. "So far as they know, Colonel

Gamoudi has not yet left the city, although he might have. However, we think the situation is, for the moment, static. The French are trying to assassinate him, but he is under heavy protection from the King, and is probably holed up in one of the palaces."

"What about his family?" asked Admiral Doran.

"That may turn out to be key," said Morgan. "My own view is we should snatch them, using SEALs and helicopters if necessary, and get them the hell out of France. That way we got some chips. Then we somehow let Gamoudi know we got everyone safe in the U.S.A., and all he has to do is locate us, somehow, somewhere, and he's safe, too.

"Then we put him in front of the UN, he cuts the balls off the lying French, and we give him a new identity and a new life. That's when we go and take over the Saudi oil, because no one can deal with France, and the towelheads can't do it without us."

"Neat," said Admiral Doran. "I'll tell you something, that Gamoudi character just became the most important man on this planet. And we got the added problem of the French trying to kill him."

"If I were French, I'd be trying to kill him," said General Scannell. "All I can say is we better get Mrs. Gamoudi real quick, and try to avoid breaking more than about a hundred international laws while we're about it."

"You're right there," said Morgan. "We screw this up, we're in more trouble than France. Because without Gamoudi we can't prove a damn thing. Anyone know what time John Bergstrom is due in?"

"Thirteen hundred," said Frank Doran. "He left San Diego at o-five-hundred this morning."

Tuesday, April 6, 1330
The White House

Two armed, uniformed guards were waiting at the helicopter pad on the White House lawn, staring into the skies way down across the eastern bank of the Potomac. They could see it now, the big U.S. Marine guided-missile gunship, the Super Cobra, clattering in over the river.

On board was the Emperor SEAL, Admiral Bergstrom, Commander in Chief of SPECWARCOM, the top Special Forces unit in the U.S. military. The Marine guards watched the helicopter bank right and then settle gently onto the White House landing area. The loadmaster was out before the brand-new four-bladed rotor even slowed down. He opened the door for the Admiral, who stepped down and returned the rigid salute of both guards.

"This way, sir," said one of them. And beneath the steady gaze of a fully armed SWAT team, positioned with machine guns primed on the White House roof, the three of them headed up the short, grassy slope to the West Wing entrance. Today's meeting, comprising just Adm. Arnold Morgan and Adm. John Bergstrom, would be, as ever, a strategic discussion, for "action this day," between two of the toughest men who ever wore shoes.

They greeted each other like old friends, and Morgan outlined the situation, stressing the critical nature of the capture of Colonel Gamoudi, and the even more critical nature of the kidnapping of Giselle and the two boys.

Admiral Bergstrom was thoughtful. "I do see the problem," he said. "If we have the family members, the Colonel will *want* to come over to us. If we don't, he will not want anything to do with us."

"That's right," said Morgan. "And it's likely to be ten times easier to find a man who is trying to find us, than to find a guy who's essentially on the run."

"And you are proposing to send a team of SEALs into a tiny French town in the Pyrenees and snatch Giselle and her boys?" John Bergstrom looked highly doubtful.

"You think that's a problem?" said Morgan.

"It's not a problem to grab them. And it's not a problem to get them away. It's the sheer ramifications that bother me. First of all, it's plainly illegal. Second of all, it's damn nearly a declaration of war—the U.S. military going into action against innocent foreign civilians in full public view."

"Well," said Morgan, "How about we put the SEALs in plain clothes?"

John Bergstrom was deeply unimpressed. "Arnie," he said, "you can't hide or disguise SEALs."

"Why not?"

"They're not the same as other people."

"What do you mean?"

"They look different."

"In what way?"

"They just stand out. Their powerful physiques . . . crew cuts. They just look too hard, too healthy . . . the way they carry themselves . . . the way they walk . . . straight backs, erect . . . fantastic posture . . . they look like they're marching even when they're going for lunch. And they have this alert, wary look about them, like wolves. Arnie, they can't help it. They're trained killers.

"And Mrs. Gamoudi's going to be under escort, and those escorts will recognize my guys at a hundred paces. You want a nice quiet grab at three civilians, you gotta do it with civilians. My guys could cause a fucking uproar. Trust me. They're not trained in subtlety."

Admiral Morgan nodded. For a few moments he paused, then he said, "I'm getting kinda used to making shaky judgments on this operation. Guess I must be getting old."

"The best of us make shaky judgments," said John Bergstrom. "And it doesn't matter a damn. The only thing that matters is how quickly you recognize the problem, and how ready you are to make the change."

"I'm ready," said Morgan. "What do you suggest?"

"Okay. We got a nice French lady and her two young sons. They're effectively under house arrest, right? By the French Secret Service, somewhere near the town of Pau, in the Pyrenees. We have to hand this to the CIA and they have to locate her and watch the house for a couple of days. When they pounce, they do it quietly, in the street. A diversion. The grab. Getaway car. Escape by helicopter. No problem. Very fast. No one knows what the hell has happened."

Admiral Morgan visibly brightened. "Got it," he said.

"You're right. But what about when we grab the Colonel himself?"

"That has to be at a seaport or on a beach. Then my guys can move in and complete the operation. But if the French are trying to kill him, we may have to be pretty darned brutal in our execution of the mission."

"The stakes are about as high as they can get, John," said Morgan quietly. "We better get a full team of your guys on standby, probably in the Mediterranean. Because we're gonna find the ol' Chasseur in there somewhere."

"Who the hell's the Chasseur?" asked Admiral Bergstrom.

"Oh, that's Colonel Gamoudi's nickname. He's had it a long time. Le Chasseur. It's French for The Hunter."

"That's not good," replied the SEAL Chief.

"Why not?"

"Because guys don't get names like that unless they are damned dangerous. Was he ever in the Special Forces?"

"Sure was. First Marine Parachute Infantry. And the French Foreign Legion. And the French Secret Service, on active duty in North Africa."

"Jesus Christ," said John Bergstrom. "That's a trained professional fighter. You don't want to try and take him against his will. Otherwise someone's going to get killed. You have to get Mrs. Gamoudi and the kids. And you have to get 'em real quick."

Four Days Later, Saturday Morning, April 10
Pyrenean City of Pau

Andy Campese and a CIA team of some fifteen field operators, including his colleague Guy Roland, had been tracking, watching, and logging the life of Giselle Gamoudi for several days. It had been a simple matter to trace her to her mother's house, north along Montpensier Avenue, to a tree-lined residential area near Lawrence Park.

But she was never out of the house for more than a half

hour, and she was never without two plainly armed escorts, one of whom was, quite often, the same Secret Service officer Andy had met at her own home back in the village of Heas.

The boys were always with her. But Campese had seen no sign of their attending school. This was plainly an enforced break, courtesy of the French government. He had expected it to be a mission packed with tension, since the French Secret Service obviously wished to keep her away from any intruders. But thus far he had been mildly surprised at how relaxed his quarry and her "minders" seemed to be. Right now Campese and young Roland were sitting in a parked car watching the driveway of Giselle's current residence. She was in the car with a driver, but the left, rear passenger door of the car was open, awaiting, Campese guessed, the arrival of the two boys.

He was correct about that. The older one came running out first, followed by the yelling Andre. They both piled into the backseat, and the car pulled out into the south-running avenue that led to the central area of Pau, almost a mile away. An identical car, parked in the street right outside the house, immediately fell in behind them.

Andy Campese hit the buttons on his mobile phone, making three short calls in less than a minute. At the same time he ordered his driver to track Giselle's Peugeot and her escort car. All three of them moved out into the Saturday-morning shopping traffic.

In the center of town, at the junction of Place Clemenceau and Rue Marechal Foch, the lead Peugeot slowed to a stop, and Giselle and the boys climbed out. Two men climbed out of the escort car, and Andy Campese's man pulled into a no-parking area of the adjacent Rue Marechal Joffre.

He and Guy Roland disembarked and moved quickly into the Place Clemenceau, from where they could clearly see Giselle and her sons walking slowly past the shops, with their two escorts strolling along around ten feet behind them.

Campese hit the buttons on his mobile again. This time

he made two calls, and he finished only one of them. For the next hundred yards he walked with the phone held to his ear.

Giselle reached a large pharmacy and ushered the two boys inside. Her escorts did not follow her, but hung around outside, smoking, in front of the large window next to the main door.

It was a busy street, and neither of the guards seemed to notice three more CIA men disembark from a black Mercedes that was now double-parked twenty yards beyond the pharmacy. Neither did they notice two more tough-looking characters wearing heavy dark blue sweaters and Breton fishermen caps, walking slowly along the street from Rue Marechal Foch.

They did however notice a very pretty blonde woman in the passenger seat of another double-parked car on the other side of the street, who seemed to be giving them a broad smile—but that might have been mere wishful thinking. The French do quite a lot of that where women are concerned.

The minutes ticked by. Then five more. And finally, Giselle Gamoudi emerged from the pharmacy with Andre, but not Jean-Pierre, who showed up fifteen seconds later. As the three of them stepped out into the street, Andy Campese raised his right arm.

The blonde woman stepped out of the car, showing legs up to her panties, and let out a piercing scream. It had taken Campese two hours to persuade Agent Annie Summers to wear a skirt that short and then to scream the place down in the middle of Place Clemenceau.

Both of Giselle's escorts moved instinctively toward the blonde, one of them literally running to her aid. And as he did so, the first of the men in the Breton caps raced forward and intercepted him, kicking his legs out from under him and slamming a boot into the back of the man's head, knocking him senseless.

His colleague did not have time to move. The second man in the Breton hat was on him, slamming a fist into the guard's solar plexus and driving a knee straight into the man's jaw as he fell forward. The men from the Mercedes rushed forward, dragged the inert figure out of the road, and stood guard over both unconscious bodies.

A few passersby noticed the commotion, and stopped to stare at the two fallen men. But Annie was still yelling and she managed to distract the entire area.

Simultaneously, Campese, Roland, and the two "fishermen" grabbed Giselle and the boys and carried all three of them, kicking and trying to scream, along the street to the black Mercedes. Powerful hands covered their mouths, but soothing voices were telling them—*take it easy . . . don't scream . . . you're safe with us . . . get in the car. We're here to rescue you.*

Only twenty seconds had passed since the CIA men had launched their attack, and now Guy Roland hit the gas pedal on the big automatic Mercedes. The car rocketed along Rue Marechal Foch and swung right down to Boulevard Barbanegre, hurtling along to the main entrance of Beaumont Park.

By now, Andy Campese had slipped handcuffs loosely onto all three of his prisoners. For their own sakes he did not want any of them to do anything reckless. The car slowed, turned right, and Roland drove into Beaumont Park.

With the doors and windows shut, they could not hear the helicopter heading in to a wide clearing beyond the magnificent building of the Municipal Casino, which dominated the park. Right now Andy Campese was talking to the pilot who was hovering twenty feet above the tree line.

Roland flashed his headlights, and the helicopter came on in and touched down lightly, to the astonishment of two park groundsmen. The Mercedes ran right up close, and Roland cut the engine. He and Andy Campese whipped open both passenger doors and hauled Giselle and the boys out.

While Roland hung on to Andre and Jean-Pierre, Andy ushered Giselle toward the open door of the eight-seater helicopter, which looked like a civilian aircraft but contained two United States Navy Lieutenants and one Chief Petty Officer.

Giselle felt strong arms lift her bodily into the cabin, and then Jean-Pierre came flying through the door as if on wings. He landed in the rear seat, followed by Andre, who landed on top of him, laughing his head off. Last man to board was Andy Campese, who was needed because of his fluent French.

Then the door slammed, and one of the Lieutenants, Billy Fallon, removed the handcuffs and told them to fasten their seat belts.

The chopper was in the air and climbing, less than a half minute after it had touched down. Young Andre looked out of the window and waved at Guy Roland, who had time to wave back, and then everyone was gone, the car moving back toward town to pick up two of its passengers, the helicopter beating its way up to a flight path ten thousand feet above the Pyrenees.

Lt. Fallon sat opposite Giselle and the boys and he spoke calmly. "Mrs. Gamoudi, you were in the most terrible danger. The French Secret Service has already made an unsuccessful attempt on Jacques's life, but if they should manage to assassinate him, you and the boys would . . . well, just disappear.

"We are United States Naval officers and we are taking you to a place of safety. We are also desperately trying to save your husband, but we are uncertain where he is."

Andy Campese translated swiftly, and Giselle Gamoudi's hand flew up to cover her mouth, as if to stop herself from crying out.

But Billy Fallon was not finished. "You must answer my questions," he said. "Now tell me, is your money safe? I imagine we're talking several hundred thousand?"

"Sir, it is much, much more than that. But it is safe in our account in the Bank of Boston. They have told me no one can touch it."

"Okay. But we better get it out of France, fast, because these guys might put a freeze on it."

Andy translated. And Billy asked for the account number, the Bank branch, and password. For some reason, Giselle trusted him and gave him the information.

Billy punched the buttons of his cell phone's direct line to the ship. He spoke briefly to the comms room and relayed the banking information to the Commanding Officer, who would now call the private emergency number of the

President of the Bank of Boston on the Champs-Elysées, Paris.

By some miracle of detection, Lt. Commander Ramshawe had traced the bank that held the Gamoudi money. And by special orders from the President of the United States, the bank was empowered to wire-transfer the entire account to the branch in State Street, Boston, Massachusetts.

Six minutes later, Billy Fallon's cell phone rang to inform him that $15 million had just crossed the Atlantic from Paris to the United States.

And now they were high above the Pyrenees Atlantique, and the great mountain range was rapidly flattening out to the west, into the Basque country, which ran right to the shores of the Bay of Biscay.

It took only forty-five minutes to reach the coastline, which they crossed, still making 200 knots and flying at 10,000 feet, five miles north of Biarritz. Twenty minutes later they could see a tiny gray shape in the water way up ahead, and the pilot immediately began his descent.

They came clattering down through 2,000 feet, then 1,000, and now they could see clearly the outline of the 10,000-ton guided-missile ship U.S.S. *Shiloh*, a Ticonderoga-class cruiser, the world's most dangerous combat warship.

The sea was calm, and the ship rode fair on her lines, making seven knots behind a light bow wave. On deck they could see the landing crew signaling them in. The pilot banked right around to the east and came in over her stern, hovering slowly over the Harpoon missile launchers, over the five-inch guns and then the SAM launchers, touching down on the flight deck, directly above the torpedo tubes.

"Sorry, guys. This is gonna be your home until we get Dad out of Saudi Arabia," Lt. Fallon told Gamoudi's sons.

Generally speaking, Andre Gamoudi, age eleven, considered this as probably the best day of his entire life.

Saturday, April 10, 1400
French Secret Service Headquarters
Caserne des Tourelles, Paris

GASTON SAVARY COULD not believe what he was hearing. He leaned forward on his desk, resting on both elbows, the telephone pressed to his right ear. In a working lifetime in the Secret Service, he had never been quite so shocked, not even when he was first told that the CIA was inquiring about Col. Jacques Gamoudi.

"What do you mean, they've gone? Gone where?"

They've just gone, sir. Several people attacked our men, who are both in hospital.

"But where the hell is Giselle Gamoudi, and the boys?"

They vanished, sir.

"What do you mean vanished?"

They left in a big Mercedes-Benz.

"Anyone get the number?"

No, sir.

"Well," said Savary helplessly, "which way was it going?"

Sir, it headed into Parc Beaumont.

"Did we follow?"

No, sir. But someone saw the helicopter land.

"WHAT HELICOPTER?"

The one in Parc Beaumont, sir.

"Is it still there?"

No, sir. It only stayed a few seconds, then it left. The chief groundsman was watching.

"But what about Giselle Gamoudi and her sons?"

They left in the helicopter, sir.

"Holy Mary, Mother of God," said Savary, and gently replaced the telephone.

Two minutes later—two minutes of stunned silence in his empty office—and Savary called back his Toulouse agent, the luckless Yves Zilber, who was now somewhat hopelessly drinking coffee in the bar of the Hotel Continental, on the Avenue Marechal Foch in Pau, just along the street from Place Clemenceau.

"Yves," said Savary, "may I presume you have told the appropriate authorities to try and track the helicopter?"

Yes, sir. I have. I told them the park groundsman saw it flying very high, heading due west, toward the Basque region and the coast.

"I bet it was," muttered Savary, replacing the receiver without a word for the second time in three minutes.

This was bad. This was absolutely diabolical. If Colonel Gamoudi already knew that agents of the DGSE were trying to eliminate him, and he somehow now knew that his wife and children were safely out of France . . . well, he'd never need to return to his home. Maybe we should freeze his money.

Gaston Savary had no idea what to do. He stood and walked to his office window, staring out of the bleak ten-story building at the depressing view of *la piscine*, the indoor municipal swimming pool.

Was this really as bad he thought it was? Yes. Worse, if anything. And was he, Gaston Savary, the only one of sixty million French citizens who understood the appalling consequences of the events in Place Clemenceau today? Yes again.

The loss of the Gamoudi family in the Pyrenean city of Pau was a crisis that could see mass sackings, both in the government and the Secret Service. Worse yet, his head would almost certainly be the first to fall.

Standing there alone on this gray, rainy Parisian day, Gaston Savary had a fair idea how Louis XVI's Queen, the vilified Marie Antoinette, felt in the hours before the guillotine in October 1793. Wearily he picked up the telephone again and instructed the switchboard to contact the French Foreign Minister, Pierre St. Martin, and get him on the line. "Don't hurry," he muttered, softly enough for the operator not to hear.

Just then his telephone rang angrily. At least it sounded angry to him. Yves Zilber again, still at the Hotel Continental.

"Sir, I just heard from Biarritz Airport. An unannounced helicopter, flying at more than ten thousand feet, left France and flew straight out to sea over the Bay of Biscay. They alerted the Air Force Atlantic Region HQ, but since the helicopter was transmitting nothing, they decided pursuit would be a total waste of time.

"Ten minutes from that phone call, the helicopter was beyond French air space anyway, and heading west, out over the Atlantic. The Air Force said it was no business of ours, since the aircraft was not flying into France."

Savary thanked Agent Zilber and replaced the phone. "They should have shot it down," he muttered unreasonably. "Then we'd all be out of trouble—even though we'd be at war with the U.S.A."

One minute later his call to the French Foreign Office was through. Pierre St. Martin listened without a word as the Secret Service Chief recounted the disastrous events in the main town square of Pau.

At the conclusion of the dismal tale of French mismanagement, he just said, "And where does the French Secret Service think the helicopter is headed? Washington?"

"Since its range is probably around four hundred miles, I doubt it. More likely a U.S. Navy warship, well beyond our reach."

"So where, Monsieur Savary, do you think that puts us?" asked St. Martin.

"In approximately as deep an amount of trouble as we can be," Savary replied.

"Which means we have just one option," stated St. Martin flatly. "And I am instructing you to achieve that objective, no matter how much it costs in lives or money. You will find Le Chasseur and you will eliminate him. Because if you do not do so, the United States of America will destroy French credibility in this world for twenty years."

"But, sir . . . what about Madame Gamoudi?"

"Gaston. Get into the art of realpolitik. Stop chasing shadows. Madame Gamoudi has gone. There's nothing we can do about that. What she knows, she knows. What she tells, she tells. But anything she says is about a hundred times less important than anything her husband has to say.

"He alone can sink us. Get after him, Gaston. And silence him permanently. You may assume that is an order from the President of France in person. And, Gaston, if I were in your shoes, I would bear in mind that it was your organization that first leaked to the CIA the whereabouts of the Gamoudi family. It is now your organization that has absolutely failed in its allotted task to keep Madame Gamoudi well out of the way of the CIA . . ."

"But, sir," pleaded Savary, "I had eight armed men guarding her twenty-four-seven . . ."

"Perhaps you should have had one hundred and eight," said St. Martin none too gently. "In matters of this importance, the cost does not matter. Only success or failure. And I say again: You will find Jacques Gamoudi, and you will have him executed. Is that clear?"

"Yes, sir. It is," replied Gaston Savary. "One last thing, do you still want the Gamoudi family to have all that money, or shall I have the bank freeze it?"

"You may leave that to me," replied the Foreign Minister calmly.

But there in the great building on the Quai d'Orsay, St. Martin was trembling, both with anxiety and fright. He knew this was probably the end of the line. He knew this might spell the end of his own finely planned political career and his hopes to attain the presidency of France.

He had of course listened intently to the speech made by the President of the United States a few days ago. He had helped to draft his own Prime Minister's reply. But in his heart, Pierre St. Martin knew the Americans were on to them. It was obvious by the way Paul Bedford had spoken with such panache and daring. He said he knew. And he did know.

Pierre St. Martin had no doubt about that. And he also knew of the recall to the White House of Adm. Arnold Morgan. The newspapers and television stations had been full of it.

When he had first read it, every hackle he had rose in alarm. And now his worst dreams were coming true: the United States knew precisely what France had done to help the Saudis.

Pierre St. Martin stared out across the River Seine from one of France's great offices of state. He realized he may be in his final days in there. The final days of his lifelong dream.

"Damnation upon Arnold Morgan," he said to the deserted room. "Damnation and blast the man to hell."

110930APR10. 25.05N 58.30E, Course 270, Speed 7, Depth 200

The brand-new Virginia-class hunter-killer *North Carolina* was running slowly west through the clear warm waters that led up to the Strait of Hormuz. Capt. Bat Stimpson had just ordered the fastest possible satellite check, and the jutting ESM mast had split the surface waters for only seven seconds.

Now the great dark gray hull was back where she belonged, running silently, as quiet as the U.S. Navy's peerless Seawolf-class ships, betraying no wash on the blue waters of the Gulf of Oman.

In his hand, fresh from the comms room, Captain Stimpson held the critical satellite signal that would soon summon his ship to action stations. It read:

102300APR10. WASHINGTON. VLCC Voltaire, *ON CHARTER TO TRANSEURO CLEARED ABU DHABI LOADING PLATFORMS 092200APR10. ASSESS CURRENT POSITION 25.20N, 57.00E., SPEED 12.* Voltair *300,000 TONS BOUND FOR MARSEILLE THROUGH SUEZ. COMPLY WITH LAST ORDERS. DORAN.*

Bat Stimpson knew what his last orders were: *SINK HER*. And he gave an involuntary gulp. The Louisiana native had never sunk anything before, but he'd had a lot of practice in U.S. Navy simulators. He knew, on this early morning, how to put a huge oil tanker on the bottom of the Gulf of Oman. He knew that as well as he knew how to eat his cornflakes.

He turned to his executive officer, the veteran L.A.-class navigator Lt. Cdr. Dan Reilly, and said quietly, "This is it, Danny. She'll be about a hundred miles northwest of us right now. And they were not joking. This is from Admiral Doran himself. How long we got?"

"Probably about five hours, sir. That tanker will speed up soon as she rounds the Musandam Peninsula and starts heading into open waters. She'll probably be making seventeen knots when we locate her. I'm guessing she'll be in our preferred range at around fourteen-thirty, maybe a little earlier."

"Under five miles, right?"

"Uh-huh," replied the XO. "But we'll need to go inside a half mile to read the name on her hull. We can't risk hitting the wrong ship, and we won't see it much over nine hundred yards."

"No," said the CO. "After that we better retreat fifteen miles to our launch area. We don't want to be any closer. But we don't want the birds to miss."

"You think a couple of those sub-Harpoons will do it, sir?"

"Oh, sure. Remember what two French Exocets did for the Brits' *Atlantic Conveyor* during the Falklands war? She was just a very large freighter, but she burned for hours, glowed red hot in the water, and she wasn't full of oil."

"She was full of bombs and missiles, wasn't she, sir?"

"Yes. But they didn't explode for a long time. The *Conveyor* just burned from the sheer heat of two big missiles crashing through her stern."

"And these sub-Harpoons can't miss, can they?"

"No, they can't. Everything in this ship is damn nearly perfect."

He referred to the flawless conduct of every working part

in this sensational new submarine. The *North Carolina* was on her first operational voyage, after two years of sea trials and workup in the North Atlantic. And if there'd ever been a better underwater ship, Capt. Bat Stimpson had not heard of it.

They would pick up the *Voltaire* right after lunch, with a couple of radar sweeps. Only then would they close in and check her out at periscope depth. It was always slightly more awkward identifying a merchant ship, because she transmitted just regular navigational radar. Merchant ships did not have a clear-cut "signature" like a warship, which transmitted active sonar, pinging away, probably with her screw cavitating. And a modern nuclear submarine's ESM mast would intercept her radar and identify the pulse immediately.

"We'll head for her direct line of approach," said the CO. *"Helmsman. Captain. Make your course two-seven-six."*

"Aye, sir."

The President of France had been circumspect about the Gamoudis' money. He was plainly furious at the loss of the family to the CIA, but he recognized that nothing could be done about that. His Foreign Minister was now quite rightly wondering about the $15 million paid to a man France was now obliged to eliminate.

"There is a moral issue here," said the President. "And I suppose it would be wrong to leave Madame Gamoudi absolutely destitute. After all, she did not ask to be kidnapped by these damn cowboys from Washington."

"No sir, she did not."

"My suggestion is that we freeze the money, temporarily, and then retrieve ten million of it, leaving Madame Gamoudi with five million. I think that would be fair compensation for the loss of her husband. We should also make it known to her that she is welcome back to live among her own people in France. She is, after all, innocent."

St. Martin sounded doubtful. "I agree it would be more comfortable to have her on our side," he said. "And when the Colonel is gone, we could take steps to bring her home. Just so long as she doesn't know what happened to her husband," St. Martin reminded the President.

"Oh, she'll never know. An accident in a far-off land. Meantime, I should get to work on freezing that money. Ten million U.S. dollars is rather a lot to waste on a dead man, *n'est-ce pas?*"

For the next half hour the Foreign Minister put ten aides onto the task of opening up a bank on a Sunday afternoon. It took only a short while to locate the emergency number of the bank president via the Paris Gendarmes.

But when the call was finally made, the news was not good. "I'm sorry, sir," said the banker. "But that account was removed from Paris and relocated in Boston, Massachusetts."

"But when did that happen? And why were we not informed?"

"Sir, this account was set up deliberately fireproof. Only Colonel Gamoudi and his wife could issue instructions by means of a password. The money was removed about four hours ago, with a call from the United States Ambassador to France. The envoy had every necessary detail, and informed us that Mrs. Gamoudi was in the care of the U.S. government, and, if we checked, there was an edict from the President of the United States instructing the Bank of Boston to transfer the money to a different branch.

"Of course, sir, we made the checks. We even phoned back the embassy, and everything was in order . . . and, sir, it's not as if the money has disappeared. It's still in the Bank of Boston, still in the same account. It's just been moved to a different city."

"A different planet, I am afraid," replied St. Martin, wishing the bank chief good afternoon and pondering the sheer futility of phoning a bank in the United States and asking to have access to a $15 million account controlled by two private customers.

"Hopeless," he muttered. "This operation is becoming more and more impossible, every hour."

111330APR10
Gulf of Oman

The *North Carolina* was still steering very slightly north of due west. It was four hours since the satellite signal had been received, and they came once more to periscope depth.

One sweep of the radar located a major ship seven miles off their starboard bow. It was a hazy Sunday afternoon, and it was not possible to get a visual. So the submarine went deep again and continued to close, holding course two-seven-six, making seven knots through the water.

Ten minutes later the navigation officer put the oncoming ship at 24.40N, 58.02E, and again the *North Carolina* came to periscope depth. And this time they could see the ship, a VLCC, a black-hulled tanker of at least 250,000 tons, riding low in the water, making around seventeen knots.

From here they could see her bright scarlet upperworks through the periscope, but they would have to close in much nearer to read the name high on her port bow.

The Captain ordered her deep again, and the *North Carolina* accelerated underwater on a direct course to the tanker's line of approach. They came in at over twenty knots for another nine minutes, and the Captain ordered them again to PD. And now they could really see her, less than a mile away, and every bit of 300,000 tons. But the name, in white lettering just below the massive sweep of her bow, was still not sufficiently clear to be read.

They slid back under the surface and ran forward for another half mile before returning to PD. They were actually just astern of midships, which made it slightly more difficult to read the letters.

But the name was unmistakable. This was the *Voltaire*, right on time, barreling through the calm water off the coast of Oman, laden with Abu Dhabi's finest crude and bound for the port of Marseille.

Captain Stimpson ordered the *North Carolina* deep again, and he ordered a speed increase and a course change . . . *make your depth one hundred, speed twenty-two, come left to course zero-seven-zero.*

The *North Carolina*, now running easterly for the first time, was moving much faster than the tanker, on a course that would take her slightly north of the oil ship. On this diverging course she would be fifteen miles away inside forty-five minutes, but she would still be directly off the port beam of the *Voltaire*.

Final missile check.

Captain. Missile Director. Both weapons programmed . . . course one-eight-zero to target.

At precisely 1425, Capt. Bat Stimpson, with his ship now two hundred feet below the surface, ordered the missiles away. And one by one the sub-Harpoons ripped out of the underwater launchers, pre-programmed and unstoppable—at least by an oil tanker.

They swerved upward toward the surface and burst clear of the water, cleaving their way into the clear skies, still swerving until they settled down on the course fed into the computer brain of each weapon.

These were not sea-skimmers, but they flew low over the water, coming in toward the *Voltaire* at over 1,300 mph. Flight time for their fifteen-mile journey: forty-one seconds.

No one saw anything. The ocean was deserted in this part of the Gulf, and the crew of the tanker was paying scant attention to anything out on the port side. Those who were on watch were gazing steadily ahead when the big heat-seekers smashed into the hull seventy feet apart, twenty feet above the waterline.

The missiles exploded with sensational impact, sending two fireballs clean through the mighty ship. Each one of them blew the bulkheads separating the oil tanks. The heat was so incinerating, it immediately set fire to the gasses above the actual fuel, which exploded violently, blasting upward two massive holes in the deck.

The deck pipelines were blown to smithereens, and in a split second the crude oil itself, unable to resist the terrifying heat of the missiles' warheads, burst into flames, the fire racing across the surface of the oil. It was a vicious, roaring fire.

Within twenty seconds the great tanker was doomed. She began to list to her port side, and the fires were so intense the entire upperworks was becoming too hot for human survival. The French captain ordered the ship's company to abandon, and lifeboats were lowered on the starboard side and over the stern.

Miraculously, no one had been killed, because there was no one for'ard at the time. The crew was either on watch, sleeping, or eating in the towering aft section. The nearest missile hit one hundred yards for'ard of this. But the fire would not be quelled for three and a half days, and would melt the midships section of the deck and upper hull.

One minute after she had unleashed the missiles, the *North Carolina* turned away from the datum and ran southeast at twelve knots, leaving behind a puzzle that would confuse the world's tanker industry for several days. But in France, military leaders were highly suspicious of an involvement by the U.S.A.

Indeed General Jobert, C-in-C of France's Special Forces, on that same Sunday evening, convened a meeting with his friend Adm. Marc Romanet, the Navy's Flag Officer Submarines. The General came in by helicopter to the dockyards in Brest, and they talked through dinner.

There was just one question: would the United States have dared to sink a French tanker?

Admiral Romanet was absolutely certain the all-powerful U.S. Navy could most certainly have done it. "I could have done it," he said, "in a halfway decent attack submarine."

"Leaving no trace and no clues?" asked the General.

"Not a problem," replied Admiral Romanet. "Mind you, with all the trouble for the U.S. at the United Nations I think it extremely unlikely they would have done something like this. I mean . . . that censure motion was very serious last Thursday. But I expect you noticed the American representatives at the UN refused to attend any of the three Security Council meetings, or indeed to recognize formally any censure by anyone."

"I did notice that, of course," replied the General. "They

are quiet, but defiant. It would still be very extravagant just to go out and blow apart a three-hundred-thousand-ton tanker in the Strait of Hormuz, in complete contempt of world opinion."

"Yes. It would," said Admiral Romanet slowly. "But my fellow former submariner, Admiral Morgan, is in the White House at the President's side. And he is a very dangerous man to any enemy of the United States. And, whether we like it or not, at this moment, he perceives us to be in that category."

Monday, April 12, 0530
The Red Sea, South End

Capt. David Schnider, commanding officer of the U.S. Navy's second brand-new Virginia-class SSN, the *Hawaii*, was waiting 200 feet below the surface, thirty-six miles north of the Bab el Mandeb. His ship was making a quiet racetrack pattern, moving at only five knots in a surprisingly deep stretch of water, almost 700 feet, twenty-five miles off the remote desert seaport of Al Mukha, on the Yemeni coast.

This is where the Red Sea split into two buoyed channels, both of them with in and out lanes, one heading along the Yemeni coast, the other swerving toward the Eritrean side. Captain Schnider did not know which lane his quarry would choose, which was why he was lurking quietly in deep water, positioned to hit in either direction. But his hit would be on a very special ship and there could be no mistakes.

Captain Schnider, who was born within sound of the old Brooklyn Navy Yards in New York, was one of the most able SSN commanding officers in the U.S. Navy. At forty-four, he had already commanded the Los Angeles–class attack submarine U.S.S. *Toledo,* and there was a degree of envy among his contemporaries when SUBLANT had appointed him to U.S.S. *Hawaii.*

David Schnider was a short, swarthy man with a crushing

grip on facts and situations. He would have made one hell of a lawyer, but his father had served as a Chief Petty Officer in a destroyer, and his grandfather, a gunnery Chief, had died in the blazing hulk of the battleship *California* at Pearl Harbor.

The Navy was in his blood. Despite a certain rough edge to his method of command, and indeed his somewhat black humor, his men loved serving under him, and there were those who thought he might rise to the highest pinnacles of the U.S. Navy.

Captain Schnider knew what he was looking for here at the south end of the Red Sea—an 80,000-ton red-hulled gas carrier, distinguished by four massive bronze-colored holding domes, which rose sixty feet above the deck, with a long gantry crossing the length of the ship, nine hundred feet, above all four domes, and then descending to the foredeck.

David Schnider agreed with SUBLANT. She was damned hard to miss, so long as you were positioned in more or less the right place. His plan was to let her run by and then slam his missiles into the hull below two of the holding domes. The water here was plenty deep enough for a safe and efficient escape, but Captain Schnider had decided he did not wish to turn around, and then run back past a burning ship that, so far as he could see, was not much short of an atomic bomb.

He had the details of these LPG carriers right in front of him. The TRANSEURO ship he awaited, the *Moselle*, carried 135,000 cubic meters, that's 3,645,000 cubic feet of liquefied natural gas, frozen to minus 160 degrees. The liquid gas was compressed 600 times from normal gas and formed, without doubt, the deadliest cargo on all the world's oceans.

"Jesus Christ," murmured Captain Schnider. "That sonofabitch could blow up Brooklyn." And he made himself a promise: that no submarine in all of history had ever vanished from the datum faster than U.S.S. *Hawaii* would in the split second after he had loosed off her sub-Harpoons.

Meanwhile, the *Moselle*, which had cleared Qatar's north

gas field at the beginning of the week, had passed through the Strait of Hormuz the previous Thursday, three days in front of the *Voltaire*. Right now she had completed her crossing of the Gulf of Aden and was positioned to the left of the flashing light on Mayyun Island in the narrowest part of the Bab el Mandeb, heading north.

Captain Schnider's orders were as succinct as Capt. Bat Stimpson's had been in the *North Carolina* the previous day: SINK HER. And the only thing concerning the CO of the *Hawaii* was the temperature of his target.

"Since the Harpoons, in their final stages, are heat-seeking," he told his missile director, "how the hell are they going to find a target frozen to one-hundred-sixty degrees below zero? I mean, Jesus, that's as cold as a polar bear's ass. Like trying to find the heat in a goddamn iceberg."

The missile director, Lt. Cdr. Mike Martinez, laughed. "Sir," he said, "I promise you there's a ton of temperature in that ship. The refrigeration plants alone generate enormous heat, and the engines, situated toward the stern, generate twenty-three-thousand horsepower. Our missiles will go straight into the hull, probably at one of the refrigeration plants. We don't want to hit the domes, because they are seriously reinforced. But they won't be cool. The dome walls are too thick. The Harpoon explosions will be below the deck, right in the heart of the ship.

"And we don't need to slam one into the side of the dome: the sheer power of the TNT below decks will probably split at least one, maybe two, of them in half. And immediately on contact with the hot air, the liquid gas will flash off into normal gas, the most volatile cargo on the ocean. One spark will turn the *Moselle* into something like Hiroshima. And I just hope to hell we're well underwater and moving away fast at that time."

Captain Schnider smiled and said, "Mike, we're firing from five miles off her starboard quarter, because she's going straight up the Red Sea to Suez, and 'most all fully laden tankers moving straight through take the left-hand lane going north. We'll be so far away when that sucker goes off *bang* it'll be like we never existed."

It was actually quite hard to believe they existed now, while the *Hawaii* cruised two hundred feet below the surface, making just five knots, and leaving no trace of a wake on the surface. All through the night they had stayed on their deep, lonely station listening to the roar of ships' propellers churning away overhead, traveling both north and south. But not one of those ships, neither merchantman, tanker, nor warship, had the slightest inkling that beneath their barnacled keels lurked the most dangerous attack submarine on earth.

Two more hours went by after Captain Schnider had outlined his getaway plan to Lt. Commander Martinez. And then, at 0730, as soon as they slid up to periscope depth, they spotted her. It was the *Moselle*, moving at a steady seventeen knots north up the channel, heading slightly toward her left, just as David Schnider had forecast.

At 80,000 tons she was small enough to make the transit through the Suez Canal, and from there it was a six-day run up to the huge underground terminal for liquid petroleum gas in the port of Marseille.

U.S.S. *Hawaii* had spotted her on radar ninety minutes previously, but there had been three other paints on the screen at that time. Only now, at 0730, with the sun climbing out of the desert to the east, was it possible to make a POSIDENT. The red hull of the *Moselle* was bright in the morning light, and the sun glinted off those huge bronze holding domes.

"We got her, sir," called the XO, as he ordered, *DOWN PERISCOPE.* And then, *We're about a mile off her starboard bow. Steer course two-seven-zero until we can read her name.*

The ESM mast slid down, and the comms room confirmed there were no further signals on the satellite. The orders were unchanged.

As the *North Carolina* had done on the previous day tracking the *Voltaire*, the *Hawaii* moved in closer, but only a few hundred yards, because the light here was much better. The periscope went up one final time, and it was possible to see the huge white letters on her hull, L N G. Right below the safety rail on her starboard bow was the word, *MOSELLE.*

Temporarily, the *Hawaii* turned away, back south at twenty knots. But only for six minutes. Then she returned to PD for her final visual check. And the *Moselle* was still on course.

"Missile Director final checks," ordered Captain Schnider.

"Both weapons primed, sir. Pre-programmed navigation data correct. Course three-three-zero. Launchers one and two ready."

"FIRE ONE!" snapped David Schnider. *"FIRE TWO!"*

Seconds later, the two Harpoons came hurtling out of the calm water, one hundred yards apart, swerved as they hit the air, and then settled onto their course, both making a direct line toward the *Moselle*, one hundred feet above the surface.

Thirty-five seconds later they slammed into the starboard hull of the *Moselle*, around twenty feet above the waterline. The steel plates on this side of the double hull, both layers, were blasted apart and there was a firestorm of sparks and explosive inside the ship.

The reinforced aluminum of number two dome at first held, and then ruptured, and 20,000 tons of the most flammable gas in the world, packed with methane and propane, flooded out into the air—air that was two hundred degrees Celsius warmer than its refrigerated environment. Instantly it flashed off into vaporized gas, and exploded with a deafening *W-H-O-O-O-O-M!* Dome three split asunder, both from where the Harpoon had smashed into its shell and from the enormous explosion from dome two. This blew the for'ard dome, and before the Captain of the tanker could even issue a command, the entire ship was an inferno, flames reaching 1,000 feet into the sky, the entire front end of the ship a tangled wreckage of ruptured, melting steel.

Again, as in the tanker, the crew was, to a man, in the aft section, in the control room, the engine room, and the accommodation block. The Captain issued the totally unnecessary order to abandon her within one minute of the blast. He had not the slightest idea what had happened, and the crew who were able would have to leave in the two lifeboats on davits at the stern.

The whole length of *Moselle*'s starboard side was a blow-torch of gas, rising up off the water and fed by thousands of tons of liquid petroleum cascading out of the hull from the aft dome, which had not yet exploded but was somehow setting fire to the Red Sea.

The sheer size of the fire was already causing other ships to move in for a search-and-rescue operation, and a few men who failed to make the lifeboats were jumping off the stern, like in a scene from *Titanic*. But the waters were clear, warm, and deep, and the tide was carrying the gas on the surface to the north, away from them. Almost every one of the seamen who had crewed the *Moselle* would survive.

But the inquiries would be long and painstaking. She was the only LPG carrier ever to have a serious fire, except for one in the Persian Gulf a few years earlier that had hit a contact mine.

By the time the order to abandon ship was given, the *Hawaii* had gone deep, 400 feet below the surface, making twenty-five knots away from the staggering scene of maritime destruction. Captain Schnider had only two miles at this depth and this speed, after which he would slide into the regular south-running shipping lane, and make his secretive exit through the Strait, only 100 feet below the surface at six knots.

His satellite signal to SUBLANT in Norfolk, Virginia, would not be transmitted until they were safely in the much deeper water of the Gulf of Aden. Just one word: GASLIGHT.

Monday, April 12, 0900 (local)
Foreign Office
Paris

There was an air of foreboding on the Quai d'Orsay. News of the *Moselle*'s demise was raging around government corridors. The President was furious, the military was demanding orders, and Pierre St. Martin was trying to prevent himself doing something that might ultimately be judged as rash.

And, of course, the dark, satanic cloud of the United States of America hung heavily over the entire scenario. Had Uncle Sam just whacked out a couple of French oil tankers? Or had there just been two ghastly, coincidental accidents?

Pierre St. Martin, as a lifelong career politician, knew it would be futile to ask the United States if their Navy had been responsible. And even if they answered, the Americans would certainly use the question to berate France: *not every nation is willing to use destructive firepower in the cause of its own interests . . . do not judge others by your own infamous conduct . . .*

No. St. Martin could see no earthly reason to contact the United States. He paced his elegant office, uncertain what to advise the President, uncertain what, if anything, he could do.

He was not helped by the simple fact that no one onboard either the *Voltaire* or the *Moselle* had any idea what had taken place. So far as both commanding officers were concerned, their ships had suddenly, for no discernible reason, exploded and burst into uncontrollable flames. Which did not assist St. Martin one iota.

His tenure as Foreign Minister had always been cushioned by the comfort and elegance of the job, and its many, many *accoutrements,* not to mention the priceless antiques and furnishings from bygone days of French glory that perpetually surrounded him as France's frontline executive in the global community.

But now the whole thing was turning sour. Everything possible was going wrong. He felt powerless and vulnerable. He turned to the portrait of Napoléon, with that smug expression on his round, complacent face. And St. Martin understood, vaguely, how the Emperor must have felt as he prepared to depart for his final exile in St. Helena.

The trouble was, at this level of government, there was

nowhere to hide. Worse yet, there was no one to whom he could turn. The President, at 7:30 this morning, had been incandescent with rage. *"All I have ever asked for is secrecy . . . and what do I get? Some jackass French officer from the Pyrenees having his photograph taken on the front of a tank! It's probably framed now in the U.S. Embassy.*

"I get incompetence, betrayal. I ask for my massive highly paid security forces to guard one slim French lady and two children, not a group of terrorists. And they can't even do that. And now I have America, which appears to know everything about us, blowing French ships out of the water, and you tell me I cannot even remonstrate! Pierre, this is intolerable!"

Pierre tried to calm himself. He picked up the telephone and asked to be connected to Gaston Savary over at La Piscine. And to him he repeated the words of the President, "Gaston, this is intolerable."

But he was preaching to a man on his way back up the road from Tarsus. Savary knew that everything about this mission had turned out to be intolerable. And like the Foreign Minister and the President, he too believed that the U.S. Navy was banging French tankers out of the water.

"Is it your opinion that we should cease all oil shipments from Gulf ports to France?" asked Pierre St. Martin.

"Quite frankly, yes," said Savary. "Because if we lost another one, and a lot of people were to be killed, there would be a major uproar in France. The people would accuse the government of callous indifference to poor, hardworking sailors, who now leave widows and fatherless children, because of our own ambitions. Pierre, we cannot afford to lose another big ship. The risks are too great."

"Can nothing stop a U.S. Navy submarine from doing its worst?"

"Not really. Those things can stay underwater for eight years, if necessary. At least their nuclear reactors can run for that long, supplying all the heat, light, fresh air, fresh water, and power they need. They only come up for food when it runs out."

"And what about sonar? We have zillions of euros' worth of sonar on our ships. Can't we find the American submarine?"

"Not much chance. A nuclear boat can be anywhere, very quickly . . . you could be searching in the Atlantic and she's in the Indian Ocean. You could be searching in the Pacific and she's six thousand miles away. Give it up, sir. They think we've smashed the world's economy, and they're taking revenge. And there is not too much we can do about it, short of war with the United States, which we would swiftly lose."

"So your advice is simply to stop all tankers traveling from the Arabian loading docks to France?"

"Yes, sir. That's my advice."

"Then I shall have to seek further help from the Navy, Gaston. *Bonjour, mon ami.*"

Adm. Marc Romanet, in his office in Brest, besieged by government departments wondering what to do, or say, about the latest American outrage, was marginally more optimistic. "Foreign Minister," he said, "the Navy could provide an escort to the tankers, as the British did for the Atlantic convoys against the u-boats in World War Two."

"You mean each tanker leaving the Gulf and bound for a French port would be accompanied by a battleship?"

"Sir, we don't have battleships as such. I was thinking of a destroyer."

"*La même chose,*" said the slightly precious Foreign Minister haughtily. "Very large, very smelly, very noisy ships loaded with guns and shells and angry young men in badly pressed uniforms."

Admiral Romanet was deeply unimpressed by St. Martin's grasp of the French Navy. "Not these days, sir," he said briskly. "Very large, pristinely clean, guided-missile ships fitted with state-of-the-art electronics incomprehensible to a civilian and crewed by very calm, very educated young men in immaculately pressed uniforms."

Severely put in his place by one of the Navy's favorite sons and the head of the entire submarine service, Pierre

St. Martin beat a very fast retreat. "Just joking, Admiral," he said.

"I very much hope so, sir," replied Admiral Romanet. "Because in the final reckoning, should we ever come under attack, your life will very probably be in the hands of those young men in the pressed uniforms."

"Of course," replied the Minister. "I was only teasing."

"Naturally," said the Admiral. But he was not smiling. "To continue," he added, "we have our newest Tourville-class destroyer, the *De Grasse*, exercising in the northern Arabian Sea at present. She's our specialist antisubmarine warfare ship. If anything can protect a tanker against attack, she can."

"Against torpedoes? Which I believe is what the Americans used against the tankers."

"Tell the truth, sir, I don't think they did. The fires were too big and too sudden, in both ships. My guess is they hit them with missiles. But the *De Grasse* is a specialist. She's loaded with her own missiles, but her torpedo capacity is formidable, ten ECAN L5 antisubmarine active/passive, homing to six miles—with a hundred-fifty-kilogram warhead.

"She also carries two Lynx Mk 4 antisubmarine helicopters. She has towed-array torpedo warning, radar warnings, jammers, and decoys. You want a ship to protect a tanker from underwater attack, I'd request the *De Grasse*, if I were you."

"Admiral, I thank you for this advice, which I will pass on to the President. But I must ask you: can you guarantee this destroyer will keep the tanker safe?"

"There's no guarantees in my business," said the Admiral. "And, perhaps, unlike politicians, we do not like to say there are when there are not. But I'd give the *De Grasse* a fighting chance against any enemy."

"Thank you, Admiral," said the Foreign Minister, who had not enjoyed sparring with a very senior officer in the French Navy who had managed to make him feel faintly absurd.

Nonetheless, he called back the President, and, attempt-

ing a career-saving final throw of the dice, told him he
could absolutely guarantee the safety of French tankers on
the high seas if they were accompanied by French Navy
warships, particularly Tourville-class destroyers like the *De
Grasse*.

"Perhaps organize them into half a dozen groups," he
said ambitiously. "Six of these Tourvilles would probably
do the trick," he added jauntily. "Antisubmarine specialists,
of course."

The President did not know any better than St. Martin
that the French Navy owned only two of the Tourvilles, and
the other one was on sea trials in the north Atlantic. Instead
he trusted the word of his Foreign Minister, which would
not do him much good. Meanwhile, St. Martin continued
his rock-steady progress toward the gallows.

Wednesday, April 14, 1430 (local)
Strait of Hormuz

Capt. Bat Stimpson had the *North Carolina* in the identical
position he occupied on Sunday morning just before he
sank the *Voltaire*. The Virginia-class hunter-killer was
steaming slowly up the Strait of Hormuz, two hundred feet
below the surface, awaiting the arrival of another tanker,
chartered by TRANSEURO, this time a ULCC, the
400,000-ton *Victor Hugo*, fully laden with Abu Dhabi sweet
crude bound for Cherbourg.

The coded signal from SUBLANT had been retrieved
from the satellite in the small hours of that Wednesday
morning. It read: *140400APR10. ULCC* Victor Hugo *heading east along Trucia coast from Abu Dhabi loading platforms. Escorted by French ASW DDG De Grasse. ETA your
datum Strait of Hormuz 1600. Eliminate them both.*

Bat Stimpson did not bother to gulp this time. The orders
were succinct and perfectly straightforward. The *Victor
Hugo* was already around the Musandam Peninsula and
past Oman's rocky headland of Ra's Qabr al Hindi.

The *North Carolina* ops room knew it was their approaching target because the sonar room had picked up the sonar transmissions of the *De Grasse*, unmistakable on D-Band, Thompson-Sintra DUBV 23. French warship.

At 1510, the operators picked up the *De Grasse*'s military air/surface search radar transmissions, right at the end of its sixteen-mile range. Again unmistakable, beaming out from the top of the destroyer's mast, Thompson-CSF DRBV 51B on G-Band.

The Torpedo Director deep below the ops room in *North Carolina* was already making his final checks. He had prepared two weapons in case there was a malfunction. But Captain Stimpson was confident they could sink the destroyer with just one wire-guided Gould Mark 48 ADCAP fired from seven thousand yards. They would take the destroyer before they hit the tanker because, again, they would use submerge-launch Harpoons against the ULCC, in order to burn the colossal amount of crude oil.

Right now the ops room had the *Victor Hugo* and the *De Grasse* steaming on a south-southeast course, at seventeen knots, 200 yards apart, the destroyer positioned off the tanker's portside bow.

And on they came, hard on their course, headed for the mouth of hell.

Ready number one and number two tubes, 48 ADCAP.

Aye, sir.

Fifteen minutes passed, and the sonar room called, "*Track 34 . . . bearing one-seven-zero . . . Range six miles.*"

And now the guidance officer was murmuring into his microphone constantly. The *North Carolina* seemed to hold her breath as the sonar team checked the approach of the French destroyer, calling out the details in that hypertense calm that grips a submarine in the moments before an attack.

The XO had the ship, and Bat Stimpson stared at the screen. Then he called, *STAND BY ONE! Prepare to fire by sonar.*

Bearing one-two-zero . . . range 7,000 yards . . . computer set.

FIRE! snapped the CO. And everyone felt the faintest

shudder as the big ADCAP thundered out in the ocean, instantly making forty-five knots through the water, straight toward the projected line of approach of the *De Grasse*.

Weapon under guidance, sir.

Bat Stimpson ordered the torpedo armed, and 5,000 yards away, still running fast through the water, it began to search passively for the warm hull of the destroyer.

Three minutes after firing, the Mark 48 switched to active homing sonar, pinging its way toward the destroyer. Now it could not miss, and it locked onto its target.

It was just 300 yards from the warship, when the French sonar room, taken by surprise, caught the torpedo flashing in toward the stern, where the four huge turbines drove the twin shafts.

TORPEDO! . . . TORPEDO! . . . TORPEDO! . . . RED ONE SEVEN FIVE . . . ACTIVE TRANSMISSION . . . RANGE THREE HUNDRED YARDS.

Too late. Too close. The Mark 48 slammed into the stern of the *De Grasse*, detonated with barbaric force, blew the stern clean off the ship, split the shafts asunder, and blasted the engine room to rubble.

Eight men died instantly, and within moments the ship began to sink, stern first, as water cascaded through the open aft end of the warship. No one had been expecting anything like this, and there were several bulkhead doors and hatches left open.

This might have been construed as shortsighted, since the destroyer's entire raison d'être was to protect, and perhaps fight, as she moved through a possible war zone.

However, 200 yards away, onboard the tanker, men stood at the rails on the high bridge and gazed in astonishment at their mighty escort, which had not only blown up but also appeared to be on fire at the aft end, and sinking as well.

And as they watched, incredulously, several of them saw the unthinkable, as two sub-Harpoon missiles came scything through the crystal-clear skies and smashed straight into the hull of the *Victor Hugo*. They blew most of the 1,000-yard-long deck 100 feet into the air, straight out over the starboard rails like a can of sardines, opening sideways.

Again, the crew was largely saved by the great distance between the upperworks and the long front end of the ship, which housed the oil. Four men, who were working for'ard, were of course killed instantly, and the ensuing fires were unimaginable. From the bridge, it looked like a lake of pure flame roaring up into the stratosphere. Crude oil is hard to ignite, but when it does it's extremely difficult to extinguish.

As with the *Voltaire*, the Master of the *Victor Hugo* had no option but to abandon her. There were two gigantic, thirty-foot-long jagged holes in the tanker's port side, close to the waterline, and there was oil leaking out into the ocean but burning fiercely.

The fire was growing hotter by the second. If the Captain and his crew did not get off this massive ship in the next ten minutes, they would surely fry.

At that point, with the lives of everyone onboard the two ships hanging in the balance, Captain Stimpson elected to leave the area. He made one final visual observation of the havoc he had wrought, and then ordered the *North Carolina* deep again, instructing the helmsman to turn away, south.

"Bow down ten... depth two hundred... make your speed twenty... course one-three-five...

In his seaman's heart, he hoped that rescue would be prompt and thorough, using every possible ship and helicopter the Omani Navy possessed. For the catastrophe was closest to their shores. But he could not afford to dwell on the unfairness of the sailors' fate. France had transgressed the natural laws of survival on the planet earth. And she deserved every last bit of vengeance the U.S.A. chose to inflict upon her.

The warship, and the men who sailed it, was the responsibility of the French Navy and the politicians in Paris. Captain Stimpson believed the survivors should be well compensated. Like him, they were only carrying out their orders.

Same Day, 1600 (local)
Elysée Palace
Paris

The President of France had been this angry before, but not in living memory. He twice banged his fist down upon his Napoleonic sideboard, which made the Louis XVI Sevres porcelain cups dance up and down on their saucers and the silver Napoleonic coffee pot bounce on the polished inlaid surface of the sideboard.

Another couple of whacks like that and the burly little former communist mayor could have done about a million dollars' worth of damage.

"I AM NOT PUTTING UP WITH IT," he roared. *"THEY CAN'T . . . THEY . . . THEY . . . THEY CAN'T KEEP DOING THIS. IT'S . . . IT'S LUNACY . . . WHO THE HELL DO THEY THINK THEY ARE?"*

"That, of course is the main trouble, sir," replied Pierre St. Martin. "They know who they are."

"Well, whoever they are, they can't just keep sinking ships and killing people."

"Sir, they can. And I believe they will, until we stop trying to ship oil out of the Middle East. They have issued a very firm warning, and with that dreadful bastard Morgan in the White House, they are going to continue."

"Then you are saying we must stop trying to keep this country running?"

"No, sir. I am not. But we have to find other ways of importing oil than with tankers out of the Persian Gulf—"

"But, Pierre," interrupted the French President, "that's just not acceptable. We cannot just lie down and give in, like a . . . like a . . . poodle." The President was so angry he could hardly speak.

"Sir, we have to, because those submarines of theirs are impossible to deal with. You cannot even find them, far less destroy them. And even if we did, the Americans could probably produce fifty more."

"FIFTY!" yelled the President. "FIFTY! That's ridiculous."

"Sir, I have told you already. The U.S. Navy is invincible."

At which point the President of France lost all semblance of control. *"YOU ALSO TOLD ME THAT DESTROYER WOULD PROTECT THE TANKER . . . YOU . . . YOU GUARANTEED IT . . . YOU SAID IT WAS A SPECIALIST ANTISUBMARINE WARSHIP . . . AND IT TOOK THE UNITED STATES ABOUT ONE MINUTE TO BLOW IT IN HALF! FUCK YOU, PIERRE. DO I MAKE MYSELF CLEAR? F-U-U-U-U-CK YOU!"*

"I was only repeating naval advice."

"GAZING AT YOUR NAVEL . . . THAT'S THE NEAREST YOU GET TO KNOWLEDGE!" he bellowed. "I am surrounded by lunatics. My friends and my enemies. Imbeciles and killers. And I am sick to death of it."

At which point, the butler entered the room to announce the arrival of Gen. Michel Jobert's staff car at the main door downstairs.

"Bring him straight up," said the President, not even looking at the man.

And three minutes later, the Commander in Chief of France's joint service Commandment des Opérations Spéciales walked into the room. General Jobert had presented himself with the task of trying to prove what had happened in the Strait of Hormuz and in the Red Sea. He instantly announced that he was the bearer of important information, which was just as well, given the general atmosphere in that room—the President fit to be tied, his Foreign Minister cowering before the onslaught.

"Sir, as you know," said the General, "we were unable to discover anything about the *Voltaire* or the *Moselle*. However, today's atrocity is very different. Most of the *De Grasse*'s ship's company survived, that's 20 officers and 294 men.

"Their sonar room caught an incoming torpedo three hundred meters out. They even had its bearing. They have the recording and the software, with someone calling out 'Torpedo! Torpedo! Torpedo!'

"It's the first time we have had incontrovertible evidence that our ships were hit by a malevolent enemy. And, sir, it gets better: Four of the crew of the *Victor Hugo* were watching the destroyer burn when two guided missiles came in and smashed into the tanker's hull. They saw them in the air, aimed straight at the ship, sir. They were right there on the high portside rail.

"Mr. President, we are in a position to go to the United Nations with irrefutable evidence that the United States has committed at least two most terrible crimes on the high seas."

The President smiled for the first time that morning. "Paul Bedford may have thought he had enough to accuse us publicly, but we *really* have enough to nail the Americans."

"Except for one thing," said St. Martin. "The Americans will deny it flatly. They'll just say it was the Japanese or someone."

"Not quite," interjected General Jobert. "When a sonar search system acquires an incoming missile or a torpedo, it instantly bangs it into a software program that identifies the type of sonar the enemy is using."

He saw the President's slightly puzzled face, and simplified the matter. "Sir," he said, "if I walked out of that door and shouted something from the other side, you would know it was me. You'd recognize my voice. Same with a sonar system. When it receives a radar or sonar beam, its computer can identify the source of that beam. In this case, according to the *De Grasse*'s ops room, a Gould Mark 48 ADCAP transmitting active. That's American. And, sir, the Omanis are just helping us to airlift the entire contents of the destroyer's operational computer system, before she sinks."

Again, the President smiled. "Then we have them, General?"

"Yessir."

"Then we shall humiliate the mighty U.S.A. publicly. I shall broadcast to the entire world, tonight, condemning their actions. I'll describe them as cold-blooded killers, cowboys, bandits. Irresponsible. Reckless. I'll say the United Nations should not even be in New York. It should be in Paris. Center of the world . . . where people are . . . well, civilized, not madmen."

"Steady, sir," cautioned St. Martin. "The Americans would be glad to be rid of the UN. What do they call it . . . ? Yes, the Chatterbox on the East River."

"Hmm," said the President. "We shall see, Pierre. We shall see."

And that night the roof fell in on international relations between France and the United States of America. The French President made his broadcast at 7 P.M. in Paris, in precisely the terms he had outlined in the Elysée Palace for St. Martin and General Jobert. It was theatrical, accusing, rude in the extreme, and political to the nth degree.

The French President threw at the U.S.A. every insult every French President has longed to utter since World War II. Not even De Gaulle, at his most insufferably imperious, had ever let fly at the world's policemen with quite that much venom.

And he ended it with this jackhammer flourish: "As from this moment, the envoys of the United States are no longer welcome in this country," he thundered. "I hereby expel them all. I hereby close down their embassy, which pollutes the beauty of the Avenue Gabriel, not three hundred yards from where I am standing.

"I know that under international law that building and that land is officially designated land of the United States of America. As from this week, it is restored to its proper title deeds. Gabriel Avenue, in its entirety, belongs to *LA FRANCE!*" And he raised both arms in the air and signed off with the joyous shout: *"VIVE LA FRANCE! . . . VIVE LA FRANCE!"*

When he marched off the wide upper landing of the Elysée Palace, stepping between the television arc lights, he entered once more his private drawing room and clasped the hand of General Jobert, who had sat and watched the performance onscreen with the Foreign Minister.

"Well, General, how was that?" he demanded. "Did your President do your country proud?"

"Oh, most definitely, sir," replied the General. "That was a speech from the very . . . er . . . heartbeat of the French people. It needed to be said."

St. Martin once more sounded a word of caution. "It was perfect, sir," he murmured softly. "Just so long as the Americans don't get to Col. Jacques Gamoudi before we do."

And that night the stakes were raised yet again. At 10 P.M. President Paul Bedford formally expelled every French diplomat from their embassy on Reservoir Road in Washington, D.C. And while he was about it, he ordered the following French consulates to close down: New York, San Francisco, Atlanta, Boston, Chicago, Houston, Los Angeles, Miami, and New Orleans.

It was the lowest point of relations between fellow Permanent Members of the UN Security Council since the Russians shot down the United States Air Force U-2 spy plane almost a half century previously.

And with the East Coast of America operating six hours behind Paris, the U.S. newspapers and television stations had ample time to rearrange their front pages and the top story that they had been planning all morning. That was the one about the state of the world economy, the one that had dominated the world's media ever since the fateful March night when the French Navy had flattened the Saudi oil industry.

Every night things were globally bad, but tonight was especially dismal. There had been a complete electricity blackout in Tokyo, lasting from 11 P.M. to 6 A.M. Not one flicker of a neon light penetrated the blackness, and the Japanese government stated that this might be happening every night until further notice. They warned the population of Tokyo to be patient. The lights had been off for three days in the cities of Osaka and Kobe, as the electric-power generators used the last of the fuel oil.

Hong Kong, another voracious user of oil-fired electric power, was into its emergency supplies, and Rome, the Eternal City, was headed for eternal darkness. The northwest of France was running out of gasoline, and the great seaport of Rotterdam was virtually closed down.

There was a complete blackout in Calcutta. Traffic was grinding to a halt in Germany, and there was no power in Hamburg, with brownouts in Berlin and Bremen. In England the refineries in the Thames Estuary were slowing right down, and the government had banned all neon lights in London. In the county of Kent, particularly southeast of Ashford, there was absolutely no electricity—at all.

On the East Coast of the United States the situation was becoming critical, as the refineries along the New Jersey side of the Hudson River, opposite New York City, began to fail.

That ought to have been enough to keep the most insatiable news editor happy, but the standoff between France and the United States knocked every other story off the front pages, and from the leadoff spots on television news.

Back in the National Security Agency, Lt. Cdr. Jimmy Ramshawe was trying to hold together a great spider's web of agents all over the Middle East, all of them trying to find Jacques Gamoudi.

And the situation was not greatly assisted by a phone call every two hours from Admiral Morgan, which always started with the words *Found him yet?* And always ended with *Well, where the hell is he?*

If they had but known it, the U.S. operation was way behind the eight ball in the battle with France to find the missing assault commander, because France had inserted five top agents into Riyadh as assistants to Colonel Gamoudi in the runup to the attack on the palaces. Throughout his preparations, they had kept him informed of developments, and all five of them had enjoyed free and easy access to the ex–French Special Forces Commander. Three of them were still in Riyadh, just observing on behalf of the French Secret Service, and all three of them were regular visitors to the splendid white-painted house that King Nasir had made available for the Colonel as long as he needed it.

And suddenly, as both the U.S.A. and France stepped up the pace to locate the Colonel, the game changed. Gaston Savary, the only man with access to these three French spies, called the senior officer, former Special Forces Major Raul Foy, and instructed him, in the fewest possible words, to report to the French Ambassador in the Diplomatic Quarter.

Somewhat mystified, the Major drove over to the embassy, where the Ambassador's secretary told him it would be necessary to wait for new orders, direct from Paris, which would be given to him by the Ambassador in person. His Excellency would be free in ten minutes.

In fact he was free in five, and Major Foy was ushered into the office. The two men shook hands, but the Ambassador did not invite his guest to sit down. He just said simply, "Major, I do not wish you to remain here for one second longer than necessary. I have just been speaking for the second time this morning to Gaston Savary. I am instructed to tell you, in the most clandestine terms, that you and your men are to assassinate Col. Jacques Gamoudi this day, on the direct orders of the President of France."

If the Major had been given the courtesy of a cup of coffee, he would have choked on it. "B-but . . ." he stammered.

"No buts, Major. My own instructions are to call the Elysée Palace the moment you leave, to confirm I have passed on the orders. I don't need to tell you how serious this is. But I am asked to inform you that there will be an excellent financial reward for you upon your return to Paris. We're talking six figures."

Major Foy, a man who had faced death more than once in the service of his country, just stood and gawped.

"I'm sorry, Raul," said the Ambassador in a kindly tone. "I know that you are certainly a very good colleague of the Colonel's, if not a friend. But I think I mentioned, this is supremely important. The blackest of black ops, you might say. Good-bye."

The forty-one-year-old Major turned away without a word, and walked out of the building to his car, parked outside the main door. He climbed into the driver's seat and just sat there, stunned. He was not, of course, the first soldier to bridle at an order, and perhaps not the first to tell himself, *I did not join either the Army or the Secret Service to kill my fellow French officers.*

But he may have been the first to be told he must assassi-

nate his own boss. And all he could think of was Colonel
Gamoudi's decency, professionalism, and understanding of
his own problems working undercover in the city. When he
first arrived from France, he had dined with Jacques
Gamoudi on two or three occasions. The two men had spoken every day, always with immense dignity and respect.

Major Foy, who like the Colonel had served with distinc-
tion in Brazzaville at the height of the Congo revolution,
was not at all sure about this—six figures or no six figures.
But then, he thought of all it would mean for him, and for
his wife and children.

He started the car and drove away, back toward his own
apartment in the center of the city. He resolved for the moment to tell no one of his five minutes with the Ambassador.
He just needed some coffee, and some time to think. He
glanced at his watch. It was almost eleven o'clock on that
hot Thursday morning, which gave him a lot of time to con-
template, since there was no way he was going to shoot
Colonel Gamoudi in cold blood in broad daylight.

Thursday, April 15, 10:00 P.M.
Diplomatic Quarter
Riyadh

Major Foy parked his car approximately two hundred yards
from the "grace and favor" home awarded by King Nasir to
Jacques Gamoudi. He had made up his mind now. He
locked the car door and walked quietly up the deserted
street, beneath the trees and the fading pink and white
spring blossoms still hanging over the high walls of these
impressive houses.

When he reached the wrought-iron gateway to the Colonel's Riyadh home, he tapped on the window of the guardhouse outside and was pleased to see that the men inside
both knew him. They waved him through, opening the electronic gates.

At the front door, he faced two more Saudi armed guards
whom he knew even better, and they too directed him in-

side. And there the duty officer greeted him. "*Bonsoir*, Major. I am afraid the Colonel has retired to bed for the night. I don't think he wants to be disturbed."

"Ahmed," said the Major, to a young man with whom he had been on friendly terms for more than four months, "I have just come from the French Embassy. I have a message for the Colonel that is so secret they would not even commit it to paper. I have to tell him in person. I'd better go up. He's probably reading."

"Okay, Major. If it's that important, I guess you better."

Raul Foy walked up the wide staircase and along the left-hand corridor. At the double doors to the master bedroom, he hesitated and then knocked softly. Jacques Gamoudi heard the knock and slipped out of bed, positioning himself behind the door with his bear-slaying knife in his right hand.

But Gamoudi did not answer. The door opened quietly, and Major Foy came into the room and closed the door behind him. The Colonel heard him whisper, "Jacques, wake up," in a somewhat hoarse voice.

The Colonel did not recognize that voice, and he leapt forward into the darkness, seizing the intruder by the hair and flattening the blade of his knife hard onto the man's throat.

Raul Foy almost died of shock, for the second time that day. "Jacques, Jacques," he cried. "Get off. It's me, Raul. I've come to talk to you—urgent. And get that fucking knife out of my neck."

Colonel Gamoudi released him and switched on the light. "Jesus, Raul, what the hell are you doing, creeping around in the middle of the night?"

"Jacques. Do not interrupt me. Just listen. This morning I was given personal instructions from the goddamn President of France to assassinate you, at all costs. I don't know why but, Jacques, you are a marked man. They are determined to kill you. They even offered me a financial reward to do it. A big one too."

"Christ, you haven't come to shoot me, have you?" The Colonel grinned.

"Not while you're holding that fucking knife," Foy

replied. "No, Jacques. Seriously. I'm not even armed. I haven't even told my team. I'm here to warn you. Honestly, you have to get out of here. Now. These guys are not joking. Run, Jacques. You've got to run."

"And you, Raul. Now you have neglected to kill me, what will you tell them?"

"Jacques. You are going. Now. I'm going to tell them I got here to obey their orders, and you were gone. Do you want a lift to the airport or somewhere?"

"No," replied Colonel Gamoudi. "The King will arrange my transportation. I'll just round up General Rashood, who's in the billiards room, and we'll be on our way. And thank you, Raul. I mean that. Because I just cost you a lot of money, in a way."

The French Secret Service man smiled, and told him, "Earlier today, I made a decision, based on a few lines written by the distinguished English novelist, E. M. Forster."

And with that, Raul headed toward the door. But when he reached it, he turned back and embraced his former boss, with genuine concern. "Good-bye, Jacques," he said. "For Christ's sake, be careful and . . . and God go with you."

"Well," said Jacques wryly, "before you go, you might tell me the lines which caused you to spare me."

Raul Foy looked quizzical, as if nervous to utter the sentence that would confirm his loyalties. But then he said carefully, "Very well." And he recited, to the best of his memory, Forster's words: *If I was asked to choose whether to betray my country, or my friend, I hope I'd have the courage to choose my country.*

Thursday, April 15, 11:00 P.M.
Arabian Desert

THEY PRAYED AT sunset, out on the edge of the desert, southwest of Riyadh. King Nasir of Saudi Arabia and all of his most trusted council members turned east toward Mecca and prostrated themselves before God in accordance with the strict teachings of the Koran.

Tonight would see the ancient ritual of the *mansaf*, and the prayers were as much a part of the rite as the dinner itself: the rice served on the flat whole wheat crust of the *shrak* and the succulent boiled lamb poured upon it, with a sour-milk sauce.

Tonight the King would dine with his advisers, six of them gathered in a circle around the great circular feast, eating with their bare right hands, selecting pieces of lamb and rolling them expertly into rice balls with the dexterity of a group of cardsharps.

These nights, in the opening days of the new King's reign, the prayers were particularly poignant, because Nasir demanded that Islam and its teachings pervade every aspect of Bedouin life.

I witness there is no God but God, and Mohammed is the messenger of God . . . The murmured prayers of the most powerful men in the kingdom were spoken with firmness, and the words hung heavily on the warm night air.

The tall, bearded ruler of the kingdom, on his knees in the center of the vast brightly patterned Persian rug spread out on the sand, epitomized the strength that lay in the fellowship of faith. In all of their conferences since he had assumed power, King Nasir had made it abundantly clear that he was dedicated to a return to the ancient ways, and not merely in the creed of personal faith and piety.

King Nasir wanted to restore Muslim life back to the correct code of ethics, the one passed down through the wisdom of the Koran. He wanted a culture, a system of laws, an understanding of the function of the State—Islamic guidelines for life in all of its dimensions.

And there was not a man on the great carpet in the desert who did not believe that the King would achieve his aims. Nasir was a strong leader, unbending in his beliefs. He still refused to sleep in an ornate, lavishly decorated bedroom, preferring his plain, white, almost bare room, which was more like a cell.

And he preferred to dine in the desert, sitting outside his tent, ensuring that everyone had enough to eat, including all of the fifteen servants who attended him. On this night, he had characteristically invited four perfect strangers, mere passersby, to join the gathering.

And now the robed figures were preparing to sit up long into the night indulging in that most ancient of Arab rituals—sipping coffee freshly roasted on an open fire while dinner was consumed and served from a long-beaked, blue enameled pot with pale cardamom seeds.

It was an unchanging scene, out here beneath a rising desert moon: modern men upholding their Bedouin past as if time had stood still down the centuries. Except that at twenty-two minutes before 11 P.M. the King's cell phone rang loudly from somewhere in the folds of his robes. His expression changed from content, to startled, and then to irritated. It was as if someone had offered him a cup of instant coffee.

But he answered the call. Because it must be critically important. No one could remember anyone having the temerity to interrupt Nasir al-Saud during the ceremony of the *mansaf*, not even when he was only Saudi Arabia's Crown Prince.

The gathering was hushed as he spoke.

"Why, hello, Jacques. Are you safe?"

And then there was silence while Colonel Gamoudi explained there was about to be a second attempt on his life, how the French Secret Service man had arrived in his bedroom with the warning.

They all heard the King ask, "And that saved you? Those wonderful lines from *Two Cheers for Democracy?*" And they saw him smile, fleetingly, before adding, "Yes. I do know them. I know them quite well." But the King's face was grave when he said, "Jacques, when you leave here it will be as if I have lost a brother. I am deeply disappointed in the conduct of my allies in France, but I agree you must go, because no security is one hundred percent.

"I will have you collected from the house and taken to the airport where a private Boeing will take you anywhere you wish to go. I want you to keep it for as long as it takes, until you are safe." He then asked quietly, "Does this mean that General Rashood will leave as well?"

And it was clear from the sad expression on Nasir's face that the Hamas leader was also going to fly out of Saudi Arabia. "You both go as my brothers, and my comrades in arms," he said. "Your names will not be forgotten here, and you have my support and my help until the end of my days. Jacques, go in peace, and may Allah go with you."

Thirty minutes later, an amazing clatter split the night air of the Diplomatic Quarter as a Royal Saudi Navy helicopter, an Aerospatiale SA 365 Dauphin 2, came in low over the houses and put down with a tremendous racket on the wide lawn outside Colonel Gamoudi's bedroom.

Gamoudi almost had a heart attack at the sight of the French-built Dauphin, assuming briefly that it was Gaston Savary's hit squad coming to finish him off. But when he looked closer, he could see the insignia of the Saudi Navy and the crown painted near the stern that signified it was for the use of the King.

The loadmaster who came to the front door was immediately admitted, as if the guards had been forewarned of his arrival. Both Gamoudi and Ravi Rashood traveled light, each with just one duffel bag, a machine pistol, four magazines of fifty rounds, and their combat knives. Suits, shirts, and uniforms were left behind for another time.

The Dauphin took off instantly, the moment they were aboard, and eight minutes later it put down at the head of the runway at King Khalid Airport, right next to a fully fueled Boeing 737, its engines running.

They thanked the helicopter flight crew and bolted up the stairway into the big private jet. The doors were slammed and, with immense dignity, the second officer came through to inquire, "Where to, sir?" as if the Boeing were a taxi.

General Rashood's mind raced. He considered Damascus was not a good option—not on a direct flight from Riyadh. Jordan was not far enough; neither was Baghdad. Tel Aviv was too dangerous. And so was Cairo.

"Beirut," he said. "Beirut International Airport."

"No problem," replied the co-pilot.

Three minutes later they were hurtling down the runway, climbing above the sea of light that is modern-day Riyadh. The only difference being, since they arrived, there had been a change in management.

Same Night, 9:00 P.M. (LOCAL)
DGSE HQ
Paris

Gaston Savary hardly left his office these days. And mostly he just sat and fretted, unshaven, praying for the phone to ring, praying it was someone with the news that Col. Jacques Gamoudi had been eliminated.

So far he had been out of luck. And tonight was no different. Maj. Raul Foy was on the line from Riyadh, imparting the precise information Savary did not wish to hear.

"Sir, I gained entry to the house at ten-thirty tonight. I entered his bedroom only to discover he had already left and was not expected to return. The guards there of course know and trust me. One of the guards told me Gamoudi had left Saudi Arabia; I understand the King himself organized his escape."

The name of the Major's target was naturally never mentioned, but Gaston Savary did not need reminding of it. *"Merde,"* he said. "Do we have any clue where he's gone?"

"Nossir. All we know is one of the King's private jets took off from King Khalid Airport shortly before midnight, and that our man may have been aboard."

Major Foy, treading the treacherous line between traitor and efficient undercover agent, added helpfully, "It's damned hard to trace the King's aircraft, sir. They never file a flight plan from his own airport, and of course no one has any idea where it's headed."

"Merde," said Savary. "What now?"

"Sir, that Boeing can fly more than twenty-four hundred miles. But General Rashood may also be onboard. He was staying at the Colonel's house. I suggest we place agents in the Middle East airports where we think they might be going. I'd say Jordan, certainly Damascus, where it's possible the General lives. Cairo, which is a hell of a good place to hide. Maybe Djibouti, because that's where General Rashood came in before the attack. Certainly Tripoli, because Rashood could get help there, and possibly Beirut, which is often beyond the rule of law."

"How about Baghdad, Kuwait, or Tehran?" suggested Gaston Savary.

"Not Baghdad, because the General might have enemies there. But perhaps Tehran. He is, after all, from Iran. And Kuwait . . . I don't think so . . . it's too close. It's like going nowhere."

Gaston Savary scribbled the names on a pad in front of him. He told Major Foy to stay in touch, and he prepared to put at least two DGSE agents into the airports where the Boeing might land. That would be his first call. The second one would be to Pierre St. Martin. Savary was not looking forward to that one.

Friday, April 16, 0030
25,000 Feet Above Al Nafud Desert

General Rashood had regained his composure. Relaxed here in the first-class compartment, he pulled out his state-of-the-art cell phone and for the first time in almost four months dialed his wife's number in Damascus.

Shakira answered immediately, despite the late hour, and was overjoyed to hear from him. She told him she had been at her wit's end to know whether he was alive or dead, but she understood he could not risk calling her.

And was it safe now? Could someone be listening in?

"Since I'm calling from a passenger jet about five miles above the desert, it's unlikely," he said.

"Are you coming home?" she asked. "Please say yes."

But Rashood's answer was stern. "Shakira, I want you to get a pen and write some things down. Meet me tomorrow afternoon in the town of Byblos; that's less than thirty miles up the coast road from Beirut. To get there, you'll drive sixty miles along the main Damascus highway, straight over the Lebanon Mountains. It's a good road, but you should allow four hours from home to Byblos.

"When you arrive, you'll find the main attraction is some Roman ruins right at the edge of the town. You get into them through an old crusader castle. I'll meet you in there, in the castle, at three P.M.

"Before you start, please go to the bank and get money. A minimum of fifty thousand U.S. dollars, a hundred thousand if you can. We've got five million on deposit in the Commercial Bank of Syria. I'm guessing you'll be out of the bank and on the road by ten-thirty in the morning.

"And, Shakira, bring an AK-47, hide it in the compartment I had built into the Range Rover. There are a few checkpoints on that Damascus highway, but they won't be thorough. Use your Syrian passport, and bring your Israeli one.

"Shakira, just tell me you have your notes correctly written down, and then ring off. I'll see you tomorrow."

"Are we in trouble, Rashood?"

"Not yet."

"Well, I love you anyway. Wait for me."

Earlier, Thursday, April 15, 1700 (local)
National Security Agency

The eight-hour time difference meant it was still late on Thursday afternoon in Washington when Colonel Gamoudi's Boeing roared up into the midnight skies above Riyadh.

Within minutes, there had been a check call from the CIA's duty officer at King Khalid Airport, informing the Riyadh embassy that one of the King's private aircraft had taken off with just two unknown passengers. As always with the Saudi royal family's personal transports, its destination was unknown.

The embassy in Riyadh was very quickly off the mark, and on the phone to the CIA's busy Middle East Desk in Langley, Virginia. They already knew a Navy helicopter transmitting military radar had landed in a well-guarded private residence near the Diplomatic Quarter just before midnight, and had taken off immediately.

Inside the NSA, Lt. Commander Ramshawe already had a report from the CIA's man at the airport who had photographed the chopper with night lenses as it arrived at King Khalid, and he had seen the Boeing take off. The assumption in Riyadh, Langley, and Fort Meade was that Le Chasseur had been airlifted out of Saudi Arabia and that he was somewhere above the desert in the Boeing.

The Americans, after all, knew the French had already tried to assassinate him once, and it was now obvious the King was taking steps to protect him, in return for the enormous favor he had done the kingdom.

The question was, where was he going? The CIA did, more or less, what the French DGSE had done: they posted men at the likely Middle East airports, watching and waiting for King Nasir's Boeing to touch down.

There was, however, one major problem. Beirut was last on the Americans' list, and their man did not arrive there until 4 A.M., by which time General Rashood and Colonel Gamoudi had been whisked away to the new Saudi embassy in Beirut, by orders of the King.

It took the CIA agent an hour to ascertain that the Boeing had indeed landed, which left him with little to do except sit and watch until it took off again.

The French agents were, however, on time. And while they never got anywhere near the two passengers, they were able to follow the diplomatic car to the embassy, so at least they knew where the fugitives were. Whether or not they would be lucky enough to get a sniper shot in was very questionable.

Nonetheless, the French were plainly winning this race. And when a different, smaller vehicle pulled out of the embassy the following morning, with a chauffeur driving and darkened rear windows, the four French agents now involved in the chase elected to tail it—all the way up the coast road to the ancient city of Byblos.

Friday, April 16, 12:30 P.M. (LOCAL)
Outskirts of Beirut

Shakira Rashood had been an active member of the terrorist organization Hamas since she was twelve years old. She was rarely out of reach of an AK-47 rifle and she had served on combat operations ever since she was seventeen.

She and Rashood had fled a battle in the Jerusalem Road, Hebron, in the hours after they first met four years before. He saved her life, then she saved his. Their subsequent marriage was conducted inside the deepest councils of Hamas, of which General Rashood swiftly became the Commander in Chief.

They had thus met and married in the harshest of environments, a place without sentimentality, only a brutal desire for victory. But theirs was a love match, and the beautiful Palestinian Shakira, stuck now in a diabolical traffic holdup five miles out of Beirut, was beside herself with worry.

She sensed danger. Why did Rashood want so much money? Why had he been so reluctant to talk after all these weeks apart? Why had he told her to be sure to bring her rifle, when he knew she never made a journey without it?

Every inch of her sensed that something terrible was happening. Again she leaned on the horn of the Range Rover, like everyone else. There were few places in the Middle East where traffic could snarl as comprehensively as around Beirut.

As ever, the holdup was caused by a young man driving at a lunatic speed, zigzagging in and out of traffic, and then managing to hit a construction truck head on. The young man was of course the only driver who no longer cared one way or another whether his car started or stopped.

But about three hundred other drivers did, especially Shakira, who was held up for forty minutes, which seemed like six hours. There may have been a better way around the city, but if there was she missed it. Shakira headed north toward the coast, straight down the Rue Damas, and swung right onto the Avenue Charles Hevlou, a wide throughway that became jammed solid after a half mile.

The clock ticked on. It was almost two o'clock. And again they were dealing with an accident. Much of Beirut was still a building site, while contractors attempted to rebuild the shattered city in the long aftermath of the civil war. The crash on Avenue Hevlou was caused by a young man who, apparently inflamed by two huge trucks double parking, had made a break for it around the outside and hit a crane *bang* in the middle of the road.

By the time the accident was cleared, Shakira Rashood had twenty-eight miles to cover in forty-five minutes. Eventually she was compelled to start driving like a native, speeding up the coast road, with the blue Mediterranean to her left and the endless coastal plain in front of her.

The Range Rover raced along in the traffic, often making eighty miles per hour. And the last miles were endless. She sped into tiny Byblos from the east at 3:05 P.M. and followed the tourist signs to the ruins.

It was raining when she reached the parking area and got out of the car. Right next to the entrance was a stationary Peugeot, its hefty, tough-looking occupant just heading into the main door of the castle.

Shakira's sixth sense, the one that had kept her alive in tougher spots than this, took over. One hundred yards from the man, she began to run, her feet pounding through the puddles, her breath coming in short angry bursts. Her AK-47 was tucked under her right arm, beneath her raincoat, and could not be seen. She was sobbing as she ran inside the castle. Beside herself with fear, she bolted into the dark passageway. Rashood, she knew, was in desperate danger.

3:07 P.M.
Crusader Castle, Second Floor

Rashood and Gamoudi were cornered, flattened against the stone wall on either side of the door. Their three armed French Secret Service pursuers were gathered outside, and had already decided the best way to get this over was for two of them to come in firing. There was no escape, and whatever happened, there was a two-man backup outside.

There were no windows in the room, but there was a former window, just the bricked-up stone frame five feet above the ground to the left of the doorway looking out. Jammed inside the frame, his feet rammed into the lower corners, was Jacques Gamoudi, in position, on higher ground than his attackers.

The two French hit men came in together. And Gamoudi shouted, "This way!" The man on the right coming in turned, and Gamoudi shot him clean between the eyes. The second man, on Rashood's side of the doorway, also swung around to his right in search of the person who had shouted.

That was not smart. Rashood blew away the back of his head with a sustained burst from his machine pistol. Both the men slumped down onto the stone floor.

On the steps leading up to the corridor Shakira heard the shots and was gripped by a cold terror she had never before experienced. She kept repeating Rashood's name over and over, as if it would somehow keep him safe.

The trouble was, Rashood's cover was blown. Whoever else was outside in the passage now knew that both he and Gamoudi were in there, one on either side of the doorway. Secret Service combat officers have a way of dealing with such matters—possibly a couple of grenades.

The third man who waited outside did not have them. The fourth man coming along the corridor had three. Very calmly he passed one over to his colleague and began to loosen the firing pin.

At which point the near-hysterical Shakira came racing around the corner, tears streaming down her face, but now with her AK-47 raised to hip height.

Both men spun around at the same time. The man she had followed dropped one of the grenades, mercifully with the pin still tight, and swung his rifle straight toward her. Too late. Shakira Rashood opened fire, pouring hot lead into both men, neck and head, just like General Rashood had taught her.

"If you've killed him . . . I swear to God . . . if you've killed him!" The words tumbled from her without reason. She stumbled over the two bodies and carelessly rushed into the stone room where her husband was still flattened against the wall and Jacques Gamoudi was still jammed into the granite window frame.

"I told you not to be late," said the General, in that modulated Harrow School accent. "You could have got us all killed." Which proved, in a sense, you can take the officer out of the British Army, but you can't take the British Army out of the officer.

Shakira did not actually care what he said, so long as he was still breathing. She rushed across the floor and hurled herself into his arms, allowing her rifle to drop with a clatter. Over and over, she said, "Thank God . . . thank God."

Meanwhile, Jacques Gamoudi, who was still positioned halfway up the wall, cleared his throat theatrically and suggested that they had all better get out of there very fast, before someone charged them with four murders.

He jumped down from the ledge and led the way out into the corridor and down the stone stairway. The place was deserted aside from two groups of tourists. Beirut and its environs had retained its dangerous reputation over the years, and that coastline was still not especially popular among visitors, who thought they might be kidnapped. God alone knew what the first group to go inside would think when they stumbled on the four French hit men lying dead on the second floor, covered in blood and surrounded by hand grenades and rifles. Ravi Rashood mentioned that he was not anticipating a unanimous vote of thanks from the local tourist board.

Rashood told the embassy driver to head straight for the airport. He then used his cell phone to call two of his aides in Damascus and asked them to drive over to Byblos to pick up the Range Rover. The extra key was in the house on Bab Touma Street. Then he called the Saudi pilot and told him to file an immediate flight plan to Marrakesh, refuel the King's Boeing, and be ready to take off in a real hurry, about one hour from then.

They had traveled six fast miles south before the Hamas General found time to introduce Jacques Gamoudi to his wife. Of course, as a red-blooded Frenchman, or at least a French citizen, Gamoudi had scarcely taken his eyes off the neck-snapping, walnut-eyed, gazelle-legged Palestinian goddess, and when he muttered, *"Mon plaisir,"* he *really* meant it.

But the situation here in Beirut was now menacing. The three of them sat in tense but companionable silence most of the way to the airport.

"Does anyone know why we're going to Morocco?" asked Shakira finally.

"Well, it's been a difficult decision," said her husband. "Jacques is probably in more danger than we are, because he has the entire French Secret Service trying to kill him. You and I are in no more danger than usual. But Colonel Gamoudi has to get out of the Middle East, somewhere he can lie low for a few months, get his breath back. And his instinct is to fly back to Morocco, to his home up in the Atlas Mountains. No one's likely to find him there. He and his father were both guides."

"Are we going too?"

"Uh-huh. We're staying with Jacques until I know he's safe."

"Is that why you wanted all this money—for airfares?"

"No. We've got a plane."

"Will it hold three?"

"It'll hold two hundred, plus crew."

Shakira just shook her head. "Well, that's okay then," she said. "I was able to get a hundred thousand U.S. dollars from the bank."

"Shakira," said Rashood. "Aside from the lateness, I'd have to say you have excelled this morning, as a wife, a financier, and a marksman."

"Thank you, General," said Shakira, laughing. "It's been my pleasure to work with you."

It was amazing how thoroughly this Palestinian beauty had absorbed that British sense of irony from her husband. It's not a natural way of thinking for any Arab, but Rashood thought it definitely suited her.

He leaned back in his seat, having cheated the Grim Reaper once more, and told her, "In the last twenty-four hours, I can say I owe my life to the former Shakira Sabah, and Jacques reckons he owes his to E. M. Forster."

"Who's Eeyem Forster?" demanded Shakira. "I never even heard that name Eeyem before?"

"He's not Eeyem," said Rashood carefully. "He's E. M. Letters. The initials of his Christian names."

Shakira thought about that for a moment, smiled, and

said, "You mean like G. A. Nasser, or O. B. Laden?" knowing full well it sounded ridiculous. "Anyway, you still haven't told me. Who is he?"

"He's a very famous English novelist. My school insisted we read a couple of his books for A levels."

"What books did he write?"

"Well, I suppose his best-known one is *A Passage to India.*"

"I've seen the movie," cried Shakira in triumph. *"Mrs. Moore! . . . Mrs. Moore! . . . Mrs. Moore!"*

"So you have," replied her husband, chuckling gently. "Forster had a very sensitive touch with subjects like loyalty, treatment of those less fortunate, and, I suppose most of all, friendship."

"Yes, but . . ." said Shakira, employing her most reliable form of questioning, when she was starting to dig deeply into a subject. "How did he save Jacques's life? Does he live in Saudi Arabia?"

"No, he's been dead for forty years," said Rashood. "But his words inspired a colleague of Jacques's to treat their friendship more seriously than he treated a government order."

"Was he ordered to kill you, Jacques?"

"Yes, Shakira. Yes, he was."

"And he didn't because he remembered the words of Eeyem?"

"Yes, that's what he said," replied Gamoudi.

"Hmm," said Shakira. "You too have read his books?"

"No, I have never read them. But I think I will now."

"Then I think you'd better get started," said Shakira gravely. "This Eeyem, he's a very influential man."

By this time they were within a couple of miles of Beirut International Airport. The traffic was terrible, and General Rashood again called the pilot on his cell phone and told him to be ready.

The embassy driver turned in through the cargo area and made straight for the runway where private aircraft were parked. The car pulled right up to the waiting Saudi Boeing 737, and the three of them rushed up the stairway.

The flight attendants, who had been hanging around all

night, not disembarking, greeted them cheerfully. "Marrakesh, nonstop?" one of them said.

"If you would," replied General Rashood.

"It's almost twenty-three hundred miles," the flight attendant replied. "And that'll take us almost five hours. But we pick up three hours on the time difference. We should be there around five-thirty in the evening."

By now the aircraft was rolling, thundering down the runway. The flight attendant, a young Arabian would-be pilot, hastily sat down and clipped on a safety belt, which was not a complication since there were close to 200 spare seats.

The Boeing screamed up into the blue skies above the eastern Mediterranean and set a westerly course. And as it did so, the CIA agent in the airport, the one who had arrived too late in the small hours of the morning, reached for his cell phone and hit the buttons to Beirut flight control.

He spoke to his airport contact. Twenty seconds later he knew the Saudi King's aircraft was heading to Marrakesh, with three passengers who had arrived in a Saudi embassy car.

There was one difference between the two latest departures of the Boeing. In King Khalid Airport, Riyadh, the captain had not been obliged to file a flight plan. Here in Beirut, he was. And that put the Americans ahead of the game, because the six French agents in Lebanon were temporarily stymied. Four of them were dead inside the Crusaders' Castle. The other two were still parked outside the Saudi embassy.

The U.S. field agent dialed Langley direct, and reported that the King's Boeing had just taken off, heading directly for Marrakesh, no stops. Langley moved swiftly. They immediately contacted Lt. Commander Ramshawe and asked him for a degree of certainty on his report that Col. Jack Gamoudi had been born in the tiny village of Asni.

Lt. Commander Ramshawe, who had spent days searching through computerized French military data, had managed to file away a copy of Jacques Gamoudi's birth certificate, courtesy of Andy Campese in Toulouse and a

Foreign Legion filing clerk in Aubagne, who had reacted favorably to Campese's five-hundred-dollar bribe.

Ramshawe pulled up the photocopy of Colonel Gamoudi's birth certificate and read off: "Born Asni, Morocco, June twelve, 1964 . . . Father Abdul Gamoudi, mountain guide . . ."

"Beautiful," said the voice from Langley.

"You guys got a lead?" asked the Lt. Commander.

"Sure have. The Colonel's right now in a Boeing 737 owned by the King of Saudi Arabia, and he's heading for Marrakesh, nonstop."

"My boss will want to alert the Navy about that, but . . . wait just a minute. I have some extra data on Asni that may help."

Jimmy Ramshawe's fingers hit the computer keyboard like shafts of light, until Jacques Gamoudi's early military record came up: "He worked as a mountain guide with his father in the High Atlas Range around his home village . . . He also worked in the local hotel and . . . this is interesting . . . the owner of that hotel, a former Major in the French Parachute Regiment named Laforge, sponsored him in his application to join the Foreign Legion . . ."

"Hey, that's great, Lt. Commander."

"Guess you guys think Jacques Gamoudi's going home, right?"

"We're thinking if the French Secret Service are trying to kill him, the Atlas Mountains are not a bad place to take cover. Christ, you'd never find him up there, not in those high peaks, where he knows the territory backward, and where he probably still has friends."

"That'd be a tough one," replied Ramshawe. "But we're not trying to kill him, and we've got two damn good leads in Asni—his dad and his old boss at the hotel. If one of them's still there, we might be in good shape."

He rang off and headed immediately to see Admiral Morris, who listened to the latest twist in the saga of Le Chasseur. When Ramshawe was through, Admiral Morris pulled up Morocco on a computerized wall map, four feet wide.

"Let me just get my bearings, Jimmy," he said. "Right, now here's Marrakesh. Where the hell's Asni? Is it close?"

"Yeah, right here, sir."

"Ah, yes. Right astride the old mountain road between Marrakesh and Agadir, on the Atlantic coast . . . see this place here . . . where it says Toubkal? That's one of the highest mountains in Africa. Guess that's why Asni became a major mountaineering village. That's where Jacques Gamoudi's dad made his living."

"So did Jacques, for a while."

"Hell, those French killers have their work cut out. Can you imagine chasing a professional mountain guide through that range? You'd never find him."

"You been there, sir?"

"I've been to Agadir. That's how I remember Mount Toubkal. A bunch of our guys had shore leave for a week and they were going to climb it. It's damned high and extremely steep—something like thirteen thousand feet."

"You didn't go yourself, sir?"

"Jimmy," said George Morris. "I might look kinda stupid, but I've never been crazy."

Ramshawe laughed. "So what do we tell the Big Man?"

"We tell him both the CIA and the NSA consider Le Chasseur is going home to the Atlas Mountains, to hide out from the French assassins. And we tell him it's going to happen fast, and it looks like our best bet to grab him might be off the dock in Agadir."

"We're assuming he wants to be grabbed."

"Jimmy, we've rescued his wife and family, his money's safe in the U.S.A., and the French are trying to kill him. He'll come, and he'll do as we ask. He has no choice. Because if we don't get him, the French will eventually take him out."

"But how are we going to find him?" asked Ramshawe.

"Why don't you call Admiral Morgan and see what he says?"

"Okay, sir. I'll do that right away."

He marched back down to his office and went through on the direct line to the White House at a particularly bad time. Admiral Morgan was wrestling with a statement from the

United Nations condemning the action of the United States
of America in sinking at least two, maybe three, and possibly
four French ships. The statement was withering for the UN,
which spent a certain amount of time each year expressing
"dismay," a small amount of time being "disappointed," and
considerable time finding things "incomprehensible."

But, essentially, the UN did not "condemn." As a word, it
was too inflammatory, too likely to make a bad situation
worse, and too difficult a word from which to retreat.

Today, however, the United Nations not only condemned,
it issued a paralyzing anti-American statement that read,
*The probable actions of the U.S. Navy in the Strait of Hor-
muz represented bullying on a scale totally unacceptable to
the rest of the world.*

It added that the Security Council intended to summon
the United States representatives to appear before the General Assembly, the main debating chamber of the UN. And
there, every Member State, all 191 of them, would be invited to cast a vote in favor of the severest censure the UN
had issued in a quarter of a century.

*There was no state of war existing between France and
the United States,* the statement said. *Therefore the action
of the U.S. Navy must fall under the heading of, at best, a
reckless and careless attack or, at worst, cold-blooded murder of innocent seamen."*

Either way the UN could not condone the actions of the
U.S.A. The General Assembly would also be asked to decide whether substantial damages, possibly $1 billion, ought
now to be paid in reparations to the French government.

When he read it, President Bedford shuddered at the
enormity of the ramifications. Not many U.S. Presidents
have been accused of "murder" by the UN. And Paul Bedford was not much enjoying his place in that particular
spotlight.

Since Admiral Morgan had masterminded the entire exercise, he asked him to come into the Oval Office. And
that's exactly where they were when the phone rang with
Lt. Commander Ramshawe on the line from Fort Meade.

Arnold Morgan just growled, "We got him yet?"

"No, sir. But we're in better shape than we were yesterday. We know where he is, and we think we know where he's going." He outlined to the Admiral the developments of the day and the new significance of Morocco, and then posed the question he had asked Admiral Morris.

"If we want to pick him up in Agadir, sir, how the hell do we find him?"

"Jimmy," rasped Morgan, "we got to get him a cell phone, one of those little bastards with a GPS system attached. That way we can hook him up with his wife onboard the *Shiloh*, and he can show us where he is. Do the guys at Langley think the French are in hot pursuit?"

"They don't know whether Paris understands yet that Gamoudi is on his way to Marrakesh. But I guess we'll find out soon enough."

"Right. Meanwhile you better get Langley to deliver one of those phones to Le Chasseur."

"How and where, sir?"

"If the CIA can't get a telephone to a guy who's trying his damnedest to get into the U.S.A., they might as well close the fucking place down," snapped Morgan, slamming down the phone.

President Bedford was extremely relieved to see that his main man had not lost his nerve in the face of a frontal assault by the UN. "This is very serious, Arnie, don't you think?" he said.

"Serious!" growled Morgan. "You think we ought to be nervous about some half-assed, know-nothing Security Council that contains among its fifteen members the Philippines, Romania, Angola, Benin, and Algeria. Jesus! These guys are pressed to feed themselves and plant fucking soybeans, never mind have a hand in running the goddamn world."

Even President Bedford, in the darkest moment of his presidency, was compelled to laugh.

"And I don't want you to lose your nerve, Mr. President," added Admiral Morgan. "Remember what we know has happened: the French, in partnership with some kind of a robed nutcase, have forced the world into its worst economical crisis since World War Two. With reckless disregard for any other nation's plight, they cold-bloodedly smashed the Saudi oil industry with naval explosive, and then provided two Supreme Commanders to force the surrender of the Saudi armed forces and then assault the royal government in Riyadh.

"Now half the world's without oil, and not everyone realizes, yet, that the French did it, for some sleazy financial deal with this Nasir character . . . that's a guy dressed in a fucking bed sheet.

"And *we* have to get the industrial world out of this. And if that means sinking a handful of French ships, that's the way it's gotta be. They're goddamn lucky we haven't sunk 'em all."

"But, Arnie, what about this United Nations censure?"

"Sir, this is a momentous chain of events. It's something history will judge in the fullness of time. Ignore the short-term rantings of a few nitwits who only know about a tenth of the facts. Sit tight, don't crack, and we'll win this. Probably in the next week."

"You mean if we can get this Colonel Gamoudi to testify at the General Assembly for us?"

"Absolutely. And he will, because his own land has turned against him, he's been betrayed, and he only has one set of friends in the world—that's us. We've rescued his family and his money, and we'll save him. And when we've done it, he'll sing—that curly-haired little French Moroccan will sing like Frank Sinatra."

"You've only seen a picture of him in his Arab kit," said the President. "How do you know he's got curly hair?"

"North African, sir. All North Africans have curly hair. Christ, most of them live in the Sahara Desert. If they didn't have thick, curly hair for protection, their heads would blow up."

"Which of Darwin's theories of evolution are you currently studying, Arnie?" asked Paul Bedford wryly.

"Right now I'm concentrating on the bit about the ever-evolving diabolically devious nature of the French," retorted

Morgan. "I'll tell you what. I'll just call Alan Dickson, we'll have a couple of cups of coffee, and we'll hear more. This is hotting up, and I'm darned sure we're out in front."

Friday, April 16, 1730 (local)
Royal Navy Dockyard, Gibraltar

The eight-man U.S. Navy SEAL team, which had been air-lifted from a joint exercise with twenty-two SAS in Hereford, England, arrived in a red-painted Royal Navy Dauphin 2 helicopter in the great sprawling British base that stands guard over the gateway to the Mediterranean.

Moored alongside, on the North Mole, the great break-water that protects the strategically important harbor, was the 10,000-ton Ticonderoga-class cruiser U.S.S. *Shiloh*, fresh from a 900-mile run down the Portuguese coast from the outer reaches of the Bay of Biscay.

Back in Norfolk, Virginia, Adm. Frank Doran had reasoned that if they were going to haul Le Chasseur out of some Middle Eastern banana republic, they were going to need a big U.S. warship on hand to deal with the problems. The middle of the Mediterranean, somewhere east of the Italian peninsula, seemed as good a place as any to set up shop.

However, the way things were now moving, there had been a major change of direction. *Shiloh*, complete with the Gamoudi family and the SEAL team, would leave the Med within two hours, heading 428 miles south down the Atlantic, along the long sand-swept coast of Morocco. Latest orders, direct from the Pentagon, recommended that the SEAL team go in and grab the French Colonel sometime in the next three or four days.

Capt. Tony Pickard had been ordered to make all speed from Gibraltar to an ops area 100 miles off the Moroccan seaport of Agadir. When SEAL Team Number Four, home base Little Creek, Virginia, was safely aboard, U.S.S. *Shiloh* would cast her lines and leave immediately.

The SEAL's team leader was Lt. Cdr. Brad Taylor, the

Virginia garrison's resident iron man, one of those SEALs who pins the Trident on his pajamas before he goes to bed. A veteran of the Iraq war, thirty-one-year-old Brad Taylor was a graduate of the U.S. Naval Academy, Annapolis, and leading classman in the SEALs' brutal indoctrination course BUD/S, known in the trade as "The Grinder."

His father was a U.S. naval Captain from Seattle, Washington, and his mother, a former actress who had spent much of her life wondering how she could possibly have given birth to this miniature King Kong.

Brad was six foot two, but every stride he took looked as if he were just out of the gym and on his way to a world heavyweight title fight. To complement that natural-born swagger, he had wide shoulders, massive forearms and wrists, and thighs like mature oaks. He seemed shorter, but he looked like a young John Wayne, with slightly floppy brown hair worn longer than the standard SEAL hard-trimmed buzz cut.

Brad Taylor had won collegiate swimming championships, over 100 yards, a half mile, and one mile. He also won a U.S. Navy cruiserweight boxing championship, flattening all three of his opponents in the quarterfinal, semifinal, and final. Only injury had prevented him from playing free safety for the cadets in the Army-Navy game.

Brad Taylor was one of those people born to service in the U.S. Navy, born to lead a combat SEAL team, born to carry out SPECWARCOM's orders, no matter how difficult. And today his orders were short and succinct, straight from the White House, via the Pentagon: *Get the French Army Colonel Jacques Gamoudi out of Morocco.*

The U.S. guided-missile warship cleared Gibraltar at 1930 (local) and made all speed through the Strait and into the Atlantic, turning south on a course that would keep her 100 miles off the Moroccan coast, steaming past Tangier, Rabat, and Casablanca.

At thirty knots, it took the *Shiloh* five and a half hours to cover the 165 miles to a position off the capital city of Rabat—which was where the first activity of the night took place. At midnight (local) one of the two boarded helicopters, the SH-60B Seahawk LAMPS III, took off into the night, and headed directly into Rabat.

Clasped in the first officer's hand was a cardboard box containing the cell phone Admiral Morgan had ordered. It was satellite-programmed to connect with the comms room of U.S.S. *Shiloh* from any point on the globe. It also had a built-in GPS system, operational via satellite, that would pinpoint its user's position accurate to thirty yards.

Furthermore, that position could be relayed to the *Shiloh* without the user's even speaking. With the phone held in the open, one touch on one button would automatically inform the warship's ops room precisely where the caller was standing.

The LAMPS III took twenty-five minutes to reach the city. It made a long sweep to the north and, following the lights, came clattering up the river before banking right and putting down in the expansive grounds of the U.S. Embassy on Marrakesh Avenue.

On the strict instructions of Admiral Morgan, the Moroccan authorities had been fully informed that a U.S. military aircraft would make this night delivery to the embassy, the normal courtesy between countries. Right now Admiral Morgan had a golden chance to humiliate and embarrass the French, and he did not wish the United States to put a foot wrong diplomatically.

Which was the principal reason why he had insisted that the rescue of the French Colonel should be a clandestine grab by the SEALs, rather than a winch-out by a U.S. Navy helicopter operating illegally over deep Moroccan sovereign territory. As the Admiral had stated it, "When you want to play the knight in shining armor, you don't walk around with a goddamn blackjack."

And now, awaiting the helicopter, next to the flashing landing light on the embassy lawn, was the U.S. Ambassador to Morocco and one of the CIA's top North African field officers, Jack Mitchell, a native of Omaha, Nebraska, who kept a careful eye on Algiers and Tunisia from his Rabat base.

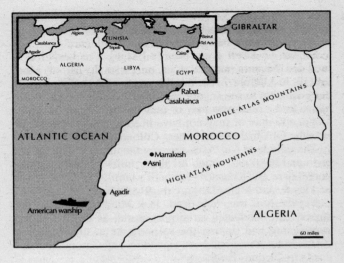

The helicopter never even opened its door. The cell phone was tossed out into the waiting hands of agent Mitchell and the pilot took off instantly, not even bothering with his northern detour, just ripping fast above the city and out into black skies above the Atlantic.

No one beyond the aircrew, the Ambassador, and the CIA knew of this swift insertion—which was precisely as planned. Because Morocco leaks. And Morocco has deep French connections. It had been, after all, a French protectorate for half of the twentieth century, and at this critical time the Americans understood full well that the French Secret Service were bound and determined to end the life of Le Chasseur.

Jack Mitchell, watching the departing Navy chopper climb away to the west, was now awaiting a flight of his own, due here on the embassy lawn in twenty minutes. This would be a nonstop 145-mile flight to Marrakesh, where Mitchell, a divorced former Nebraska State Trooper, would pick up his Cherokee Jeep and head into the Atlas Mountains, in search of either Jacques's father, Abdul Gamoudi, or the proprietor of the only hotel in the village.

So far, he knew King Nasir's Boeing had landed at a crowded Menara airport, four miles southwest of Marrakesh, just before 7 P.M. But the young CIA man there had not been able to see anyone disembark, and it was impossible to find a man who may or may not have been traveling alone, and may or may not have been in Arab dress. Right now the CIA had no idea where Colonel Gamoudi was.

The only lead was Asni, the tiny mountain village of his birth and boyhood, which lay thirty miles south of the airport. There was a chance Gamoudi's family might still be in residence, and Major Laforge might still be at the hotel.

But the trail was very dead. Jack Mitchell's man at the airport had conducted an airport search as best he could, questioning and tipping the sales clerks at the rental car desks. But nothing had been signed by any Gamoudi, or indeed any Jacques Hooks.

For all Jack Mitchell knew, the Colonel could have decided to hide out in Marrakesh. Although he doubted that because of the strong French presence in the city. There was no doubt Asni was the key. That's where Agent Mitchell would have headed if he had been on the run. There was a lot on his mind as his helicopter took off from the embassy grounds. He was clutching the little super cell phone which would be, ultimately, the lifeline of Le Chasseur, if Mitchell could deliver it.

Same Friday Night
Marrakesh Airport

From the first moment they disembarked from the Boeing, Rashood, Shakira, and Jacques Gamoudi split up, making for three separate destinations inside the terminal.

They had no luggage except duffel bags. Shakira with her several passports and driver's licenses made for the Europcar desk in the arrivals hall, Rashood went to the bank to try and change $10,000 into local dirhams (10.5 to the dollar), and Gamoudi went to a coffee shop for supplies for the journey.

They met in the Europcar parking lot and threw their stuff into the trunk of a small red Ford. It was 10 P.M. before they were ready to go. Gamoudi took the wheel, heading south up the old mountain road to Asni, where the French Colonel knew his father would be, even though they had not been in contact for several months.

Gamoudi had no intention of going into the village, where the French might be waiting. But he intended to contact his father by phone. The old man would arrange for all three of them to get kitted out tomorrow with good mountain gear, for their journey into the still snow-covered peaks of Jacques's boyhood.

This was certainly the one place on this earth where the odds favored them against a determined military pursuer. All three of the fugitives knew the French Secret Service could not be far behind. As yet they had no knowledge of the intention of the Americans, and Gamoudi had not the slightest clue about his family's kidnapping in the main square of the Pyrenean town of Pau.

Gamoudi had decided they should trundle up into the mountains, call his father, and then wait for the dawn. Banging on the door of his father's house in the small hours of the morning was out of the question. In a place like Asni, that would most certainly attract the attention of someone, somewhere, who might suspect who it was.

As it happened, Jack Mitchell got there first. He slipped into the Moroccan tunic and hat he always kept in the rear of his car and inquired at the local bar where he might find Abdul Gamoudi. His house was only fifty yards away. Mitchell went to it and tapped sharply on the front door.

The man who faced him was lean and tanned, a true Moroccan Berber of the mountains. He was in his mid-sixties and he was wearing jeans and no shirt. He confirmed readily that he was indeed the father of Jacques Gamoudi.

Mitchell explained rapidly that he was expecting the Colonel either to arrive there within the next few hours or, somehow, to make contact. Either way, the CIA man said, Gamoudi was in the most terrible danger.

Gamoudi's father nodded, almost as if such a scenario were not entirely foreign to him. "Ah, Jacques," he said slowly, in French. *"Mon fou, mon fils fou."* My crazy son. *"Malheureusement, vous êtes en retard."* Unfortunately you are late. Abdul Gamoudi admitted that his son had been in contact during the past hour, but that he was not coming to the house.

"Est-ce qu'il vous téléphone encore?" Will he call you again? Jack Mitchell's French was passable, but nothing like fluent.

"Bien sûr, demain." Of course, tomorrow.

This was no time for idle chatter. Still speaking in French, Mitchell told Abdul that there was a hit squad somewhere behind him, searching for Gamoudi, determined to assassinate him. He told him that the Americans had the Gamoudi family, and their money, safe. Gamoudi was to use this cell phone, which would connect him direct to the U.S. warship where Giselle and the boys were waiting to speak to him. The Americans would get Gamoudi out of Morocco, with the help of this cell phone. Jack Mitchell struggled through the French verbs, informing the old man about the phone's GPS, which would beam its position to the ship's communication room.

"Les Américains sont les amis, Abdul," said Mitchell. With some heavy gestures he made it clear that everything would be fine, if the Colonel could reach them. He hoped his final, dark warning was understood by Mr. Gamoudi. *If the French find him first they will kill him.*

Abdul Gamoudi nodded gravely. *"Je comprends. Je lui donnerai le téléphone et votre message."*

Jack Mitchell handed over the phone, and hoped to hell that old Abdul would remember everything.

In fact the French were some way behind. They did not even learn that the Saudi Boeing had left Beirut until after 10 P.M., when the local radio station announced the death of four French agents in the Crusaders' Castle. The two men still on duty outside the Saudi embassy heard this, and tried to contact Paris.

That took longer than usual. From then it took four more hours to establish that the Saudi Boeing had left, probably carrying the passenger who had fled Riyadh.

The flight control office was closed and it was not until seven o'clock on Friday morning that the French Secret Service established that the Boeing had gone to Marrakesh, almost certainly with Col. Jacques Gamoudi, a native Moroccan, onboard.

Back in Paris, Gaston Savary was furious. He had always felt "out of the information loop" on this case, ever since the operation began, as if he were always trying to catch up. But now in his military/policeman's mind, he knew a few things for certain: (1) His men had failed to eliminate Gamoudi in the car "accident" in Riyadh; (2) his men had not been in time to catch him at his residence in Riyadh; (3) having successfully tailed him to a little town north of Beirut, all four of his agents had got themselves killed; (4) his men had failed to detain Mrs. Gamoudi in the town square of Pau; (5) his Beirut team had somehow failed to track the Boeing without a delay of almost twelve hours; (6) the CIA wanted Colonel Gamoudi as badly as he did; and (7) Pierre St. Martin was going to have a blue fit when he found out that, right now, no one knew where the hell Gamoudi was.

He picked up his phone and went through on the direct line to Gen. Michel Jobert at the Special Forces headquarters in Taverny. It was the middle of the night, a fact that was not even noticed by either of the two men. General Jobert needed to move from his bedroom, and his sleeping wife, into his study next door. But that was the only delay—twenty seconds. At which point Gaston Savary recounted the entire sorry tale of the failure of the French Secret Service to put this matter to rest.

"And now, Michel," he said, "we have this armed, highly dangerous military officer loose in the High Atlas Mountains, in an area in which he grew up, giving him every territorial advantage. And I'm supposed to catch him."

Savary paused, and then said, "Michel, this is no longer a Secret Service operation. The President of France wants this man eliminated, and my organization is not equipped to stage a manhunt in the mountains. This has suddenly become military. People can get killed. We need helicopters, gunships, search radar, maybe even rockets, if we are to catch him.

"Michel, I am proposing to hand the entire operation over to the First Marine Parachute Infantry Regiment. Quite frankly, I hope you'll agree, but anyway I am proposing to recommend to Monsieur St. Martin that the Special Forces take over from here. You do, after all, have two helicopter squadrons under your permanent command . . ."

"Gaston," said the General, "I am in agreement with you. If they want Gamoudi killed, it will have to be Special Forces. I imagine that will also mean getting rid of the body?"

"Oh, certainly. They want Gamoudi to vanish off the face of the earth and to stay there."

"Well, I have no doubt that can be arranged, Gaston," said the General. "What's our focus point for the operation?"

"Little village called Asni, thirty miles south of Marrakesh. It's way up in the Atlas Mountains, and that's where we think Gamoudi is hiding out, until we tire of trying to track him down."

"You know, Gaston, it's over a thousand miles from Marseille. We'll make the journey overland, across Spain, with a refuel before we cross to North Africa. We have three of those long AS532 Cougar Mark Ones ready to deploy instantly, they hold twenty-five commandos each, and they're well armed—machine guns, canons and rockets. Plus tons of surveillance. I can have them in Marrakesh tomorrow morning. Do I speak to St. Martin, or do you?"

"I will, now. I'll tell him you're on the case. And I'll send detailed briefing papers via e-mail in ten."

"Okay, Gaston. Let's go and silence this troublesome little bastard once and for all."

Saturday, April 17, 1100
High Atlas Mountains

Abdul Gamoudi had made an excellent delivery. His closest friend owned the main ski shop in the area. He borrowed equipment and met his son at the foot of a high escarpment, 500 feet below the ice line. Gamoudi's father arrived cross-country in a piekup truck full of equipment—boots, socks, climbing trousers, sweaters, weatherproof jackets, and, as requested by Gamoudi, nothing in bright modern colors, all of it in drab, almost camouflage coloring. There were sleeping bags, gloves, rucksack bergans, ice axes, crampons, hammers, nylon climbing ropes, and a small primus stove to heat food and water.

Abdul had followed Jacques's instructions to bring everything three people would require to stay alive up there for a week. He had also brought the "magic" cell phone.

Abandoning the hired Ford, Rashood, Shakira, and Gamoudi climbed aboard the pickup. Rashood, sitting on the sleeping bags in the back, handed over 60,000 dirhams to Abdul, who now drove them even higher into the mountains to a point east of the ski-center village of Imlit.

This was their last stop-off. They unloaded the truck and gladly put on warmer clothes, and distributed the climbing equipment, while Abdul drove into Imlit to collect food and water. When he returned, they dumped their old clothes and bags into the pickup and made their farewells.

Abdul smiled and shook hands with Rashood and Shakira, and he hugged Jacques. There were tears streaming down his tough, weather-beaten face as he stood alone on the mountain and watched them trudge off to the northeast, uncertain whether he would ever see his only son again.

Gamoudi had selected a familiar but lonely route that would swiftly bring them into a rugged stretch of hillside with deep escarpments and plenty of cover. After two miles they stopped. Gamoudi sat on a low rock and fired up the cell phone.

He pressed the power switch and then hit the single button that would relay him and his satellite position to the comms room in the U.S.S. *Shiloh*. He felt an instant tremor of excitement when the call went through immediately and a voice responded, *"Comms."*

However, Gamoudi's excitement hardly registered compared to the exhilaration onboard the *Shiloh*.

We got him! 33.08N 08.06W. He's on the line. Captain. Comms. We got him right here . . . get Giselle . . . it's Colonel Gamoudi, and he's damn close.

The words *We got him* were repeated about 200 times in the next half minute, Comms to Captain Pickard. Comms to the XO. Giselle. The ops room. Navigation room. The SEAL boss Lt. Cdr. Brad Taylor. Sometimes you don't even need a telephone in a warship—everyone just finds out, from the engine room to the foredeck, from the galley to the missile director. It's a bush telegraph on the high seas, perfectly reliable and very fast.

Captain Pickard spoke carefully. "Colonel Gamoudi, my ship is about eighty miles off the coast of Morocco, in the port of Agadir. How far are you from the port?"

"I'm in the mountains, around one hundred miles east of Agadir."

"Are you in significant danger?"

"Negative right now. But the French Secret Service has made three attempts on my life, and I have reason to believe there will be others."

"Are you alone?"

"No. Two friends."

"Can you make Agadir?"

"I think so."

"How long?"

"Maybe five days' trekking."

"Can you remain in communication?"

"Affirmative. Say, every twelve hours?"

"From now. Let me connect you with Giselle . . . but don't waste your battery."

Jacques Gamoudi gave himself one minute on the line to his wife, who had recovered fully from being kidnapped in

Pau and now wanted to know only that he was alive. There was no time for details, no time for explanations, just the overpowering sense of relief they were both safe, in his case temporarily, but for the moment safe.

The Colonel shoved the phone in his pocket and climbed to his feet, leading his little group up the steep slopes of this craggy, barren moonscape. It was now clear that Agadir was their destination. Gamoudi selected a route that would take them off the beaten track, away from other trekkers and mountain guides.

Over the next four hours they climbed almost 1,800 feet and a total of six miles. Here they took a rest and drank some water, and very slowly, Jacques Gamoudi turned to Rashood and said, "You don't have to come any farther with me. I can find my way to the seaport. You have both done enough."

The Hamas General grinned and said, "If it hadn't been for you, old friend, I'd be in a grave in Marseille. I'm not leaving you until we reach the dockyard. Besides, you never know when the French hit men are going to arrive."

"They'll never find me," replied Gamoudi.

"Maybe not. But I'll bet they'll try. And they might get lucky."

Down below them they could see the climbers and walkers on the regular trail, almost all of them with guides, and some of them with mules carrying their baggage.

"We just need to avoid being seen by any of them," said Gamoudi. "The country's steep and rough, but we must avoid the villages of Ouaneskra and Tacheddirt—that's where everyone is headed. We'll stop at a summer settlement called Azib Likempt. It won't be open yet, but there's shelter in some old stone huts."

They camped in there for the freezing cold night, cooked some sausages, and thanked God for the quality of the sleeping bags Abdul had purchased. By mid-morning on Saturday they were up beyond the snow line, through the windy mountain pass at Tizi-Lekempt, and on their way to the flat pastures high above the Azib.

Right then, Ravi Rashood heard the first sound of a huge

military helicopter, its massive rotor lashing noisily through the mountain air. The high peaks completely obscured the view, but the sound was so intense General Rashood guessed there were more than one.

"Jesus," he said. "Jacques, we have to find cover. Which way?"

"That way," snapped Le Chasseur, pointing southwest. "Come on . . . run . . . run . . . run."

Carrying their heavy burdens, all three of them set off down the escarpment, heading for a great rocky overhang they could dive behind. Gamoudi kept urging them forward. They reached the rock just as two AS532 Cougar Mark Ones came rocketing around the high southern slope of the mountain.

The noise was ferocious, but the pilots were going slowly, making short low-level circles above the terrain, obviously in search mode.

"Holy shit," said Rashood, looking up. "Those fucking things have search radar, infrared heat-seeking and Christ knows what else."

"I'm too cold to register," volunteered Shakira.

"Quick, get under there!" yelled Gamoudi. "You too, Ravi. They're headed straight toward us."

All three of them dived for cover, Jacques Gamoudi in last place. But it was immediately obvious that the helicopter surveillance crew had seen something. They circled around at low speed, one after the other, flying back only fifty feet above the ground, above the enormous rock that provided shelter for the three fugitives.

Rashood, Shakira, and Gamoudi flattened themselves onto the ground, praying that the helicopters would not land and begin a ground search. There was no doubt in Colonel Gamoudi's mind: the French could operate with impunity in Morocco, which was a privilege the United States did not have. *Not good,* he thought.

The helicopters circled for twenty minutes, before clattering off, dead slow, almost reluctantly, to the west. "We have to get the hell out of here," said Rashood. "Didn't you get the feeling they thought they'd spotted something?"

"I did," said the Colonel. "And in my view they've gone to get permission to stage a military search up here."

"From the Moroccans?" asked Rashood.

"No, no. Just from their superiors. But they might want to touch base with the Moroccan military before they go ahead. It's a serious matter to start operations in a foreign country, especially if people are going to get shot."

"You're not referring to us, are you, Jacques?" asked Shakira.

"I hope to hell I'm not."

"Well, where do we go?" said Rashood.

"I know somewhere, two miles west. The country's pretty flat getting there, so we'll have to be fast across the ground."

"How about if those wild men in the helicopters come back and start searching?" said Sharira.

"That's what bothers me," said the Colonel. "If we stay here and they come back and land, we're dead. We have to run and we have to run now, while the coast is relatively clear."

"That's my view also," said Rashood. "Come on guys, let's go. Jacques, lead the way!"

Running fast with the big packs was out of the question. Shakira carried less and could manage a decent jog, but it was very tough for the two men, who kept going at a steady military pace that would not break any records, but would probably have caused a person of normal fitness to drop dead.

They made the shelter of a big shadowy rock face to the northwest, and fought their way along a mountain trail that was really not much more than a ledge. All the way along, the stones and dust beneath their feet shifted and crumbled. And all three of them tried not to look to the right, to the almost sheer drop of 2,000 feet to the floor of the valley.

The helicopters returned when the three were at least a

slow 200 yards from the destination Jacques Gamoudi had planned. Out of breath and holding on to any foliage that occasionally sprang out of the face of the mountain, they were now inching their way forward, grabbing with their left hands, trying not to slide over the edge.

The mountain shielded them from direct sight of the pilots, unless the copters suddenly swerved westward and began searching the granite wall of this escarpment—which they very well might, at any moment. The fact was, there was no cover, and the only hope was for the French pilots to continue searching the reasonable side of Mount Aksoul, rather than bother with the sheer rock face on the west side, just below the summit—the side upon which only a lunatic would venture.

The racket from the rotors was still echoing, unseen, in the mountain air when the three of them reached a point where Jacques Gamoudi told them to unclip their packs and haul out the mountaineering gear.

He swiftly uncoiled the ropes, hammered in the securing crampons, and made the lines fast. He then looped the harness expertly around Rashood's chest, clipped on the climbing ropes, handed over the gloves, and told Rashood to assay over the edge and down the rock face for forty-seven feet exactly and then swing into a cave.

"Who, me?" said Rashood. "What if there isn't a cave?"

"There is," replied Gamoudi. "I've been in it dozens of times. Go now, feet first, and hang on tight to both lines."

Rashood slithered over the edge, leaned back, and began, effectively, to walk backward down the sheer cliff face.

"You're secure up here . . . this'll hold you, even if you fall."

"I'm not going to fall," Rashood called back. "I'm going straight into that bloody cave when I find it."

Colonel Gamoudi chuckled and watched for the little black sticky tape he had attached to the line to reach the edge. When it did so, he called, "Right there, Ravi! Right in front of you."

"Got it!" yelled the General. "I'm in!"

"Great work!" called Gamoudi. "Now unclip and send the line back. Okay, Shakira, you're next . . . and I want you to understand: I have the spare line attached to your belt, and it's playing out through this fitting. You *CANNOT* fall. Even if the rope broke, which it wouldn't because you weigh less than a ton, you still could not fall."

Shakira was terrified. She watched Gamoudi clip on the harness, then the lines. She pulled on the gloves and slithered backward to the edge. However, the thought of leaning back was too much and she just kept scrabbling at the rock face with her feet, until she felt her husband's hands grab her and haul her into the cave. She was trembling like a songbird's heart.

Gamoudi checked that the lines were set for the climb back, and then he went over the edge, hot-roping it down in five long strides, landing dexterously on the front ridge of the cave.

"Have you done that a few times before?" asked Rashood.

"Just a couple," grinned the French Colonel. "I could do that when I was nine years old."

Ten minutes later, the first of the Cougars came rattling around the mountain, about 400 yards from where the three fugitives sat at the back of the cave, thirty feet from the entrance. It was impossible for anyone to see into the cold gloom of the place, and the dark brown of their lines outside made their climbing equipment invisible. Even the crampons were black.

But Rashood feared the heat-seeking radars, and he told the others to flatten themselves against the floor of the cave as far back as possible. The lead helicopter came past twice more, and intermittently, throughout the afternoon, they could hear the search continuing.

Just before dusk both Cougars flew once more, slowly across the west face of the mountain. Rashood was relieved they did not fire a couple of rockets straight into the cave, as he himself would most certainly have done if he'd had even an inkling that his quarry was inside. But perhaps they didn't.

As night fell, Jacques Gamoudi hammered one of the crampons into the hard rock of the wall and made the climbing rope fast. He clipped on, and with a bag of crampons attached to his belt, he moved out onto the rock face, left of the entrance. Secured now by two ropes, he began the climb up, hammering in a stairway of steel crampons for Rashood and Shakira to use to follow him.

At the top he dropped the rope down for Shakira and called for her to clip it to her harness. He half pulled her, and Shakira half climbed her way to the top, following the zigzagging line of crampons expertly smacked into the mountain by Jacques Gamoudi.

Rashood brought up the rear, faster than Shakira but not like a true mountaineer. In fact, the Hamas C-in-C looked mightily relieved to be standing on firm ground rather than in an eagle's nest, 2,000 feet above terra firma.

The next leg of the journey was a long four-day haul through the wildest lands, over the Ouimeksane Mountain range and down to the deep blue waters of the d'Ifni Lake. But they were no longer being pursued, and the days passed easily. They hit the tiny village of Taliouine on the morning of April 23, purchased a hot meal of spiced lamb and rice in the town's only restaurant, and bought the proprietor's car for 30,000 dirhams.

Three hours later, after a fast run down the P-32 highway, they reached the outskirts of Agadir. It was 3 P.M. Gamoudi touched base with the *Shiloh*, suggesting that they send in the ship to meet him on the dock in five hours, after dark.

The comms room informed him that the cell phone would now be connected to that of the SEAL team leader, Lt. Cdr. Brad Taylor, who was bringing in an eight-man squad for the getaway. "Just keep hitting the GPS beam so we know exactly where you are—every few minutes after 1930."

Colonel Gamoudi thanked the American communications officer and spoke briefly to Lt. Commander Taylor.

"Try to get down there and get your bearings before we arrive," he said. "But don't risk anything."

"I'm afraid I have no idea what the place looks like, and I have no chart or even a map," replied the Colonel. "How about I touch base in three hours? I'll know more then."

"Perfect," replied the SEAL boss. "And remember, they've got a couple of Moroccan Navy warships at one end of the harbor. We'll be staying well away from them. Check out the other end, to the north. We'll talk in three."

Out there on the edge of the town, Gamoudi could see no sign of his French pursuers, but of course that did not mean they weren't there. He gassed up the car and parked it in a deserted, unobtrusive square above the town. Then they all changed out of their mountain gear and into the light pants, sneakers, and shirts.

It was much warmer down here. They strolled down to the port, where they were shocked to see maybe twenty or even thirty French commandos standing around in small groups all along the docks.

They instantly turned back up the narrow, busy street, secure in the knowledge that no one knew them, no one would recognize them, and no one had any idea they were traveling as a group of three. Nonetheless, it might not be easy to make a break tonight, and board a boat in the harbor, not even with the help of the fabled U.S. Navy SEALs.

And so they waited, out on the edge of town. At 7:30 Colonel Gamoudi beamed up his GPS position, and told Lt. Commander Taylor he was about to walk down to the dock, and would meet the SEALs, as agreed, on the south side of the north harbor, the one filled with little blue fishing boats and surrounded by a rocky sea wall.

Gamoudi had seen a tall yellow crane on the shore side. They would use that as a beacon.

"We're less than a half mile offshore," said the Lt. Commander. "We're gonna cut the engine and row in."

"Copy," said the Colonel.

In company with Rashood and Shakira, he walked on down toward the water. Out in the offshore waters, Brad Taylor, in company with four other SEALs, went over the side, complete with wet suits, Draeger breathing apparatus, flippers, and sealed waterproof automatic rifles.

There were 400 yards left to swim. They headed straight for the crane, all five of them, maintaining a depth of twelve feet below the surface. Brad Taylor wanted an armed guard on that dock, and he was not going to get one by driving the big inflatable up to the jetty and tying up beneath the lights, in full view of anyone who might be watching.

They landed on the pitch dark beach, around the corner from the seawall, and took off their flippers, clipping them to their belts. Each man kept his black rubber hood on, which was damned uncomfortable but rendered them almost invisible.

They hovered in the darkness, taking up positions in the construction areas that seemed to surround the entire place. Taylor checked the GPS. So far as he could see, Colonel Gamoudi was walking within 200 yards, straight toward him.

Taylor hit the button of his phone and Gamoudi answered. "How many of you?" asked Brad.

"Still three. My two friends," replied Gamoudi.

Suddenly, the SEAL boss could see them walking through a shadowy narrow gap between two buildings. As he watched, an armed patrol of three uniformed men stepped from the shadows and challenged them.

"Shit," muttered Taylor, and signaled for two of his team to follow him along the other side of the alleyway. He watched from the darkness. Gamoudi and his companions appeared to be answering the uniformed men's questions.

Taylor knew these soldiers were French, and his orders were to take no chances. He hissed to his team to open fire. No mistakes. The chatter of the submachine guns was instant. The three French commandos went down like three sacks of laundry.

Lt. Commander Taylor burst out of his cover and crossed the rough ground. "GAMOUDI!" he snapped. "Which one?"

"Right here," replied the Colonel.

"Let's go, buddy!" And with that, all four of them took off toward the water, leaving an astounded Rashood and Shakira gawping at the running figures, three of them with scuba kit on their backs.

Out of sheer habit, General Rashood leaned down and seized one of the rifles on the ground and led Shakira back into the construction site and toward the town. Their waiting car, up in the square above town, would take them back down the main highway to Marrakesh airport. For them it was over.

It was not, however, over for Jacques Gamoudi. Two more French commandos came racing along the dock following the sound of the gunfire. One of them kept going straight into the rough ground, toward his dead comrades. The other drew his pistol and came straight at the U.S. SEALs. But that was like charging a full-grown Bengal tiger: they cut him down in his tracks.

The SEALs reached the edge of the seawall. *"JUMP, GAMOUDI, JUMP!"* yelled Brad Taylor. All six of them leaped over the side and into the harbor, bobbing up in the middle of the front row of fishing boats. Gamoudi, gasping for air, was not that great a swimmer, but the others were experts.

Behind one of the boats, they clipped on their flippers and rifles, which were stowed in waterproof back holsters, and began to swim, kicking fast for the harbor mouth, each of them with one hand on Jacques Gamoudi. The Colonel was lying motionless on his back, being dragged through the water faster than an Olympic one-hundred-meter freestyler.

There were only three hundred yards to go—that was thirty powerful kicks from these guys. And at the end of that, Jacques Gamoudi was dragged inboard the twenty-four-foot-long inflatable.

They kicked the twin Yamaha outboards into life, and the boat surged to the west, making almost forty knots across the calm water, the lights of Agadir growing fainter behind them.

Taylor took the cell phone off the dashboard and hit one button. And for the second time in a week there was a loud burst of applause in the comms room of the U.S.S. *Shiloh*, for the same three identical words . . . *We got him.*

Epilogue

COL. JACQUES GAMOUDI stood before the General Assembly in one of the most extraordinary sessions ever to take place inside the great round hall of delegates. He was surrounded by bulletproof glass on all four sides.

There were seventy-four different interpreters in the UN's operations room. The glass was the idea of Adm. Arnold Morgan, as a continuous world precaution against the lawlessness of France, whose representatives were not present. The Admiral had also framed the questions that would be directed to Colonel Gamoudi by the soft-spoken North African diplomat who now served as Secretary-General.

The interrogation lasted for two hours, and by the end of it the international reputation of the Republic of France lay in shreds. Among the exchanges, which were heard around the world, was the following:

> *Q: And did you personally command that large assault force in Riyadh that overthrew the Saudi King?*
> *A: Yes, sir, I did.*
> *Q: And who hired you to do so?*
> *A: The French Government, sir.*
> *Q: And how much were you paid by the French Government?*

A: Fifteen million dollars, sir.

Q: And could you prove that beyond any doubt what-soever?

A: I could.

Q: And who was responsible for the destruction of the Saudi oil fields and the loading docks?

A: The French Navy, sir. Two submarines, the Amé-thyste and the Perle. Frogmen and submerged-launch cruise missiles.

Q: And the destruction of the King Khalid Air Base?

A: French Special Forces, sir. Ferried in from Dji-bouti. Specialists, trained in France, blew the air-craft to pieces.

Q: And could you name the French Commanders?

A: Yes, sir, if you wish.

Q: And why have you decided to betray your country?

A: Because they have tried to assassinate me after I carried out my orders, direct from the President, to the letter.

Q: And how were you saved from the assassins?

A: By the United States Navy, sir. I owe them my life.

Q: And do you know why they saved you?

A: Yes, sir. In order that the world should know the truth of France's actions.

Q: And will you ever be returning to France?

A: No, sir.

At 3:25 that afternoon, on behalf of the General Assembly, the United Nations Secretary-General apologized uncondi-tionally to the President of the United States for the previ-ous directive condemning the actions of the U.S. in the Strait of Hormuz and the Red Sea. This was formally ac-cepted by the U.S. Ambassador to the UN.

The following morning, Admiral Morgan himself opened negotiations with King Nasir for the U.S.A. to take future charge of the Saudi oil industry. The Saudis would still re-ceive the same money, but the U.S.A. would be responsible for security and the marketing of the product worldwide.

Admiral Morgan was in fact surprised by the ease with

which the negotiations proceeded, the relaxed way the King cut the French right out of the equation, confirming, for the moment at least, that he wanted nothing more to do with the Republic of France.

Arnold Morgan thought the King's attitude bordered on treachery toward his old partners in crime, in the overthrow of the free-spending former Saudi royal household. But then, he was not party to a conversation between the King and the French President, which unhappily ended thus:

"I am afraid, Mr. President, your conduct toward a very close friend of mine is entirely unacceptable to me. As a Bedouin, I cannot condone such betrayal of a good and loyal soldier and, I believe, a friend to us both.

"If it helps you, I should remind you I was a student of the works of E. M. Forster. I wrote my English literature thesis on him at Harvard. That, perhaps, is all you need to know."

But the French President did not know. And probably never would.

Two Years Later
Boise, Idaho

The two Royal Saudi Air Force Boeings touched down lightly, one after the other, on the runway at the little airport south of the state capital of Idaho. Here, in one of the great mountainous regions of the American Midwest, was the new home of Mr. and Mrs. Jack McCaffrey.

Jack and Giselle stood in the doorway of the tiny arrivals lounge awaiting their guest, who was, incidentally, accompanied by an entourage of forty-seven family and staff members—kid's stuff compared with the retinue of 3,000 that had often traveled with his predecessor on the Saudi throne.

The guests would be filling the biggest of the local hotels, but the King himself insisted on staying at the McCaffreys' home for three days. *We fought a great battle together, I stay under your roof.* And, it was a pretty reasonable roof for the King to . . . well, pitch his tent: a beautiful white-columned colonial at the edge of the small city, with the snowcapped

Sawtooth Mountains rising spectacularly to 6,000 feet to the east and then, beyond, to 11,000 feet.

The family had come here to Idaho with their two boys immediately after the United Nations hearings were concluded. Gamoudi, in different but soon to become beloved mountains, had never been happier.

With his great fortune, he had bought the big house and a large ski chalet over in Sun Valley, and set up a chain of three ski shops and mountain guide centers, which immediately prospered.

The boys, now Andy and John, had settled in swiftly in American schools. Gamoudi spent hundreds of cheerful hours with them and Giselle, exploring the great Idaho peaks above the hundreds of cold, blue lakes.

There were a few very large bears up there, which meant he never ventured far without his old hunting knife, the one that long ago had ended the life of the Mossad hit man at the Marseille restaurant, in a faraway country to which he would never return.

Gamoudi and Giselle had found a special place in the southwest of the state where so many Basque immigrants had once arrived from the Pyrenees in search of cheap land to raise sheep on the mountainside.

There was evidence of Basque culture everywhere here in Idaho—food, restaurants, and timeless stories handed down among the local farmers. You could even buy the famous Basque spicy sausage *chorizo*, specially made by fourth-generation immigrants, in nearby Payette County.

The McCaffreys had found an earthly paradise among people of a distant but often shared culture. Even the towering mountains, in certain light, looked much the same as the Pyrenees.

And suddenly, here was the King of Saudi Arabia, dressed in Western clothes but waving the distinctive greeting of the Bedouin as he walked down the aircraft steps. He wore the smile of a man whose oil economy has been rebuilt and is back on track and he walked onto American soil as the confident political partner of the U.S. President.

A few local photographers took pictures as the King

walked straight up to his old rebellion tank commander in Riyadh and hugged him. *"JACQUES,"* he exclaimed, beaming with camaraderie. *"COLONEL JACQUES GA-MOUDI!"*

In his left hand the King carried a gift—a gilt-edged, leather-bound first edition of E. M. Forster's *Two Cheers for Democracy*. Inside he had inscribed the words: *For Le Chasseur, my friend . . .* as salaam alaykum, *upon you be peace, Nasir.*

Look out for

GHOST FORCE
by Patrick Robinson

The year is 2011, and one of the largest oil fields on earth is discovered on the Falkland Islands. Argentina, with the secret assistance of the Kremlin, invades the islands for the second time in 30 years, and an outraged Great Britain dispatches a battle fleet to the region. Waiting for them is a Russian nuclear submarine capable of destroying the Royal Navy aircraft carrier.

With a conflict brewing in its backyard, the United States, in the person of the indomitable Arnold Morgan and the Navy SEALs, must act, and when it does the consequences are as unexpected as they are devastating.

Ghost Force is classic Robinson—suspense, harrowing action, and authentic detail set against the backdrop of an uncanny "what if?" scenario.

As a GENERAL RULE, Admiral Arnold Morgan did not do state banquets. He put them in the same category as diplomatic luncheons, congressional dinners, state fairs, and yard sales; all of which required him to spend time talking to God knows how many people with whom he had absolutely nothing in common.

Given a choice, he would rather have spent an hour with a political editor of CBS Television or the *Washington Post*, each of whom he could cheerfully have throttled several times a year.

It was thus a matter of some interest this evening to witness him making his way down the great central staircase of the White House, right behind the President and his guests of honor. The Admiral descended in company with the exquisitely beautiful Mrs. Kathy Morgan, whose perfectly cut dark green silk gown made the Russian President's wife look like a middle-line admin clerk from the KGB. (Close. She had been a researcher.)

Arnold Morgan himself wore the dark blue dress uniform of a U.S. Navy Rear Admiral, complete with the twin-dolphin insignia of the U.S. Submarine Service. As ever, shoulders back, jaw jutting, steel-gray hair trimmed short, he looked like a CO striding toward his ops room.

Which was close to the mark. In his long years in service as the President's National Security Adviser, he believed the White House *was* his ops room. He always called it "the factory," and he had conducted global operations against enemies of the United States with an unprecedented free hand. Of course, he had kept the President posted as to his activities. Mostly.

And now, with the small private reception for the Russians concluded in the upstairs private rooms, Arnold and Kathy stood aside at the foot of the stairs, alongside the Ambassador and a dozen other dignitaries, while the two Presidents and their wives formed a short receiving line.

This was deliberate, because the Russians always brought with them a vast entourage of state officials, diplomats, politicians, military top brass, and, as ever, undercover agents—spies, that is—badly disguised as cultural attachés. It was, frankly, like seeing a prizefighter's goons and bodyguards dancing a minuet.

But here they all were. The men who ran Russia, being formally entertained by President Paul Bedford and the First Lady, the former Maggie Lomax, a svelte, blonde Virginian horsewoman, fearless to hounds, but nerve-wracked by this formal jamboree in support of U.S.-Russian relations.

So far as President Bedford had been concerned, the presence of Arnold Morgan had been nothing short of compulsory. Although the telephone conversation between the two men had been little short of a verbal gunfight.

"Arnie, I just got your note declining the Russian banquet invite . . . Jesus, you can't do this to me!"

"I thought I just had."

"Arnie, this is not optional. This is a Presidential command."

"Bullshit. I'm retired. I don't do State Banquets. I'm a naval officer, not a diplomat."

"I know what you are. But this thing is really important. They're bringing all the big hitters from Moscow, civilian and military. Not to mention their oil industry."

"What the hell's that got to do with me?"

"Nothing. 'Cept I want you there. Right next to me, keeping me posted. There's not one person in Washington knows the Russians better than you. You gotta be there. White tie and tails."

"I *never* wear white tie and tails."

"Okay. Okay. You can come in a tuxedo."

"Since I don't much want to look like a head waiter, or a goddamned violinist, I won't be wearing that either."

"Okay. Okay," said the President, sensing victory. "You can come in full-dress Navy uniform. Matter of fact, I don't care if you turn up in jockstrap and spurs as long as you get here."

Arnold Morgan chuckled. But suddenly an edge crept back into his voice. "What topics concern you most?"

"The rise of the Russian Navy, for a start. The rebuilding of their submarine fleet in particular. And the exporting of submarines all over the world."

"How about their oil industry?"

"Well, that new deepwater tanker terminal in Murmansk cannot fail to be an issue," replied the President. "We're hoping they'll ship two million barrels a day from there direct to the USA in the next few years."

"And I guess you know the Russian President already has terrible goddamned problems transporting crude oil from the West Siberian Basin to Murmansk . . ." Arnold was thoughtful. And he added slowly, ". . . And you know how important that export trade is to them."

"And to us," said President Bedford.

"Give us a little distance with the towelheads, right?"

"That's why you gotta be at the banquet, Arnie. Starting with the private reception. Don't be late."

"Silver-tongued bastard," grunted Admiral Morgan. "All right, all right. We'll be there. Good morning, Mr. President."

Paul Bedford, who was well accustomed to the Admiral's excruciating habit of slamming down the phone without even bothering with "good-bye," considered this a very definite victory.

"Heh, heh, heh," he chortled, in the deserted Oval Office, "that little bit of intrigue on a global scale. That'll get the ole buzzard every time. But I'm sure glad he's coming."

Thus it was that Arnold and Kathy Morgan were now in attendance at the State Banquet for the Russians, gazing amiably at the long line of incoming guests entering the White House.

So many old friends and colleagues. It was like an Old Boys' reunion. Here was the Commander of the U.S. Navy SEALS, Admiral John Bergstrom, and his soignée new wife, Louisa-May, from Oxford, Mississippi; Harcourt Travis, the former Republican Secretary of State, with his wife, Sue. There was Admiral Scott Dunsmore, former CNO of the U.S. Navy, with his elegant wife, Grace. The reigning Chairman of the Joint Chiefs, General Tim Scannell, was with his wife, Beth.

Arnold shook hands with the Director of the National Security Agency, Admiral George Morris, and he greeted the new Vice President of the United States, the former Democratic Senator from Georgia, Bradford Harding, and his wife, Paige.

The Israeli Ambassador, General David Gavron, was there with his wife, Becky, plus, of course, the silver-haired Russian Ambassador to Washington, Tomas Yezhel, and the various Ambassadors from the United Kingdom, Canada, and Australia.

Arnold did not instantly recognize all of the top brass of the Russian contingent. But he could see the former Chairman of the Joint Chiefs, General Josh Paul, talking with the Russian Foreign Minister, Oleg Nalyotov.

He vaguely knew the Chief of the Russian Naval Staff, a grim-looking, ex-Typhoon-class ICBM Commanding Officer, Admiral Victor Kouts.

But Admiral Morgan's craggy face lit up when he spotted the towering figure of his old sparring partner, Russian Admiral Vitaly Rankov, now C-in-C Fleet, and Deputy Defense Minister.

"Arnold!" boomed the giant ex-Soviet international oarsman. "I had no idea you'd be here. They told me you'd retired."

Admiral Morgan grinned, and held out his hand. "Hi, Vitaly—they put you in charge of that junkyard Navy of yours yet? I heard they had."

"They did. Right now, Admiral, you're talking to the Deputy Defense Minister of Russia."

"Guess that'll suit you," replied the American. "Should

provide ample scope for your natural flair for lies, evasions, and half-truths . . ."

The enormous Russian threw back his head and roared with laughter. "Now you be kind, Arnold," he said in his deep, rumbling baritone voice: "Otherwise I may not introduce you to this very beautiful lady standing at my side."

A tall, striking, dark-haired girl around half the Russian's age smiled shyly and held out her hand in friendship.

"This is Olga," said Admiral Rankov. "We were married last spring."

Admiral Morgan took her hand and asked if she spoke any English since his Russian was a little rusty. She shook her head, smiling, and the Admiral took the opportunity to turn back to Vitaly and shake his head sadly. "Too good for you, old buddy. A lot too good."

Again the huge Russian Admiral laughed joyfully, and he repeated the words he had used so often in his many dealings with the old Lion of the West Wing.

"You are a terrible man, Arnold Morgan. A truly terrible man." Then he spoke in rapid Russian to Mrs. Olga Rankov, who also burst out laughing.

"I understand we are sitting together," said Arnold. "And I don't believe you have actually met my wife, Kathy."

The Russian Admiral smiled and accepted Kathy's outstretched hand. "We have of course spoken many times on the telephone," he said. "But believe me, I never thought he'd persuade you to marry him." And, with a phrase more fittingly uttered in a St. Petersburg palace than a naval dockyard, Vitaly added with a short bow and a flourish, "The legend of your great beauty precedes you, Mrs. Morgan. I knew what to expect."

"Jesus, they've even taught him social graces," chuckled Arnold, carelessly ignoring the fact he was a bit short in that department himself. "Vitaly, old pal, seems we both got lucky in the past year. Not too bad for a couple of old Cold Warriors."

By now the guests were almost through the receiving line and a natural parting of the crowd established a wide entrance tunnel to the State Dining Room. Within a few moments, President and Maggie Bedford came through, escorting the Russian President and his wife to their dinner places, with all of the guests falling in, *line astern*, as Arnold somewhat jauntily told Vitaly.

The President took his place next to the former KGB researcher directly beneath the Lincoln portrait. Maggie Bedford showed the boss of all the Russians to his place next to her at the same table, and everyone stood until the hostess was seated.

The banquet, on the orders of Paul Bedford, was strictly American. "No caviar, or any of that restaurant nonsense," he had told the butler. "We start with Chesapeake oysters, we dine on New York sirloin steak, with Idaho potatoes, and we wrap it up with apple pie and American ice cream. There'll be two or three Wisconsin cheeses for anyone who wants them. California wines from the Napa Valley."

"Sir," the butler ventured, "not everyone likes oysters . . ."

"Tough," replied the President. "Russians love 'em. I've had 'em in Moscow and St. Petersburg. Anyone who can't eat 'em can have an extra shot of apple pie if they need it."

"Very well, sir," replied the butler, suspecting, from vast experience, that Arnold Morgan himself had been somehow in the shadows advising Paul Bedford. The tone, the curtness, the sureness. Morgan, not Bedford.

As it happened, there had been one short conversation when the Oval Office called Chevy Chase to check in on the menu content. "Give 'em American food," Arnold had advised. "Strictly American. Big A A A. The food this nation eats. We don't need to pretend sophistication to anyone, right?"

"Right."

And now, with the apple pie just arriving, the Strolling Strings, a well-known group of U.S. Army violinists, began to play at the rear section of the room. It was a short miniconcert, comprising all-American numbers, such as "Over there!" . . . "True Love" (from *High Society*) . . . a selection from *Oklahoma* . . . "Take Me Out to the Ball Game" . . . and concluding with "God Bless America."

Finally the President rose and made a short speech extolling the virtues of the Russian President and the new and close trade links developing between the nations.

The guest of honor then stood and echoed many of the Presidents' statements, before responding with a formal toast "to the United States of America."

At this point the entire room stood up and proceeded toward the door that led out to the Blue Room, where coffee would be served, followed by entertainment in the East Room, and then dancing to the band of the United States Marines in the White House foyer.

Everyone was on the move now, except for one guest. Mikhallo Masorin, the senior minister from the vastness of Siberia, which fills one-twelfth of the land mass of the entire earth, had suddenly pitched forward and landed flat on his face right in front of Arnold, Vitaly, Olga, and Kathy.

In fact, the huge Russian Admiral had leaned forward to break his fall. But he was a fraction of a second too late. Mr. Masorin was down, twisted on his back now, his face puce in color, gasping for breath, both hands clutched to his throat, working his jaws, writhing in obvious fear and agony.

Someone shouted, *"Doctor! Right now!"*

Women gasped. Men came forward to see if they could help. Arnold Morgan noticed they were mostly Americans. He also considered Mr. Masorin was very nearly beyond help. He was desperately trying to breathe but could not do so.

By now two or three people were shouting, *"Heart attack! Come on, guys, let the doctor through . . ."*

Within a few minutes there were two doctors in attendance, but they could only bear witness to the death throes of the Siberian head honcho. One of them filled a syringe and unleashed a potent dose of something into Mr. Masorin's upper arm.

But there was no saving him. Mikhallo was gone, in rapid time, dead before the Navy stretcher bearers could get to him. Dead, right there on the floor of the State Dining Room in front of his own President and that of the United States.

President Bedford asked one of the doctors if the Siberian could be saved if they could get him to the Naval Hospital in Bethesda.

But the answer was negative. "Nothing could have saved this man, sir. He was gone in under four minutes. Some heart attacks are like that. There's nothing anyone can do."

Of course, only those few in the immediate vicinity realized that one of the Russian guests had actually died. More than 120 other dignitaries quickly became aware than someone had been taken ill, but were unaware of the fateful consequences of the heart attack.

And the evening passed agreeably, although the White House Press Office did feel obliged, shortly before eleven P.M., to put out a general press release that the Chief Minister for the Urals Federal District, Mr. Mikhallo Masorin, had suffered a heart attack at the conclusion of a State Banquet, and was found to be dead on arrival at the United States Naval Hospital in Bethesda, Maryland.

Admiral Morgan and Kathy made their farewells a little after midnight, and Arnold's driver picked them up at the main entrance and headed northwest to Chevy Chase.

"Terrible about that poor Russian, wasn't it?" said Kathy. "He was at the next table to us, couldn't have been more than fifty years old.

Must have been a very bad heart attack . . ."

"Bullshit," replied Arnold, not looking up from an early edition of the *Washington Post*.

"I'm sorry?" said Kathy, slightly perplexed.

"Bullshit," confirmed the Admiral. "That was no heart attack. He was writhing around on the floor, opening and shutting his mouth like a goddamned goldfish."

"I know he was, darling. But the doctor *said* it was a heart attack. I heard him."

"What the hell does he know?"

"Oh, I am so sorry. It entirely slipped my memory I was escorting the eminent cardiovascular surgeon and universal authority Arnold Morgan."

Arnold looked up from his newspaper, grinning at his increasingly sassy wife. "Kathy," he said, formally, "whatever killed Masorin somehow shut down his lungs instantly. He could not draw breath. The guy suffocated, fighting for air, which you probably noticed was plentiful in the State Dining Room. But it was beyond his reach. Heart attacks don't do that."

"Oh," said Kathy. "Well, what does?"

"A bullet, correctly aimed. A combat knife, correctly delivered. Certain kinds of poison."

"But there was no blood anywhere. And anyway, why should the CIA or the FBI or whatever want to get rid of an important guest at a White House banquet?"

"I have no idea, my darling," said Arnold. "But I believe someone did. And I'll be mildly surprised if we don't find out before too long that Mikhallo Masorin was murdered last night. Right here in Washington, D.C."